LESIDI'S COIN

A Serpent's Coil Time-Travel Romance
Book 2

KAT DRENNAN

DEDICATION

Lesidi's Coin is dedicated to my husband who does all the heavy lifting while letting me indulge my greatest dream, writing the stories of my heart.

ACKNOWLEDGMENTS

Many thanks to my Saturday Zoom Writers group, Lark Batteau, Sharon Hall, and Paulette Mahurin. We made the best of the Covid pandemic by forming an amazing partnership. I could not have finished Lesidi's Coin without your support. I can't wait to see the other books born in this group.

A special thanks goes out to my dear friend and biggest fan, Sally Crawford for going on this journey with me. Your constant encouragement has been invaluable.

Thanks again for the dedication and thoroughness of historian, Dena Pollard, without whose meticulous scrutiny this manuscript would be sorely lacking. Any remaining historical discrepancies or technical errors found in this manuscript are entirely my responsibility.

LESIDI'S COIN

CHAPTER 1 - BAGGAGE CLAIM

Newport Beach, California - 2019 CE

Alexis Hill stood before the dusty gray rollup door of her storage unit. The last thing she wanted was to paw through the flotsam of the life she'd deliberately left behind. Now, she cocked her hip and sent her best friend and long-time roommate, Tessa a reluctant frown. "Do we really have to do this?"

Tessa frowned right back at her. "How many times have you recommended your patients clean out their crap and make a clean start?"

"Because they were running away from something."

"Uh huh. And so…" Tess rolled her hand to encourage a reply.

"So…, maybe some things are better left in the past."

"Not in my experience," Tessa said, and Lexi couldn't argue. After all she'd been through this past year, Tessa should know better than most. "Besides," Tessa crooned. "Who was it who said, *Physician, heal thyself?*"

It was getting serious when Tess quoted the Bible. Lexi jangled her keys in her hand.

"Unless," Tessa went on, "you want to put your stuff in my garage. I'll only charge you three hundred a month. You'd save a hundred bucks. Why, in two years, that would be enough money to take that dive trip you're always talking about."

That wasn't going to happen. She was ready to move on. She was ready for that illusive Closure thing. And it only made sense to stop putting this off now that she was moving into her own place.

While her psychotherapy practice was gaining momentum, she still had to watch her finances to make ends meet. This was Newport Beach, after all, and office space near the prestigious harbor was at a premium. With this last thing on her list of things to do before the move, the days of choosing between groceries and a decent pair of shoes would be gone, with maybe enough left over at the end of the month to think about having an actual life.

"Oh, all right." Lexi shoved the key in the lock, twisted it, and … nothing. "Damn."

"Sure it's the right unit?" Tessa asked.

Lexi backed up and checked the numbers of the unit, as well as those on either side.

"Twenty-five." She remembered because that's how old she had been when she'd locked her past life away in this little corrugated metal cave.

As if on cue, the lot attendant barreled toward them in a shiny red golf cart, his foot half out of the vehicle, a pair of bolt cutters on the cracked seat next to him. He hefted his huge bulk off the seat and hitched up his belt, beads of sweat budding on his face with the effort. His name badge read *Rob*. "Problem?"

Lexi held up the key and lifted a shoulder. "I don't know, *Rob*. Worked the last time I was here."

"Yeah? And when was that?"

"Five years ago." Almost to the day.

Rob harrumphed. "Salt air clogs up the lock's moving parts over time."

Indeed. It was hard to believe that much time had passed. She'd been wrapped up in her master's dissertation and a very messy breakup with an even messier man, when all her childhood belongings arrived on her studio apartment doorstep with a COD shipping bill for $2,000 and note from her mother: *You're father and I are through. I sold the townhouse in DC and I'm going back to Gaborone.*

Gaborone. Her mother wasn't even from Gaborone. But her sister had married a goldmine superintendent from Botswana and Gaborone was the closest town that passed as what she considered civilization, so it halfway made sense.

Still, the letter, and the pile of stuff on her doorstep had come as a complete shock. She rarely heard from her mother since she'd gotten her BA, and when she did, there was never anything personal, such as, *Hey, miss you, maybe you could come home for a visit,* let alone *I'm leaving the country.*

Now that she thought about it, her mother had occasionally threatened to move back to Africa with her sister, but Lexi had never taken her seriously. With mixed blood like her own, her mother often complained about not fitting into either world, though Lexi never understood. Her *mother's* African blood came through loud and clear. It was Lexi whose race was ambiguous. With her father's Anglo complexion and reddish hair, her mother's high cheek bones and peridot green eyes, neither of Alexis's feet were planted firmly in one culture or the other.

Althea Tedese-Hill had always had the choice to step back to her roots. But, honestly, what self-respecting black woman with a PhD in economics would leave her *chichi* job at Georgetown University and fancy DC townhouse with a respected diplomat husband for a tiny apartment in Gaborone? A jilted one, maybe? Or guilty for leaving her family for the states? Or some other unexplained and deeply personal reason she had no intention of sharing with her daughter.

More likely, she had simply burned out. Tired of all the hype.

Life in DC had its pressures and standards. Looking back with adult eyes, Lexi could see the signs of fatigue in her mother, both mental and physical. Newport Beach wasn't so different, after all. It was something Lexi saw in her practice every day. A surgeon's wife, maybe, caught up in the competitive world of philanthropy, or an A-list athlete pressured to perform week after torturous week, or the CEO of a fortune one hundred corporation. Some women thrive on success, others fall apart.

Lexi on the other hand, had a lot to be grateful for. Despite the fact that she hadn't seen her parents since they'd shipped her off to the West Coast, they had paid her tuition at an exclusive private school and had set up a trust to pay her college tuition through graduation with her degree in psychology. She'd paid for her masters on her own nickel, a fact that while it left her a pile of debt, was still a source of personal pride.

With the money she'd saved working night shifts at Orange County's Mental Health Center she'd loaded her entire past into the ten by twelve storage locker without so much as peeking inside a single box. It was easier to pay the rent each month than deal with the tsunami of emotion that assailed her whenever she considered cleaning out the boxes.

Out of sight, out of mind; and that's the way she liked it.

Now, mild panic worked its way up the back of her neck with creepy little fingers. "Maybe we should call those Storage Wars people? Rob here looks like he's aching to use those bolt cutters."

Attendant guy's eyebrows lifted. He looked her up and down. She could almost read his mind.

What is she?

Most people landed somewhere between Caucasian and Pacific Islander. She could thank her mother for that. Her eyes had a distinctive heavy lid that gave her a sultry look. But it was her hair that threw them off. Dark brown with hints of her father's red, but you couldn't ignore the distinctly African kink. J Lo she was not. She'd stopped straightening the day she left her mother's constant insistence. Today's natural, springy twists came easier and fit her personality.

Rob grinned like the Cheshire Cat. "I could take the whole thing off your hands, for say, five hundred?"

Tessa slid her sunglasses down her nose and peered at Lexi, her hand gently squeezing her arm. "We'll just have a look first, right Lex?"

Lexi spewed out a breath. "Easy for you to say, girl. That's not your smelly history all up inside there. Maybe I don't *want* to look at it."

Tessa was right, of course. She always had been. And … there it was, the foot tapping. "I didn't come here without unpacking my own honeymoon luggage to bring you home empty handed."

Lex could never hold out long once Tessa's foot started to tap. "Okay. Let's do this."

Rob shot a look between them, and then, shoulders slumped in resignation, turned back to the task of jiggling the lock. He pulled a small can out of his tool kit and sprayed something oily into the keyhole, then stepped back, wiped his hands on his pants. "Try that."

Lexi shoved the key in the lock, and it gave way with a click that seemed to mock her. "Fine. Okay. We're going in."

Rob climbed back into his golf cart. "Take your time. Let me know if you need anything else," he said, nodding down the row. "I can unlock that dumpster down there for anything you don't want. There's a twenty-dollar fee."

Right. She lifted her eyes to take in the asphalt alley way. If she knew what was good for her, she'd *schlep* everything down there and be done with it.

He waved over his shoulder and scooted down the row toward a young couple—the woman balancing a baby on her hip--unloading a rental trailer full of furniture into an empty locker. Lexi wondered briefly about their circumstance. She couldn't help it. People and their baggage were her jam. Her own baggage was another story. One she'd been avoiding way too long.

Once inside Lexi's Junk Cave as she'd come to call it, Tess, the ultimate organizer, set up her trusty card table. "We'll sort through everything here. That way you won't take home anything you don't really want."

"Easy for you to say. We're not ripping open your veins right now." The first stab of anxiety prickled in the middle of Lexi's chest as she knifed open the seam of a box marked 'bedroom' in her mother's loopy script.

Tessa sent her a reprimanding look under raised brows. "At least one of us will be objective."

Lexi folded back the flaps of the box and pulled out a set of Barbie[R] bed sheets and a pilled-coated pink teddy bear with the stuffing coming out at the neck. Tessa pointed to the place on the floor where she'd chalked out three squares labeled TOSS, KEEP, and DONATE.

Lexi tutted. "You've done this before."

Tessa shrugged. "Mom was a compulsive hoarder. *I* know how to get rid of stuff."

Lexi had to smile, remembering their first apartment together. Lexi and Tess had both started from zip. She stuffed the sheets and bear back in the box and let it drop on the floor with a loud thunk inside the TOSS pile. "Right."

The next few boxes produced the same junk. "I can't believe I've been paying to store this crap for five years."

So far, the only thing surviving in the KEEP pile was a little pink jewelry box with two tiny ballerina dancers inside, still in their cellophane wrappers: one's body a rosy pink, the other a warm, brown. Neither had been placed on the twirly spring in front of the beveled mirror.

She closed the box with a long sigh. They'd only been at this thirty minutes and already she was exhausted. She lifted a shoe box to the worktable, absently cutting through the packing tape around its middle before she noticed it was marked May 2005. Odd. None of the other boxes were dated.

The prickle again. In her fingers. Down her spine. She glanced up a Tessa who gave her that look.

"You're doing great. Keep it going."

Lexi lifted the shoe box lid. The scent hit her hard. Fragile, sweet cherry blossoms on the Potomac…home in another life. A place she really didn't care to be right now. She dropped the lid back in place, her fingers shook a little, resting on top of the box. "You know, I'm hungry. Let go get some tacos."

Tessa moved in behind her, peeking over her shoulder. "Hit a raw spot, did you?"

Lexi's heart compressed into a tight fist; she pressed her hand against her breastbone. "Not raw. Scarred, maybe."

She had never told Tessa the real reason she'd been shipped off to private school. At sixteen. Never told her much of anything about herself prior to meeting her.

Tessa squeezed her shoulder. "It's like a Band-Aid. Better to rip it off all at once."

She was right, of course. She would have to face her past sooner or later and it was better to get it over with.

She lifted the lid off the box and laid it aside. Folded on top was a colorful scarf her aunt had sent her from Botswana, a yellow, blue, and gold Kente cloth wrap an African woman might wear to a wedding or graduation. It had been a thoughtful gift, a nod to her roots, and one she cherished; although at the time, her mother had turned up her nose. All the more reason it belonged in the KEEP pile.

Thinking to tie it around her head, she unfurled the scarf. She didn't notice the tiny pink knit cap that fell out of it until Tessa scooped it off the floor.

Lexi's face burned. She extended a shaky hand to grasp the soft knit, then her throat closed tight, the date suddenly making sense. Her daughter's day of birth; an event she could never celebrate, but sometimes noted on her calendar with a tiny heart. Her knees went liquid and she pressed a fist on the table, heading off a crush of remorse she knew would waylay her if she let it.

"Lex?"

The memory of that day paraded in storm boots through her heart. Hats. Blankets. A brief moment of clarity clawing up from an anesthetic fog — running shaking fingertips through black peach-fuzz hair on her baby's tiny head. The next moment her mother snatching the baby away like a crow stealing an acorn from its neighbor. *It's for the best*, she had said, *caw, caw,* and flapped out of the recovery room without a backward glance. Lexi had never seen the little girl or the hat again. *Until now.*

A deep sense of betrayal sat cold and heavy in her stomach as she tightened her grip on the little knit cap. She should have taken good old Rob's offer of five hundred bucks for the lot.

Tessa leaned in and caught her eye. "Do you want to talk about it?"

Lexi swallowed a hard knot in her throat and shook her head.

She peered into the box, where a half dozen objects wrapped in newspaper nestled. What other land mines had her mother set for her? Her gut tightened at the thought. Without touching the rest of the contents, she tossed in the hat, folded the scarf on top of it, and replaced the lid. No amount of talking would ever change the past. She shook her head. "Let's just … get this done."

"O-kay." Tessa ratcheted the postal tape noisily across the box lid and set it gently on the KEEP pile. "You're right. We have a job to do, and we'd better get to it because I promised Phillip I'd make dinner for his folks tonight. You're invited of course. I don't want to have to go through all our honeymoon pictures more than once."

Lexi closed her eyes. No way was Tessa going to let her slide forever. But for now, she was relieved. Better to get this job over with before taking that misery train.

She brushed suddenly sweaty hands down her jeans, re-gathered her hair into a poof on top of her head. "Right. Honeymoon pictures."

Tessa pushed her toward a pile of boxes against the wall. "Open, sort, toss, repeat."

Lexi exhaled, grateful for her friend's persistence. The shoe box aside, she couldn't think of much else that would shock her. Beyond the few boxes, there wasn't much left—A few odds and ends, her old dive equipment, and a pretty *big girl* bedroom set she got on her twelfth birthday.

Open. Sort. Toss. Repeat. She could do this. And then it would be over.

Thank god for Tess. She was more family than anyone of her own blood. From the day they'd met at the boarding school, they'd been connected at the hip in a way she'd never experienced with another person, including her family. Now, she could see the disappointment on Tessa's face. Since discovering the pink hat, her eyebrows had never quite gone all the way down to normal. Guilt lurked at the top of Lexi's lungs, keeping her from a much-needed exhale. As close as they'd been, Lexi had kept a glaring secret from Tessa. It was time to come clean.

Lexi lifted another box to the worktable and zipped open the seam. All right. Better to get it over with here, while it was just the two of them. She owed her friend that much.

"Okay," Lexi said on an exhale. "The truth is, I probably never would have met you if it wasn't for that little hat. It's how I ended up in California in the first place. It was the farthest away my mother could send me without shipping me out of the country." Her voice came out softly on that last bit; she wasn't sure she'd said it aloud until she saw the look of compassion on Tessa's face.

She slit open another box and pulled out a honey blond, wild-haired, half-dressed doll, one eye stuck shut.

Tessa grabbed it out of her hands and hugged the doll to her chest. "Wow! I had one just like her! Stuck eyeball and everything."

"TOSS," Lexi commanded, stretching a long finger toward the pile.

They'd been fifteen when they met. From that day on, they had shared every moment of their lives. Lexi had never shared much of her life before California. In fact, she had buried that wound so deep she had almost forgotten it. Almost.

Tessa looked at her expectantly, hands resting atop another box marked *shoes*.

Lexi went back to sorting boxes. "My father was a US ambassador to Botswana. My mother had worked as an intern at the Embassy. They fell for each other hard. They continued their relationship when she came to Georgetown University to get her doctorate. They were married and she got her citizenship and had me not long after. It was a pretty good life for them in DC. They enjoyed all the benefits of the Expat community. All the foreign diplomat's kids were in private school, lots of events and traveling abroad; partied together, vacationed together. The adults were living the lifestyle of the rich and famous, and I suppose, that's what they were. Hobnobbing with the heads of state, lobbyists, corporate moguls. Making money, making deals, furthering their own livelihoods. We kids were left pretty much on our own, with *money to burn*, as they say."

Tessa started to open the box marked shoes and Lexi shook her head. "I can't imagine I'd wear any of those today. Let's just donate 'em to the women's shelter."

"Great." Tessa plunked the box on the DONATE pile and lifted another to the table.

Lexi watched her work a moment, before she picked up the story.

"Anyway, in the summer of 2004, we vacationed with a friend of my mother from Ethiopia. The husband was a prominent hotelier with deep ties to the coffee export business and deeper pockets. I met their son, Zaire on a diving trip we took in the Mediterranean."

She closed her eyes a moment, remembering the first time she saw him smile. It was like a shot of lightening straight to her heart.

"He was eighteen. Introduced me to scuba. Our parents were more interested in basking in the sun and sipping martini's. Zaire and I were left to entertain ourselves and we didn't waste a minute."

"There was a small launch at our disposal. Next thing I knew, we were off on an adventure of our own. At fifteen I hadn't had much experience with boys. Zaire was like a god. Deep brown skin, amber eyes, tall and wide chested like an Olympic swimmer. His name, Zaire, meant River, he told me, and the sound of it on his lips made me tingle all over.

That summer was the perfect storm of teenage lust, testosterone, and complete abandon."

"Having lived most of my life in DC, I'd known plenty of boys; but I'd never met anyone like Zaire. He was at once familiar and mysterious. I could have watched him simply sit and breathe for hours."

"My mother warned me away. Zaire is *too old for you, Alexis.* No context, no detail. Just *not for you.*"

Tessa tilted her head and gave her an accusing frown. "Like you needed context."

Lexi let go a little laugh. "Right. One look into those wolverine eyes and I had all the context I needed. I was drunk in love. We spent every waking moment together, staring through rainbow sunbursts on perpetually wet lashes into the depths of each other's souls. Or so I told myself."

The remembered image of Zaire stopped her. The mesmerizing blue-green underwater world and their bodies wet and shining in the sun … the gold coin necklace his father had given him after his first dive flickering against his dark-walnut skin, his fingers working a spiny whelk shell from the sand.

"I swear I can't look at a man's hands without seeing his fingers entwined in mine, dark and light, male and female. Strong and … yielding."

Tessa tied off a plastic bag of t-shirts and pants for the DONATE pile. "So, you did the wild thing."

"Like bunnies." Lexi couldn't help smiling at the thought. She was too young, and he was from a completely foreign world. Never in all the time since, had she made love with such abandon, such conviction, such desire. She shrugged the memory away. She'd counseled enough teenage girls to know the same could be said of any young affair. There was nothing special about hers.

Liar.

"Anyway, by mid-September, he returned with his family to Ethiopia — Bole, near the capital I understand — to the largest of his father's elite hotel complexes. I headed back to school in DC."

"I thought I would die without him. Begged my parents to take us there during Christmas break. But they had moved on to Fall and the next round of holiday galas and fundraisers. By late November I knew I was in trouble."

Tessa sank into a tired bean bag chair, shaking her head. "So, you went through with the pregnancy."

Lexi sat on a pile of boxes, propped her elbows on her knees. "I was terrified. I didn't tell a soul until it was way too late to talk about options. My parents barely paid attention to me anyway. I was four months in before my belly started to pooch out, and then a big slouchy sweater covered it up. Between working at Georgetown and our housekeeper acting as nanny, my mother probably hadn't seen me naked since I was five years old. By the time she realized what was going on, I was nearly six months gone."

"My parents were understandably furious. Their reaction was predictably all about them. *They* were humiliated. What would *their* friends think? How could *they* attend events of state knowing everyone saw them as failed parents?"

"What about Zaire? His parents? What did they say?"

Lexi wiped the backs of her hands at the sting of tears in her eyes, even after all these years. She shrugged. "That last day on the dive boat was the last I ever saw or heard of any of them. Zaire never called, never wrote, nothing. It was as though our time together never happened."

Those old feelings rose up unbidden, injustice, anger, despair. And her mother's words came back to haunt her. It was just as she had warned. Zaire — tall, handsome, irresistible Zaire — who swore he would never love another — had only wanted one thing — his first piece of ass.

She shifted her gaze to focus on the KEEP pile. "They took away my phone, took me out of school, practically locked me in my room. They told me they contacted Zaire's parents and it was all decided. I would have the baby in isolation, and it would be adopted. They never even took me to a doctor."

"Seems a little risky."

"Not as risky as tarnishing their reputation, apparently." Lexi shook her head. "I went into an early labor and the first doctor I saw was in the emergency room, and then, only long enough to see her nod at my mother before they put me under for a C section. Not my choice either."

"I'm so sorry, Lex. It may have been the right thing for you and the baby, but it was harsh and cruel to have to feel punished over it." She reached out and cupped her hand over Lexi's. "You could have told me, you know."

There weren't enough sighs to empty out the shame. "I know that now. When I first got to

California, it was all so fresh, so painful. I was just as determined no one knew my disgrace as my parents. I buried it deep. Pretended it never happened."

She got up and went to the box with the little cap inside, rested her hand on the lid. "I'm actually kind of surprised my mother kept the hat. I would have expected her to throw everything connected to the incident away."

"It was her granddaughter, after all."

Lexi slowly shook her head. She would never understand either. "She was only thinking of herself and how a baby would affect *her* life."

Lexi let her gaze slip to the roll up door. "I honestly think they were both glad to have a reason to be rid of me. They shipped me off two weeks after. You know. We went through the school summer session together--and I rarely heard from them again. They paid for school, sent money to the clerk to give me on my birthday, but never a *How are you?* Or A*tta girl* for getting straight A's."

Those old feelings crept in again, making her chest ache. "I'm not sure what was worse, going through that pregnancy or being ejected from their lives." She shrugged. "I suppose I was better off on both counts."

Tessa studied her face a bit before she answered. "She must have had second thoughts, though. Your mother. She kept the hat."

Lexi closed her eyes again.

"And," Tessa went on "Whatever else is in that box."

Lexi stared at the box, the taped lid taunted her. "I should just toss it," she said, reaching for the box.

Tessa grabbed her hand. "Let's just … give it some time. If you still feel that way after the earth takes a couple of turns, you can chuck it in the trash then. Meanwhile, let it steep like good tea."

In a flash of fancy, Lexi imagined herself chucking the box overboard miles out to sea. Instead of sharing, she let it go and moved on to a messy tangle of masks, weights, and other items in the dive box.

"At least you learned to dive out of it."

Lexi lifted a shoulder. "I suppose. I haven't dived since I loaded the storage unit. That guy I dated right before I moved in with you? He was a diver, remember? His parents ran a tour boat to Catalina. The idea of diving again drew me in, like a beach lover longs for the coast if they move away. But it didn't take. Diving reminded me of Zaire and not in a good way." Truth was, Lexi had never met anyone who could erase the memory of Zaire.

"Do you know what happened to him? Did he take over his father's empire? Go into politics? Start a revolution?"

Lexi chuckled. "You mean, have I Googled him?"

"Everybody does."

Lexi dragged herself up and tackled the next box in the pile, determined to move on. "He's a filmmaker. The Nat Geo kind. I saw his name referenced in an article in the Smithsonian about rare gold coins found in the Bosphorus. Apparently, he's some kind of expert. But nothing personal."

"No pictures? Family? Wife?"

"My aren't we nosy."

Tessa shot up a knowing brow.

"Like I said. I never found any direct connection to him; only a reference, but it doesn't surprise me. You see that a lot with politicians and diplomats. They put a big block on that branch of the family tree. His family was extremely private. Not anxious for anyone to know the extent of their wealth. The last thing they would want is their son's shady past coming back to bite them."

"I suppose. But it's hard to resist, isn't it?"

"What? You mean seeking him out? No. I'd just as soon move on. Forget about it." She closed her eyes. The image of Zaire stared back at her, beckoning her across the bridge of time. He had been three years older than her, but really, they were both just kids. If he had offered so as much as an *I'm sorry*, she might have forgiven him. She let go another sigh. "I really don't want to talk about it anymore."

Tessa scrunched out of the chair. "What about this," she asked, her cutter poised over a box of old school notebooks.

Lexi pondered a moment. Was there anything about her young life worth remembering? A prom? A dance recital? A friend? Her heart squeezed into a tight fist, then to her own surprise, relaxed. This time, she would listen to her own advice. It was all in the past, and there wasn't a damn thing she could do to change any of it.

"Drop it in the TOSS pile."

20

Chapter 2 – A Spiny Whelk

Phillip was waiting at Lexi's garage. With parking at a premium on Balboa Island, they'd need to get unloaded quickly before some Air B&B visitor complained. Funny. Lexi still thought of her house as Audrey's, even though she had the deed tucked away in her safety deposit box and had emptied it of all but a few pieces of Audrey's furniture. She still half expected the old girl to shuffle out of the bedroom in a threadbare bathrobe with some wild story about the island's history to tell. She had only known the old woman for the last year of her life, but Audrey had left an indelible tattoo on her heart: *I promise to always take care of your home.*

With Phillip's help, they unloaded the van onto one side of the garage, leaving just enough room for her Volkswagen on the other. The tired Beetle would be replaced, too, as soon as Lexi could manage.

"Dinner is at seven," Tessa told her as she and Phillip climbed the back stairs to their house next door. Rags, the cat she'd inherited with the house, hustled to follow them up the stairs. Since the day they'd moved into Tessa's Uncle's home, Rags had let them know, he owned both houses. With a big smile and a sense of belonging she hadn't felt since, or maybe never, Lexi hoisted herself into the U-haul's driver seat and blew them an air kiss.

If ever a couple deserved to be happy, it was those two. And by leaving her house to Lexi, Audrey had ensured the three of them would remain close.

"I'll bring some good wine," she called out as she pulled away. Very good wine. Her family may have dumped her, but her friends had come through. They deserved something special. It was four o'clock. She'd have just enough time to get the U-haul back with a one-day charge, stop by the wine shop for something sparkly and expensive, and get a soak in Audrey's claw-foot tub before she had to dress for dinner.

In the tub, she tried to relax, without much success. No matter how hard she focused on emptying her mind, her thoughts crawled doggedly back to the shoe box. Her fingers tingled at the thought. What else had her mother hidden away from her all these years? No doubt, it was the reason she'd shipped the whole frickin' mess to her doorstep. Whatever it was, it was clear, she needed to face it now, head on, before she could move on. *Physician heal thyself.*

She dried, dressed, and clumped down the stairs to retrieve the box from the garage and bring it back to her bedroom.

Lifting the lid, she quickly plucked the pink infant cap off the top and tucked it in the back of her nightstand drawer where it couldn't ambush her. Laying the Kente scarf aside, she unfolded the newsprint from a fist-sized package. It was a single strand of red, cherry-tomato-sized beads separated by smaller ones — silver and brass enameled in red and yellow. Gorgeous.

She fastened the heavy beads around her neck then wrapped the scarf around her head, letting her tight dark curls spring out over the top.

Now there's something you don't see every day, Lex.

But there was something missing. She tipped her head at her reflection, then scrunched up her mouth, inspired.

She pawed through a box of mostly unused make up on her dresser to find the tube of shiny red lipstick she rarely had the guts to use, then added a swipe of color to her lips and pressed them together.

The effect was not as much startling as transformative. The woman who stared at her from the mirror was exotic. Beautiful. And a complete stranger. In her entire life, Lexi had never embraced her African roots, unless she counted her habit of wearing giant hoop earrings.

Her mother's words echoed in her head: "With your father's pale skin and my gorgeous green eyes, you can pass for whatever you like." The memory pricked a sore spot in her soul she thought she had worked through. Her mother had always described her skin as pale. Not white, or peach, or light, or caramel, or mocha or any other beautiful color people used to describe a mixed complexion. No, her mother described her as pale, somehow lacking, missing something important. A something she had realized over the years was her mother's problem, not hers.

Anger tinged her cheeks scarlet, she shook off the old hurt. The scarf emphasized her tousled hair, the necklace brought out a hint of amber in her skin and amplified her lightly freckled cheekbones, and the lipstick made the whole thing pop. She stood up to her full five foot ten and tried on her biggest toothy smile. A bold statement. One she didn't quite feel entitled to make.

That thought deflated her. She was an impostor. She'd never even set foot in Botswana or Ethiopia, or whatever African soil her mother claimed. She huffed out a laugh. She couldn't even claim ex slave status.

She blinked at herself. The dark and unfamiliar weight of her mother's blood pounding in her ears. Who did she think she was?

Who indeed?

She slid the scarf off her head, removed the necklace and lay them aside. The next package was larger but lightweight and wrapped in three layers of newspaper. A spiny whelk like the one's they'd found in the Med. On reflex, she put it to her ear, but instead of hearing the ocean, she heard a clink and rattle. Hum.

She tipped it over, turned it several times to free from the spiral whatever was inside. Expecting loose sand or tiny particles of shell, she gasped when a thick gold chain poured out onto the duvet. She reached out a finger to touch it. At the base of the chain a round bezel held a bright, shining coin. One she recognized immediately.

Zaire's necklace. The one she'd seen him wear every day they'd been together — pressed between them when they'd made love, dangling over his shirt at dinner. Her lips went suddenly cold; she covered her mouth, holding back a cry. How did it get here? Her mother had said they'd never heard from Zaire again.

But she'd lied, hadn't she? She picked it up. The proof lay in her hand.

Lexi draped the chain against her neck, lifted her eyes to the mirror, and everything she thought she knew about her life dissolved in a blur of tears.

How on earth had it gotten here? The shell alone was a mystery. Her mother had refused to let her pack any shells from their trips because "they'll stink to high heaven by the time we get home."

There was only one explanation. Zaire had sent her the shell and necklace as a message that he cared, and her mother had kept it from her.

Anger throbbed at her temples. Everything she'd believed for the last fifteen years had been a lie. A terrible, cruel lie.

She held the coin to the light and there was no mistake. It was the coin Zaire's father had given him from the small treasure they'd discovered on his first dive in the Bosphorus. She draped it around her neck and fastened the clasp. The coin hit squarely between her breasts, jumping slightly at her quickening heartbeat, a hypnotic ba-bump, ba-bump, ba-bump.

She stood mesmerized, caught up in the sensation. Her gaze lifted slowly to the mirror until she saw with a rolling shock a young woman smiling curiously back at her. At first, she recognized her own familiar features, but now, as she stared into her own green eyes, the woman's features began to change — to tilt as her cheekbones rose a little higher, their color deepening to a glowing brown, her hair losing its reddish hue to a cobalt blue-black.

With shaking fingers, she touched her burnished cheek. The image did the same. Then, like when a rogue wave suddenly lifted her tiny sailboat on a swell and drove her forward, her stomach lurched; the floor dissolved beneath her feet, and she slid through a void so empty it had no color or shape. She rolled and rolled until she had to squeeze her eyes tight to block out the sensation.

A moment later, it was over. She opened her eyes. The necklace lay cool against her skin. She pressed the coin between her thumb and forefinger. Nothing.

She stood a moment longer in an eerie silence.

What the hell just happened? Who was the woman in the mirror? What did the necklace have to do with it?

Her phone chimed a text notification, breaking the spell. Rags was back in her bedroom, batting at discarded newspaper from under the bed skirt.

She picked up the shell and set it gingerly on her dressing table. Unsure why it mattered now, after all these years, one thing was clear to her. Zaire had cared once. And that thought warmed a tiny corner of her heart that had never quite healed.

The phone chimed again. Tessa.

Lex? Where are you? We're waiting to start the picture deck.

She picked up her phone, her fingers still trembling as she texted back:

LESIDI'S COIN

On my way...

28

Chapter 3 - A Little Back Story

Lexi arrived at the Koenig home to find the image of Tessa and Phillip's faces pressed together in a kiss gracing the entire wall of the great room. Their glowing smiles helped dispel the images reeling through Lexi's head. Her heart rate had slowed closer to normal, although she wasn't sure she would ever feel normal again. What she thought had been normal had been all wrong. She was going to have to find a way to live with that. But not now. Not tonight. It was Tessa and Phillip's night and she wasn't going to let her baggage interfere with their happiness.

She slipped off her over-sized bag, retrieved the bottle of sparkling rosé wrapped in a festive crinkle of pink cellophane, and joined the newlyweds and Phillip's parents at the bar. Phillip's mother Jenessa clasped her hands together like a child given a Christmas present. Her expression made the extra stop at the wine shop on the way over from the island worth all the fuss.

Cortland Koenig, an ex-airline executive who had worked his way up after piloting Caribou troop planes in Vietnam, twisted the wire off the bubbly and worked the cork almost out, sending Jen a quick wink before popping it. The sound drew a little yelp out of her that made him grin. Those little things — the tender, caring moments that came fewer and farther between — were the ones Lexi'd hoped someday would be in her life.

Jenessa McGuire-Koenig, once one of the first woman Ob Gyns in Orange County, had slipped to a mental plateau where speech mostly eluded her. Lexi had helped Phillip deal with the emotional fallout in private counseling before his wedding to Tess. But tonight, in the company of her family, Jen's eyes still sparkled with delight, hinting at the woman she had once been. As hard as it was to face the devastation of dementia, this was real life and Lexi was happy to have it surround her and take her in. These were real people. People who cared about each other. People who cared about her. The only family she had.

Cort filled champagne flutes all around. "So, are you all moved in, Alexis?"

Lexi grasped the tall flute, hitched a hip onto a high bar stool, and hooked her boot heel on a rung, feeling steady for the first time since she'd discovered the necklace.

On a slow exhale, she leaned back against the bar. "If by *moved in* you mean the boxes and bags containing my past life are inside the building, then yes, I'm moved in. Unpacking those boxes will be another story." One she wasn't sure after what she'd just found, she was ready to face. "At least all my worldly possessions are finally under one roof."

"I'll drink to that," Phillip said, drawing Tessa under his long arm. "We've got a ways to go."

Phillip and Tessa had agreed to split their time between Tessa's Balboa Island home and Phillip's apartment atop his family's garage in order to help his father care for his mom. Tess had been researching dementia care nearby. By the dark circles camped out under Cort's kind eyes, it was likely it would be needed very soon.

They toasted, and the sense of camaraderie eased her soul. Since Lexi's best friends in this world had tied the knot, they had each resigned their positions with their former employer, Cauldron Industries. After exposing the owner's family — at least what was left of it — as long-time jewel thieves, there was no point in prolonging their employment. Phillip had already put out his shingle as private investigator. For him the creation of Koenig and Associates was the start of fulfilling a lifelong dream.

Tessa had decided to hold off her search for new employment. There was little doubt in Lexi's mind Tessa would have no trouble finding another position as research analyst; however, before she leaped back into the corporate world, having been inspired by her latent connection to the Cloisonné Brooch, Tessa wanted to spend some time on her college passion, that of making artisan jewelry. Working from home would also free her up to help Phillip's mom through the next phase of her life.

Lexi sipped her bubbly, fending off her own doubts. The fact that she'd buried the memory of her early pregnancy so well suddenly hit home. Hadn't she made a career out of counseling young women in trouble? Like she had been counseling her young self all along. Well, except for moving into the house she'd inherited from Tessa's neighbor. That serendipitous event still blew her away.

Cort raised his glass, catching the eye of each one of them in turn for another toast. "To new beginnings."

Lexi blinked back a tear. Was it a new beginning for her? Or was hauling out the junk from her past just dredging up and poking at old hurts she thought had healed over? She had spent the last five years helping others deal with and heal from all kinds of personal trauma; and all the while, she'd been avoiding her own.

"To new beginnings," she chimed in on a forced smile. Pink fizzys prickled the back of her throat then went down like sharp stones.

She watched the images on the great room wall flash by as Phillip clicked through a series of wedding photos. He and Tessa taking their vows on the yacht of one of his father's fishing partners, the Cloisonné Brooch Tessa had uncovered on her uncle's property gleaming at the center neckline of her pearl-white dress.

Cort stopped the projector and zoomed in. "Talk about wearing something old at your wedding. That piece was truly extraordinary."

Tessa lifted her glass. "I have Lexi to thank for that. She had our friend at the Getty hold off meeting with Immigration and Customs until after the wedding."

"Pure luck," Lexi said. "From the moment our friend, Alana at the Getty guessed the true nature of that jewelry, the pressure was on." Lexi took another sip of her bubbly, letting the sizzle calm her nerves and forget her own troubles. The memory of the Getty meeting still struck fear in her soul.

Cort leaned in, his interest perked. "How so?"

Lexi shook her head slowly. She shot her eyes to Tessa.

"Go ahead," Tessa said. "We're all family now. I'm sure Phillip has told his dad most of it anyway."

Phillip shrugged. "Not really. We weren't sure what we uncovered until recently ourselves."

Lexi rested her champagne flute on her knee. "That was probably a good thing, or we would all have gone a little crazy. The moment Alana had knowledge of the existence of stolen artifacts, she was responsible to report it. So, when I started describing it, she stopped me. I hadn't even gotten to the brooch yet and she was getting goose bumps. Apparently, ICE has an office at the Getty, so it could have all gone down much differently." She raised her glass. "The toast should more rightly go to Alana. I mean, she literally put her fingers in her ears and said *Lalalalala*, so she couldn't hear anymore. That's why we delayed the official appointment."

Tessa laughed with delight. "Oh, no. You don't get off that easy. Without you, I might never have learned the truth about the jewelry before we had to give it up."

Lexi tipped her glass. "That's what friends are for." Sipping, she settled in to watch the slides. But while the images on the wall clicked through a series of her friends' smiling faces in the sunset glow in

Belize, her thoughts were thousands of miles away. Discovering Zaire had sent her the necklace was a two-edge sword that made her question the value of learning the truth. How might her life have been different if she'd known about the necklace? Was it always better to know the truth? Or were some things better left hidden away in the dark?

"Lexi?"

Lost in thought, Lex sat up in her seat, startled to find the slide show was over and Tess was standing in front of her. "You all right?"

"I—sure. Fine." Now wasn't the time to dump on her friend.

"Cort wants to know if you want surf or turf," she asked, then her eyes popped wide. "Wow. Where did you get that?"

Lexi glanced down at her hand to see she was holding the coin between her fingers again. And like before, she'd seen… something. A woman standing at the stern of a small sailing vessel rested her hand on a graceful tiller, a white gown drifted around her feet. The wind billowed a single square sail, the vessel lifted, slid forward, and just before it headed away, the woman turned and gazed right at Lexi, a gentle smile curling at the corner of her lush mouth. It was the same face she'd seen in the mirror at home.

"I—oh. It's just … uh. Nothing."

Tessa sent her a look that said she didn't believe her. Lexi's face heated. The patio was bathed in the peach glow of sunset across Balboa Island. The projector had been put away and the table was set just inside the sliding wall of windows, Jenessa Koenig was already seated at the table, pushing pieces of steak around her plate with her fingers. Clearly, Lexi'd lost some time.

How long had she been standing here at the terrace railing, staring off into the void? She smiled weakly at Tessa now, confused. "I'm … sorry. What did you ask me?"

Tessa smiled at her, hooked her arm through hers. "Alexis Hill, I do believe you've had a bit too much of that bubbly."

That would be some kind of special bubbly because she'd never been known to check out on half a flute of it. She shook her head. "I'm not much of a guest. I should have offered to help with something."

Tessa sent her a sideways glance. "Sure you're all right?"

Lex nodded. "No worries."

"Okay then. I'll go get the pasta."

But Lexi *was* worried. It was the second time in the last few hours she'd drifted from reality. Drifted. Hell.

She was G.O.N.E. Gone.

Fugue up the wazoo.

Enough of a slip out of time that Tessa had noticed. What if she'd been in session with a patient? Or worse yet, driving? What if some kind of madness ran in her family? She always thought her mother was a bit mentally fragile. She bit her lip, trying to appear casual, while inside she was churning with an anxiety she could only attribute to … what?

She'd never experienced anything like it. And if she had, she'd have called one of her colleagues and had herself checked out. Maybe she'd had some kind of psychotic break. She'd had a shock, after all, discovering her mother's betrayal. But, seriously, was that enough to totally lose what must have been fifteen or twenty minutes of her life? She didn't think so, but her hands were icy cold.

Tessa gave her the fisheye again. With a shrug, she slipped the coin necklace under her shirt, shoved her hands into her side pockets, and grinned back at her. *Nothing to see here.*

She studied Tessa's beaming face, flushed with color and all smiles after returning from a lovely honeymoon trip. She'd placed a hand on her mother-in-law's shoulder on the way to the kitchen and whispered something in her ear that made the older woman smile. Her friends were celebrating their new life, their parents doing what they could to preserve what was left of theirs. Whatever was going on with herself, now wasn't the time to get into it.

"Well, Lex? What will it be?" She turned to see Cort strolling toward her holding his tray of barbecued delights aloft like a waiter. "We've got Tri Tip or lobster. Or both," he said, beaming.

What will it be, indeed? Was she going to let a little trip into the Twilight Zone destroy her present moments? Throw her off track? Or was she going to put on her big girl panties and carry on? Her gaze cut to the table, the mingled aromas of steak sizzling on the platter and buttery lobster settled her galloping stomach, feeling suddenly hungry like she hadn't eaten in days. Whatever had just happened, it was over now, and she wasn't going to dwell on it. She slipped her hands out of her pockets and rubbed them together. "Why thank you Chef Koenig, I'll have a little of both, please."

Dinner brought back a pleasant glow of comfort, and after a scant second helping of macadamia nut ice cream pie, Lexi settled into a friendly kitchen clean up while Phil and his father tended to Janessa. It had been almost a month since Lexi'd moved out of Tessa's and into Audrey's — her place — next door. With planning the wedding and their trip, and managing the minor repairs the old house needed, Lexi had been too busy to focus on the fact that their *separation* had left such a big hole in her life. Philip and Tess were a married couple now. Now, standing in the Koenig's kitchen, each wearing one of Janessa's homemade aprons, she realized how much she missed Tessa Madigan-Koenig.

"I miss this," Tessa said, reading her thoughts.

"Yeah." She'd always known one day it would happen. One of them would get married, start their own separate life. They were grownups after all. But if you counted the years in school and the last five, they'd spent at least some part of their day together, shared nearly every thought, finished each other's sentences for ten years. "I miss you, too."

Tessa hip-bumped her, drying a plate and slipping it into open slots above the dishwasher. "Things will get back to normal now that we're back home."

Lexi shifted her gaze to Janessa's kitchen window overlooking the street, nasturtiums cascading down the steep hill across the road. Again, that woman's face superimposing itself over her ghosted reflection in the window. She blinked it away. "Yes. Of course. I noticed Rags hasn't wasted any time making himself at home at your house again."

Tessa laughed. "We should make him a little catwalk. You know, between our two front decks."

"That would be really cool. As long as we enclosed it somehow. So he doesn't fall."

Tessa scrunched her mouth up. "I'll put Phil right on it. He's almost done with my workshop downstairs and until he's admitted to the California State Bar, I'll need something to keep him busy."

"I thought he already passed the bar."

"He did. A long time ago. But he's been inactive for a while. The guy has been a professional student most of his life. He got his AA degree in police science, then sat for the bar, but decided to switch to engineering."

Lexi glanced over at Phil who was cutting up pieces of lobster for his mother. "He's a multitalented guy."

He sent his status in with his application to the FBI before we left for Belize. He'll apply for the license once that comes through, but in the meantime—"

"He's all over you."

Tessa smiled. "That can actually be a good thing, but I'm not getting anything done."

Lexi polished the last glass and folded a hand-embroidered dish towel over the rack. "I'm so happy for you two. Glad you're next door."

Tessa leaned against the counter, folded her arms over her chest. "So, are you going to tell me about that little trinket hanging around your neck?"

Lexi's chest tightened. Small talk over. "What do you mean?"

"You aren't your usual bubbly self."

"I'm never bubbly."

"Maybe not, but you're definitely not yourself."

Lex drew in a slow breath, let it out. She was right about that. "I'm … good. Nothing to worry about."

Tessa raised a brow.

"Well, okay. I need to talk to you about some things. But not now. Not tonight. No big deal."

Tessa untied her apron and hung it on one of the hooks by the back door. "How about next week, after we get settled back into our routine?"

"Tess? Lex? You ladies done yet?" Phillip's voice sounded cheerful but urgent. His mother was beginning a sundowner phase and Lex suspected she was heading for bed. She also suspected it wouldn't be long before they'd need heavy assistance.

"Coming," Tessa called, resting her hand on Lexi's forearm. "I'll call you in a few days. We'll have lunch or something."

Lexi looped her apron over a hook. "Right. I'm going to take off. Let you guys take care of Janessa." She glanced over her shoulder to see that poor Janessa was taking off her blouse. "I'm so sorry."

Tessa shook her head. "I know. Phillip is really broken up."

Lexi pulled her in for a hug. "Talk soon."

Chapter 4 - Grand Theft Auto

Out of habit, the first thing Lexi did on entering her office was sprinkle a pinch of food into her saltwater aquarium and say hello to Elvis and Loki, the clown and damsel fish whose gentle movements along with the bubbling purr of the filter helped to mask the highway sounds outside, adding a layer of calm to the space that helped put her patients at ease.

Monday was always busy in Lexi's office. The teenagers of Newport Beach predictably carried out their drama on weekends, prompting frantic calls from distraught parents first thing Monday morning. Lexi reserved Mondays for making appointments later in the week to let all but near suicidal have time to cool down.

Her online schedule for Mondays was typically blocked out for "Community Outreach", which meant, she was in the office catching up on correspondence, paying bills, and working on classes to keep her license current.

With her usual Chai Latte poised on an ocean-themed coaster, she had propped the gold coin in its bezel setting against the open screen of her laptop. She had no idea the history of the coin beyond the fact that the beautiful boy who had stolen her heart had always worn it around his neck. Or one like it.

Zaire. Just the thought of him sent a pulse of heat to her body that made her feel like a teenager again. Her fingers tingled, and then she was typing his name in the Google box: Zaire Negatu. The cursor blinked its accusatory warning in time with her fluttering heart. *To Google or not to Google.*

It had been years since she'd followed the impulse. Years since she'd hit the impenetrable wall. The last time she'd tried it, there was a minor hit that resulted in little but a disappointing dead end. If she were one of her clients, she'd advise against going down that road. But, with the gold coin gleaming at her, she was perched on the precipice preparing to dive. All she had to do was hit ENTER.

And why not? It was different now, right? Circumstances had changed. She was no longer a helpless teenager, steeped in sorrow and shame. She had a different perspective: Hindsight.

Until now, she had accepted things at face value. Zaire had let her go without a word. Their parents had handled the situation. Each year on May 27th she secretly acknowledged the birth of her daughter, and each year confirmed she had done the right thing giving her up. Even if Zaire had acknowledged what happened, it had been the right thing to do.

But he *had* cared. He'd sent her the necklace; a token he'd have known would touch her heart. The fact that she'd never received it was her mother's betrayal, not his. She cringed at the thought. What mother does that?

And does that give you the right to peek into his life now?
Her fingers tingled again.
It most certainly does not, her conscience sang.
She leaned back in her office chair, gripped her hands safely in her lap. The cursor blinked. Blinked. Blinked.
Her phone pinged, giving her a sharp start. It was a text from the building's shared receptionist.
"Mrs. Tran is in the lobby. I told her you don't see clients on Monday, but she insists it's an emergency."
Lexi drew in a deep breath and slowly exhaled through. Tran's daughter, Minh, AKA Minnie to her school pals, was a sweet sixteen-year-old whose mother was gorgeous, well educated, and married to a prominent Orange County oncologist. Impressions meant a lot to her and her expectations for Minh were high. Her daughter was everything she'd hoped — beautiful, smart, popular, and ten times more assertive than her mother. Add what Lexi thought of as the battle of the big E vs little e — Estrogen waning on one side and raging on the other — and you have the classic mother/daughter apocalypse that played out in her therapy room at least twice a week. Both sides were at their most vulnerable.
Lexi sighed. In most cases she would have insisted her boundaries be respected. The Trans had signed her services contract that included respect for their agreed-upon schedule: arriving on time, notifying cancellations 48 hours ahead, and no unscheduled visits. But there was something about Minnie that wheedled into Lexi's heart. Something endearing that went way beyond the boundaries she'd set for her

practice. There were moments when the teen sat in the comfy lounge chair in her "interview" office she felt somehow akin to the girl.

Lexi had the certain sense that behind the hot pink streaks in Minnie's jet-black hair, the lips outlined in dark contrast to bright pink lipstick, and the clunky lace-up ankle boots below tattered skinny jeans, there was a vulnerable teen heading down a difficult road.

Unlike Lexi's mother, who'd absorbed adulation like a black hole and never gave back a hint of light, Minnie's mother looked on her daughter with a palpable love, one that forgave all, even when it should stand firm.

Lexi glanced once again at the blinking cursor on her computer screen, hissed out a breath. Instead of being interrupted, she was likely being saved.

She scooped the necklace into her pocket, closed the lid on the laptop, and pushed it to the side of her desk.

There was a real-life girl who needed her now.

Yuperoo.

She picked up her phone and thumbed her reply to the front desk: **Send her in.**

Clad in a jacquard suit of plaid pants and jacket likely Gucci and worth enough to pay Lexi's office rent for the next three months, Cam Tran appeared in her doorway, her usually perfect mascara smudged under her eyes.

Lexi inclined her head, expecting to see Minnie come teen-slouching along behind. Before she could comment, Mrs. Tran turned and closed the door behind her, leaned against it eyes closed, and exhaled. She stood there for a good count of five seconds before she recovered herself and slumped into the rose-colored upholstered chair on the patient side of Lexi's desk.

Lexi leaned forward, folded her hands in front of her, and let the silence speak between them while Mrs. Tran's breathing settled.

When she raised her chin and opened her eyes, anguish twisted her mouth into an uncharacteristic frown. "Minh is in the Orange County Juvenile Detention Facility."

Lexi's heart took a little dive. That made three times in as many months Minh had been in trouble. In their last session, Minnie had promised she was turning over a new leaf. The second time, she had shoplifted a bottle of cheap foundation makeup and a set of false eyelashes from Sephora, the value of which was less than fifty dollars; but the store manager, having recognized her from the first time, alerted store security and refused to be bought off by the return of the items plus a generous purchase from her mother.

Minh had been adamant when Lexi asked her how she had come to shoplift again, knowing she would get into trouble. "Mom took away my credit card," she'd told her on a shrug. "I had to have that foundation for my Facebook Live."

Lexi had seen Minnie's Facebook videos. Fairy lights surrounded her bedroom mirror in the background as she patted foundation over a complexion as clear and perfect as an American Girl doll fresh out of the box, right down to a pale smattering of freckles across her nose, all the while chattering about technique.

She had to give it to Minnie, whose Facebook persona wore an over-sized polka dot bow in her hair, the video was cute and captivating, and had over a thousand followers. It wasn't enough to get Minnie a big sponsor yet, but she had a leg up on most of the girls her age.

That time, Mrs. Tran took away Minh's cell phone, grounded her from Facebook for a month, and made her do her homework in the kitchen under strict supervision, despite the fact the girl was an A student.

Apparently that approach wasn't working.

Mrs. Tran sucked in a ragged breath and held it until Lexi thought she might explode. And then she did.

"She's not my daughter." Her voice was a painful wail. Tears pooled in her eyes; she threw her head back to stop them leaving wet tracks down her powdered cheeks.

Crap. This was exactly why Mondays were reserved for non-contact work. She pushed a box of tissues to the edge of her desk. The woman pulled a sheet from the box and dabbed at the corners of her eyes.

"Believe me, Mrs. Tran. You are not the first mother to speak those words in that chair. It's hard to fathom sometimes what our teens are thinking when they do something they have to know is wrong."

Tran blotted her eyes and leaned back in the chair. "No. I mean. She's really not my daughter. She's … adopted."

"Adopt — Oh."

"From Vietnam. Fourteen years ago."

Lexi was stunned. Not only that she hadn't known Minnie was adopted (you'd think as a regular counseling patient, her mother might have mentioned it), but that Lexi had made a most regrettable assumption based on appearances. Of all people, she should have known better. While Minh was too young to be among the group called Children of the Dust— the result of American GIs spending time in country in the seventies — she could certainly be the daughter or granddaughter of one.

"My husband wanted me to tell her when she was small. Her eyes are like ours; but, I'm sure you noticed, her skin is a shade or two darker than...Well, children can be cruel…" She trailed off, plucking the last of the tissue from the box to blot her eyes again.

She shredded the tissue in trembling fingers. Lexi regulated her breathing, careful not to react. The truth was the only thing she'd noticed about Minh was she was strikingly beautiful. She'd never seen her father and just assumed…

"My husband was right, though. We couldn't keep it from her forever. My sister's kid told her in one of her jealous snits. I'd like to ring her nasty little neck."

Nasty indeed. Lexi resisted the urge to commiserate, feeding her statement back to her instead. "So, her cousin told her."

"Yes. And when Minnie grabbed her purse and jumped in her cousin's Beamer and drove away, leaving her stranded at the mall, Veronica called 911 and said she'd been carjacked. Minh got as far as Little Corona before they pulled her over."

Lexi let out a sigh. This was a family issue that could easily be solved by a call to the girl's parents. So why didn't she feel relief? She plucked out a tissue of her own, feeling the sting in her eyes. Tran's story pulled at her heart like a painful cut that never healed.

Did her own daughter know she was adopted? And if she did…

She pushed the unspeakable question down deep. This is what they paid her the big bucks to do right? Help *other* people fix *their* problems, not get derailed by her own. Besides. *That* problem had been solved a long time ago.

Taken out of her hands.

Bam.

Over.

She claimed a reset moment, took a sip from her chai, and wiped her hand over her lips, then glanced up. Cam Tran stared at her, curiosity creasing her neatly tattooed brows, her nose glowing raw pink where her foundation had been wiped away. "What is it? What's wrong?"

Lexi smiled back at her. "Nothing. I just…" She pushed back from her desk a little, rolled her hand. "Please. Go on."

Tran's gaze shifted to the window, her chin puckered. "My husband says it's all my fault. I'm a lousy mother. I suppose he's right. I just don't know what else to take away from her. I can't just lock her in her room."

Lexi's heart softened. She could feel Tran's pain. Her husband was right about one thing. They should have told Minnie a long time ago. It was a fact that could not be changed. Now her reaction bore the weight of teenage angst. In this case, they may have gotten off easy. This whole thing was a misunderstanding that wouldn't likely stick Minh with a serious crime. The emotional fallout would be a different story.

Lexi stood, paced to the window, weighing her options. It never paid to get too close to one's patients. A rule she had never broken. Maybe it was time.

She turned, folded her arms over her chest, and cleared her throat.

Tran stared at her, her eyes wide.

"Mrs. Tran, Cam. I don't normally share personal information with my clients. But I think in this case, it might do us both some good."

Tran inclined her head, her dark eyes questioning.

"I just passed an anniversary of sorts." She pictured the little pink cap shoved to the back of her dresser drawer. "We would have celebrated my daughter's birthday in May. She would be fifteen."

Tran's hand went to her lips. "Would be? Oh my gosh, she's—"

Lexi held up her hand. "Oh, no. She's okay. At least I have no reason to think otherwise. I ... gave her up for adoption the day she was born. I haven't seen her since."

Tran blinked, shaking her head.

"I was only fifteen myself when I had her. So, I have to hope that she has a much better life than she would if I had tried to raise her on my own." She sank back into her chair. "My parents had the means and the lifestyle that could easily have managed another child. Could have even passed her off as their own. They could have been the kind of parents who loved their kid so much that they would support her no matter what mistakes she'd made."

"But they weren't. Instead, after the baby was born and—disposed of—they shipped me off to California. Out of their hair. Haven't seen them since."

Tran's lips were pressed tightly together, her chin puckered and trembling.

"You have given Minh a wonderful life. Likely much better than she would have had, right?"

Tran nodded slowly. There was fear in her eyes. Fear and guilt and maybe a little shock, but Lexi went on. There was no turning back now. She needed to make her point.

She got up and came around to Tran's side of the desk, scooted in front of her and took both her hands. "They were right, of course. I knew better than to have sex with Zai— that boy. But I did anyway. I had no business having a baby. And they shouldn't have had to pay for my mistake by raising another kid. But the rejection. Sending me away? That did permanent damage."

"I don't…understand. What does all this have to do with Minh? She's not pregnant."

"All I'm saying is parenting is tough. Adoptive, single, bi-racial, different faiths — But the one thing all parents have in common — hopefully — is they love their kids. No matter how angry or frustrated you are, you've got to keep that connection — or repair it if necessary. Put yourself in her shoes. What would you want right now if you were her?"

Tran gripped her hands in her lap, squeezing her eyes shut. She sniffed. "I think I would want my mother to come and get me and hold me tight." She looked up, anguish in her eyes. "But I'm not her mother. She was going to run away. She doesn't want me." The words came out in an agonized croak.

Lexi leaned across her desk, got a fresh box of tissue, and handed it to Tran. "She's angry. And rightly so. She wasn't expecting such a shock. But right now, she needs you. You might not be her biological mother, but you're the only mother she's got."

"She has a mother somewhere. Like you."

"Oh? Has she contacted you?"

"No. It was a closed adoption. She couldn't contact us, she—"

That specter again, peeking into Lexi's soul, pumping her heartbeat faster. "And what if she did?"

Tran pressed her lips together in a thin line, her eyes going obsidian dark. "Minh is sixteen. I wouldn't have a choice in the matter."

Lexi stared at those dark eyes a moment longer, seeing the anguish there. Then she reached out a hand to cover Cam's.

"If her mother leaves word with the adoption agency, Minnie is old enough to make that decision on her own. No doubt, she is already wondering about her real mom."

Lexi's own throat closed now. The sooner she got Tran and her daughter reunited, the better for all of them.

"One step at a time, right? Meanwhile, I want you to be thinking of something you can give back to her, rather than something to take away."

Tran nodded, once again her eyes cast to her hands folded in her lap.

Two hours, a skipped lunch date with one of her outreach partners, and a trip to OC Juvenile Hall later, Minnie had been restored tearfully into the arms of her mother, cousin Victoria and her parents agreeing it had all been a misunderstanding.

Hollowed out and alone, Lexi watched them drive away, the weight of her tiny little daughter resting in her arms taking over her senses.

Back in her office, Lexi opened her laptop, Cam's words echoing in her head. *She has a mother somewhere. Like you.*

It had never occurred to her to reach out to her daughter. What would be the point? She'd had nothing to do with the adoption when it happened. Without her own mother's help, she wouldn't even know where to start. The teenager was probably just like Minh, happily unaware of her adoption or at peace with it. What right did Lexi have to upset a fifteen-year-old's world? Contacting her daughter would be a selfish act. One she couldn't take back. It was a time in her life better left in the past.

Determined to shake off the empty feeling, she opened her laptop, the lighted screen reminding her where she'd left off. The cursor in the search bar behind Zaire's name taunted her. A slippery slope.

No way would she let her past overtake her life.

With new resolve, she hit the backspace key on the keyboard, erasing his name one letter at a time until the Google search bar was empty.

The moment the letters were gone, a sudden heat spread against her thigh, right under her pocket. She flattened her hand against the area, feeling a small, hard shape. The necklace. She slipped it out of her pocket and rubbed the image embossed on the coin with her thumb, feeling the tingle she had when she'd done the same thing at Phillip's parents' house.

She couldn't help thinking of Tessa and her bracelet. Hadn't the snake bracelet heated to her touch? What if now she directed her energy, her intention, while holding the necklace? Would it take her back in time?

She stared at the face on the coin, the image worn thin. Pulling a plastic magnifying glass from her desk drawer, she stepped to the window and held it to the light. She couldn't quite make out the words on the coin, but over the noise of the highway below and fish tank filter bubbling, the face she'd seen in the mirror floated to the surface of her thoughts. And then the name came on a whisper, gently lyrical, transcendent, so near her ear, she could almost sense the hair standing at her nape: *Lesidi.*

She closed her eyes, breathed salt air, and let herself go with the images tumbling through her mind.

Chapter 5 – Lesidi Waits

The Bosphorus - 327 CE

Lesidi stood silent near the cabin of her transport ship, her hand resting on the wood-carved swan's neck at the stern. She let herself drift into a remembered childhood dream of riding the back of a giant swan, strong and silent over the water to the ends of the Earth, unseen by human eyes.

She had so loved to sail. When her father, Negasi commissioned this newest ship of his fleet, he'd let her name it. And she had christened it The Isis, a goddess who was believed to bring the dead back to life, on the prayer she could keep her ailing father in this world with her a little longer. But it was not to be. Isis was a beautiful myth, nothing more.

A wave of melancholy swept over her, tightening her chest. Turning her thoughts outward, she focused on the shoreline under a sky burnished purple as the night advanced. A sprinkling of torchlights dotted the quay nearest the Emperor's palace. Her twin brother's ship, the Leto, had been moored all day at a lesser dock. *Stand at the ready, and soon*, he'd promised, *we will return home to Auksum with riches beyond our dreams.*

He reminded her more and more of her father— ambitious dreams the fire that drove him ever toward some time when he would at last be satisfied. Only

Lesidi knew, as sure as night follows day, for her brother that day would never come.

Amari was born, quite by surprise, only a few heartbeats after Lesidi on a sultry morning and a difficult birth that had left her mother nearly dead from exhaustion. Except for their near identical physical features, and of course the fact they were male and female, they were as opposite as two siblings could be.

He was anxious, reckless, and bold; she was patient, methodical, and cautious. He acted on impulse, never giving a care for the consequences of his actions; she stood like a statue before a challenge, her mind spinning probable outcomes, playing out like Greek Theater.

Comedy or tragedy?

Fair or foul?

Leap or stand her ground.

At times her indecision was debilitating; other times, holding back had prevented disaster.

Now that their father had passed into the next realm, and their mother lay infirm back in their mansion in Auksum, they had only each other in this world. They were two sides of a coin that had until the present moment seen them safely from the Red Sea down the canals to Alexandria, and into the Mediterranean bearing their cargos of ivory and olive oil and wine.

Once their holds were empty, and the Gods willing, they would join forces one more time with the greatest of Negasi's merchant ships, The Demeter, before the winter set in, transferring life-giving wheat up the Tiber river to distribution centers at Ostia.

Their reunion would be bittersweet, for their father no longer captained the biggest freighter in the fleet. Her only consolation was knowledge that Keleb, the young Auksumite commissioned by her father before his death, would be at the helm.

Not that Keleb would notice her. At twenty-five years old, a man of his rank would scarcely look at her, let alone consider her an appropriate match. But that hadn't stopped Lesidi from daydreaming about him.

Now, as she strained to detect any sound or movement across the water, fine hairs stood alert at her nape. The only sound was the soft lapping of a gentle current against The Isis's hull and the muted voices of her small crew taking their evening meal near the prow.

Ordinarily, she would welcome the calm. But tonight, the silence only heightened her sense of impending disaster. A mission Amari assured her would bring them back together by the time the sun was at its apex had extended well into the twilight; and now the day was nothing but a violet memory on the horizon. Her patience was running thin.

It didn't help that her dreams the night before had been filled with thunder and fire. Her father's words echoed in her mind. *You are blessed with the gift of sight,* he'd told her the last night they were together. *You are a Seer, like your mother.*

Her mother saw her power as a gift; Lesidi saw it as a curse, for rarely did her visions portend anything wonderful or uplifting. Quite the contrary. There would be drought, there would be flood, a loss of fortune.

She had cried over her visions, worried that her thoughts, her dreams, were the cause of people's misfortune.

Sometimes, her mother tried to console her. "It is only because we live in a volatile region. Anyone can predict a flood because there will always be one, and the flood is always followed by drought. It is the way of our land."

Her father had tried to console her in other ways. "Ah, but after the flood come the water lilies and the elephants and the egrets with their long-legged babies."

Other times, her mother told her the gift was because Lesidi was descended from Queen Zenobia, a powerful ruler of Syrian descent. "Your gift will be misunderstood, and one day, you may have to risk everything because of it. However, combined with patience and wisdom you will learn as you mature, you will be vindicated and gain what is most important in this world."

What her mother said was true. Their family had been blessed with much wealth, having grown rich in the ivory trade, but there was no proof of any connection to Queen Zenobia, unless it was the fine cut of her nose and her sea-green eyes. Her hair held a reddish hue like her mother, and she was long-limbed like Negasi, a tall, Auksumite merchant who had carried himself like a king.

Despite their efforts, as Lesidi grew into a young woman, most often when it was her moon time, she stayed awake late into the night for fear of what she might dream.

One stormy night shot with thunder and lightning and torrential rain she dreamed of a child born without fingers and toes and the next day in the village she learned her vision had come to pass. The girl child was born in the storm, then hidden away for fear the people would do her harm. Lesidi stopped sharing her dreams with her family after that.

So far in this life, her only gift seemed to be the ability to draw trouble and grief to those around her, which was why she'd begged her father to let her take the corbita, Isis out on the sea so she could no longer be a detriment to the people closest to her. But it hadn't worked. The last night of her journey she saw him laid out on his death bed. She arrived home to find that he was gone. The pain of his loss would forever ride heavy in her heart.

Now, she refocused her attention, ignoring the complaints of her empty stomach, listening for any sound that could signal her brother's return. The night before she'd dreamed once again of thunder and fire, torment and treachery. It wasn't the first time she'd *seen* their transports attacked, their goods stolen, their fortune lost. It was a natural fear, she'd told herself. The more responsibility one bore, the more worry.

She had accepted the fact she would never quite be free of worry as long as they sailed the sea. But they were on the Mediterranean now, controlled by the great ships of the Roman Empire. There were pirates on the Red Sea, but none dared attack the Emperor's ships in their own territory.

Still, she had been up a full day and night, and until Amari returned safe to her, she feared sleep on the chance her dreams might produce the exact outcome she most dreaded. Better to stay awake, think of good things, and keep her wits about her.

Seeking a sense of calm, she turned her thoughts to Keleb. The way his voice rolled warm and resonant over her when he spoke reminded her of home in Auksum. The first time she'd seen him was on the veranda of their villa overlooking a harbor crowded with great ships from far off lands. She was hardly a woman, but old enough to feel her blood hum when she overheard his conversations with her father.

With her beloved father gone, and her mother grown weak with melancholy, Lesidi was charged to carry on her family's legacy, transporting ivory from her beloved Africa's interior and spices and silks from the East across the Red Sea, through the canals of the Nile, through the Kingdom of Kush, and on to Alexandria; then across the great sea all the way to Ostia in Rome, fulfilling government contracts Negasi had negotiated years before. So far, Amari respected her leadership, accepted her first-born authority. So far, she had been able to hold his recklessness in check. For now, at least she could not do it without Keleb's help.

"Will you take some food, Lesidi?" Her first mate Cyril approached, proudly displaying a trencher of boiled snails he had kept alive for the entire trip. "This is the last of them. I fear it will be gourds and pine nuts from here until we meet up with the fleet."

Lesidi had lost her appetite. Her stomach roiled with apprehension. But she accepted his offering, for refusing would be disrespectful to the one who kept them all fed and healthy during their long journey. "Thank you, my friend."

"Will there be anything else? The men talk of retiring soon."

Lesidi gazed again across the water, her dream replaying in her head. "I would bid them stay alert a while longer until Amari returns with the Leto."

"Oh?" Concern deepened the trenches in his sun-burnished face.

To calm his fear, she selected an olive-oil-smothered snail from the trencher and popped it in her mouth, barely tasting the delicacy through her anxiety. She didn't want to alarm her crew, but she didn't want to be taken off guard either.

"Why don't you engage them in another round of dice? It would give me peace to know I'm not the only one awake should there be a need for…" She waved her hand vaguely in the direction of the palace. *For what?* She did not know, only that the hair still stood up at the back of her neck, she could not take her eyes off the shore, and she had the distinct sensation she was being watched.

Chapter 6 – Flame and Thunder

Lesidi continued her vigil as the night darkened, only a sliver of moon casting a ghostly veil across the still water. Nothing stirred along the docks she could clearly make out, save several small boats poling their way along the rushes near the shore away from the palace.

It was with a modicum of relief that at last the dark silhouette of the Leto slipped into view, the tall figure she could barely make out at the tiller would be her brother, Amari. His first mate, a man loyal to Negasi and who acted as a good influence on Amari was likely at the prow, working the sounding lead to measure the water's depth. Her heart rate began to settle as they picked their way out of the shallows, the sail turned leeward to pick up a light breeze.

The little corbita rode high in the water to her estimation, which made her question what cargo could be so light and at the same time so precious that Amari had promised riches. As her father always said, *It is a foolish captain who sails a light ship.* She blew out a sigh, rolling her head to release the tightness in her shoulders and the tension in her gut. The next time Amari proposed something out of the ordinary she would think better of allowing it.

Keleb would be angry at the both of them for holding up the entire fleet, something that could jeopardize her assignments in the future. Some in the fleet already believed she was only given command of a vessel out of respect for her father. It was up to her to prove them wrong.

Keleb's contract was explicit. Amari was the son, but Lesidi was the first born, and by Negasi's order (and likely her brother's reckless reputation) she was the heir of the family's business. To be sure it was not a traditional role for a woman, but as the supplier of Rome's most precious commodity—wheat—who could argue against it? Lesidi had encountered obstructions in the past, but having not backed down, she was beginning to earn the respect of the merchants.

The only way the shipping company would ever go to Amari would be as designated by her, or upon her death. For the time being, Keleb commanded the fleet and barring some calamity, would continue in that role.

The thought she would soon see him made her feel warm in the deepest hollows of her heart. To be sure he had no personal inclination toward her. She'd actually prayed to dream of him on several occasions if only to see the truth in his disinterest so she could set herself free. But her sight never brought her any visions of Keleb. Perhaps that was a good thing, considering her visions never turned out well.

She lifted her eyes momentarily to the heavens and the familiar patterns of stars overhead.

She had just let her hand slip from the swan's neck at the corbita's stern when a blinding flash lit the sea surface all the way to the nearest walls of the palace, followed by a deafening blast that shocked the air around her like some giant god had slapped his hands against her ears. Two bodies hurtled through the air, flailing in flames before they plummeted back down and hit the water with a sickening crash. A moment later the Leto was engulfed in flame.

Flame and thunder.

"Amari!" She stumbled to the prow. Her men were up, digging their poles into the water with every ounce of their strength. But without the wind in their sail, the corbita was less like her goddess namesake and more like an elephant in the water—afloat, but all bulk and no speed.

Lesidi took up an oar to help, bending her back into the effort until her muscles felt as though they would snap, but their progress toward the flaming wreck was agonizingly slow. Corbitas were never designed to be propelled by the strength of men, only by the wind in their sails.

By the time the Isis came close enough to identify splintered wood floating in the water, the ship was fast sinking below the surface, burning timbers hissing steam clouds into the night. Lesidi called out her brother's name until her throat was raw with fatigue and acrid smoke, until she hadn't another ounce of strength and all was completely still.

She gripped twisted tendrils of hair in her fist as she stalked back and forth on the deck straining to see any sign of life in the churning wreckage. Her crew joined her in the search, holding lamps aloft, though they were practically useless. The corbita itself was small and on Amari's insistence, two of her small launches had been transferred to the Leto as part of his mission.

Lesidi stood on the prow taking in the scene. There were no other ships nearby, no rescue party coming from the dock.

The Leto, along with her crew and whatever precious cargo they had procured, was lost. There was nothing left but a few empty amphora bobbing to the surface and a slick from what was most likely olive oil from the broken ones.

"Amari," she whispered, her throat closing on despair. She felt as though half her soul had been ripped from her insides and turned out raw and bleeding into the sea. They had been at odds most of their lives, but siblings still. No one was closer to her in spirit and blood. That spirit couldn't be gone. The hollow ache inside was more than she could bear.

"Lesidi!" Her first mate shouted and waved his arms from the stern. "There's someone in the water. Over here."

"Amari? Oh, by the gods, let him be all right," she prayed as she flew to the stern.

The first mate had tied a piece of hemp rope to the windlass, then tied the other end around his midsection and, filling his lungs with three heaving draughts of air, he dove courageously overboard.

She leaned over the side, pushing her hair out of her eyes. It was too dark to see exactly where he was, and she prayed she wasn't about to lose Cyril as well.

A moment later she spotted him. He lay on his back, one arm around the chest of what appeared to be a lifeless body, the other paddling toward the corbita's hull.

Lesidi shouted for the other men. "Pull them up. Hurry."

The men rushed to her aid, using the windlass to pull them in. Steadying himself with one hand on the rope and his feet braced against the hull, the mate hauled the body with him — step-by-labored-step — until two men could get a grip under the arms of the limp form.

Lesidi realized with shock and horror, that not only was the ragged creature too small to be her brother, but with round breasts straining against the cloth of a tunic and dark hair stringing down over her mate's shoulder, the poor thing was a woman.

Chapter 7 - Girl in the Water

She was blue around the lips and her head lolled back on the first mate's arm in a way that made Lesidi fear she was lost. Lesidi had witnessed enough near drownings in her sailing experience to know there was always a chance a victim might be revived.

"Lay her on her stomach, her head to the side." She dropped to her knees and pressed her hands flat on the woman's back. Using her full weight, she pumped hard. Water gushed out of the poor woman's mouth.

"Here, let me." The man who had cooked their dinner pushed her aside and passed her a lit torch. After two more heavy pumps, the young woman convulsed, vomited seawater, then coughed and gulped air into her lungs.

"Take her to my quarters," Lesidi ordered the second mate, her hope renewed. If one could survive the horror she'd just witnessed, perhaps there were more. She lifted a torch over the briny surface where she had seen her brother's ship go down, only peripherally aware of the men collecting their new passenger and carrying her into the boat house. Eyes straining into the dark, Lesidi caught a glint of light in the water, a clump of white bobbing near the bow of her ship. Hope surged in her veins once more. "Over here!"

Holding the torch aloft, she gulped her breath, chest heaving, as the men came running from behind her. Her heart raced in her chest until, with a defeating stab, she made out what the object was: the swan's head from the Leto, burned and splintered, bumped along their hull, one dark eye staring sightless into the night.

The image sent a chill through her entire body and sank deep into her soul. As much as she hoped otherwise, she had to accept what was right before her eyes. Her brother was gone and his dream with him.

And, Keleb was waiting.

They had already wasted a day on Amari's reckless adventure, only to meet with disaster. Keleb would be none too pleased for their late arrival. Winter's storms had sunk many a cargo ship that had ventured across the sea too late. Keleb's loyalty was to the fleet. Next to that, the news of her brother's loss would be secondary.

"Boatswain, call the men to task. We have to get out of here," she ordered, pulling herself together. With that order delivered, she returned to her quarters and peeked inside.

The young woman was propped in the chair next to her writing desk, wrapped in fur, a woolen wrap over her damp hair, her blistered palms swathed in lard from the galley. Her eyes were closed, but her breathing was steady.

Lesidi knelt by her side. She was very young, barely a woman at all by the look of her. Blood seeped from a gash at her forehead, but the color was slowly returning to her lips.

"We need to get you out of those wet clothes," she said gently. "I've got a wool tunic to keep you warm."

The girl startled, opened her eyes. Lesidi reached out and smoothed a hair out of the young woman's face.

"What is your name?"

The girl blinked, looked around the cabin, as if to re-orient herself. "Who is asking?"

Lesidi smiled at her. She would probably have answered the same in her circumstance. "I am Lesidi, Daughter of Negasi. This vessel is bound to Negasi's fleet."

The young woman looked her up and down, considering, then drew in a deep breath and coughed. After clearing her throat as if it hurt, she lifted her chin and answered, "My Name is Kindra. I am a goldsmith to the Empress."

Her chin quivered as she said the final words, but she fought to hold her head erect. The truth of her words remained to be proven, but Lesidi had no doubt of the veracity with which she believed her position.

"You're going to be all right, Kindra the Goldsmith," she answered, as much to reassure herself as the young woman. "Although for now, I fear you should keep that information between us."

The corners of Kindra's mouth turned up and she nodded.

"Can you stand?" Lesidi offered her hand, and the girl took it, letting the fur drop away. Lesidi turned her back, opened a deep storage basket next to her bunk, found the tunic and turned back to the girl. She stood, shivering, one hand supporting herself at the arm of the chair, the other covering her belly in the way a mother protected a child in the womb.

Lesidi held back a gasp, reserved comment, and helped the young woman on with the tunic, then found a dry wrap for her head. "Can you tell me what happened to Amari?"

"Am-ari?" The young woman coughed again.

Lesidi poured a cup of fresh water from an urn next to her bed and offered it to the girl. "My brother. He was on the Leto." She took her by the shoulders, none too gently. "I need to know what happened to my brother."

The girl drew back, fisted her hand at her mouth, shaking her head. "I don't…know, I…"

Lesidi would try another tack. "What were you doing on the Leto?"

"The Leto?"

"My brother's transport ship."

It was clear the woman was confused and afraid, but Lesidi couldn't keep the desperation out of her voice. "He was bringing a cargo back to the fleet. What were you doing on the Leto?"

"I don't know of your brother. I wasn't on the boat." She slipped the tunic over her head, pulled it down, and gripped her arms tight around herself to stop them shaking. "I was in the water."

"In the water? Whatever for?" Lesidi's desperation turned to suspicion. Did this woman have something to do with the blast? The fire?

The woman returned her searching glare. They appeared to be at a standoff. She drew herself up to stand erect. "Am I a prisoner?"

"A prisoner? Why, no. Of course not. I just—"

"May I go outside then?" Her gaze left Lesidi's and shifted to the bulkhead leading out of her quarters.

Lesidi stepped out of her way, feeling suddenly guilty for grilling the girl. "Of course."

The ship lurched as her sails harnessed a draught of wind. Lesidi moved to steady the girl at her elbow, but she evaded her grasp. She picked her way across the cabin to the doorway, bracing herself against the bulkhead as she stepped through. There was a calmness about her, one Lesidi had to admire. They had just plucked her from death's door, for god's sake and now she acted like they were out for an evening's sail. Lesidi followed her out.

The woman gripped the railing tightly, seemingly unaware of her blistered hands. She stared into the water where Amari's ship had gone down; the sorrowful countenance of her features matched the ache in Lesidi's heart. There was a sudden and inexplicable sensation of kinship, as though they had once traveled the same road, traveled it still. She moved to the woman's shoulder, gently touched the back of her hand. "You're safe with me, Kindra. I think we can help each other."

Kindra did not meet her gaze but allowed Lesidi's hand to remain atop hers; closing her eyes, she drew in a long slow breath.

Images tumbled through Lesidi's mind like a shuffled deck of cards: Amari's determined face, a tall man she didn't recognize, equally determined, and a woman, disheveled and angry, yet somehow regal and composed.

Then suddenly, the girl turned and fixed her gaze on Lesidi, a deep penetrating gaze that opened a connection. There was fear and pain in her eyes, but not malice. This woman, this girl, could never be capable of creating such a disaster on her own. Murder? Maybe. Under the right circumstances, but not random mayhem.

The young woman drew in a breath that seemed to inflate her to stand upright and confirm she had gained standing in her rescuer's eyes.

Lips set in a determined line, her hand returned to cover her stomach.

Lesidi leveled her gaze at her. "Please. Tell me what happened. How did you come to be in the water?"

The girl's eyes shifted to the surface and then to the horizon, now salted with stars. "I was looking for Marcus. But I can see now I was too late."

Still holding her hand Lesidi whispered low, "and, who is Marcus?"

The woman lifted those sorrowful eyes to hers once more. "He was the father of my child."

Chapter 8 - The Conspiracy

Lesidi stood at the railing next to the young woman, her heart twisting in two directions at once. She ached for her brother in the way only a twin can. But she couldn't help sympathizing with the young woman beside her, eyes care-worn and colorless as dry stones. She didn't need *The Sight* to understand their fates twisted together by the events of the day as surely as hemp rope anchoring their sail.

Her brother's whereabouts might be hidden from her, but she could feel him with a drifting certainty that gave her hope. If he were dead, surely she, of all people, would know. Feel his absence. Instead, she felt the reckless impudence of him mocking her doubt.

You are the one who sees, 'Sidi. Why do you not trust me?

Why indeed? Her dreams tonight might tell her otherwise, but right now, buoyed by the timbre of his confident voice in her head, a laugh bubbled up her chest, relieving a pressure there that allowed her to think past tragedy.

She focused again on the profile of the young woman they had plucked from the sea. If her brother was alive, then there was a chance this Marcus was with him.

How could she explain this to the girl without sounding banal or dismissive? Perhaps if she told her own story…

She touched the woman's shoulder. "This man, Marcus. If he is alive, Kindra, we will find him."

The girl stared out over the sea a moment longer; she slowly lifted her eyes to Lesidi's, then startled as if she'd forgotten she was there. Some of the life returned to her expression, an amber light in her eyes turned up a notch.

Lesidi took her hand. "The Leto, the ship that sank," she said, her eyes shifting to the calm sea where they had witnessed the tragedy, "…belonged to my brother, Amari. We had dropped off a cargo of olive oil at the Palace docks and were bound to meet the rest of our fleet when he informed me of a secret cargo. He had arranged with an envoy from the palace of which I was unaware until he was already engaged."

Kindra's eyes narrowed on hers as she took in the information, calculating, weighing, as if to discern whether or not Lesidi was telling the truth. "Valeria," she said with a visceral contempt.

"Valeria? You know of this person?"

Kindra turned back to the sea, pulled the blanket tighter around her shoulders. "I'm afraid your brother was caught up in a conspiracy underway long before you entered the harbor."

Lesidi's heart thudded hollowly against her ribs. Amari was drawn to trouble like flies on elephant dung.

"A conspiracy," she stated flatly. Would he ever learn?

Kindra glanced at her for a fraction of a second, then gripped the railing tight, and started to shiver.

"It's all my fault," she said, her words clipped as her teeth chattered with cold.

Lesidi shook her head. It was difficult to fathom how someone so frail and innocent looking — a pregnant girl no less — could be responsible for the explosion they'd witnessed. She slid her arm across the young woman's shoulders and turned her away from the rail.

At the touch of her bare skin, cold sliced up her arm and a series of emotions twisted through her mind in a swirling storm: humiliation, fear, murder, love, passion, blood, loss. In that fraction of a second, Lesidi knew this young woman, not more than eighteen years old, had lived through more terror and grief than most did in a lifetime.

She swallowed hard against the urge to break away. There was more to this young woman than met the eye and she felt compelled to see further. "Let's get you back inside. Cyril!"

A moment later he appeared, his eyes steadfast and trusting. She had known this man since she'd sailed with her father and trusted him without question.

"Bring us some hot tea and something to eat at once."

"Will we be heading out?"

"Not yet. Soon," she said, shifting her gaze to Kindra. "Our … guest has some information we may need before we make that decision."

"As you wish," he acknowledged, and was off.

She drew Kindra back into her quarters, pulled the fur over her shivering shoulders.

Kindra pressed her lips together against the chill, and after a moment, her shaking calmed. Lesidi's heart went out to her. Whether or not her brother's situation was her fault remained to be seen. Regardless, as captain of her ship, Lesidi was responsible for every soul on board, but after what she'd seen a moment earlier, her interest went well beyond duty. This young woman was in grave danger.

Lesidi poured the hot tea, fortified with honey, letting the heat of the liquid and the oil lamps inside her quarters warm her. The days still carried a warm breeze across the sea, but evenings turned cold quickly, a sign winter was coming on fast.

Kindra sat upright now, let the fur slip from her shoulders as she cupped her tea in both hands.

"How are you feeling, Kindra? Warm?"

"Better. Thank you." The chatter gone, the girl gave her an ashen smile.

Lesidi folded her arms and sat back on her bunk. "I want to assure you, Kindra, you are safe with us on this vessel." She sipped her tea and sat with legs crossed. "You said there was a conspiracy. Tell me about it."

Kindra drew in a breath and straightened her shoulders. Much of the color had returned to her face. Whatever doubts Lesidi may have had, the young woman was stronger than she appeared; it was clear she was ready to tell her story.

"Marcus wore the golden circlet of the Chief Praetorian guard to Emperor Constantine around his neck."

Lesidi couldn't suppress a gasp. Her father had spoken of the Emperor with less than admiration. A man does not become Emperor — indeed, unite all of Rome under his rule — by being a benevolent ruler. Constantine's Chief Guard would be someone to reckon with; someone to fear. It was difficult to imagine this fragile woman mixed up with such a one. Yet, there was a fire in those amber eyes; one that burned bright enough to compel her to cast herself into the sea to save her man.

Kindra silently sipped the rest of her tea, then set the metal cup on the shelf next to her chair.

"Whatever the Emperor bid him do; he had to obey. For this he received payment in gold, and in the care and safety of his family. His mother and sister."

"I understand," Lesidi said, respectfully. "Marcus was trusted, but also owned."

"He was also a Christian."

Lesidi took this in. Many in Auksum were joining the Christian movement, including her mother. Her father, however, was reluctant to give up his old beliefs, mostly because they were bound to the sea. "As I understand, Constantine was amenable to this."

Kindra huffed out a breath. "In theory."

"How so?"

"Well. He has ordered his magistrates not to persecute Christians as they had done in the past. And his mother, Helena, has rallied forces to replace some of the pagan temples with Christian ones. But that doesn't mean all of Rome — the Emperor included — operate by Christian principles."

"And you? Are you a Christian?"

The girl hung her head, her hand absently resting on her belly. "I don't think God would want me," she answered.

Lesidi studied her guest from a new angle. She ached to see what tormented her so, but for now, she would let her finish at her own speed. "Go on."

"Marcus was a loyal servant and proud of it. But he had always feared under the Emperor's command, he would someday be asked to do something that would test that loyalty."

Once again, their eyes met and a sharp, soul-shattering chill slammed up Lesidi's neck. This time, it was her brother's determined face she saw in a flash. She narrowed her eyes, refusing to break the connection between them. This is where their destinies collided.

Kindra stood now and strode to the doorway, rested her hand on the bulkhead. Lesidi had to admire her strength.

Now Kindra turned to face Lesidi, crossed her arms over her chest and lifted her chin. "I don't know whether you are privileged to hear such things, but it was rumored that the Emperor's second wife, Fausta, and the Emperor's son of his first wife were—" she rolled her hand in front of her.

Lesidi raised her brows. "Oh, my, no. I had not heard that. But then, I'm a citizen of Auksum, and have only just this few weeks been in the great sea with the fleet. I have little contact with any but those receiving our freight."

"The story was," Kindra continued, "Cripis and Fausta had consorted behind the Emperor's back. I knew Fausta for only a short time, but in that time she shared much. She was lonely, neglected, bitter." She stroked her belly and drew in a long slow breath, blew it out, then she studied Lesidi's eyes. "One has to ask oneself what is missing when you have all the riches in the Emperor's palace yet remain unfulfilled."

"She was an easy target," Lesidi said.

"Target?"

"The lust for power consumes all else. With the entire Roman Empire combined under the Emperor's rule, there would be little room for a son to move into a position of power as long as his father was alive." Lesidi didn't have to have the power to see the future to see where this was leading. "They were plotting to overthrow the Emperor."

Kindra nodded. "I have to admit, I was so bound to my own … situation, I did not see it coming until I was caught up in the plot."

Now that was interesting. Lesidi began to understand why the young woman had given off such a strong presence at her touch. There was far more to her than met the eye. "Tell me what happened."

Kindra lifted her chin and closed her eyes a moment as if searching for a place to begin. She started with a shiver.

"I was Fausta's chamber servant, a temporary service where I replaced her usual servant girl. It was a privilege, I was told, to serve the Empress and it came with benefits. Good food, elegant lodging, fine clothes. It was arranged by this Valeria I mentioned earlier. I had already had — a run in — with the woman. By the gods, she was a hateful sort, I can tell you. Up to no good. But once inducted into the Empress's inner sanctum, I was easily seduced. I had never lived a day in my life that I didn't have to work hard just to survive. All at once, I was traveling in her entourage, my quarters were nearly as elegant as Fausta's own."

Kindra's eyes shifted away and Lesidi sensed she was leaving out much of her personal story. She was curious, but she was more interested now in how her story meshed with her brother's disappearance.

"We left the palace at Constantinopolis and traveled to Moselle. Something I gathered Fausta did often, not only to get away from the stifling summer heat, but to escape the boredom of the palace."

Lesidi huffed out a laugh. She understood that feeling perfectly well. "A gilded cage is still a prison." She'd spent many a dull day in her parent's compound in Auksum. Her relentless begging to go to sea is what prompted her father to finally give in and take her with him. Her heart swelled at the memory. She'd never looked back.

Kindra stared at her a moment, as if reading her thoughts, then gave her a wan smile. "Fausta was pampered to be sure. Servants, the best food, travel, entertainment. Someone else to do the cooking and cleaning and managing the day-to-day work of the palace. To be sure, being the Empress is better than being a servant or a slave. But, from what I could see, she was isolated, lonely, without a true friend to trust."

Kindra slumped, her lips pressed together in thought a moment before she continued. "She opened up to me, a stranger. I was … surprised … to say the least. Maybe a little flattered. She took me into her confidence. She gave me full run of the summer palace, access to food, oils, lamps for the evening. I had never witnessed such bounty."

"When she told me I was to accompany her to the bath and guard the gate while she made her liaison, I did it without question. I had no idea of the conspiracy at the time, mind you, only that Fausta was giddy like a child to see her lover."

"Imagine my surprise and horror when it was Marcus who appeared in the Caldarium."

Lesidi's hand went to her neck on a gasp. Imagine indeed.

"I couldn't believe my own eyes. Fausta's secret lover was none other than the father of my child? I was stunned nearly senseless, which is why I lapsed into a moment of desperation before I understood what was really going on."

Those eyes clouded over a moment, her shoulders once again began to shake. Lesidi lifted the furs back around Kindra's shoulder, then lifted the brass urn, poured more tea into her cup, and handed it to her. Their hands touched; their eyes met and held, and for a disquieting moment, Lesidi saw bright red blood spattering over a stone floor, then swirling toward the bottom a lapis-tiled pool. She jerked away, startling them both.

"You do not have to go on, if it is too difficult."

Kindra lifted the cup in both hands and held it in front of her, visibly working to calm herself. "I will be all right. I have not told this story to another soul. It all happened so fast, I--" She swallowed hard. "I need to tell someone or it will eat me up inside."

She sipped her tea, her eyes turning thoughtful, then went on. "By Constantine's order, Crispis had already been killed. Constantine had sent Marcus to murder Fausta in the bath. Only Marcus could never do such a thing. It put him in an impossible situation. Kill Fausta and break the solemn laws of his God and savior; or disobey Constantine and be hunted down and murdered because he knew too much. So, at his peril, even though the man sent with him was bent on carrying out the order, instead of killing her, Marcus helped Fausta escape, which meant he would have to leave as well. He admonished me to get back to the palace however I could and promised to find me there. Take me with him."

Lesidi nodded, the outcome all too clear. "The plan went wrong."

Kindra closed her eyes a moment and lowered her head before she continued, her face was a mask of pain. "I did my best to hold off the other man as Marcus hurried through the catacombs of the baths with Fausta, but before I could escape, Valeria and her men were on me. They bound me and hauled me back to the palace in Constantinopolis in a filthy felon's cart. Apparently, she knew about my connection to Marcus all along."

Lesidi shook her head, commiserating. "By the gods, you must have been terrified."

Kindra dropped her head into her hands. After a moment, she gathered herself and straightened. "No more than I was before they took me to Fausta in the first place. My presence there was only a cruel reprieve. Valeria had always planned to hang me for murder.

86

Chapter 9 – The First Sign

Newport Beach, California - 2019 CE

The week rushed by way too fast. By Wednesday Lexi'd overbooked sessions for Friday, been sucked in to organizing a charity event for the Women's shelter and had to answer all incoming calls because the building's shared receptionist emailed from Vegas that she'd eloped and was gone for good.

Two weeks ago, she'd celebrated the fact that with Phillip moving his investigator service into one of the last two available spaces, the office building she'd scraped together every last penny she could to afford to buy a majority share was nearly fully occupied. That meant, with the receptionist gone, she was responsible to fill in for no less than eleven tenants until she hired a replacement.

The good news was that with Lexi's regular appointments and answering calls for the other tenants in her building, she'd been too busy to get waylaid by her personal problems. The bad news was it was Thursday morning, she'd interviewed six prospective receptionists, and in the meantime, had been roped in to forwarding all the front desk calls to her own phone so she wouldn't have to work from the lobby. She promptly sent all those calls to Voice Mail.

The only person who came even close to what the rest of the tenants wanted in a receptionist — being there top on the list — was a young man who had shared during the interview he was recovering from gender reassignment surgery. Of all the candidates, she'd liked him the best. True, he could use some lessons from Minh to really pull off a girly look. His eyeliner was trying too hard, and his man bun was a bit overdone, but he had a gorgeous triangle nose and a winning smile that could turn anyone's head no matter what their preference.

"The next time you see me, I'll be … myself," he'd said with all the confidence in the world.

But, dammit, when she'd made the call, his recording said the number had been disconnected and there was no new listing. To say she was disappointed didn't come near covering it.

She was seriously considering making a call to a temp agency. She was so disgruntled, she realized now she'd forgotten to feed Elvis and Loki. They were circling just below the surface of their tank where she usually sprinkled flakes of food the minute she came in. She had just started the task when the voice mail notification dinged.

"Alexis Hill?" At least the call was for her, and the voice was familiar, though she couldn't quite place it. "It's Robbi Glassman. With an i? I interviewed with you Monday for the receptionist position?"

The transgender kid. Hallelujah. She hit the callback number. "Robbi with an i. Yes. I'm so glad you called. I tried to get a hold of you and—"

"I know. I'm sorry. I had to get a new phone number and…You know how it is."

Lexi did know. Some of her favorite clients had been through sexual reassignment and people, even family, could be asshats. Sometimes the best thing was to diss them all together. She hoped whatever assholiness Robbi had been through was over for now. He had no experience as a receptionist, but even a twelve-year-old was adept at answering the phone these days. Robbi with an i had two years of college under his belt. And that smile. What more could she ask?

"We had a good interview, so I thought I'd just follow up in person."

"In person?" Lex heard the ding on the foyer door and popped her head out of her office. Yep. There he was. Or rather, *she*. He had obviously undergone a makeover since Monday. The *taller-than-most* young woman standing at the reception desk with a clutch bag in one hand and two barista style coffee cups in a cardboard holder in the other, glanced up at her with that smile. A new, short, auburn bob framed her face. She wore a white shirt open at the neck under a tweed jacket, and a pair of dove-gray pants that looked really great on her slim-hipped frame. Perfect.

"I saw you had a Chai Latte Monday, so I got you one," she said, holding up the tray. "Shall I bring it upstairs?" Her hair swung at the quick tilt of her chin like she'd been a girl forever. Well, yes. That's what it was all about, wasn't it?

"Good instincts, Robbi Glassman. Can you start right now?" *God, please say you will.*

"That's what I was hoping. My parents are a little…disturbed…right now and I need to get my ass … I mean. I'm saving to get my own place."

Creeps. She had counseled enough parents to know a situation like this could be handled with dignity and respect. She hoped the rest of the tenants in her building could do that, too. As for herself, she was all in.

"Stay where you are. I'll be right down."

Ten minutes later, with Robbi at the helm of the lobby desk, she heaved a sigh of relief behind her own. None of the other tenants had seen their new receptionist Monday when she had looked decidedly male. Lexi loved that Robbi was getting a fresh start. *We should all be so lucky.*

First on her agenda today was checking in with Mrs. Tran and Minh, whom she'd scheduled for a meeting in two weeks. Hopefully, the two of them were back in each other's good graces and ready to move forward. She scooted away from her desk to open her blinds and let in the weak light of the morning fog.

Zaire's coin, which she'd taken to wearing around her neck, caught on her desk drawer handle for the umpteenth time, a constant reminder of its presence.

Anxious to eliminate any further annoyances, she slipped it inside her sweater where it nestled between her breasts, then opened her computer to her daily planner.

The first sign something had shifted was the glowing warmth radiating into her skin where the necklace lay. Subtle at first. Maybe her latte was too hot? But then the pleasant warmth spread over her entire torso and down her arms. She leaned into it, like waking up on Sunday morning in a warm bed she didn't have to leave. And then … she just…melted, slipping like warm caramel into her chair, then spilling over onto the floor, then through, then down, down, sending her stomach into a spin. She closed her eyes and swallowed hard against the sudden urge to heave up what little was in there. And then, as quickly as it had overtaken her, her stomach settled. Her feet were once again on solid ground.

She opened her eyes on … Wait. What's this? She was in her office chair, but this was definitely not her office. There was a translucent wall just in front of her, behind, all around. She reached out to touch it, but instead of revealing its nature, it simply expanded out of her reach. The enclosure shimmered all around her, sealing her in a soft cocoon of muted light.

And then, from behind, a woman's voice. Strident, determined. "I'll do nothing of the kind!"

*   *   *

Lexi spun toward the source of the voice. The cocoon cleared to glass revealing four people only a few feet away. They were definitely not from around here.

Three men huddled around a flat rock, their clothing wet, their hair stringing in their eyes. A woman glared at them, her breasts clearly visible as her chest heaved under a shredded gown; wet, torn, and burned. Two of the men, heavily muscled and mature, wore leather hauberks over plated skirts like

Roman soldiers in some Ben Hur revival. The third was much younger, his clothes clean and dry.

Lexi sucked in a breath. What the Fu— She lifted her latte slowly to her nose and sniffed, because surely she'd been slipped a shot of something.

The young man, a sultry, disinterested frown at the corners his mouth, was stacking gold coins on the surface of the rock like a nervous craps player.

Lexi closed her eyes, rubbed hard, and opened them again. He was still there.

"You paid for two passages to Auksum, my lady, so I'm obligated to keep my part of the bargain. But if you wish to cancel that part, more the profit for me."

A handsome hunk of a soldier shed his wrap and attempted to drape it over the woman's shoulders.

She pushed him away. "Leave me alone. You can run if you wish, but I refuse to be shuttled away like garbage."

The soldier rested his hand on a short sword at his belt, his expression sympathetic. "I understand your frustration, Lady Fausta, but if you remain here, and the Emperor gets word of it, he will hunt you down and finish the job. There are targets on both our backs. As of now, Valeria thinks we're dead. I recommend we keep it that way. At least until we're out of the Empire."

Wait. Fausta? Lexi couldn't believe what she was witnessing. It was Tessa's dream, or past life, or whatever the heck it had been. And not just Tessa's dream. A part of her recognized this story on a personal level. Like she should know these people. She stood transfixed a moment, then lifted her hand to see she pinched Zaire's gold coin so tight between her fingers, all the blood had squeezed out of them. The heated conversation spun around her, pulling her out of her reality and into theirs.

The man who had addressed Lady Fausta — tall and imposing--glanced in Lexi's direction, but his gaze passed right through her to focus on the trembling, angry woman.

Lexi put out her hand; the barrier once again moved just out of reach. Damn. She was there, but not there, just like Tessa had been. "Cool" she said aloud, then clamped a hand over her mouth. But it didn't matter. It was obvious they couldn't see her.

The woman pushed past Lexi to stand nearly chest-to-chest with the hunk of a man.

She glared at him. "I suppose you expect me to be thankful for you sending me into exile?"

"At least you will have a life, my lady, which is more than I can say for the crew of that transport ship." He lifted his arm to indicate the surface of the sea behind them.

Wait. A ship? But yes, there it was, in the background, a wide, open sea. Lexi could almost smell it.

"That was not my doing," Fausta accused, defensive. "As I recall, you, Marcus, were the one who made the arrangements."

The man's expression turned cold. "Indeed. We were lucky to escape before Valeria's plan was carried out. Going back now would mean those men died in vain."

"What do I care for those men? As far as I'm concerned, they can all rot in Hades!" Her face flushed crimson; her hands clinched into fists.

The younger man scooped the gold coins from the rock into two leather bags with a distracted casualness, then tied them at his waist with a leather thong.

"Well, whatever you wish to do, get on with it. My sister probably thinks I am dead. She will not wait forever. If we fail to join the fleet by morning, they will leave without us, and I wouldn't blame them."

The handsome hunk took hold of the woman's arm. "We are going to Auksum, as planned, where you will be safe."

Fausta silenced him with a look. "Safe? You know me so little. That cur Constantine murdered my Crispus and tried to get rid of me. If you thought I would simply run away and hide without taking revenge, you are sadly mistaken."

She removed his hand from her arm. Turning to the young man she said. "Your fleet is all the way from Auksum?"

Her eyes narrowed, pinning the man under intense scrutiny.

If Lexi could take a step back, she would have, but she was glued to her chair.

"What is their cargo and destination?"

The young man straightened, his chin raised. "Our fleet is the largest on the sea, the great ship carrying wheat all the way from Alexandria. She will offload to our transports at Ostia, taking the cargo up the Tiber, bound to Rome."

The woman crossed her arms over her chest. "It is a little late for that now, is it not? The weather will be turning vicious."

"True," he said, his eyes searching a starry sky overhead. "Ours will be the last to make safe passage before the winter storms set in. If we fail, the people of Rome risk starvation."

Her eyes shifted, darkened by a cold gleam, until, like an actor changing character, the corners of her mouth quirked in a wry smile. She slipped her arm through the soldier's and turned him back toward the small launches beached nearby.

"What if I were to tell you I could pay you more to take me with you?"

The young man rolled his eyes, impatiently. "More than the Emperor would pay in bounty if I returned both of you to the palace?" he crooned.

Whoa, this guy is a player.

Fausta blanched at his threat, then turned it back on him. "Ten times more my greedy little friend."

This woman was bold. Scary, bristling with resentment and an inherent power. A bad ass combination. Lexi held her breath.

The young man's expression lost its insolence and warmed to Fausta; the gleam in his eyes matching hers.

Lexi shivered, clinging to the coin as the strangers argued. The gold grew icy hot and she let go of it. Their voices were slowly replaced by insistent chiming.

*   *   *

The images faded as the cocoon shimmered, then clouded, then disappeared.

She was back in her office, her heart pounding like kettle drums in her ears. There was a chiming, vibrating, irritation nearby, pushing at her. *What does it want?* Her thoughts, herky-jerky, sifted from past to present.

She squeezed her eyes tight a moment, then lifted her gaze to the window. Outside, the sun had lowered almost to the horizon. How long had she been gone this time? What the holy crap just happened?

The chiming again, finally making sense. A Voicemail message dinged. She picked up her phone and listened.

"Hey Lex. Phillip is doing some repairs over at his parents' tonight. It's perfect timing for us to grab a bowl of chowder. Call me back."

Lexi blinked at the screen, attempting to clear her head. More accurately, bring her thoughts into focus. It had been years since she'd had anything near a panic attack that would make her heart pump out of bounds. And never had she come out of one of those having lost time.

She pulled the necklace out from under her sweater. A frisson of anxiety tripped across her nape, then down her back. Had the coin something to do with her racing heart? Probably not a good idea to speculate. She hadn't had breakfast, except for the Chi. That much she remembered. Maybe she had slipped into a low blood sugar state. A bowl of chowder cupped inside a hunk of sourdough bread would take care of that quite nicely once she settled herself down. Being with Tessa would do the rest.

She deliberately slowed her breathing, eased herself into a calmer place, then thumbed her cell phone.

Lex: Okay. Meet you at the Crab Cooker.

Tess: Uh. They're still closed for reconstruction.

Lex: Damn. Butterfish?

Tess: See you there in a half hour.

Chapter 10 – The Kindra Collection

Lexi pulled her jacket tighter against a chill winter wind coming off the ocean. Sunny California was a bit of a misnomer at the beach. While warm weather nights could stretch deep into fall, riding on Santa Ana winds, the January sun during the day at the beach could be deceiving. By late afternoon, fog could come rolling in, shrouding the low-lying harbor under a heavy, wet blanket. All week, the weather got colder, until today it felt like Winter had set in. A welcome rain would scrub the air crystal clear, and result in mountain snow which would likely be seen on Mt. Baldy when the clouds cleared.

At the restaurant she found a booth near the window overlooking the parking lot where in the not-so-distant past, fishermen hauled their dories up on the sand, laden with the day's catch. She sat back against the faux leather banquette, the aroma of chowder tweaking memories of her father, making her heart pinch a little.

Tessa waved at her from the door. Thank god. The last thing she wanted was to remember those days. She'd been a young, innocent, fool.

Tessa plopped down next to her and dropped her over-sized bag by her feet. "What's up?" she asked, concern drawing her brows together.

"Up?"

"You look… faraway."

Lexi shrugged. "I was just thinking about the last time I had a conversation with my father. We had chowder at Old Ebbitt's Grill."

"Sounds like a DC thing."

Lexi nodded. "I was probably three months pregnant at the time. We were both blissfully ignorant." She folded her hands in her lap and stared down at them. She was still daddy's little girl then.

When she looked up, there was Tess, her eyes all glittery and excited. It was what Lexi loved about her bestie. No matter how far down the rabbit hole of despair Lexi went, Tessa could always reach like a magician into her top hat and yank her out.

She had missed her since she'd moved out of her house, even if it was only next door. They were still neighbors, but after boarding school and rooming together for nearly ten years, living in different homes was an adjustment.

"I brought you something," Tessa said cheerily. She dug in her bag, plucked out a shiny pink store-bought gift sack, and scooted it across the table.

Lexi sent her a quizzical look. "*Whatsis*?"

"Just a little *somethin'*. My first attempt at lost wax since I ordered some casting grain to work with. Thought you might like it since we had to turn the originals I gave you over to the feds."

"Casting grain?" she asked, fingering the bag.

"You know, the little granules of 14 karat gold you melt down? They come in a little sack?"

Lexi knew Tessa made gold jewelry in college, but she'd never actually seen the process or the raw materials. She'd take her word for it. She dug a little box out of the bag and opened it, suddenly realizing what Tessa meant. When they'd discovered the cache of ancient jewelry in the wall of the house Tessa had inherited from her Uncle Theo, they'd innocently divvied up the treasure. Tess had given Lex a pair of heavy gold earrings fit for a queen, only to learn from their friend at the Getty, the entire collection — ten pieces in all — was reported stolen from the British Museum after World War II. Except for the serpent bracelet that wasn't part of the find, they'd had to turn the entire lot over to the ICE team at the Getty, including the fabulous earrings.

Lexi turned them out into her palm. They were large discs, about the size of a silver dollar, with concentric rows of tiny gold beads surrounding a smooth red stone in the center just like the ones in the original collection.

"Oh my god, Tessa. These are exquisite. If I didn't know better, I'd say you held them back from the collection."

Tess waved away the complement. "Not the quality of the original, but I'm pretty proud of them for a first try. I haven't actually cast anything since I was an undergrad. They're gold filled, not solid. I want them to be accessible to people, you know. People like us. The first in my 'Kindra' collection."

Lexi turned one over. They had the delta stamp on the back like the original, but with Tessa's stylized "T" inside. "They're amazing. I'm impressed."

Tessa wiggled her shoulders like an exited puppy. "Put them on."

Lexi removed her go to large gold hoops and replaced them with the discs. They were lighter than the originals, which was a good thing. "Whadaya think," she said, turning her head left and right.

"Perfect."

"So, you're going to reproduce the whole collection?"

"Going to try. Phil set up my kiln in Theo's old studio downstairs."

Lexi grinned, almost jealous. "He's definitely a keeper."

"Yup. And he really doesn't want me to go back to a full-time job, so it was to his benefit to get my shop up and running."

Francine, the server they knew both from the Island and regular trips to this restaurant approached the table, nodded to the women.

"The usual? Wait. Wow." She bent over to get a better look at Lexi. "Those earrings. Where did you get them?"

"Oh, I just —" Tessa started in before Lexi put her hand on her arm.

"They're part of a new collection by an up-and-coming designer specializing in ancient jewelry replicas. You like?"

"I *love.*" She straightened and filled their water glasses.

Lexi winked at Tessa and gave the server one of her broad, *I'm-letting-you-in-on-a-secret* smiles. "I'm pretty sure she's going to be doing a Preview show. I'll let you know when."

Tessa's face went crimson.

Francine shook her head. "Want your usual bottle of Pinot Grigio?"

"I'll have a glass, and my friend here will have a glass of milk."

When their friend left, Tessa punched Lexi in the knee. "Why did you do that?"

"With baby on board, you're having milk, missy."

"Not that, the 'Preview'," Tessa said making air quotes.

"Why not? Who's going to blow your horn if you don't?"

"Maybe I'm not ready."

"Maybe you're scared, need a little push."

Tessa shook her head. "So, you're my self-appointed promoter."

"Why not?"

Francine plopped a platter of fried calamari on the table between them with three different dipping sauces. "These are on the house. Cook made extra today, for our regulars."

Lexi forked up a crispy morsel and dipped it in some cilantro lime sauce, then plopped it in her mouth. "God, I love living at the beach."

Tessa joined her in chowing down on the pile. They feasted and licked their fingers, until Lex blotted her napkin on her lips. The events of the last few days playing in her mind.

"So, girlfriend," Tessa said, sliding the empty plate to the edge of the table. "What's going on with you? And don't tell me you miss your dad."

Chapter 11 - Lexi Shares her Vision

Lexi squirmed in her seat. "First, tell me how you're feeling."

Tessa wrinkled her brow. "What do you mean?"

"I mean, after the incident on the balcony, then the wedding. The trip. Phil's mom. How are you coping?"

"No way, sister. You're not deflecting. I asked you first."

"Deflecting?"

"You don't live with a shrink for five years without picking up some of the lingo."

Lexi laughed. She'd had a white-knuckle grip on her spoon. She put it down and stretched out her fingers. She had to let this feeling out. All of it, or it would eat her up inside.

She caught Francine's movement toward the table, milk and wine in wine glasses on a tray.

"Hold on," she said, nodding at her best friend. She shifted her hands to her lap.

Francine unloaded the tray. "The chowder will be here in a minute."

When Lexi glanced back to Tessa, she was giving her the raised eyebrows.

Lexi lifted her wine, Tessa her milk and they clinked. Might as well get straight to the point. "I saw Kindra."

Mid sip, Tessa sputtered. "What?"

Lexi spewed out a long slow breath. "The last time we — you — saw her, she was floating on log in the Bosphorus?"

Tessa gave her a slow nod.

"So. I saw her. Rescued. From the water." Her throat closed off, squeezing out the words.

Her chin quivered as Francine slid the steaming bread bowls in front of them. "Will there be anything else?"

"Thanks, Frannie. We're good." Tessa waited until their friend was out of ear shot. "What do you mean, you *saw* her?"

Lexi blew stray hair off her forehead and glanced out the window, looking for a better place to start. A place that made some kind of sense. Maybe it was best to go all the way back to the beginning.

She dipped her spoon into the creamy chowder and lifted out a fragrant bite, steam ribboning up between them.

"Last year. When you very first noticed something was off? That something was different? What exactly happened? From what I remember, you put on that bracelet and you sort of zoned out for a few minutes. How did you feel during all that?"

Tessa poked at her chowder, then let herself fall back against her seat. "I've been trying to forget."

Lex lifted a shoulder. "I know. And I'm sorry, but—"

"No. Don't be sorry." Tessa's gaze slid to the window. She rubbed her arms like she felt cold. "The first time? It was like a veil dropped around me, separating me from the present moment. I heard you and Phillip calling to me, but I couldn't see you. I felt isolated, removed."

Yes. Lexi swallowed hard. "And then what?"

She pursed her lips, closed her eyes a moment. "The bracelet started to burn my bicep and then Phillip's hands gripped my arms, and it was over."

"And you never saw anyone."

"No. Not then. Just that feeling of being closed off from the present."

"So, when was the first time you actually saw Kindra?"

Tess considered a moment while she crushed oyster crackers into her chowder, tasted, savored, wiped a drip off her chin. "Sorry. With the baby on board, I'm famished all the time. This stuff is really hitting the spot." She put down her spoon.

"The next time was later that same night. Phillip and I were making love." She took a sip of her milk. "I felt the heat in the gold again, squeezing my arm, and I slipped away from the present. But I have to say, I didn't *see* her. I felt her." Her brow knitted. "I *was* her."

Lexi was squeezing her fingers together in her lap so tightly, she had to shake them out. Then she fisted them under her chin.

Tessa frowned at her. "You sure you're okay?"

"No," she said forcing herself to pick up her spoon. She pushed a cracker below the surface of her chowder. "Go on."

Tessa eyed her suspiciously but went on. "It was like I had slipped into her skin and was looking out through her eyes. I think she was aware of me, too. It was creepy but also, sort of — I don't know — powerful. She acted on some of my thoughts."

Tessa leaned in and eyed Lexi suspiciously. "Come on. What's this about?"

Lexi slipped the necklace out through the neck of her sweater, lifted the chain over her head, and laid it on the table. She watched it for a moment as if it would somehow move of its own will. It did not.

Tessa's eyes went wide. She picked it up and studied the face on the coin, then read the letters around the edge. "This is an Auksumite coin if I'm not mistaken. King Ezana I, fourth century."

Lexi nodded. "Yes. Best I could figure, doing a quick Internet search. I thought you would know better."

Tessa shrugged. "They're pretty common in collections. Lots of 'em found in shipwrecks around the Mediterranean and as far as the Red Sea. The Ethiopians — well, Auksumites at the time — were the first sub-Saharan culture to mint their own coins." She poured it back into Lexi's hand. "I'm assuming you found it in the shoebox?"

Lexi nodded. "It's Zaire's." It was the first time she'd said it out loud and the truth of it took her breath away.

Tessa shook her head. "Your mother kept it from you like the knit cap."

Lexi's throat stung, the anger she'd felt earlier giving way to hurt. "That would be my mother. Yes." Her lips quivered when she pressed them together.

"Take a breath. Eat some more chowder."

Lexi looked out the window at the pier a beat, then dumped probably too much Tabasco into her soup. When she'd had a chance to breathe and collect herself, she started in again.

"So, the other night at dinner, when I was standing at the balcony? I had the necklace in my pocket. I felt like I was somewhere else. A daydream, I don't know. It was like watching a movie or reading a book. I was witness to … an event." She told Tessa about watching Lesidi, about how she was afraid of her gift, about the explosion.

"So, the necklace is like the bracelet," Tessa mused.

"I felt the heat between my fingers, yes. And this Lesidi pulled Kindra out of the water. I mean, it had to be her, right?" She put her hand over Tessa's. "She told the woman, Lesidi, Marcus was the father of her child."

Now Tessa was shaking her head. "And you felt connected to this Lesidi?"

She sat back, considering. Had she? Or was she simply a witness? She needed to talk it through. "Yes. I mean, no. I… well, I suppose I was observing from her point of view. It happened again later. In my office. I held the necklace between my fingers. Waited. And it happened again. But a little different."

She told Tess about the three men and the woman, the stacks of coins, the thick membrane separating her from the people. She shivered at the memory, a set of chills running over her shoulders like frantic ants. "Not sure I like the direction their plotting was headed."

"So, you were musing, finishing off the story in a satisfactory way, like we talked about in the regression."

"Making it up? I know. I thought that, too. I mean, who would believe what happened to you really happened?"

Tessa drained her glass. "No one but you."

"Right. So I think we have to admit, there is some kind of connection. Audrey, Theo, the houses, the bracelet…"

"But your necklace has nothing to do with them. You say it belonged to Zai."

"I know, but… Kindra. It was her. Who else could it be? What if — now keep an open mind, here — what if the bracelet is still in play? It picked up on the coin."

"You weren't wearing the bracelet."

"That's right. And I wasn't really in the scene. When I was at Phillip's parent's house, I was just an observer. Back at home, I got closer. I mean, the Cloisonne Brooch was out inside that pedestal in the yard when it came into play, but it was close enough to influence the bracelet. Maybe, directed its focus."

Tess started to tip her head, but her phone vibrated on the table. She glanced at the screen, grinned at Lexi. "It's Phil. Do you mind?"

She had already hit the green button.

"Sure. Go ahead." Lexi poked around in her sourdough bowl, scraping at the remaining goodness there, trying to give her friend privacy.

"Oh my god! Is she all right?" Tess lowered the phone and Lexi saw the concern in her eyes. "Phil thinks his mom had another stroke."

Lexi lay down her spoon. "Oh, no."

Tessa scooped up her purse, talked holding the phone between her ear and shoulder. "Okay. Okay. I'm on my way, bud. I'll meet you there." She dropped her phone in her bag. "Lex, I gotta go."

"No problem." Concern for her friend and her new family built in her chest. "I've got this," she said, pointing at the table.

Tess was up and gathering her coat. "I'll be at Hoag Hospital. I'll call you from there. Oh no!"

"What is it?"

"I'm not sure whether I turned off my kiln. I was going to pour another piece when I got home—"

Lexi held up her hand. "Don't worry. I'll go in and check. Just keep me posted, okay? And let me know if you need anything."

Lexi parked in Tessa's garage and went straight through to the downstairs studio. She pulled out the key to Tessa's home still on her keyring, but as it turned out, she didn't need it. She was going to have to remind Tess they had no garage door on the carport. Anybody could walk right in, just like she was doing. An L-shaped space bounded on two sides with old casement windows, the large room that had been loaded floor-to-ceiling with odds and ends and boxes when they'd first moved into the house had been completely reorganized. Phillip had built a long work bench against the front windows, taking advantage of the light. Built-in bookshelves flanked a twin-sized day bed that served as a couch. It was evident the two were sharing the space: There was a clam digging shovel and a pair of large rubber boots by the back door and Phil's quiver of surfboards were stacked against the long exterior wall.

Next to the work bench was a utility shelf with a dozen little drawers and cubby holes, and a variety of jewelry-making tools and supplies. Tessa was obviously serious about her new enterprise.

At the far end of the workbench, on a piece of slate, sat a miniature furnace. No lights glowed on its control panel. Tessa had turned it off after all. Good. She might have left the back door open for anyone to walk in, but at least the house wasn't going to burn to the ground while she was gone.

She had, however left on a small fan sitting on top of the cubbies. Lexi had just reached up to flip the switch when the fine hairs pricked up on her forearms along with that crazy feeling you get when you feel you are being watched.

She glanced outside to the front yard. Nothing. Hum. She glanced around the small room — from the day bed to the flatscreen TV on the wall above, a beaded curtain between the work area and the hallway to the modest bathroom. Nothing. But still a chill grabbed the back of her neck.

She turned back to the cubby cabinet and caught her breath. The serpent bracelet, a bright glint in its ruby red eyes, seemed to look right at her. Where had that come from? It hadn't been there when she flipped off the fan, she would have seen it surely? But there it was, coiled against the base of the fan like it was resting.

"No way," she said aloud. Not THE serpent bracelet sitting out here in the open where someone might grab it. It belonged in a safe. Or a museum. It most certainly did not belong lying here, haphazard.

Then Lexi laughed. Of course. It was a copy. Tessa hadn't mentioned it because Tessa had always been Frodo-ish about that damn bracelet. She had made a copy and kept it to herself.

She grinned at the thought. It made perfect sense. That would have been the *first* thing Tessa made, now that she thought of it. Relieved, she picked it up, turned it over to look at its underside. No markings.

No delta, no "T". Huh. Tessa said she was going to…

She turned it back over to lay on her palm. The rest happened so quickly she couldn't remember the details; only that the serpent heated, uncoiled, and streamed up her forearm like liquid gold to circle her biceps.

The sensation started deep in her chest, a sharp contraction of her diaphragm that should have produced a guttural scream worthy of a Steven King horror show as it rose white hot up her throat, but Lexi never heard a sound.

Chapter 12 - The Hitch Hiker

The Bosphorus - 327 CE

The sea had calmed as it did for a time each day with the setting sun. Lesidi gave up her bunk to her passenger who had collapsed in exhaustion the moment she lay down her head.

Poor thing. She had been through hell and likely there was more to come if indeed, she carried the child of a traitor to the Emperor.

At Lesidi's request, Cyril brought furs and made her a palette near the ship's tiller, leaving Kindra to rest inside. Lesidi could duck into shelter if need be, but for now, she was warm and safe, and welcomed the view of the entire night sky overhead.

She doubted she could sleep despite the heavy fatigue weighing her down into the pile of furs. Events of the day had left her in a bit of a quandary. She was no longer worried about her brother, despite the outward signs. She sensed his heartbeat incorrigibly nearby. Of that fact she was certain. And if he was alive, then it stood to reason this Marcus was with him. Perhaps, and this was a stretch, but Lesidi had a feeling it was so, Marcus and Fausta were indeed the cargo Amari had undertaken to transport. Or, to take her thinking in a different direction, would be a source of a bounty should he return them to the Emperor.

The question remained. Was the explosion an accident? or part of the plan? It was difficult for Lesidi to believe Amari would sacrifice his ship for any amount of gold. She knew deep in her soul the only person more gratified to be away from the compound at Auksum other than herself was her brother. Having his own vessel made that possible. If the explosion was a plan, it was definitely not his.

I'd worry more about Fausta if I were you, Lexi said.

Lesidi sat up, glanced in the direction of her quarters, expecting to see her guest. "Kindra?"

Wait, you heard me?

No movement, no reply. She levered herself up and made her way back to her quarters. Kindra lay on her bunk in the same reposed position she'd been when she'd left her there.

Les-i-di.

The voice said her name like a poem. Reverent, lyrical, as if voicing it out loud for the first time. Lesidi stopped. Listened. There was nothing but the sound of a light breeze stirring the ropes of the sail.

The men had retired to their cramped bunks below deck, except for the night watch, who stood silent as a marble statue at the bow of the boat, his hand gripping the rigging. Not a sound or movement, only the shadow of the swan's neck cast across the boathouse by the nearly full moon. She ghosted to the swan, took comfort in the feel of its neck against her fingers. And then the voice came again in a woman's whisper: *Les-i-di.*

All right. There was no one on the ship but her sleeping guest and her five-man crew. And none of them female, so she had to accept what seemed impossible. The voice was inside her own mind.

"Who are you?" she queried into the dark, more curious now than disturbed.

Lexi swallowed hard. It was like Tessa had said. She was no longer watching the mariner woman, she was peering out at her world through her eyes.

I am Lexi. Goddess of … um … I'm … not from around here.

The words were preceded by an echo that wrapped around Lesidi like a scarf. A streak of light chose that moment to cut across the sky and disappear over the horizon. Many thought of the fiery streaks as omens portending some momentous event. To one who lived her life on the sea like Lesidi, a night rarely passed without witnessing at least one star sign, if not many. They never ceased to dazzle and inspire. Did they portend anything other than the great mystery of the heavens? Lesidi didn't think so. There were forces in the universe she did not understand, but they existed none the less.

"Lexi. The Goddess of Shooting Stars?" She scanned the sky for another.

The echo, and then, a series of musical notes that sounded like laughter, then:

If you have the gift of sight, then you should use it to your advantage. Just sayin'.

Lesidi's heartbeat fluttered in her chest. Use it? It was true. Lesidi had never deliberately applied her gift to any specific situation or desire. The sight used her.

Spoke through her. The images just came, mostly when she slept. As a little while ago, when she touched Kindra. She hadn't sought to know her mind, the images it stored were simply revealed to her. She didn't ask, didn't wish it. It just happened.

Tonight, with her brother missing and the presence of the mysterious woman onboard, and the inspiration of the glittering stars overhead, a voice called her by name. A voice apart from her own originating inside her mind? "Who are you? Where…are you?"

And then it came again, preceded by a soft echo. *I am Alexis. I speak to you from the future.*

"Alexis," she whispered as she slid to her knees. Her gift? Speaking to her while she was wide awake? It had never happened that way before. She was at once frightened and amazed. "You see my future?"

I see only what you see. For now. Your eyes are my window to your world. But I can tell you your passenger, Kindra, is in grave danger, and you and your fleet, by association.

Lesidi breathed in the cool night air, lifting her chest high. "I would see the next steps I should take. How shall I continue?"

Lexi bit her lip. This wasn't a game. What if she gave some twenty-first century advice and it backfired and caused a tsunami of change? Especially since she wasn't sure of the information she'd gleaned.

You're the one with the vision. I'm just a hitch hiker here.

The voice lost some of its volume, the last words fading away like fog under the morning sun. "Wait. Don't go. What is this hitch hiker?" Nothing again. "Alexis?"

But the voice, along with the ethereal connection to it, went silent. One thing was increasing clear as she witnessed another shooting star in the sky. She was not alone in her vision as she had been in the past. She had an ally. Granted, she had no idea why or how, but she was there, as free and easy as breathing.

She closed her eyes and was immediately flooded with a rush of warmth, like arms enfolding her, lifting, soothing. And like dipping into a warm bath, images emerged in her inner vision. Amari, two men, and a woman.

They argued, as Amari stacked gold coins on a rock. The largest of the men, broad shouldered and thick muscular thighs like Keleb's, wore the heavy gold circlet of the Emperor's service. High ranking, trusted, deadly. The woman was tall as well, and of obvious wealth by the gold belt and bracelets she wore, even though her clothes were torn and soiled.

She wished she could hear their words, but she could only read by their actions: it was a heated discussion, and the woman would have her way.

Suddenly overtaken by cold, Lesidi shivered. The sensation of being enveloped in a warm bath gave way to the cold, dark of a surrounding sea. She felt as though she were drowning. If she didn't lift her head above the cold, she would swallow her death.

She gasped, then held her breath, a great weight bore her down, down, into a darkening depth. Her lungs burned and she grabbed at the tightening force around her waist. But it was no use. She opened her mouth, the water gushed in.

*　*　*

She floated in a sea of fear for a few moments before she came to herself and opened her eyes. The sky was completely black; no moon, no stars, nothing. No. Not the sky. The wood roof over her quarters.

"Feeling better?"

Lesidi turned her face toward the sound of the voice to see Kindra seated next to her bed, a tray of bread and oranges on the table.

"How did I get inside?"

"Cyril brought you in."

She propped herself up on her elbow. She didn't remember that at all, only the sensation of drowning in a cold, dark sea. She drew in a deep breath now and blew it out. A dream? Or one of her visions? She closed her eyes, willing her heart to slow down its panicked beating.

"Take this," Kindra said, and she opened her eyes. Kindra handed her a cup. Steam twisted off the surface. "And now I have the chance to repay your kindness, it seems."

Lesidi sipped, her heartbeat settling. "So, you are on a first-name basis with my first mate?" she asked, trying to focus on the here and now.

Kindra blushed, then offered a shy, half smile. "He is kind and thoughtful."

Lesidi nodded. "That he is. He was a close friend of my father."

"And your father assigned him to your crew."

"Indeed, he did, although I expect it was a concession to make up for the fact that I am a female, and females 'have no business on a transport ship'."

"You seem to be performing the job quite admirably." Kindra broke the hunk of hard bread in half and passed a piece to her. "You must miss your father terribly."

Lesidi held on to the bread. Her stomach complained of being empty, but she still felt a bit queasy. "He was my heart."

"You are lucky. I don't remember my father, other than he sold me."

"Sold you?"

Kindra chewed her bread crust thoughtfully. "It's … not important." She shooed Lesidi's concern away with a flick of her wrist. "Listen," she went on. Leaning closer, she took Lesidi's hand in hers. "If you are recovered and need no further service from me, I bid you please take me to shore. I need to get to Marcus's mother. She should know about Marcus. I need to inform her of his loss, and that I carry his son. It is the kindest thing I can do for her. Also, she is … the only family I have." She covered her belly. "Valeria is a vengeful woman. She knows where Flavia and Anastasia abide. Indeed, she is jealous of the home the Emperor provided for Marcus and his family. It was an amenity that had illuded her. But his protection is gone now. I've got to warn them."

Alarm set Lesidi's heart pounding in her temples again. The voice in her head had told her of this already.

"Of course. I will take you myself. But listen. I don't know where your Marcus is, but I can tell you with a certainty, he was alive after the explosion.

Marcus, Amari, and Fausta I presume were all alive and well and plotting their escape."

"But how can you know this?"

"Trust me. It is my gift."

Lesidi had seen them all alive after the explosion, but that wasn't the end of it. There was tragedy ahead. She had seen it. Felt it in her bones. Could she prevent what was to come? No point in bringing that up to Kindra now; she had enough to concern her.

"At any rate, I've decided to stay in the vicinity for at least another day. We'll take a position away from the main quay. There's a landing not far from here. How far is the home of this Flavia?"

Kindra sat straight, more animated than she had been since coming aboard. "Near the city center, an upper-class district, not far from the palace gates."

She took Lesidi's hand, her skin light olive against Lesidi's dark walnut. Their eyes met and it was clear Kindra had the same thought. "They'll be looking for me. I'm an escaped criminal in their eyes; and you will stand out, Lesidi. There are many like you in the marketplace, but not in Flavia's sector."

"Do not worry on my account, my lovely friend. I have lived in my skin all my life and know how to conduct myself."

Chapter 13 – Reunion with Flavia

Lesidi stumbled as she stepped down off the cart, her sea legs adjusting to the solid feel of earth under her feet for the first time in what seemed like months.

Kindra, dressed in men's clothing, a heavy linen cloak pulled well over her head, led the donkey and two-wheeled cart to a trough of water.

She had to give Cyril credit for knowing what was needed. Having arrived at a marshy shallow well away from the merchant's dock, he had waded to shore and disappeared, returning a short time later in a narrow craft, just big enough to carry the two women back to shore without getting wet, where the cart and beast awaited.

Flavia's dwelling was further into the city than she imagined; the two women would have had a much more difficult journey without the cart. Kindra had assured her they would have no trouble once they passed through the marketplace. Women traveling un-escorted, according to Kindra, were not welcome in the city. But she had traveled as a young man in the past. Once they entered the part of the city near Flavia's home, they would be among friends.

They wound their way through ever narrowing streets, until at last they entered a square where a group of women washed clothes in a pool fed by a single-tiered fountain. The moment they heard the cart, all eyes turned on them.

Kindra immediately lowered her head, and following her example, Lesidi pulled her head deep into the folds of her palla.

Leaving the donkey to drink, Kindra strolled up to the group of women, and to Lesidi's astonishment, was met with calls of delight. She pointed at Lesidi, and all faces turned to look.

Leaving their laundry on the stone wall edging the pool, they surrounded her, drew her to the wall, bid her to sit.

"Here. We have bread and olives and dates," said a woman with a sleeping child tied across her back. Her teeth were yellowed, but her smile was wide as she passed them a wooden plank with the morsels spread across it. *Peasants*, Lesidi thought, by their dusty feet and hard calloused hands. Yet each in her own way had a healthful glow about her cheeks, and welcoming smiles.

Kindra helped herself to a date, her eyes taking in each entrance to the square in turn, her senses on high alert. Valeria was aware of her prior location at Flavia's home, and it would not be out of character for her to assign spies to watch the area. For the moment, all appeared normal. A number of youngsters pitched stones against a wall, setting up a cheer at intervals as they played their game. Other than that, the only sounds were the soft murmurs of the women going about their chores and the gently dripping water from the fountain.

Still, she stayed in her role as a young man. She handed the plate to Lesidi, making sure not to let down her disguise.

Lesidi followed her example. "Many thanks. You are very kind to offer."

"But what are you doing here?" asked the eldest of the bunch. "We heard you were in Moselle with the Empress when she was killed."

Kindra's eyes flashed to Lesidi, carrying a silent warning. "Indeed, I was in Moselle, in Anastasia's place."

The woman with the baby twisted a garment in strong, gnarled hands and laid it over the edge of the pool to dry. "It is true. The Emperor is tearing his hair. Someone killed his eldest son by Minerva, and the mother of his young children. It is a great tragedy."

"Constantine's heart must be broken," another woman put in.

Tearing his hair that his plan was foiled, more like.

Lesidi's stomach clenched at the intrusion once again of the inner speaker coming unbidden into her head. She trapped her hands in her lap and let Kindra take the lead in what she realized was a deeper deception than she anticipated.

"It was his Emperor's own man, Flavia's son, Marcus, they say is responsible. A terrible betrayal. Flavia was in agony when she heard."

Kindra drew close to the women, leaning her head. "Shhhhhhh. That is why we've come. I must see her."

The women's eyes grew wide, glancing at each other. "Then you don't know?"

"Know?" asked Kindra, clearly disturbed by the news. The cover fell off her head, revealing her cropped hair. "Know what?"

"She and Anastasia. They're gone."

"Gone!" Now it was Kindra's eyes gone wide. "No. It can't be. We were going to her chambers just now."

The woman shifted her baby to her other hip, lowered her voice. "To be sure, their apartments are empty, ransacked by the Praetorian Guards. They came galloping through the streets and broke down her door."

Kindra stared at her in disbelief. "This can't be true." Her hands clenched in her cropped hair, her face a mask of pain, her green eyes wild.

Lesidi took her by the arm and urged her back a step, pulling her cloak back over her head. "All right, listen. We will go, see for ourselves." She nodded to each woman in the group in turn. "If you care for Flavia, and I can see that you do, you mustn't tell anyone we were here."

The women stood dumbfounded, their eyes darting back and forth between Kindra and the woman with the child.

Lesidi straightened, revealing her full height, the twisted hair piled atop her head, gold circlets around her wrists and gold chains cascading down the front of her garment; the dark walnut of her skin gleaming against white plaster walls surrounding them. She searched their faces once more, settling on the mother. She strode to her, slipping a gold ring studded with red and black stones off her small finger as she went. She lifted the woman's hand and slipped the ring on her finger.

"Tell no one," she ordered in a firm command as one comfortable with giving orders she expected to be carried out.

The woman stared in disbelief at the gift of the ring, then closed her gaping mouth and nodded energetically. The others quickly followed her example.

Lesidi pulled her cloak around her shoulders and climbed into the cart. With a last glance around the square, Kindra led them through the widest passage away from the women's stares and into what was obviously a higher-class section of the city.

They stopped in front of an archway frescoed with a rose covered vine. Lesidi watched pensively as Kindra entered the private courtyard. Inside, potted herbs had been upended, a large amphorae smashed, olive oil pooled at its base; the head of an Aphrodite sculpture lay staring at the bottom of a small pond sullied with spilled flour.

Kindra dropped to her knees. "Flavia's garden," she said. Her voice twisted tight with anguish.

Lesidi went to her, rested her hand on her shoulder. She didn't know this woman, Flavia, but she could feel the depth of Kindra's despair. This destruction was not the work of vandals. Whoever did this wanted to cause pain. Hatred had ruled their soul; the air around them was foul with it.

After a long moment, Kindra lifted her head, wiping her tears away. She cast her gaze beyond the garden to the small keep. There was a glimmer of hope her eyes. "Their cart is gone, and their donkey. Maybe they escaped before the guards arrived."

Lesidi felt the rounded top of the small brick oven. Warm. She picked up a small cake from the ground where a half dozen were scattered, sniffed.

"Honey cakes." Kindra brushed the dirt off one and took a bite.

Lesidi did the same. It had been hours since they'd eaten the small chunks of bread they'd taken with them. "It appears they left in a hurry. Whether captured by guards or slipping away on their own it's impossible to tell."

Kindra scanned the hearth area again. "Or maybe they left food because they wanted someone to *think* they were coming back."

Lesidi simply nodded; there was no point in drawing conclusions for the young woman. It was clear she wanted Flavia to be safe and her peace of mind depended on the possibility. Is that not the same hope she was holding out for her brother?

Once again, their eyes met in understanding. Kindra turned on her heel and headed toward what looked to be sleeping quarters. Lesidi followed a pace behind. In each of two rooms, baskets were emptied, clothing strewn on the floor. In a third, smaller room with a cot built into a window alcove overlooking the street, there were several crocks broken, water spilled, and a basket of yarn emptied into the middle of a small throw rug. Bedding was pulled off the cot and tufts of straw poked through the torn mat. Kindra stood still as a statue for a moment, holding her arms tight around her stomach.

"That was my bed," she whispered. "They did not do that to the other mattresses. Only mine."

Lesidi moved to her side. Touched her hand. "We should go. If they come back—"

"No. Wait. Just--" She knelt and looked underneath the mess, pushed broken shards of pottery out of the way. She flattened herself on the floor and scooted half under the cot, then pulled out a damaged, but unopened basket.

Lesidi knelt beside her. "What is it?"

She held up a ragged, linen dress that looked like something Cyril might have used to mop the floor of his galley.

"This is the only thing I have of my life with my mother," Kindra said. "Everything else I had—my tools, the gold pieces I was going to sell to the Empress—are all gone."

"Gone?"

"My tools and clothes are all at the palace, so not much chance of getting those back." She snorted out a breath. "The rest is at the bottom of the sea." She crossed her legs in the middle of the floor and dropped her head in her hands. "The jewelry is nothing. The empress had more than anyone could ever want. I came to learn it meant little to her. But my tools..." She raised her eyes to Lesidi's and the sadness she saw there nearly broke her heart. "Without my tools, I have no way to support myself. I am nothing."

Lesidi stared at her a moment. "You are not nothing. Look at all you've accomplished. Why from just what you've told me, I have to believe you are probably the bravest woman I have ever met."

She stood and offered her hand. Those green eyes took her in, testing her trust. "I'm like you, Lesidi. A woman in a man's world." She let Lesidi pull her to standing. "You were never sold as a slave, but you know of what I speak."

"I do." Lesidi knew even when her father was alive, she got nowhere without Cyril at her side. And Keleb. Her heart squeezed a moment as she thought of he and his fleet. Waiting. Was he angry? Was he worried about her personally, or only on behalf of the fleet? Did he think of her at all? The notion that she let her thoughts stray that far off course in this moment sent a cringe of shame through her and brought her back to her senses.

Kindra's eyes scanned her again, landing on the gold chains at her neck before they darted away. "I was sold as a slave to a palace goldsmith. He never put me in chains, but he might as well have. I would not have survived without him. I learned his trade to replace his rheumy hands."

"And you survived."

"Lived well enough. Decent food, a roof over my head. That is, until he thought I betrayed him."

Lesidi caught her breath. "So, he is the reason you were wanted for murder?"

Kindra's eyes took on that steely look Lesidi had seen on her boat. The one that told her there was more to this young woman than a dirty tunic and a baby in her belly.

"He deserved it," Kindra hissed, closing her eyes on what must have been a frightening image. "I had no choice." Her voice broke.

Lesidi squeezed her shoulder. "There's no shame in defending yourself, Kindra."

"I'm nothing without my tools. What will I do now? Clean slops for some magistrate?"

And now she is going to be a mother. We've got to help her, Lesidi.

Lesidi straightened, squinted against a shimmering light in the doorway. Appearing in particles of flickering light, there was a woman dressed in clothing of a type she had never seen before, her hair, twisted like her own, springing over the top of a brightly colored head wrap. Her amber eyes pinned Lesidi with conviction. *Kindra is in danger. We've got to get her out of here. Now.*

Lesidi pointed at the apparition, then asked Kindra in a desperate whisper, "Do you see that?"

Kindra lifted her gaze in the direction of the doorway, her brows knitting together a moment, then shook her head.

The image flickered again. *Frickin' get moving, sister. This thing could go south any second.* The woman shot a glance over her shoulder, then as quickly as it appeared, the shimmer wavered and was gone.

There was a loud clatter near the home's entrance. Kindra grabbed Lesidi's arm and pulled her down behind the cot. They flattened themselves on the cold tiles and held their breath.

*   *   *

"They haven't returned, I tell you." A young man's voice, urgent and pleading.

Lesidi glanced at Kindra. Kindra pressed her finger to her lips and shook her head.

"How could you possibly know, you halfwit? I should have known better than to trust you. You were asleep when we came upon you." A woman. Impatient, her words tortured in anger. Lesidi flinched as a chair overturned and clattered across the tiled floor. "I should have left you tied with the hounds," the woman snarled.

"Yes, my lord, I mean, my lady. You are absolutely right." Footsteps scurred further away. "Nothing here," he offered, his voice echoing against the plastered walls.

"They're in the atrium," Lesidi mouthed to Kindra in a whisper.

Kindra nodded. "I know that voice; that boy; he's a friend," Kindra whispered close to Lesidi's ear.

Footsteps came near the bed chamber doorway. They could hear someone breathing hard. Lesidi pressed her lips together and flattened herself closer to Kindra, her jaw clamped tight to keep from chattering.

"Oh, honey cakes," the boy called.

Footsteps retreated beyond the threshold. "Quiet!" the woman scolded, then stood a moment longer as if listening, until after what seemed like forever, she stepped away, mumbling. "By the gods, I am surrounded by fools."

*   *   *

Lesidi and Kindra lay frozen, their eyes locked on one another's, ears straining for several minutes of silence before they dared move.

Kindra pulled herself up to sit on the cot. "You should go back to your vessel. Your fleet. Before you are associated with me."

Lesidi, you can't leave her here. Not now.

The goddess was right. Kindra was in grave danger. The woman, Valeria, was obviously out to get anyone associated with Marcus. Which, if she carried it out to the ultimate end, already included her brother and the rest of the fleet. Her own survival depended on their reunion. They were linked. All of them. And the only way out was seeing this through to the end, wherever that path took them.

"I'm not leaving you here, Kindra. We will go back to the Isis together."

Kindra merely ducked her chin in response. She strode out of the bed chamber, flattened herself against the walls until she stopped near the atrium, then peeked around the corner. She signaled Lesidi forward and as she did so, she picked up a piece of folded cloth near the base of the oven.

Lesidi moved to her side. "What is it?"

Kindra unfolded the cloth. Inside was a single gold coin. "This wasn't here earlier. Dracis left it as a sign."

"He knew we were here?"

"It appears so. I've got to find him. He likely knows what happened to Flavia and Anastasia."

"But, he is in service to that woman. How can you trust him?"

Kindra stepped to the outside vestibule, scanned the courtyard, her hand gripping the coin in a fist. "He has risked his life for me more than once. Left the only thing of value he has ever possessed."

"But how will you find him?"

"Let us return to the Isis. If I know Dracis, he will find his way to us."

Chapter 14 - The Wrath of Keleb

Keleb stood in the prow of his launch, the vision before him feeding his fears. From the deck of his merchant ship, the Demeter, anchored as near as he dare to the port of Constantinopolis without running her aground, he could make out only one of the two transport vessels he'd dispatched the day before. They were to deliver their cargo of olive oil and wine and return at dawn to rejoin the fleet for the final delivery to Rome before *Mare Clausum*, the end of the good weather. After that, those who ventured forward across the Mediterranean did so at their peril. Whether the missing ship was the Isis or the Leto should make no difference to him. He needed every last one of his transports to make his deliveries to Pozzuoli and on the Tiber and Ostia. Missing even one vessel would cause delays that could prove costly, both in cargo and personnel. They were all assets he could not afford to lose.

Unease clenched his insides, challenged his priorities. It wouldn't surprise him to learn that Amari had somehow sunk the Leto. The young man had all of Negasi's courage but none of his wisdom. It wouldn't be the first time he had risked a vessel on some fool's gambit. There were times Keleb sincerely felt the youth was more trouble than he was worth.

But the Isis, he realized to his dismay and not a small measure of shame, carried a more precious cargo than oil and wine. And this knowledge — clarified the moment he'd watched her sail away from the fleet toward the Palace — set his gut on edge. From the first moment he'd seen Lesidi, he had known their futures were bound together; and not just because she would soon be an heiress to Negasi's fortune.

Lesidi had been only fourteen on the day he had received his commission. She stood erect at Negasi's side, discerning eyes set wide above regal cheekbones, tall and stately as any queen of the Nile. It had been a solemn moment, one he took more seriously than any before in his life; yet, she had managed a subtle smile meant only for him. The memory of that moment burned a tattoo deep on his soul as surely as he had been struck from above by Zeus himself.

Three years later, he had agreed only grudgingly to let her sail her own transport. He would have much preferred she stay safe with her mother in Auksum. He had no doubts he would be able to protect her as he would any one of his fleet. He had even dared to dream of bringing her mother back a gift of wealth that could only result in her giving her consent to take Lesidi as his wife. Instead, Lesidi had insisted she captain her own vessel, as stipulated in Keleb's contract with Negasi, "…with all the rank and privilege of any other sailor in his fleet."

It was true, Lesidi met all the prerequisites; she was as brave and skilled as any of his men. And to her credit, unlike many of the men, she was not drawn to gamble or drink. But the sea itself was inherently unpredictable and dangerous, especially this time of year when the season was changing.

A fluffy cloud resembling a gentle sheep could rise and turn into a dark bull, then rampage into a squall that could trample and sink an entire fleet. He had no control over that, other than to take care of business and get his fleet home before the weather rose against him. It was difficult enough to worry about the fleet, but Lesidi… When he closed his eyes to sleep, he could see nothing but her eyes, that face, that subtle, secret smile.

With a knot in his throat, he thrust an oar deep into the water and pulled hard, head twisted over his shoulder to stay on course toward the little corbita they could see hiding in a reed-filled cove away from the main Palace docks. The vessel bore the mark of Negasi's fleet, an obelisk. But was it the Isis or the Leto? The low-lying fog made it difficult to see the detail of the name carved on the prow.

As they drew nearer, his mate shipped his oar. "Something is off, Commander."

Alarm rang deep in is belly, amplifying his fear. "Off?"

"This isn't a standard mooring," the sailor went on. It was true. Normally they would have put in at a small quay, or further offshore. With its shallow draft and narrow prow, a corbita could nose in close to shore to make transfer of goods easier. But it was still heavy, especially when loaded with cargo. Once run aground, it would be nearly impossible to free. "You cannot see the lesser quay from here," he observed, "only from our vantage point. She's afloat, though barely."

Keleb nodded. "Agreed. Put in over there." He indicated an area thick with reeds where the little launch would be out of sight. "We go in on foot."

*   *   *

"What do you think you're doing?"

The boy jumped nearly out of his skin as Keleb approached from behind, his sword drawn in a menacing arch. The boy fell, arms flailing, into the water below where he'd been clinging by his fingertips to the vessel's side planks. A moment later, he came up sputtering. "You've killed me! I cannot swim."

Keleb's mate waded out into briny reeds, caught the young man by the scruff of his neck, and dragged him to shore.

At the commotion, a man with a face familiar to Keleb shoved his head and shoulders out over the side. "Keleb! By the gods, what are you doing here?"

It was Cyril, the man he'd assigned on Negasi's advice to accompany Lesidi on any journey she undertook. He scanned the prow to confirm this indeed was the Isis.

"The Isis and Leto were due to rejoin the fleet at dawn. What did you think I would do? Sit quietly on the Demeter and pray her to find the Golden Fleece?"

Cyril threw a rope ladder over the side and scrambled down. "What's this?" he demanded, wading to the shore, deflecting the onus away from himself and on to the boy gasping for breath in the mud. "You challenge my authority over my own vessel?"

Keleb glared at him, undeterred. "Tell me at least, you've managed to keep Lesidi safe."

Cyril's face, though darkened and creased by many years on the sea, reddened nearly crimson before he fisted his hands at his hips and scuffed his feet. "I—"

"Cyril? What's going on?" Lesidi's voice, strident, demanding. And welcome. Relief washed over Keleb when he looked up to see her leaning over the side. Next to her was a woman he did not recognize. A Roman by the look of her, fair olive skin, dark hair cropped to her chin. Curious.

"Keleb!"

"Dracis!"

The women's voices overlapped. Lesidi lifted a leg at the top of the rope ladder.

"No." Keleb sheathed his sword. "Stay there. We'll come aboard. It seems we all have some explaining to do."

Chapter 15 - The Goddess Lexi Speaks

Lesidi pulled a fur tighter around her shoulders, the early evening air turned cold under a creeping fog. She couldn't keep her eyes off Keleb who had his back to her, staring into the waning light. They had gathered outside her quarters around a small brazier tended by Cyril. He had taken advantage of the time she and Kindra were in the city to replenish his supplies. The distinct aroma of saffron rose in the steam of a thick shellfish soup. The boy, Dracis, hands lashed behind his back, had been tied to the base of the mast. He eyed the brazier like someone half starved. Her own stomach rumbled, but as she watched the muscles ripple across Keleb's back with each slow breath, she wasn't thinking of food.

Cyril poured wine in cup and passed it to her, then offered wine to Keleb. "Commander?"

Keleb turned and accepted a cup, then joined them, sitting down, making eye contact with Lesidi first, then directing his attention to Cyril. "Tell me about the loss of my vessel, the Leto."

Cyril nearly choked on his wine. He glanced at Lesidi, his eyes wide. The first line of command was the captain of a vessel. Keleb had skipped rank. Lesidi straightened, pushing down the urge to challenge.

Keleb's choice was either an affront to her command of her ship, or a kindness born of his recognition of the possible loss of her brother. She had no way of knowing for sure, but she was grateful for the relief. She would hold off on judgment for now. She nodded at Cyril to go ahead.

"Amari spoke of a special cargo he had contracted at the quay." Once again, he glanced at Lesidi. The transports were free to conduct business while en route, as long as the captain of the vessel agreed and there was no danger to the fleet. The additional revenue was welcomed, and the ability to procure such commerce was considered when assigning command of future ventures.

"Leave nothing out, Cyril," Lesidi said. "We have no secrets from the fleet commander."

Cyril took a long drink of his wine, then recounted the events he witnessed from the moment the Leto separated from Isis.

At his account of the explosion--the fire, the bodies in the air, Kindra's rescue--Keleb rose and retreated to the railing, hunched over his wine. Lesidi could well imagine what was going through his head. For all he knew, Amari and the Leto were lost, along with any payment for the goods he was responsible to deliver, regardless of any additional cargo he took on. He would be mourning the vessel and the man. But the loss would go deeper if she was right about him. He would believe he had let her father down. The fleet would be compromised. He would blame himself in the same way she did.

Lesidi knew this moment would come—the reckoning for Amari's act and her failure to return to the fleet at the agreed upon time. She expected it would come at some future moment once the fleet's business was finished. What she hadn't expected was Keleb leaving his fleet to come after them. How little she really knew of the man.

There was something in the carriage of his shoulders, the lift of his chin, the remorseful gaze revealed in his profile, which compelled her to speak to him privately.

There was more to the story than Cyril had knowledge to relate. Would Keleb listen to her? Believe what she had to say?

With a side long glance at Kindra to see she had moved to Dracis' side and was sharing her soup with him, Lesidi rose and went to Keleb.

"This is not your fault, Keleb." It felt natural to address him in the familiar. This was the way she thought of him in her mind. An equal. Someone to which she could bare her soul. She rested her hand over his on the railing as she'd done with Kindra the night before. Her fingers looked small and frail over his sea-hardened grip.

He cut a brief, enigmatic glance at her that for all her skill at seeing into the future, was impossible to read. Then he pulled his hand from under hers and gripped her wrist so tightly she feared it would break.

"I should have insisted you stay back in Auksum with your mother," he growled in his commander voice, his brows slanted over a stern expression.

He released her as quickly as he'd grabbed her. She rubbed her wrist, but his words cut worse than his grip. Stay with her mother like an inconsequential hen? The thought of it went against everything she and her father had set in place.

"You have so little faith in my skill you'd rather I stay home with the women? That isn't the agreement you had with my father."

"Your father is dead."

The words hit her like a physical blow to her stomach. Heat rushed up her neck and over her cheeks. Whatever made her think she could share a private moment with this, this brute? She should have known better. One didn't become fleet commander without feeling they were in charge of the universe.

He scrutinized her now, making no apologies for looking her up and down, those obsidian eyes hovering at her breasts before they lifted to hers. "You are a woman, are you not?"

She lifted her chin, willing her lips into a hard line. "I am a sailor. The captain of this vessel, in case you've forgotten."

"Yet here you are, a day late, your vessel hiding in a marsh, *alone*."

His emphasis on alone sent a cold stab through her heart. Clearly, he blamed her for the loss of the Leto.

You going to let him talk to you like that?

Lesidi closed her eyes. No. She was not alone. She clenched her fists to stop her hands shaking. To Hades with his arrogance. Ignorance. She straightened, letting the fur fall off a shoulder. She aimed a finger at his chest.

"Listen to me, Fleet Commander," she said, returning to formal address. "It is not my vessel at the bottom of the sea, so you can stop the—" *...holier than thou...* "'Holier than thou' attitude right now." *Thank you.*

She took a step forward, daring to actually poke her finger against his chest plate. "My hold is empty and there's a bag of gold coins in my quarters in its place. What more do you want?"

Keleb leaned in close enough she could feel heat rolling off his body. Close enough to see a heavy gold chain around his neck, the terminus of which dipped below his hauberk. She hadn't noticed it before. When her gaze reached his eyes, he took her in again, this time with more intensity. His gaze seared her as it moved up her body. When it came to rest on her lips, she felt a twinge between her thighs that nearly made her stumble.

Whooo, he is all up into you. Take a high five on that one, girl.

High five? The Goddess's words could be puzzling. All she knew was this encounter with Keleb was heading in a direction she did not intend. She swallowed hard and clenched her hands together. The message was in his gaze when it moved to her eyes. He wanted her. At the same moment this thought came to rest in her soul, he broke the erotic link, moving out of her space.

He blinked as if stepping into a bright light from the dark. "Forgive me." He held his hands behind his back as if they'd offended him. "I have lost a vessel, but you have lost a brother. One that I know you were very close to."

Once again, she was off balance. She studied her sandaled feet on the deck.

Go ahead. Tell him. We can't go forward unless you do.

The Goddess Lexi was right. What did she have to lose? If Keleb didn't believe her, she would carry on in spite of him.

She leveled her gaze on his. "You have heard what they say about me, right?"

He looked askance at her. "That you can predict the future?" Skepticism laced his tone. She would have to prove herself to him.

"There is much more than meets the eye here, Keleb.

Ha-ha. Oh, hell yeah.

"I need you to listen to the rest of the story before you make up your mind."

Lesidi picked up the narrative where Cyril left off, detailing the events at Flavia's home.

"So, Dracis was expected, Keleb." Lesidi glanced in the boy's direction. Keleb's first mate stood next to him as though he expected him to slip out of his bindings and jump ship.

"He is not a thief or an assassin, as you have treated him, but a friend to Kindra." She returned her attention to Keleb who was fingering a stubble of dark beard at his chin.

"And I," she said, "that is, Kindra and I need to hear what he has to say without his having to fear for his life, if you don't mind."

Keleb stood and paced again, something she had seen him do on the decks of the Demeter. He studied Dracis a moment, then deepening his frown, he folded his arms over his chest. "Tell me again. What makes you believe Amari and this Marcus survived the wreck?"

My Star Goddess, you fool. The man was incorrigible. It was apparent he trusted no one. The feeling of sinking below the water washed over her once more, pulling her down. She shook it off. He wasn't ready to hear all that she had to say. Might never be. She trusted her instincts. For now, that was all that mattered. She sipped her wine and used the diversion to recover her resolve.

"As you know, Amari is not just my brother, he is my twin. This condition, in conjunction with my gift provides a connection most people do not possess. I would know if he were lost to this world. Do you understand?"

Keleb searched her face a moment, considering her words. "You receive messages from him? Directly into your thoughts?"

Lesidi held back a derisive laugh. More like a thorn in her foot. "I feel him with every step."

Keleb moved in closer, towering over her.

"You feel him?" His voice was low and held a challenge. He leveled a skeptical gaze on her that made her take a step back. "Why would I turn my entire fleet away from our goal because you have a feeling?"

He was fleet commander; she was one of his captains. She had been in his presence many times, always at a distance. She listened to his orders, obeyed without question, and kept her midnight fantasies to herself. Once again, he threatened her by virtue of his sheer proximity. Now, he was so close she could see a vein pumping at the side of his neck, the hard planes of his cheekbones under sunbaked skin, the flinty grey of his eyes. He was not the gentle giant of her dreams who took her in his arms and revered her as a goddess.

No.

This man could have been carved from the ebony tree trunks her father had freighted up the Tiber to Rome; his hands were vices, his fingers, talons, his shoulders hard as stone. The leather hauberk over his chest could not conceal the bulk of muscle and sinew sliding under his skin as he closed the distance between them.

He might be commander of a merchant ship, but he had the bearing of a warrior. She had been naive to even dream of the notion he would take an interest in her as an equal. He could crush her in one hand. At the moment, he looked like that was exactly what he wanted to do.

Why did he not believe in her? Had her father not told him of her gift?

Paper covers rock, Lesidi. It's that simple.

Paper, what? Sometimes the goddess in her head didn't make any sense.

He's afraid of you. He's a big strong bruiser, but your gift is a power he does not possess and never will. You frighten him, challenge his supremacy.

Well now. That made perfect sense. Could this be the moment her mother had warned her about? There would come a day when her gift would be questioned, and she would have to make a stand. Her body wanted to cower under his threat; ached to take another step back, but with her new goddess's help, and the words of her mother, she held her ground. She was not alone.

She took a deep breath and went on. "The Leto is lost. We all watched it sink in flames." She waved her hand to indicate those around the brazier and the rest of the crew who stood nearby, waiting for their share of the chowder. "But from what I have seen, there is much more at stake." She kept the vision of drowning to herself. There was no point in adding a layer of doom over the top of what was already a grave situation. She hoped Keleb would listen and take action before it was too late.

150

Chapter 16 - Keleb Faces the Truth

Keleb fixed his gaze on the young man. What was he, a mere child? The boy's hands were shaking hard enough to worry he would spill his soup, but the young woman, Kindra, returned his gaze with an intensity that bordered on suspicion.

He lifted his chin and studied each of them in turn. He had been trained to see every detail, evaluate the risks, and make quick, correct, decisions. He was a born leader in whose hands had rested the lives of hundreds of sailors.

Loyalty, honesty, integrity, and strength were not simply part of an oath he had taken in service of Negasi's fleet; they were the essence of his being and traits he sought, expected, of those who served him.

This young woman looked exhausted, the burns on her arms must give her much pain, but in her eyes he saw all that he needed to trust what she had to say.

The boy, not more than twelve if he were any judge, appeared half wild, without one extra pinch fat on him. He was like the dock rats that lived on the quays of every port he had ever visited. Canny and fast and able to evade every trap. Yet, this young woman, Kindra, trusted him with her life. There was something in that.

"All right. Let us hear what you have to say and be quick about it. Tell me why I should not put the Isis under sail immediately before we lose the rest of the fleet to bad weather."

Kindra waited for a nod from Lesidi, then started in. "You may or may not know there was an attempt to overthrow the Emperor Constantine. It was unsuccessful and Constantine ordered those involved put to death. They were his eldest son, Crispus, and his second wife, Fausta."

"When Fausta escaped, Constantine ordered the death of the Praetorian Guard who allowed it to happen, Marcus," she said, her eyes taking on a liquid sheen, "along with his entire family. Fausta and Marcus were captured."

Keleb stood silent, considering. "And how do you know all this?"

She covered her stomach with her hand. "I was there, in the baths when they fled together. Marcus said he would come back for me, but he never did. I was captured at Moselle and imprisoned by one of Constantine's soldiers, Valeria at the palace. Dracis assisted my escape."

His eyes focused on her abdomen; the way she caressed it meant only one thing. "And you carry his child."

Her eyes lifted to his, then she closed them and nodded. "After my rescue, Lesidi accompanied me into the city to warn his mother and sister."

The muscles deep in his gut began to tighten. He made it a policy to maintain neutral relationships with the rulers of the various ports he served; as a merchant, it never paid well to involve oneself in the politics of one's clients. This was not good news. "And how does this involve my transport ships?"

Lesidi stepped forward. "I believe Amari was paid to spirit the prisoners aboard the Leto, ostensibly to get away from the Emperor's guards."

"It was Valeria!" Dracis shouted excitedly, wiping his mouth in the crook of his arm. "I overhead the whole thing. The Leto was to take them away, but her plan was to sink it and the traitors with it."

Keleb fumed. In all his days on the sea, the Romans had been protectors of the fleet, not destroyers. "Who is this Valeria to attack a merchant ship? The Emperor must know of this at once."

Kindra stepped forward. "I advise caution, Commander. I know this Valeria. She is loyal above all to the Emperor and only does his bidding. If he believed one of our vessels assisted Marcus and Fausta's escape, he would take it out on the whole fleet."

Lesidi moved to his side and put her hand on his arm. Once again, he was shaken by her boldness. "There is more, Keleb. Before you take any action, you must hear the rest."

His nostrils flared at the scent of her. There was fear and anxiety in it, but also something that twisted in his brain and sent a coil of heat through his body. "Go on."

"After I witnessed the explosion and sinking of my brother's vessel, I was visited by a vision."

"Visited?"

"I am sure my father told you of my gift."

"Yes, but—"

"Hear me out. If my words are proven wrong, then you can send me back to my mother and never have to listen to me again."

Her eyes filled but didn't spill. She meant every word. He rolled his hand, indication she should continue.

"I was shown an image of what I believe were my brother and this Marcus..." She glanced at Kindra a moment, then turned her attention back to Keleb. "Marcus and Fausta. They were in a clearing in the marsh. There was an exchange of gold coin. The agreement was to get out of the Empire and travel with the fleet back to Auksum where Fausta could live a life without fear, only--"

Dracis whooped. "I knew it. Marcus escaped! Praise the gods."

Keleb sent him a scowl. "Hush, boy. Let her continue."

Lesidi let go of Keleb's arm. She stepped away. "Fausta doesn't want to go to Auksum." She met his eyes again. "She wants revenge on Constantine for killing Crispus and trying to kill her. She offered Amari more gold than he could imagine. I fear—"

Keleb held up his hand. He needed a moment to gather his thoughts. Of all the young men who petitioned to sail with his fleet, the one he would never have engaged were it not for Negasi was her reckless brother, Amari. Loyalty, honesty, integrity, and strength; unlike his sister who stood before him now, back straight, eyes shining; Amari possessed none of those qualities. He had been and always would be the weak link in the chain. Of all his men, Amari was not above endangering the lives of all who stood before him and the entire fleet for a bag of gold coins.

"Go on."

Lesidi sent Kindra a look that was so full of compassion, his heart clenched tight. "If…when…word gets back to Valeria that Marcus and Fausta survived, they will be hunted down, along with Marcus's family."

Kindra closed her eyes and slowly shook her head. "If they haven't taken Flavia and Anastasia already."

Dracis lay down his cup and scrambled to his feet. "Forgive me, captain, I mean, commander —"

The gawky boy looked like he was about to explode. He had to give the young man some credit. He'd apparently followed the women to the Isis unseen by either them or the Roman soldiers and climbed bare handed up her sides. The boy had courage, and strength. He could use a young man like that among his crew. It remained to be seen whether he had honesty and integrity.

"Speak, boy, and make it quick. I need to get back to the fleet."

His eyes shifted between Keleb and Kindra. "Flavia and Anastasia are safe. At least, when I last saw them. Valeria posted me near the square and ordered me to watch their home and inform her when they returned." He looked at Kindra. "I owe Marcus my life. There is no way I would turn his mother and sister over to that horror of a woman."

"So you lied to your commanding officer," Keleb said, fixing him with his sternest stare.

Dracis straightened, stared right back at Keleb. "I am no soldier, sir; I am a slave." He glanced at Kindra once more. "Valeria serves only herself and her own ambition. If I am loyal, then it is to Marcus who has always treated me fairly." He reached into his pouch and brought out a bright gold coin. "He gave me this to get a message to Kindra."

Keleb held back a chuckle. He liked this boy. Blind loyalty is no virtue. He had to respect someone so young who sought virtue even at risk to his own life. "So, you are a spy working inside the palace against the Emperor."

"No sir. I mean…" The boy cocked his head, fingered his coin, and stuck it back in his pouch. The initial frown that crossed the boy's features gave way to a half smile. He straightened his back and looked Keleb right in the eye. "I suppose I am."

Kindra stepped forward. "Enough," she said, glaring at Keleb. "While you toy with this boy, Flavia and her daughter are in grave danger." She grabbed Dracis by the arm and spun him to face her. "Where are they?"

He dragged a cap off his head and worried it in his hands. "They were going to Anastasia's betrothed." He shot a look at Lesidi, then back to Kindra. "Probably not a good idea, now that I think of it. I don't know if Valeria knew of their relationship, but if she did…"

Kindra turned to Lesidi. "If she did, there is yet another layer of revenge in play."

Keleb made eye contact with everyone around the brazier now, as the plan formed in his head. After a moment of reflection, he drew a gold coin from his pouch and held it up between his fingers. "All right, Dracis. You are no longer a slave to the palace. You are, if you wish it, under the employ of my fleet." He pinned him once more with his Commander's stare. "Once you accept this coin, you are under my command."

Dracis returned his stare. "And, what…what if I don't wish it?"

Again Keleb held back a laugh. He shot an amused glance at his first mate. "Then, I am afraid we would have to strap you to the mast of my ship until we are well away from shore and then toss you off the prow."

Dracis eyes rounded. He swallowed hard, visibly shaken. "But I…"

"Cannot swim? I know."

Keleb watched him intently for another moment, holding the coin high. After a moment, realizing they were toying with him, Dracis shoulders relaxed. He stepped forward and took the coin. Then he stepped back and saluted. "You will not be sorry, commander."

Keleb hoped that was true, as the gravity of the situation reasserted itself. "I cannot afford to stay here and look for everyone involved in this…scandal… whatever it is. My business and my fleet have to come first. Neither can I risk one of my captains going back into the city to a possible ambush."

He stood and paced the circle. "Dracis, you and Kindra are free to go into the city and find the ones you seek." He raised a brow when Dracis didn't answer.

"Yes, sir," Dracis said, realizing he had been given an order.

"Lesidi," Keleb went on, acknowledging the fear he held in his heart for her safety. "You will stay here no longer than twenty-four hours, at which time you will return to the fleet, with or without your friends."

Lesidi nodded then fixed him with her gaze. "And Amari?"

The look in her eyes—half hopeful, half disapproving—sent a shock to his heart. She would do what he said because he was her commander, but she didn't fully trust him. He lifted his gaze to the horizon a moment, gathering strength from the deepening color there. "If Amari is alive, it is my hope he will find a way to reconnect with the fleet before we have to leave the area."

He leveled his gaze at her. "You have had a rough few days. If you were wise, you'd go to your quarters and get some sleep."

Chapter 17 - Keleb Makes His Move

Lesidi sat on her bed, working oil infused with crushed rose petals *into* the twisted tendrils of her hair. *If she were wise?* Keleb's words stung her like a bee. How dare he insult her on her own boat? She lay back, arms fanned behind her head, eyes wide open, defying sleep. The faint murmurs and coughs of the others subsided as they settled into their sleeping quarters. Only Keleb remained at the prow, taking the first watch.

Kindra and Dracis had left immediately after their meeting at dinner, leaving Lesidi to worry about their safety. The girl had proven her strength on their trip into the city earlier; but at dinner, fatigue had shown in her eyes. She was still recovering from her burns and the ordeal she had faced in the water. One thing was clear: she was determined to find her friends— her family. Lesidi had no doubt if she forbid Kindra to go, she would sneak away the first chance she got. Better to let her go with Dracis than to venture back into the city on her own. Besides, what control did she have over the girl? None. Lesidi was bound to the service of the fleet; Kindra was free to do whatever she wished.

She closed her eyes tight but could not settle. Keleb's words would not let her rest. She might owe allegiance to the fleet, but this was her boat and she would damn well do as she wished on it. She slipped into a heavy palla and stole out of her quarters, her bare feet navigating the dips and flaws the wooden decks by rote.

Keleb stood at the prow, his tall frame silhouetted against the deepening purple horizon — commanding, untouchable. Lesidi pulled her palla around her as much to fortify herself against his reaction to her disobedience as to thwart a chill breeze making its way across the Bosphorus. Would he treat her differently when there was no one else to hear them?

Before she reached him, he shifted his stance, but did not turn around. "You should be getting some sleep, Lesidi." He said her name gently, without his commander's edge.

Hope fluttered in her chest. "How did you know it was me?"

He turned slowly, silently pinning her with his gaze until her insides started to squirm. This was the Keleb of her dreams.

She fingered the coils of oiled hair tied loosely at the side of her nape, heat crawling up her neck.

He stepped into her space, traced his fingers along her jawline, pressed his huge palm against her cheek. She drew in a slow breath and held it as heat inflamed her cheeks. And there was the smile she'd dreamed of. He nuzzled her neck, his breath warm against her skin. "None of the others smell like roses."

Like the moments in her dreams, Lesidi tipped her head to give him access, then rolled back as his lips pressed against the hollow of her throat. She let out a soft cry. This was a little more welcome than she had expected.

Then his shoulders stiffened. He dropped his hand and stepped away. Had her cry of pleasure broken the spell? Why?

She retook possession of herself and gazed into that face. His lips were full and strong, his chin determined, his jaw stony.

In all her dreams of finally meeting the man on her own terms, she'd never anticipated he would be so distant, so unapproachable. Even after his admission that he knew her scent, he could not — or would not — let down his armor. What had happened to him in his life that he had so many hard edges? What had he lost? She longed to reach out and touch him now, but fear of what she might see held her back.

This new part of her gift — an unexpected glimpse into a person's story just by a casual touch — was different than simply seeing images in a dream. She had no more power over it than she had over the sun and moon. She pushed away the dark, sinking feeling she'd had earlier: Sometimes it was better not to know what lurked in your future.

It was enough for now to see a battle raging behind those molten grey eyes. She didn't have to touch him to understand she played a role in that war. They stood, eyes locked for what seemed like forever until at last he blinked and exhaled like he'd been holding his breath underwater.

They had a moment; the moment had passed.

Disappointed, she stepped past him and rested her hands on the ship's railing. The purple sky had surrendered to black, the moon a slender crescent low on the horizon. At her back she could smell the scent of him—a musky blend of raw masculinity and briny sea. It reminded her of her father and something else. Something she could not name but longed for. Something at once forbidden and within her reach. She breathed it in slowly, closing her eyes, until she thought she might never exhale again.

"When will you leave?" Would he hear the longing in her words?

"We will wait for full dark, when the palace lights dim." His voice had lost its commander's edge. Was it tinged with regret? Or was that her wishful thinking?

"So. A couple of hours at the most?" Precious little time to get to know more about this enigma of a man. Perhaps it was folly to try.

And then she felt him. Close. He moved in behind her.

"Lesidi." His voice was a raw whisper. She kept her gaze on her hands, afraid to turn around and break the spell again. He moved closer still, his breath a warm flutter at her ear. She gasped at a surge of chills rolling up from her toes, through her belly and over her shoulders.

We only live one moment at a time, Lesidi. Don't let this one pass.

Lesidi took the words in. They reminded her of something her mother had said a long time ago. Never be afraid to ask for what you want, my love. Life is short enough without getting in your own way. Her Star Goddess seemed to agree.

Without another second of hesitation, she turned, and despite the warning clanging in her ears, she rested both her hands on Keleb's bare shoulders.

The first sensation was the hardened bulk of him, then the heat. It started with her fingertips, then spread to her palms. Oh, by the gods, this was a mistake. She thought to let go, but she could not move. The heat spread like oil on water, then burst into flame, overtaking her entire body, a fire so white hot she was blinded. She clenched her eyes shut against it but it was no use.

"Lesidi!" His voice sounded far away, but she could feel his hands clamped tight at her waist. He shook her and her eyes flew open. The fire was gone and his face was only inches from hers. He gazed into her eyes as she'd always dreamed he would. And then his gaze shifted from her eyes to her mouth, and without hesitation he bent to her and covered her mouth with his. His arms circled under her rear and lifted her up, clamping her against his heated body. His kiss deepened and went on and on until they were both breathless. Then he kissed her forehead, her cheek, her mouth again.

"Lesidi." His voice was a growl against her neck. Then he lifted her face to his and held it in his sea-toughened hands.

"I have thought of little but you since the first time I saw you with Negasi. He wanted to pledge you to me on that day." His eyes narrowed and darkened. "But my father…"

And then she knew. Her fingers spread on his shoulders like they were melted into his skin. Her heart thumped wildly in her chest as the visions came. His father had pledged him to another—a political match that would cement relations between his father's spice trade in the east and the woman's family gold mines in sub-Saharan Africa. When he returned from his maiden voyage as commander of Negasi's fleet, he was to have been wed and take control of the mines.

His pain bled into hers. A deep ache overtook her. "He wanted you to leave the sea for the interior. For gold."

Keleb dropped his forehead to hers, a frustrated growl issuing from deep inside his chest. She put her hands to his face and tipped it to look in his eyes. "And you never went back. I'm right, aren't I?"

"There isn't enough," he moaned, an agonized sound so raw and vulnerable she thought her heart would break.

"Enough what?"

He shook his head. "There isn't enough gold to take me away from the sea…" He looked into her eyes again. "Away from the possibility of …you."

Her throat closed on a cry welling from deep within. Their connection was real as she had imagined. She pulled his face to hers again and kissed him gently, then more ardently as he melded his body against her.

Her fingers slid down over his shoulders, down his arms and took his hands. Then she pulled him away from the railing toward her quarters.

Their union was a revelation. She was not ignorant of the ways of life and love. Her mother had been direct with her about pleasing a man and of getting pleasure in return. But the actual event was a thousand times more rewarding than her mother had described.

She forgot about the dreams, the gift, Kindra and Marcus, her mother, the fleet, even her father. There was nothing but swirling fire and smoldering flesh. They moved together as if they were one, on and on as the night enveloped the earth, rolling in her bed, drinking each other in; savoring, blessing, starting again, until they lay, bodies slick and sated in each other's arms. For the first time since she reached puberty, she slept without worry of what she would see in her dreams.

The images did come, however.

A golden dawn, the fleet sailing toward Ostia. Demeter in the lead, Keleb at the helm, followed by the Isis and the rest of the fleet. The sensation of power and love blossomed in her breast. On they sailed until, in the near distance and anvil of dark cloud gathered and spread over the water.

She tossed in her bed, gasping for breath. "No, please. Stop," she cried out. But the images kept coming, faster and faster until they spun into a freezing river of cold, dragging her down, down, down into the dark depths; only this time she was not alone. She stared helplessly into Keleb's eyes until the molten heat she had come to love slowly faded as they were swallowed by the murky water.

"Keleb!" She sat up, her heart pounding in her ears. But he was gone. She felt hollow, nothing but the memory of him moving inside her like a god. And then she saw it. On the fur next to her where he had lain, was the gold coin he had worn on a chain around his neck.

She picked it up, her fingers tingling at its touch. He had gone before dawn, leaving what she could only hope was a promise to return.

Holy shit, came the voice within, and then that was gone, too.

There was a loud clatter, like stones against the hull of her ship. "Lesidi."

She threw the fur around her shoulders, fled her quarters, and ran to the side of the ship. On the shore was the knobby-kneed boy she'd sent on a man's mission. Dracis. Kindra and another tall, stately woman stood in the reeds behind him.

He swept the hood of his robe back. "Throw down the rope ladder."

Lesidi ordered it done, the brazier lit, and returned to her room to dress.

A few minutes later, hearing their voices on deck, she emerged to find them gathered around the brazier. Cyril had brewed a pot of tea and laid out a faire of bread and olive oil and dried figs as the rest the crew prepared the vessel to leave their hiding place, loading the launch, organizing the ropes on deck to hoist the sail. Dracis scurried with them, fulfilling his promise to Keleb to make himself useful.

Kindra and the woman who must be Flavia huddled under blankets in the morning mist, using the few small bundles they'd brought with them as seats.

Lesidi studied the newcomer's face as she poured them each a cup of tea. She didn't need to lay on her hands to feel the woman's pain. "So, your daughter will be safe with her man?" she asked respectfully.

Flavia bit her lip. "She believes so."

Kindra put her arm around Flavia and pulled her close, then lifted her gaze to Lesidi. "Dracis found them at the young guard's family quarters. She refused to leave the country without him. Her loyalty is that of a woman in love."

Flavia closed her eyes and breathed in deeply. "What woman hasn't put aside what was best for her to please a man?"

"I am sorry, Flavia," Lesidi said softly.

Flavia gave her a knowing smile that reminded her of her own mother. "It was bound to happen soon." She shot a glance at Kindra. "I believe she was with child, so…"

Lesidi rested her hand on Flavia's shoulder. "Keleb is convinced my brother will find a way to return to the fleet. If Marcus is with him, as I have seen in my … visions … he will be safe. He has also guaranteed transport to Auksum once our grain has been delivered to Rome."

Flavia nodded. "Never in my dreams did I imagine I would have to leave my home. Especially sail away to a place about which I know nothing." She lifted her gaze to the swan's neck behind them and followed it to the shiny obsidian eyes.

Lesidi had never felt more at home than on the sea, never really longed to be anywhere else, even her home in Auksum.

"I am truly sorry. But if what Dracis says is true, there is a bounty on Marcus's head, along with anyone associated with him. Until at least this Valeria is vanquished, none of you will be safe at home."

Flavia nodded. "I fear you are right about that. And that I will never see Anastasia again."

She stood now, went to the swan and ran her fingers up its stately neck the way Lesidi had often done when deep in thought. Then she straightened, sipped her tea, and forced a smile.

"But, I have forgotten my manners. Thank you Lesidi. I am grateful for all you have done, both for Kindra and me…" She moved to Kindra, knelt in front of her, pressed her hands against her belly. "…and our baby—"

She gasped, her eyes flashing to Kindra's then Lesidi and back to Kindra. She bent her head to Kindra's belly and pressed her ear against it. "Babies! By the gods, daughter, you are going to have twins."

Kindra rubbed her hand over her belly and let go a laugh for the first time since Lesidi had fished her out of the sea. The sound of it lightened Lesidi's heart.

Lesidi turned away from the warm scene when Cyril cleared his breath behind her, the sounding lead looped over his shoulder. "I've prepared an area in the hold for our extra passengers as you requested, captain. We are ready to go as soon as the tide comes in."

Lesidi nodded. It wouldn't be the best of accommodation for the two women. It wasn't difficult to share her quarters with Kindra. However, the little corbita was designed to accommodate only five sailors, the rest of her space was designed for cargo. Now they were eight. "Did you cordon off the space in case we are boarded?"

"As instructed, behind a row of amphorae."

"Good. How long before we are free to depart?"

Cyril looked to the horizon. "We should be able to safely leave the reeds by dark, which works in our favor."

Chapter 18 - Ruby Eyes

Newport Beach California - 2019 CE

Lexi lay on the floor in Tessa's workshop, the serpent bracelet cold and loose at her wrist. She tried to prop herself up, but her head was heavy, off balance like a watermelon ready to roll off a kitchen counter, her stomach a little queasy. She scooted back to the workbench shelving, leaned against it, closed her eyes tight, her palm pressed hard into the cold tile floor. At least it was solid.

"Lex? You here?" Tessa's voice again. Coming from upstairs. She opened her eyelids a crack. The gray pink of near sunset stole low through the casement windows opening on to the front yard. My god, how long had she been here?

Curling her legs under her, thoughts tumbling in a muzzy haze, she clawed her way back to something that made sense. *You came down here to … Oh. Yes. Make sure the kiln was off. Tessa was called away to help Cort with Jenessa, and you came down here to …* That was just after lunch. Jeez. She rolled her eyes to the stained, acoustic ceiling. She'd been down here for hours.

Footsteps racing down the stairs. "Alexis?"

"In here," she called out, her voice forcing through a morning-after rasp. Still dizzy, she let her head drop back against the shelves.

"Lex? Oh my god." Tessa knelt beside her. "What happened? Did you fall?"

Fall? She wished. Her biceps tingled. She ran her hand up her arm and flinched at the sting of a patch of raw flesh. Tessa's gaze took in the burn, but she didn't say a word. She didn't have to. Instead, she offered her hand.

Still a little woozy, Lexi let Tessa help her get up and sit on the sofa bed. She'd had another…episode. That was for sure. Her entire body broke out in goosebumps as the sensation of sinking into a cold, dark place pushed for attention, threatened to take her down.

Screw that.

She scraped stray curls back across her head and huffed out a determined sigh.

Tessa cut her eyes to the bracelet, then her brows lifted again. "Is there something you want to tell me?"

Guilt warmed Lexi's cheeks. "I didn't mean to put it on. It just…happened." She slid the gold bracelet off her wrist and handed it to Tess.

"Where'd you go?"

"Honestly, Tess. I didn't mean to. It just happened."

Tessa took Lexi's hands. "Stop it. You forget who you're talking to. You touched it and it slithered up your arm, right?"

Some of Lexi's anxiety dialed back a notch. The good thing in all this was she didn't have to convince Tessa of anything. She'd been there before.

"All I remember is reaching for it, thinking maybe you'd cast a replica. Those damned ruby eyes latched on to mine and I don't remember anything else until you came in and found me."

That wasn't exactly true. The words had barely passed her lips when a memory slipped in. There was … what was his name? Keleb. A new flush of heat spread from her cheeks, down her neck and to the nether parts below. "There was a pretty damn sexy encounter with a handsome black ship commander dude in there somewhere."

Tessa laughed. "Isn't there always?"

"Maybe in your dreams, girlfriend. Mine is usually the night janitor at the women's shelter. One good thing, though. You did remember to turn off the kiln."

Tessa let go a laugh. "Oh no. You don't get to drop the hot sex bomb and walk away from it."

Lexi blew out a breath. "My memory's a little blurry." Also not true. She remembered their foreheads pressed together, his eyes burning into hers, his hands sliding down her ribcage to her hips … that's where it got fuzzy. He was with Lesidi, right? But it felt like…

"Uh huh. That's not what happened to me when that damn snake crawled up my arm."

"Yeah? And what happened to you?"

Now it was Tessa's cheeks going red. "Well, it wasn't fuzzy. The guy was one hundred percent into

Kindra and I felt every molecule and nanosecond. In fact, I wasn't sure who was running that show, if you know what I mean."

Lexi bit her bottom lip. It was pretty clear Lesidi was a virgin. Had Lexi encouraged her? No. It wasn't like that. Keleb was definitely in charge of that element. She had just been along for the ride. The memory sent a charge of heat to her center. "So…" she said, louder than necessary, "the bracelet is still in play."

Tessa let go a nervous laugh. "Damn pesky thing. I should have buried it with Audrey after all. We could have been done with it."

"Why'd it latch onto me? It's your trinket, not mine."

"It came with the house, Lex, remember?"

"Whatever."

"Are you wearing Zaire's necklace?"

Lexi fished it out from under her sweater and dangled it in the air.

Tessa held out her hand. "May I?"

Lexi lifted the chain over her head and dropped the necklace into Tessa's hand. She clicked on the magnifying light on her workbench and arranged the coin, face up on the black velvet pad underneath. Moving the light in to position, she took a closer look.

"I think our little serpent is picking up on its vibe. An ancient coin from the same era and close geographical location as the brooch. It's related somehow."

Lexi shook her head. "That's crazy. It has nothing to do with the jewelry found in this house. I didn't even know you when I met Zaire. And I didn't know I had the necklace until the other day."

Tessa pressed her lips together a moment then handed her back the chain. "Yet, here we are and this time, you, my friend are the time traveler."

Lexi shook her head. She twisted her arm to see the burn marks from where the bracelet had wrapped around it. A shiver worked its way through her entire body. "Yet, here we are," she echoed.

Tessa snapped off the light. "Come on. Let's go upstairs and get some salve for that burn."

The water dispenser gurgled as Tessa filled her electric teapot. "So, what do you want to do about it?"

"Do?"

The back door rattled open, and Rags shot in and jumped onto the dining room table like he owned the place. Which he did. Phillip followed behind, his jacket slung over his shoulder and a six pack of IPA's dangling from his fingertips. Realizing her mouth was still making a startled O, Lexi pressed her lips together.

Phillip stopped in his tracks. "Am I interrupting something? Want me to leave? I can go down and drown my sorrows in the workshop." He started in that direction.

"No," they replied in unison.

He gave them an appraising look. Lex was pretty sure he knew damn well he'd interrupted and thought it was funny. He leaned in and planted a kiss on Tessa's lips, sending Lexi a mischievous wink.

Newlyweds.

Lexi stood, happy for the distraction. Once the wedding was over, once the move was completed, she'd been hoping her life would settle into something resembling a responsible adult pattern. The damn snake slithering up her arm didn't fit that model. She didn't want to talk about it. Didn't want to think about it. She just wanted to put the lid back on that can of worms. She just wanted to go home and get some sleep.

*   *   *

Lexi lay flat on her bed, a dove-gray duvet clutched to her shoulders, her eyes wide open, staring at the ceiling. She'd come home, fixed herself some chamomile tea, and climbed into bed with a book of Maya Angelou poems, which usually soothed her when her soul ached.

No luck now. Words disappeared on the page, replaced by heated memories of Lesidi and Keleb. She lay the book on the nightstand, vanquished, torn in two.

Part of her wished she had never gone into that workshop. Never seen what she had seen. But another part of her—a part that changed forever when she beheld her reflection in the mirror on the day she found the coin—had her longing to see the world again through Lesidi's eyes, to sail the Mediterranean, to be the captain of her destiny. To lay with Keleb.

She rolled on her side, closed he eyes, and let go a tired sigh. Not since being with Zaire all those years ago had she felt such a deep yearning to be that close to a man. She let the memory take her deeper into the feeling of his body curled against her back, his heat radiating into her skin, his need rising with each breath. In another life she would move against him, invite him in, let herself sink deep into that warm sea of desire; deeper, deeper until she was entirely consumed…

CHAPTER 19 - OPEN THE DOOR

She awoke shaking off the ragged edges of a dream that had left her feeling both satisfied and empty. The good news was she had slept through the entire night; the bad news was she had neglected to set her alarm and was running late. She hurried downstairs to start a quick brew before she showered. Filling the pot with water at the sink, she glanced up when she caught sight of Tessa next door, hurrying down her stairs.

Lexi scooted to the door, let her in, holding the pot aloft. "Hi. Everything okay?

"Great! I'm glad I caught you," Tess huffed, out of breath..

"How's Janessa?"

Tessa sent her a confused look as she filled the reservoir, measured coffee into the strainer and closed the lid, then flipped the switch.

"Oh, she's good. That is, as well as can be expected, I guess. She wasn't too happy about being left at the care home. But, it had to be done. They advised us to let them keep her a few days before we come back to visit so they can settle her in."

"How's Cort taking it?"

"He's relieved, mostly. He'll need a while to adjust, I'm sure. But it's all for the best." Tessa fished an envelope out of her pocket. "But, that's not why I came over. I wanted you to have this before you went into the office."

Lexi got two cups from the cupboard, turned them up on the quartz counter. Tess fumbled with the envelope, suddenly at a loss for words.

"What is it?"

"Well, I. I told Phillip about…" She blew out a breath. "I told him about your daughter."

Lexi felt a stab in her heart. "My daughter? I don't understand."

Tessa shook her head. "Come on, Lex. You've been a mess since the day we found that little cap in your storage unit. I'm … we're … worried about you."

We. Of course, we. Tessa would have told Phillip everything. "You guys, stop. I don't need--"

Tessa waded in, undaunted. "You think about her. I know you do. I mean, look what you do for a living. How much clearer can it be?" She put the envelope on the counter and pushed it toward Lexi. "What if you could put all the doubt to rest? Part of your cleanup and declutter."

Declutter? Her daughter was clutter? Of course not. But worrying about her was. With every teenage girl who slouched into her office, she saw Ruby in trouble, Ruby lost and alone. She would be the same age Lexi was when she gave birth to her right now. The moan came from deep inside her body, like some painful living thing that wanted out. She sank into the bolstered bench in Audrey's breakfast nook and cut her eyes to the burgundy bougainvillea blossoms on the fence between their houses, the first gurgles of the coffee brewing.

Tess moved the envelope in front of her. "Just look at it." Her voice was a whisper, but it carried the weight of friendship, love.

Lexi lifted it gingerly off the table and scanned it.

In the top left corner was a Dick Tracy Silhouette logo underscored by the words: Koenig and Associates. She lifted her eyes to Tess. "Did *you* read it?"

Tessa shrugged, gave her a canny smile. "Just open it. No pressure. Do what you want with it. If you don't want to use it, just toss it, or save it for later. Whatever."

Lex knew Tessa's casual attitude meant just the opposite. She was excited about whatever it was. And because she trusted her friend, Lexi resisted the dose of attitude building in her shoulders. Still her fingers trembled a little. Part of her wanted to jump to the stove and set the damn thing on fire. Phillip was a friend but he had no right to stick his nose all up in her business.

But another part of her, the rational, psychologist part, pushed her finger under the envelope's glued flap and slipped it open.

Inside was a thick, tri-folded packet. With a last glance at Tessa, she slid it out and unfolded it. The cover page was a reply to Koenig and Associates email, along with a form and another page stapled to the back. She scanned the lines and boxes. Birth Mother, SSI, mother's maiden name … Her chin quivered a little. She tightened her lips against it. "It's from her adoption agency? How did he find it?"

Tessa shrugged. "Trick of the trade, I suppose."

"So, all I would have to do is fill out this form and return it to the agency?"

Tessa slipped onto the bench opposite Lexi, propped her elbows on the table and threaded her fingers together. "They won't give you any specific information about your daughter or the adoptive parents, but if your daughter ever contacts the agency looking for you, the form gives your permission to give her your information."

Lexi sat back. Was that what she wanted? Her eyes met Tessa's. She lowered her voice. "I can't believe Phillip did this."

"He's a good man. And he loves you."

Lexi huffed out a little laugh. At least somebody did. Seemed like all of her somebodies turned out to be somebody else's. *Even Keleb.* That thought sobered her. She sat up, cleared her throat. "It's a can of worms, though, right?"

"Maybe. Phil couldn't get any particulars about your daughter. Said he'd be disappointed in them if they caved. That's how it's supposed to work."

"She'll probably never contact them. I mean, why would she?"

What if she already had and hit a dead end? Would she try again?

Tessa sent her a speculative frown. "Of all people, Lex, you have to ask?"

Tessa was right. Plenty of adoptions went south, some of them ending in tragedy. The lucky ones ended up therapy like hers when they hit roadblocks, just like any other family. She didn't want to think about the unlucky ones. She wanted to think, to believe, that her daughter had gone to a loving home with parents who wanted her and made her their own. If that was the case, even if she knew she was adopted, she probably wouldn't care to meet her birth mother.

Still, curious, she read through the letter again. Attached to the form was a copy of a birth certificate.

Single Live Birth 05/27/2005. A Gemini.

The twins? She would have look that up.

Certified by Dr. Emil Rafferty. Female. 5.5 lbs. Term of pregnancy: 8.0.

A month early.

The coffee pot signaled the brew was done. She lowered the certificate and watched Tessa get up and pour them each a cup, thinking about that day. So much of it was shrouded in a fog. She had gone into labor early, complications ensued, an emergency C-section was performed. She was still groggy from anesthesia when they whisked her baby away.

She sipped coffee and kept reading.

Child's name: Redacted. Race: African/Caucasian.

She had secretly wanted to name her baby Ruby if it was a girl, after Ruby Bridges. It was a little old fashioned, she knew. But, being mixed race, her daughter would need to be strong and smart and brave.

Father, name and age redacted, race: African.

Zaire Negatu. For years she believed he never knew. She blinked against a sting at the back of her throat, threads of last night's dream strafing her heart.

Mother, age 15, name redacted, Race: Caucasian/African American.

Somewhere in the national archives an original version of the certificate would exist without redactions. Her heart squeezed into a fist.

Phillip had scribbled on a sticky note at the bottom of the certificate: *A new birth certificate is issued to the adoptive parents with the child's new name, listing their names as parents. That's the one the agency passed along.*

Lexi let out a sigh. Of course, they did.

Her baby would never know she'd been adopted unless someone decided to tell her. *For the best,* her mother had said over and over. *For the best.* But had it been? It was a question she had to push deep, deep down or it would ruin every waking moment.

Tessa stirred a small mountain of sugar into her coffee.

Lexi watched, mesmerized a moment, then closed her eyes on the image of black redaction marks on her daughter's birth certificate. It wasn't right. Black boxes on a paper might erase a person's official identity, but they didn't erase a person's existence. She was out there, somewhere. Wasn't there just a good a chance she had been placed in the perfect family? Her knowing wouldn't change any of that. She turned the papers over, stared at the blank backs a moment as if she expected some additional piece of information would suddenly decide the issue for her. Nothing happened. Of course. She wiped moisture from the corner of her eye and glance up at Tess.

"So…" Tessa helped herself to the ubiquitous bag of Oreos on the table and shoved it across to her.

"So, I don't know." Her practical, doctor side kicked in. "Why would I want to disrupt her life?" She twisted a cookie apart and scraped the frosting off with her teeth.

"You wouldn't be disrupting, Lex. You would only hear from her if she approached the agency on her own, or with her adoptive parents." She sat back a moment letting her words sink in. "The question is, do you want to disrupt your own?"

"What's to disrupt? I don't even have a boyfriend."

"So…" Tessa rolled her hand in the air in front of her. "You don't have to do anything with the papers. But there they are. It's like adjoining rooms in a hotel. You can open the door on your side. It's up to the other person to unlock theirs if they want to meet you in the middle."

Lexi sat back in her chair and stared at the letter like it was about to sprout teeth and go for her throat. Why open an old wound? That was the point of a closed adoption, right? Take the decision out of her hands and the blame off her soul. Leave the mistake behind forever. Just the thought of trying to reverse that moment — that decision — sucked the oxygen out of her lungs until she felt lightheaded.

She closed her eyes, focused on her breathing.

"Okay. Listen." Lexi finished all she wanted of her coffee. "I have to go. I've got lots of work, and I'm on call tonight at the women's shelter." Thank god, that was the truth. She'd be too busy helping others to worry about her own hot mess of a life. She took her cup to the sink. "Thank Phil for his sleuthing work. I really appreciate it. If he won't take money for his services, I can pay him in oatmeal cookies."

Tess carried her cup to the sink. "I'm sure he'll choose the cookies. He says it was good practice. Turns out tracking down adoption agencies is one of the most popular searches people want from an investigator, outside tracking down deadbeat dads."

Lexi allowed herself a laugh. "Gotta pay the bills while you wait for that really big case."

Some of the anxiety she'd felt earlier had faded under Tessa's smile. She hustled to the door and Rags leapt down to slither between her legs as she headed for her own stairway, then stopped on the first step. "Lex?"

Lexi recognized concern in her best friend's face. She leaned against her back door, the papers still gripped in her hand.

"I think you should do it."

Lexi frowned and cut her eyes to the street. "I'll think about it, okay?"

Tessa threw up her hands in exasperation. "Really, Lex? What's the worst thing that could happen?"

Lexi huffed out a sigh, closed her eyes and bit on her bottom lip, then rolled her eyes back to Tess. "Why do you always say that?"

Tessa laughed. "Just think about it."

Chapter 20 - A Hot Wind

An unseasonal Santa Ana wind whipped the bay to whitecaps and spun abandoned hamburger wrappers and dried bougainvillea flowers in angsty little circles across her office parking lot. Alexis hurried from her car to the lobby, her roller bag briefcase in tow.

Hot, gusty Santa Anas were common to Orange County. Of all the weather patterns, it was Lexi's least favorite. The atmosphere crackled with static. The air was heavy with brown dust and who knew what all. Near the beach, wind gusts sand blasted bare legs, scoured paint, and piled sand up against doors, ready to blow in the moment they were opened.

The fact that the Devil Wind arrived in March instead of October this year was a grim reminder climate change was happening in her lifetime, not some future apocalyptic moment. Her patients were more irritable and less cooperative during Santa Anas; and she had to admit, she was, too. Thank goodness it was Monday, and she had no face-to-faces scheduled.

She blew into the lobby along with a smattering of sand and struggled with the bag as she forced the door shut behind her. "Miserable wind."

Robbi glanced up from a copy of the latest edition of Vanity Fair. "Oh my God! Tavi Gevinson just signed on to do a reboot of Gossip Girl!"

"Really? I just spent an hour trying to get off the island on the ferry because a power line was down over the bridge and the first words out of your mouth are Tavi Gevinson?"

Robbi sent her a sheepish grin. "Sorry. It's pretty cool, though. I can't wait."

Gevinson — teenage fashion blogger, magazine editor, and actress by the time she was fifteen — was an idol of most of her female clients, and Robbi was no exception. She had to admit, Robbi's obsession was refreshing after her former receptionist who was in a constant phone battle with someone, usually her boyfriend, but more recently her roommate, her landlord, her mother, and AT&T.

Lexi adjusted her skirt and pulled her short-cropped jacket into place. Pants would have made more sense on a day like today, but she wasn't in the habit of thinking that far ahead. She was lucky she remembered to bring her stainless-steel water bottle. "Does this mean you'll be going blond soon?"

Robbi rolled her eyes to the stairway. "Wow. Do *ya* think it would be a good look for me?"

"Honey, everything is a good look for you." She wasn't just trying to boost the young woman's ego. Robbi had blossomed under the completion of her gender reassignment. Lexi was proud of her.

Robbi's cheeks pinked, a wedge of short-cropped hair sliding over her eyes. She reached over the counter and handed Lexi a folder. "Got a call from

Juvi. You have an interview at nine o'clock. I went ahead and booked as your calendar was free."

Lexi's spirit, already whacked because of the wind, took a steep nosedive. "Monday? Really?"

Robbi's shoulders sagged. "Oh. Right. Sorry. Want me to call him back?"

"Him?" Lexi tucked the file folder under her arm, removed a shoe, and shook a stream of sand out of it. "What happened to Marlene?"

Robbi shrugged. "Dunno. The call came from a guy." She gave her that perky smile she adored. She had been through a lot and come out the other side unscathed. In the three months since Lexi had hired her, she'd managed to master most of her duties, but more importantly, she'd been a poster child for resilience, having won over all but the most recalcitrant of the tenants in the building. And he complained when Lexi had been in charge, so he didn't count.

"Sounds like some kind of career project. He left a number in case you can't make it." She tore a pink sheet off a message pad and passed it to Lexi.

"The usual permissions?"

"I assumed…"

Lexi blew out a sharp breath, slipped into the elevator, easier than the stairway with her weekend roller bag, stuffing the number in her suit pocket before she unlocked her office door.

Elvis and Loki were circling the top of their tank when she pushed open her door.

"Hi guys. Sorry I'm late." She dropped her purse and the file on her desk and headed for the fish tank situated on a side table against her wide office window. "You guys hungry after the weekend?" she crooned. Outside, palm trees leaned toward the ocean, torn fronds piling up in the parking lot across the street. Inside, the act of sprinkling fish food flakes calmed her agitation, which she admitted had nothing to do with the wind.

Another month had passed since Tessa and Phillip had located her daughter's adoption agency and given her contact permission forms. Another month of hesitation, guilt, inaction. She just couldn't bring herself to…

The intercom buzzed. She dropped into her desk chair and pressed down the button. "Yes?"

Robbi's cheerful voice came over the speaker. "That nine o'clock is here. A bit early, but—"

Lexi checked the digital clock on her desk. Fifteen minutes early to be exact. She let out a sigh and glanced around the room. Everything was in order thanks to Robbi who came in and cleaned for her twice a week, a service she added when it was clear, the kid would need more cash if she wanted to live anywhere near Newport Beach.

She pulled at a twist of hair on her forehead. She wasn't really ready for an interview. She felt jittery, over-caffeinated, and now that she thought of it, with no time to eat the bagel she'd shoved in her briefcase on the way out the door, starved. Then she thought of the kid waiting in the lobby. Career thing? Right now, she wouldn't recommend it. No matter how hard she worked to manage her practice, her time was never her own.

She pressed the button again. "Give me five minutes, okay? Maybe get them some coffee or juice from the break room?"

A pause, then. "Got it."

She pulled her briefcase behind the desk, grabbed a quick bite of the cold bagel, and chewed thoughtfully as she scanned the file. It was basically empty, except for a name. For existing clients, she would normally call up their file on her laptop, but they used a physical file folder during introductions. She had discovered most of her clients felt better with the physical connection; a doctor taking actual notes rather than banging away on an impersonal keyboard.

The "intro" file contained a single sheet. The client was a Jamal Isiah. Student. That's it? She turned the paper over. Nothing. Curious. Health Services was very good at emailing client files ahead of a meeting even in emergencies; and Robbi was also great about including any information she could in the folder. She supposed there wouldn't be much if this were truly just an interview about her profession. But at least an age, a school, something.

She got a prickly feeling at the back of her neck; her body's way of telling her something was off. She'd have to wait and see how it panned out. She retrieved the pink message note from her pocket and clipped it to the sheet.

She silenced her cell phone, closed her eyes, and took in a slow breath, then exhaled slowly. Just. Deal.

Her office door opened, and a young man stepped in.

Lexi caught her breath. At nearly six feet tall, whip thin, with skin a light, toasty brown, the kid reminded her for a fraction of a second of Zaire. *Face it Alexis, nearly every young black man you meet sends you back to the Med at least for a fleeting moment.* But his clothes and the way he slouched in the doorway were all affluent Orange County American teenager, which comprised ninety percent of her clients.

At least he had some manners. He scooped a purple and gold Lakers ball cap off his head to reveal cornrows zig-zagged across the crown of his head, all gathered at his neck in a short tail. His clean white T-shirt — also sporting Laker's logos — and a pair of tattered jeans fit his body surprisingly well considering the trend for teens to swim in their clothes. His shoes — Nike somethings - were actually tied. She recognized the very expensive wireless headphones clamped around his neck, only because they'd been the type one of her newest clients had been in trouble for boosting from and Apple Computer store at the Plaza Mall. She guessed the latest model smart phone was shoved in his back pocket.

He closed the door quietly behind him, straightened his posture, then broke out a reserved smile. "Doctor Hill?"

Surprised he'd arrived alone, she flipped on her tape recorder, then stepped around her desk and offered her hand. "That's me. Oh!" They both flinched at the static charge when their hands touched. "May I call you Jamal?"

His cheeks flushed. "Sure."

"Come. Sit." She indicated the chair opposite her desk and pulled a side chair up to sit next to him rather than scoot around behind her desk. "Just so you know, since you are unaccompanied, I switched on my recorder."

He glanced briefly at the machine, lifted a shoulder in response.

"I understand you've been referred by The Orange County Juvenile Services?"

"Well, yes, but … I'm not, you know…"

"In trouble?" She had several referrals a month from the agency, often sessions with a psychologist are offered in lieu of time in Juvenile Hall when a teen gets himself in trouble for the first time, or under special circumstances such as parental abandonment or incarceration. Neither Jamal's clothing, nor his demeanor showed outward signs of a kid in that kind of trouble. But she'd learned from experience, looks were definitely deceiving. Still there was something engaging in his dark hazel eyes. If this were an official visit, she'd add that to her notes. On first impression, she liked him.

He glanced at the fish tank, exhaled. "I got your number from them."

Ah, that explained something. He'd made the call himself. This would be interesting. "What can I do for you, Jamal?"

He gave her the long, appraising look she often got when first meeting someone. What is she? Part black, Asian? The scrutiny, sometimes judgmental, would put her off if she wasn't used to it.

He looked away a moment, then cleared his throat. "I…I'm not here for therapy. I'm on a school project. Career research?"

He had a slight accent she couldn't place. British? No. But something. It reminded her of her mother. He hadn't grown up in Newport Beach, that was for sure. She settled more comfortably in her seat. "Oh? What school?"

His eyes flashed wide a moment, then he licked his lips. "Private school. Yes. Private," he stammered.

"I see." A private school of which he'd forgotten the name. Not likely. Her interest perked, she forged ahead. "So, you're a senior? Looking at colleges?" She was fishing in a shallow hole, she knew. He was gangly tall but judging by the obvious lack of maturing musculature at his shoulders and neck, not a day over fifteen. "I got my bachelor's at UC Irvine. Great school."

He started to shake his head. "My dad wants me to go to Scripps Institute."

"Oceanography. But let me guess. You're interested in becoming a therapist."

He lifted a shoulder. "You're a psychotherapist, right?"

"Right, and as such, I specialize in—"

His gaze explored the room as she ticked off her expertise, gliding back to the fish tank, her comfy love seat near the window, then skimmed the top of her bookshelf, and landed on the only personal photograph in the office, an eight-by-ten of Tessa, Audrey, and herself sitting at the stern of the little sailboat Tess had inherited with the house.

"You're not married?"

"I'm sorry, what?" Clients sometimes deflected by turning the tables to make the talk about her. But this didn't feel… He wasn't exactly a client. Still…

He returned his gaze to her. "You … don't have any kids?" There was something urgent in the words, the amber in his eyes going suddenly dark. He shoved his hands in his pockets and looked like he was about to bolt.

"I… no."

"So, you just didn't want any, or…"

Now that was getting too personal. There was something up with this kid and she suspected it had nothing to do with a career interview for school. She needed to steer the interview away from the personal and back to the original topic.

"Not much time for that, I'm afraid," she answered, putting on a smile, and launched into a description she hoped would satisfy him so she could get on with her Monday.

"As a career builder, you would need to get a bachelor's degree in psychology, then a master's in clinical psychology. At that point, you would seek out clinical experience in order to qualify for your license. Then if you want to go for the Ph.D., you've got research and several more years of graduate school—"

His eyes suddenly glistened wet. Their gazes caught and held a second too long before he glanced to the ceiling, then to the window. "I…I need to go."

Oh my god. What had she said?

He stood and looked around as if he forgot which way he came in, then stepped to the door and grabbed the handle. "Thank you for your time, Miss Hill."

He was out the door and down the stairs before she caught her breath. She strode to the door. "Jamal? Jamal. Wait."

He was out into the wind without looking back. "Damn."

Robbi finished a call for Mr. Cantankerous and stood up behind her circular desk. "What was that all about?"

Lexi craned her neck out the door to see where the kid went. Aside from a dust devil spinning on a construction site down the street, nothing moved. "I honestly do not know."

She leaned against the counter, pushing a queasy feeling down in her stomach. "What was your impression of him?"

"Mine?"

"Yeah. You're observant. Smart. Did you pick up any weird vibes from that kid?"

Robbi's eyebrows gathered a moment. "Well, he had no idea who Tavi Gevinson was."

Lexi opened her mouth a moment, then closed it. "Right. Listen. I know you weren't aware of this, but as a psychotherapist, it is unethical for me to speak privately with an underaged kid without parental or some kind of institutional permission. You need to check with me next time before making an appointment."

Robbi's cheeks reddened. "Wow. I'm really sorry. Want me to call Juvenile Hall?"

Lexi shook her head. "No. I mean. He didn't do anything wrong, really." There's no law against not coming off as billed. Who really knew what went on inside a kid's head? "Besides, I have a strong feeling they have no record of any Jamal Isiah."

Chapter 21 – Swarovski Eyes

Excitement lit up Tessa's face as she slid into their regular Wednesday Lunch booth at the Butterfish Grill. "Welp! It's official."

Lexi had an idea what the surprise was about when Tess called to confirm their lunch, but she let her hold on to her secret as long as she could. She knew Tess and Phillip were preggers, but until recently, he'd been dragging his feet about wanting to know the sex. People were getting a little bonkers about gender reveals and Phil wanted no part of all that craziness.

Tessa had come straight from her doctor's appointment to the restaurant, so there was little doubt as to what she wanted to reveal. Wearing a clingy tank that showed off her swelling boobs, she unrolled a hot pink T-shirt with an arrow pointing down, and the words Girl in the Oven arched over.

Lexi's heartbeat stumbled over an echo from the past. She kicked it back where it belonged. "Yay!" She high fived Tess and they hugged over the table. "I knew it." They had already predicted Tessa's baby was due in September. Life was going to take a big right turn on that day for sure.

"How did you know?" Tess smooshed the T-shirt over her head and pulled it down. She was so damned skinny there was no evidence of a bump, but under the full T-shirt, there was definitely room.

Lexi shrugged. "I don't know. Just a feeling." She had to fight to keep a little sad out of her voice. "Let's hope she gets Phillip's swimming pool blue eyes and those eyelashes."

Tess reached across the table, tapped Lexi's hand. "What's up with you, sister? You seem a little…off."

"It's nothing. I'm so happy for you." And she was. So why did she feel she was sinking into a black hole?

Tess gave her a squinty-eyed appraisal. "You know, you need to relax about Ruby." In the few weeks they'd actually discussed Lexi's child, Tessa had refused to call her anything but Ruby. "She's only fifteen. You of all people know young teens are all about themselves." She smoothed her t-shirt over her belly. "I've heard some of the most common searches for biological parents begin when the girl is going to be a mother herself."

"Oh, where did you hear that?" But she knew. Ever since Phillip had located the agency, Tessa had been emailing her links to happy endings when biological moms and kids were reunited.

She put up her hand.

"What?" Tessa asked.

"I haven't exactly sent the paperwork in."

Tessa's eyebrows raised, her mouth shaping a tight "o".

Lexi waited a beat, knowing Tess was disappointed. "Look. I know. It's stupid. But I just feel like…I just don't feel I have anything to offer, you know?"

Tessa shook her head. "Nothing to offer…"

"No. It's not that. Really. Just lately, I feel like I'm going nowhere. I'm almost thirty and I'm just, like, treading water, just keeping my head up. For what? I look to the horizon and there's nothin' out there."

Tessa cocked her head, listened. "I thought you loved your work, the house. Now you're going to be an auntie. What brought this on?"

Lexi shrugged, saw the server, and motioned her over, thankful for something to do besides try to explain herself. "The usual," she mouthed, then refocused on Tess. "You've got Phillip, now the baby. And you're getting into your own line of jewelry. Phillip is launching a new career. You've got a life. And I feel like I'm stuck in the doldrums without a rudder."

Tessa sat back. "You know, it might help if you took a break from all your volunteering in your spare time and actually did something fun for yourself. You might actually meet someone outside the system. It's not like you don't have the money." She covered her mouth, her eyes wide. "Wow. That came out harsher than I intended."

Lexi huffed out a laugh. "No apologies. You're right. I've done it to myself. I know that." She glanced up when the server, a mutual friend, approached the table.

"Notice anything?" Tessa asked, beaming. Francine gave her a puzzled look, then her eyes landed on the T-shirt and she broke out in a smile. "Wow. Congratulations! A girl."

"September 20 if she's on time."

"Ah, a Virgo. How about some tea?"

Tessa beamed her million-dollar smile. "Hot tea would be great, thanks."

And somewhere deep inside, words echoed in Lexi's head for the first time since she'd awakened in Tessa's workshop with the bracelet around her wrist. *Gemini. Twins.*

Her face drained of heat. She got up, looked around, her gaze landing on the single bathroom door at the back of the dining-room.

"Lex?"

"I…I'm going to the ladies room."

A wave a nausea had her bending over the toilet, enough to release her necklace from her shirt. She grabbed it, held it out of the way. When the sick feeling passed without producing anything, she went to the sink and splashed cold water on her face.

Nausea again. Like major morning sickness nausea. She hadn't been with a man for over a year, so that wasn't it. What was happening to her?

She leaned on the sink and breathed through her nose until the sensation passed.

She glanced up, caught her own eyes in the mirror. She'd left her office in a rush, running over time a little on her last patient, so yeah, her hair was a little wild, and her makeup… Oh, wow. Running over time did not explain away what she saw looking back at her.

Her hair wasn't just blown out of shape, it was too dry and needed a trim. Desperately. Her makeup didn't need refreshing, she'd never put it on. And her brows. She leaned in closer, ran her fingertip across the bridge of her nose. My god, she was practically sporting a uni-brow. What was the matter with her? No wonder Tessa asked what was wrong. She was a mess.

She ran her hands under the water, finger combed her hair into submission, and straightened. The nausea had passed at least for the moment.

Leaning over the sink, she grabbed the necklace to tuck it back inside her shirt, and the woozy hit her again. Hard. She swore she felt like she was going to puke, then a crushing cramp twisted deep in her belly. What the hell? The memory crowded in. The day she'd had Ruby had started just like this.

"Lexi?" Tessa knocked on the outside of the bathroom door. "Our food's ready. You okay?"

Realizing she was squeezing the bejesus out of the coin necklace, she dropped it back inside her shirt. The pain in her belly immediately subsided. Wow. That was weird.

"I'm fine," she answered, truly surprised. "I'm coming."

Back at the table, Lexi nibbled an oyster cracker. "I'm good. Really," she reassured Tessa, who was giving her serious stareface. She dipped into her chowder, tried a small bite, relaxed. Whatever had started an insurrection in her stomach had changed its mind. "I need a brow wax."

Tessa laughed. "I thought bushy brows were back in style."

Lexi scrunched up her forehead. "Not this bushy."

"I could call Gina. Maybe she has a couple of openings this afternoon?"

"I'll have to check my schedule, but it could work. I promised Robbi I'd call her with your news."

Tessa let go a little giggle. "She's somethin' else, isn't she? I can't imagine what it must have been like for her all her growing up years to feel like a girl in a boy's body. I understand from some of our discussions, her parents weren't exactly supportive."

Lexi thought about her mother, how she had manipulated her, pushed her down, pushed her away. She sighed away the thought. None of that could hurt her now unless she let it. She lifted her glass. "You and Phillip are going to make excellent parents."

"Well, we're certainly going to try. Oh, check this out." Tessa pulled a small jewelry box out of her purse and pushed it across to Lexi.

Opening the box, Lexi removed a square of cotton. Her breath hitched up in her throat. Underneath was a snake bracelet, just like the one in Tessa's workshop, only it was made of what looked like red plastic. She lifted it out of the box, sent Tessa a questioning look.

"It's casting wax. I made a mold of the original out of silicone, then filled in with the wax. It's ready for the next step when I have the time."

"The next step?" Lexi turned it over in her hand.

"I'll cast it in gold."

Lexi took a closer look. There were tiny holes cut where the eyes should be. "So, you'll mount rubies in there just like the original?"

"Well, yeah. It will be just like the original in every way."

A chill hit the back of her neck. "Are you sure you want to do that? I mean…"

Tessa pressed her teabag against the side of her cup and removed it. "Right. Get your magic time travel bracelets here. I could sell them at the Saturday Market."

Lexi put the mold back in its box and covered it up. Her stomach squirmed a little. She sat back against the cushioned booth, snuck a look over her shoulder.

She leaned forward, clasping her hands. "I'm serious, Tess. How do you know it won't…you know…do what that snake does?"

Tessa scooped the box back into her purse. "First of all, we don't know exactly what it does."

Lexi rolled her eyes. That was an understatement.

"Second, the gold in that bracelet and whatever other things are in it, were put in there thousands of years ago. We don't know where it came from or who made it." She looked around like Lexi had done a few minutes before. "The gold I'm using comes from a well-known, reputable jewelry making supply house in the Bay Area. If there were any special properties, everybody would be time traveling."

Lexi stared at her a long moment before she broke out a grin that eased her anxiety. "I don't believe you're really doing this."

Tessa smiled brightly. "Look at it this way, if the line catches on, I'll be making a living at what I love to do instead of doing someone else's research paper. And I promise you, once I make the prototype, I'll put the real thing under lock and key. Unless you want to borrow it. Then I suppose I could lease it to you."

"Lease?"

Now Tessa was laughing. "You don't think I'm just going to give it away, do you?"

Lexi's appetite suddenly returned. She crumbled oyster crackers into her chowder and chopped them in, then added a dash of Tabasco. "I don't think so. I want you to keep that thing as far away from me as possible."

"So, the prototype will have the ruby eyes, but instead of leaving it blank like the real one, I'll add Kindra's Delta mark with a T inside. So we can tell them apart. And I can assure you I won't be chanting any magic spells or hexes when I cast them."

Lexi pressed her lips together. The tingle at the back of her neck persisted. "Good of you."

"Then, the rest of them, the production version, will be hollow. Fourteen carat, but with more alloy for strength, and like I said, the Swarovski® eyes.

Francine returned, ripped the bill off her pad and slid it on the table. "You ladies need anything else?"

"No, we're good, France. Thanks."

She tucked the pad in her over-sized apron pocket and cocked a hand at her hip. "How's the jewelry making business coming along?"

Tessa reached for the bill and Lexi slapped it away from her. "My turn."

"Great," Tessa said. "We were just talking about what's next. I'll be using Swarovski® crystals for the gemstones. They're a step above rhinestones, keeping the quality, but at a reasonable price point."

Lexi's phone chimed. She slid it in front of her, lifted a finger to her friends. "It's from the office." Robbi wouldn't call during Lexi's lunch hour unless it was important. "Give me a minute."

Tessa and Francine continued their conversation while Lexi stepped out of the diner and leaned against the outside wall. "What is it, Robbi?"

"That kid who was here Monday? Jamal? I just saw him outside." She sounded excited, out of breath.

"He didn't call or come in?"

"No. He was just standing out there on the other side of the parking lot, like he was trying to make up his mind whether or not to come in."

"Did you go out there? Make contact?"

"Yeah. No. I rushed the front door, got outside, but before I couldn't get to him, a big-ass limo pulled up, he got in, and it drove away."

"A limo."

"Yeah. Not one of those airport rental jobs either. A nice one. Private."

The top of her scalp tingled. That someone-is-watching-you feeling gripped her shoulders. She glanced across the street toward the bay. Dozens of parked cars, buildings jammed together, boatyards, docks. No limos that she could see. If someone were watching her, there were a million places to hide. The idea that a client might be following her was creepy, but not unheard of in her profession. But some random teenage kid who obviously misrepresented himself? Ridiculous.

"… So, I called that number he gave, you know? I thought maybe he was just scared or nervous or something. Thought maybe we should contact the parents."

"Good thinking." Wouldn't be the first time a patient was fearful of starting a therapy relationship. What was unusual was the way it was progressing. Where were his parents? Social services? It seemed like he was in this alone.

"Yeah. The thing is," she went on, "the call went to that hair salon down on the corner?"

"Hm. Maybe his mom works there?"

"Or, he could have seen the phone number on the sign from our parking lot, just filled it in."

"Huh. Strange." She could stop in on her way back to the office. She pulled at her curls. Maybe make an appointment. At least something good might come out of it. "Do you know if they do waxing?"

"What?"

"Waxing. At the salon. You know. Brows?"

"Oh. Yeah. I don't know. Anyway, I snapped a picture of the limo as they were driving away."

Lexi laughed. "Quick thinking, Sherlock." At least somebody was. "We've got plenty of paying customers, we don't have to chase them down in the parking lot."

CHAPTER 22 - THE LIMO AGAIN

There is a screen door at the end of a galley kitchen. Outside are rows of fruit trees converging to infinity in the dusky, almost dark. There is a raven on the stoop. He pecks at the screen door, and it kicks up her hackles.

He pecks and pecks and pecks.

What does he want?

She tries to shoo him away. He squawks and flaps his wings, but he doesn't leave.

Her heartbeat races.

Another raven skitters to a landing next to the first. They are mirror images of one another. With beaks facing, wings flashed out, they look like a Rorschach Inkblot test.

"Go away," she croaks without making a sound.

Lexi woke with a start. Remnants of the dream had her sucking air. What did those crows want? Hell if she knew. The dream left her edgy, that vague nausea returning. If she were home, she'd go sit on the seawall in front of her house, let the tidal current soothe her.

But she wasn't home.

She was at the women's shelter.

Again.

Wouldn't be the first time she'd dozed off here. Weeknights could be boring as hell. Which was a good thing in the shelter. But like in her own practice, weekends could be tumultuous and disturbing on the deepest emotional level.

It had been unusually calm for a Friday night until she realized, coming fully awake: someone was pecking--knocking--on her office door.

Albert, the night attendant she'd joked about with Tessa, pushed open the door. "Hey, Lex. They need you downstairs."

She checked the time on her phone. Two-thirty a.m. Nothing good ever happened at two-thirty a.m. on a Friday night. She hauled herself to the bathroom, splashed water on her face, blotted dry, and headed downstairs. Tessa's words ran like an earworm in her head: *You could do something for fun on Friday night besides volunteering at the women's shelter.* Maybe it was time she took her up on that.

By six a.m., the twin-crow dream had faded to a bad taste in her mouth, she'd bedded down a woman and her two small kids; free, at least for a few hours, from their father's drunken rage. The *rich-girl-life-in-the-OC* dream once again shattered. Creating a safety plan going forward for the mother was the easy part. The hard part would be convincing her to use it.

By seven a.m. she was heading home, looking forward to sleeping in her own bed until noon.

She didn't notice the limo until it pulled out from the space behind Tessa and Phil's garage. It lumbered slowly past her house, and out to Marine Avenue. Its windows were tinted so dark she couldn't see the driver, let alone anyone in the back of the car, but she couldn't shake the feeling they could see her and she waited until they were fully around the corner before she opened her back door and ducked in.

Inside, she poured herself a glass of chocolate milk, climbed upstairs to her bedroom, and lay down, staring at the plastered ceiling. Images of the black limo pecked at her psyche like the crows in her dream. Was its presence a coincidence? Maybe. Maybe not. If it was the kid, how did he know where she lived? And more importantly what on earth could this kid want with her? Her mind ground out the question over and over again as a weak, liquid light slid into her room through the east windows and she heard music playing through Tessa's open kitchen window next door.

She dialed her number. "You have company last night?"

"What? No. Shouldn't you be sleeping right now, missy?"

"Right. I should." She closed her eyes and once again saw the limo slipping down the alley. "Not sure I can, though."

"What's goin' on?"

Through the phone line Lexi could hear Tessa clinking around in her kitchen. "There was a limo stopped behind your house when I pulled in."

"An airport pick up for a neighbor maybe? Flights to the East leave pretty early."

"I don't know. Could be." She yawned, thinking about what Tessa had said. "You want to go for a sail later?"

"You want to go sailing. With me." It was an accusation, not a question.

"I've been thinking about what you said. I need to get out more." She could hear Tessa's footsteps going down her back stairs like she was heading to her workshop.

"I was thinking more on the lines of maybe going sailing with some handsome hunk. In case you haven't noticed, I live with one and I don't need to fill in with my girlfriend anymore."

"Ouch."

"Sorry. That sounded bad, but you know what I mean."

Angst tightened her belly. She did. Lexi had depended on Tessa for entertainment and human bonding almost exclusively for way too long. Phillip had gone along with it, but it was time she gave them their space.

"Put it this way. I just need to talk. Some stuff has been going down at my office, and Alfred Hitchcock is directing my dreams. I just need..."

"Of course, Lex. It's just…today's not a good day for me. I fired up the kiln early this morning and I need to get as many pieces as I can through the process before I shut it down. Tomorrow?"

"You going to do the snake today?" An inexplicable dread crept up on her neck.

"It's in the kiln now. It's going to be so awesome."

Lexi shook off a chill as a pair of tiny ruby eyes glowed in her memory. *Yeah. Awesome. Right up until it slithers up your arm.* She cast her gaze around her room, landing on her desktop computer in the corner.

"Sure. Okay. Tomorrow will be good." Maybe by then, she'd have solved the mystery on her own. She yawned again, the deep, determined kind of yawn that was difficult to ignore.

"Lex?"

"Hum?"

"Get yourself some sleep."

"Okay. Bye."

*　　*　　*

Sleep? Right. What was the point of even trying? Yawns or no yawns, there was no way she was going to sleep now. She tossed her eye pillow on her nightstand, stalked wearily to her desktop, and fired it up. Her fingers hovered over the keyboard. This was probably a bad idea. She should go through the proper channels. But there was something about this kid that bothered her. Something she couldn't put her finger on. She gave in to the urge and Googled Jamal Isiah.

Not surprisingly, there were hundreds of entries in every combination imaginable. Scrolling through the first few pages of entries, she didn't see anything she could relate to the young man. And why would she? He probably gave them a fake name to begin with.

She huffed out a sigh, folded the laptop closed, went downstairs. She was better off, she decided, not knowing. As long as she was wide-eyed awake, she might as well take advantage. She had promised herself to finish going through her stuff in the garage this week.

Twenty minutes later, after dragging her dive equipment out of the pile, she had a better idea how to spend her day.

*　　*　　*

No sooner had she spilled off the side of the dive boat and let herself sink down into the light green waters off Laguna beach than her innate love of the underwater world kicked in. Weightless and drifting in sync with the golden leaves and air-filled bulbs of the kelp forest, she remembered her fascination with penetrating sun rays, flickering schools of fish, and the colorful, almost cartoon creatures inhabiting the sandy bottom.

She had headed over to West Side Scuba with the intention of updating some of her gear when she overheard the dive shop attendant take a cancellation over the phone for a dive that afternoon.

She dropped a new mask and gloves on the counter and fished her credit card out of her wallet. "So, does that mean you have an opening today?"

The attendant, a young girl with a spiky half-buzz cut and a seaweed tattoo weaving up her right arm entered her purchases in the computer on the counter, giving each poke of her black-polished finger serious consideration.

"Sorry," she said, wincing at what must have been a mistake on the keypad. "Gimme a sec. I don't usually do this."

When she was finished, she raised a thick, pierced brow at Lexi, then broke into a wide grin. "You're certified, I assume?"

Lexi hadn't dived in nearly five years, but she'd been certified since she was fourteen years old. "Yup. Where's the dive?"

"Need a bag?" the girl asked. Lexi shook her head and gathered her items in her arms. "It's a kelp forest dive off Laguna. Mostly newbies. But we're booked out three weeks, so it's a chance to get in the water if you want to go today." She stuck out her hand. "I'm Frankie. I'll be leading the dive." She plucked a card out of a holder on the counter, scribbled on the back. "Meet us here at Dana Point, one o'clock. We usually go for drinks after, if you want to come."

Lexi couldn't believe her luck. Tessa would be proud. "Sounds nice." She slid her credit card back across the counter. "I'll be there."

It was the best decision she'd made in years. In the underwater world, the chaotic noise of life on land with all its complications was shut out. She rocked in the rhythmic sounds of her scuba gear and the gentle thudding of her own heart.

Frankie beaconed her from a few feet away as the other divers dropped in, got their bearings. Together they moved through the swaying branches, long fins propelling them lazily forward, bubbles spiraling over their heads and up to the surface.

Just like riding a bike. One doesn't forget.

She couldn't help the full feeling in her chest watching a young couple shadow a red octopus as it sidled among the rocks below, their eyes reflecting each other's in excitement.

They reminded her of she and Zai all those years ago. His unbridled enthusiasm drove her to go deeper and farther than she ever thought possible—in the water and in other ways. It may have ended in a mess but getting there had been the happiest time of her life. He was still diving if her Google searches were any sign. Her heart squeezed a little at the thought. A treasure hunter. Had he ever found what he was looking for?

She floated over a bright orange garibaldi nosing around what looked like its nest, lost in her memories. Her parents, Zaire, the Mediterranean Sea…

A gentle tap on her shoulder got her attention. Frankie's bright eyes glittered behind her mask as she tapped her underwater watch.

Wow. Where had the time gone? She followed the group back to the hull of the dive boat and headed up.

She was loading her gear into a dock cart when she saw the limo parked at the top of the gangway. Suspicion prickled up her spine and gripped the top of her head.

No.

Effing.

Way.

"You coming with us?" Frankie asked. "We're heading over to the Salt Creek Grille."

Lexi sucked in a breath, cutting a glance between the dive leader and the limo. It sat like a sleek, black challenge, opaque privacy windows hiding the faces of whoever was inside. The dive had worked a little bit of confidence magic in her.

Jerk wants to follow her around? She'd keep him at it.

"Sure. Why not?" She piled her gear in the backseat of her VW and drove out of the lot without looking back.

One Huckleberry Lemonade and a plate of grilled shrimp later, she said goodbye to the last of the dive group to leave the table, a lump of anxiety stuck in her throat.

What were the chances the limo had followed her to the restaurant? She hunched her shoulders as she signed her credit card receipt. Considering her office manager saw the limo at her office and there had been one parked behind Tessa and Phillip's house the night before, and the one in the parking area above the dock? She swallowed the lump. Probably the chances were pretty good.

As the server took her receipt, she craned her neck to see that the reception area was empty. If someone were watching for her to come out, she'd be all by herself.

Could she sneak out a back entrance? It was worth a try. Down the hall to the bathrooms and past a bulletin board and a time clock, she scooted through the exit as an employee slipped in from emptying the trash. Coming around the side of the building she had a good view of the parking lot.

And … there it was, all the way in the back.

Sleek. Black. Intimidating.

A sense of foreboding collected low and heavy in her belly, anchoring her in place. It had to be Jamal. But why? He knew where to find her office. She'd invited him back. Years of training and experience told her to turn back. Exit the restaurant through the front door and go straight to her car. They had no formal agreement, no parental consent. No way should she confront him in a parking lot or anywhere else.

And then, as if to taunt her, the back window on the driver's side slid down an inch. Chills hit the back of her neck. Her mouth went suddenly dry. And that was it. She'd had enough.

She strode with purpose across the lot, passed behind the limo, and came up on the passenger side, then wrapped her knuckles hard on the back seat window. She needed to let him know he had to go through social services or bring a parent with him if he wanted to see her again…

The window slid down. Whatever speech she had planned to give stuck in the back of her throat on a muted cry. It was a beautiful black man, but it wasn't Jamal. A pair of amber eyes darkened as they stared back at her, taking her in, head to toe. All the heat drained out of her face. If the window had slid down to reveal Michael B. Jordan, she wouldn't have been more dumbstruck. Her mouth worked wordlessly a moment before she could open it.

"Zai?" His name came out of her in a breathy, disbelieving gasp.

His stern expression softened slowly into a half smile. "Hello Alexis." She'd have known that voice without seeing his face.

He opened the limo door a crack and waited for her to step back, then he unfolded his lanky body and stood. Lexi couldn't breathe. This had to be a dream. She looked over her shoulder. Nope. It was broad daylight and Zaire Negatu, like a ghost from her past, gestured toward the softly lit interior of the limo.

"Are you going to get in?"

Chapter 23 - Amari Returns

Lesidi gave Flavia a bundle of sugared ginger wrapped in waxy cloth, along with more blankets to take into the hold.

"Once we get underway, it will be safer for you to stay below. It can be pretty cold and damp once we get started, and could be a little rough going, depending on the wind. Either way, these will help make you more comfortable."

Flavia gave her a shaky smile. "I was hoping you could give me something to make me sleep until we get to Auksum."

Lesidi let go a soft laugh. "You might just find you love sailing, once you get your sea legs. But for tonight, at least, the ginger will help with any sickness."

With the last of the setting sun a thin line on the horizon, she handed Kindra a bowl of figs and hard cheese. "In the meantime, nibble on these. You may handle the motion sickness better with a little something in your stomachs."

Satisfied she had done all she could for her passengers, Lesidi made her way to the prow where Cyril's mate was hauling in the sounding lead.

"Well?"

"Looks like the tide is as high as it's going to get. If we wait any longer, we might lose all that we waited for. If it were a full moon, we might have fared better, but with a mostly empty cargo hold, and the favorable wind we have going, we should be able to get free."

"Good news," Lesidi said, setting her hand on his shoulder. "Let us join the Demeter." Ambivalence weighed heavy on her mind. There'd been no sign of Amari as her visions had predicted, and their time was running out. If they didn't leave now, she'd have Keleb's wrath to deal with and that was the last thing she wanted to happen.

Tossing the end of her palla over her head to form a cowl, she strode to the swan's neck and stood as Cyril instructed Dracis how to hold the line of the sail until they were free of the reeds. The moment the sail furled with the wind, Isis's hull scraped on the bottom and then floated free. Her knees adjusted to the shift. With luck, they could meet up with the rest of the fleet by midnight.

She breathed in a satisfied sigh and gave thanks to the gods that ruled the sea. A moment later she heard the shout.

"Isis!"

She turned to look behind her. Along the shallows, partially hidden by the deep shadows and a low-lying finger of fog, she could just make out two slender launches creeping along the shoreline. It was obvious the launches were attempting to catch up with the ship.

She backed away from the stern, wariness slowing her steps. "Cyril. We have company!"

Cyril ran down the deck, leaned over the side. "You there! Identify yourselves."

It was a man and a woman in one launch, and if she weren't mistaken, her wayward sibling in the other. "Amari? By the gods, is it really you?"

One of the launches slid up against the side of the Isis. "Cyril. Drop your anchor and throw down the ladder."

"You might have shown up while we were still on shore," Cyril growled under his breath, but he did as he was told and lifted the rope ladder over the side.

Lesidi stumbled to the railing, her heart flooding with relief. Later she would give her brother a piece of her mind, but for now, she rejoiced in his arrival.

Elation was replaced by frustration and anger as Lesidi watched three more passengers crawl up the ladder and over the side onto her ship.

The largest of the boarders who had dragged the woman up the ladder bundled under one arm, had barely set her down before Dracis shot across the deck and plowed into him at a full run. "Marcus! I knew you were all right. I just knew it."

The huge man set the boy off him and simply nodded. "And you as well."

"Dracis," Cyril shouted. "Return to the mast." The boy's chest puffed up. "Yes sir," he barked, and went back to man his post.

Lesidi crossed her arms over her chest and looked the man up and down. It was easy to see why Kindra had risked her life for him. He looked like a Greek statue. If what Dracis had told them was true, the woman had to be none other than Emperor Constantine's wife, Fausta.

Cyril lit a few lanterns so they could better see their boarders and handed one to Lesidi who moved in closer.

The poor woman would have passed for a wretched slave except for the way she carried herself and the gold chains tangled around her neck. She was wearing a makeshift palla made out of a scrap of filthy muslin, but it failed to conceal the tattered mess that was her tunic. She was trying hard not to shiver with cold.

Amari straightened his hauberk. "Lady Fausta, this is my sister, Lesidi, captain of this vessel. She will make you comfortable." He sent Lesidi a condescending look. She would address that with him later, too.

She might look like a drowned rat, but fire burned in the woman's eyes. It was apparent she wasn't happy about the accommodations, but she kept any complaint to herself.

Lesidi extended her hand. She had no idea what deal Amari had made with this woman. Whatever she was accused of it was obvious she had been through an ordeal and was in need of comfort. Being an Auksumite, Lesidi owed her no allegiance, but as a woman, her heart went out to her. She would provide whatever comfort that didn't interfere with their current mission. She would address that issue with Amari later, too.

"Of course. Let's get you into some dry clothes. Come with me."

Fausta's chin shot up, and then, as if reconsidering her circumstance, she lowered her eyes. "Thank you."

Lesidi stopped near the bulkhead to the ship's hold. "Wait here a moment? I'll be right back."

Fausta nodded, and Lesidi returned to the men who were deep into a conversation about how they had escaped the Leto before it exploded in flame. She wanted to hear all about that, but she had another more important issue on her mind.

"Excuse me, Marcus?"

He looked up. Whether he was responding to the fact that she'd been introduced as the captain of the ship, or the look of expectation in her eyes, he stood and gave her a swift bow. "At your service."

"There is a matter of importance you need to address. Come with me, please."

He glanced at Cyril who it seemed had already made a positive connection with the man and gave him an encouraging nod. She led him to the bulkhead, handed him the lantern.

"We have some other passengers below I believe you will be grateful to see."

He gave her a curious look.

She nodded. "Go on down," she said with a smile that warmed her heart. At least she'd been able to do some good on this so far hapless journey, and she had not even seen it coming. She started to leave, and that inner voice spoke to her. *Wait for it…*

Lesidi rejoined Fausta at the rail and waited only a few beats before she heard Kindra and Flavia scream together: "Marcus!"

Chapter 24 - Another Plan

Flavia came topside not long after Marcus and Kindra were reunited, giving them some privacy. Lesidi had fed and bedded Fausta down in her quarters. The poor woman held herself rigid and regal through the whole ordeal but fell asleep almost immediately when her head hit the furs on Lesidi's bunk.

Now she waited impatiently while Cyril went after Amari, who had been avoiding her. A moment later, he stood before her with an infuriating grin.

He untied two bags from his belt and tossed them on deck where Lesidi, Cyril, and Flavia huddled close to the brazier.

She narrowed her eyes on him. "So, you double-crossed Constantine's Praetorian Guard, sent your own ship and crew in flames to the bottom of the sea, and now you want safe passage back to the fleet? Do you have any idea what you've done?"

Flavia's brows shot up and she covered her mouth a moment, then stood. "Perhaps I should leave you to speak privately."

Lesidi put her hand on Flavia's forearm. "Please. Stay. We have no secrets here. What happens next concerns you and there is no point in having to tell the story twice."

She returned a scathing gaze to her brother. "Go ahead, Amari. Tell me how those bags of gold are worth your ship and the lives of four men. Not to mention the extra trip someone is going to have to make when we get to Ostia because we are one vessel short."

Amari glared back at her. "There's two more bags of denari when I return to Valeria for the other half of my fee."

"Return to Valeria? And how to you propose to do that?"

"I will take the Isis, of course."

"You cannot be serious. We are already two days late and you want to go back? There is no way I can allow it." She got up and paced the deck, her anger building to fury. "After all that has happened, you would continue to put the fleet in danger for a couple of bags of gold? Our father would take you off the fleet for this, you know that, don't you?"

Amari bunched up his lips and strode an arm's length from her. "Our father is dead, Lesidi." He spat the words with contempt. "It is time you got over it. I will take the Isis back to the palace docks to collect my fee."

Cyril shot to his feet and stepped between them. "You will not take the Isis anywhere," he growled, his nose nearly touching Amari's. "If you won't listen to your sister, then listen to me. You lost your ship. The Isis belongs to Lesidi, and I am here to make sure she keeps it. We will honor your arrangement with Marcus and Fausta and get her safety to Auksum.

Whether or not you get payment for double-crossing Valeria is not our concern."

Amari drew himself up to disagree; Lesidi held up her hand to stop him. "We made a commitment to Keleb to leave in twenty-four hours from when he was here and we're going to keep it."

Amari swallowed hard, the color draining from his face. "Keleb was here?"

Lesidi stood her ground. "When we didn't join the fleet on time, he took a launch and came looking. Only to find he'd lost a ship. He's not happy with you right now."

Amari snorted. "Keleb," he growled derisively. "I should be commander of the fleet by now, not him. I don't know why you tolerate his intrusion."

Cyril threw up his hands and returned to the brazier to sit near Flavia. The look that passed between them did not escape Lesidi's notice. She was more grateful than ever for Cyril's presence. While it was clear Amari bristled at Cyril's interference, he knew better than to cross the elder first mate on his own ship.

Lesidi followed Cyril's lead, pinning her brother with a stern gaze. "You have already done more damage than you can ever repay, Amari. If you insist on retrieving your payment from Valeria, you will have to find your own transportation to do so, including finding your own way back to Auksum. The Isis must leave now, or the tide will turn against us."

Her brother was enough of a seaman to know it was true about the tide. Still, defiance lit a fire in his eyes. His lips pressed tight together as he crowded her space once more. "You'll live to regret this, sister. It is a certainty."

The only things Lesidi knew for a certainty were that Keleb would not tolerate another delay, and the recurring vision of cold water closing over her head. Perhaps she would regret not letting Amari chase after another empty dream. Perhaps she might not live at all. But she could no longer tolerate his recklessness. "You are a fool, brother."

"We'll see who ends up with riches and who ends up at the bottom of the sea."

Lesidi's hand were shaking. She clenched them into fists. "Get off my ship now. Take one of my crew with you so there will be someone to report your demise to me when this Valeria chops off your head."

Amari glared at her a long moment before his angry countenance softened to a sulk. It would not be the first time he had puffed himself up like a blow fish only to deflate in retreat. "Perhaps we can pass through Constantinopolis to collect my due after we deliver the grain."

Lesidi eyed him suspiciously. She doubted Keleb would agree with that plan, but she was willing to agree now in order to restore peace. "Perhaps."

She hated to admit, but all this excitement had been exhausting. With her tiny ship loaded with extra passengers, she bid Cyril to make her bed up once again at the stern behind the boat house. Amari was familiar with the corbita's layout. She would leave it up to him to find his own place to sleep.

Cyril banked the coals in the brazier and stood. "I'll see Flavia to her quarters below. Dracis, trim that sail like I showed you so we can get out of here."

"Yes sir," came the boy's ecstatic reply. Never, Lesidi thought, had a young sailor been more enthusiastic to take his watch. She wondered if he would feel the same when they hit the deep, open seas.

*　　*　　*

Dracis lay on his back, arms winged behind his head, imagining he could step up onto the bright path of stars across the heavens when he heard voices lifted in front of the bunk house. He recognized the voices of Fausta and Amari, and they sounded none too agreeable. He sat up and listened, his heart thumping wildly in his chest like a trapped hare.

Cyril had awakened him from a fitful slumber near the prow and bid him take the second watch. It was cold, but with the several layers of clothing Cyril had given him over his body, he was warm enough. And, he wouldn't have missed the theater in the sky for anything in the world. The heavens were blacker than he'd ever seen in his life, making it easy to pick out the constellations. There was probably not a more peaceful place on earth, which is why, the angry voices bothered him.

Amari and Fausta raised their voices, then as if realizing they might be overheard, they quieted down. But not before Dracis made out something about riches beyond someone's dreams and revenge.

Marcus had not labeled him a spy without reason. It was in his nature. He left his post and crept closer, hanging on every word.

Chapter 25 - The Gentle Giant

Kindra slowly awakened from a drowsy dream of Marcus's warm hand caressing her belly to realize with a consuming wave of warmth and gratitude, it was not a dream after all. The gentle giant who was the father of her child was in fact curled against her back, his body a stronghold of protection she feared she would never feel again. Her doubts and fears all but vanished in the sheer warmth of him, his steady breathing stirring the hair on top of her head, and his hand spanning the width of her belly, pressing her back into his warrior's chest.

Their lovemaking had been a bit stifled under the furs in the hold, knowing there were others nearby; but there was no doubt in her mind his joy at being reunited with her matched her own in every way. The fact that she was with child only added to the poignancy of their reunion. For the first time since she was a small girl still living in her parent's apartment in the city, even though they were rolling on unknown currents on a small ship at sea, she felt completely at home.

Marcus's mother had been thrilled at their reunion as well, tears streaming down her cheeks as she held her son in her arms. But understanding their need for

233

privacy, Flavia had prevailed upon the ship's first mate, Cyril, to find her another place to bed down for the night.

Through the early hours, they told each other their stories of horror and then survival as they reacquainted themselves with their bodies.

Now, with the rest of the ship quiet except for the steady pressure of the wind in the sail pushing them forward, Marcus stirred and shifted his weight, then resettled, his hand once again resting over their babe in the sanctuary of her womb. "I am forever grateful to Dracis for helping you escape from Valeria."

Kindra snuggled deeper into his embrace. "Indeed. The boy is truly a treasure. The last time I saw the woman she was sprawled on the floor, blood streaming from the side of her head. He shut and barred the door, but I had no idea whether she was dead or alive." The image invaded her mind, stark and chilling, then took her breath away, and not because her head lay in a spreading pool of blood. Then he saved me again at Flavia's. Saved Lesidi and I."

Kindra's heart clenched in a cold fist when she remembered with clarity, the gold serpent bracelet her mother had sewn into her ragged tunic had been clamped on Valeria's arm. She clenched her fist to her mouth, bit her fingers hard.

"What is it, little one?" Marcus asked, holding her away from him so he could look into her eyes.

"Nothing. It is just..." she drew in a ragged breath and blew it out. "There was one piece of jewelry left behind at your mother's. A bracelet. Valeria had it on her arm." She tipped her head back and stared at the planks of the hold's overhead. "I suppose we were lucky to get out of the palace without being noticed."

"I do not believe in luck," Marcus said, pulling her closer still, then trailed his fingers up her torso, over her shoulders, and lifted her chin. "We cannot always see the way of things clearly, we must have faith that there is a plan."

Kindra truly wished she could be so faithful. From what she had seen, the only plans that seemed to be working were the ones that threw chaos into her path.

Do not worry, little one. Valeria will never touch you again if I have anything to say about it."

Kindra shuddered at the thought of what could keep him from having a say. If Valeria discovered the magical power her mother had told her lived in the bracelet, she would use it to carry out her vendetta against Marcus and his family. But now was not the time to voice her fears. Instead, she shifted onto her back, settling her head in the crook of his arm, and smiled at him, taking in the deep amber of his eyes.

"Lesidi says her home, Auksum, is beyond Alexandria and the Roman Empire. Beyond Valeria's reach. What do you know of it?"

He twisted a tendril of her hair lazily in his fingers. "I know the Auksumite kingdom is rich in gold and precious stones, as well as grain and oil and silks from the far east. They mint their own coins; and if Lesidi's fleet is any indication, are capable of sending their ships to far flung places."

She rolled to her side, facing him, and elbowed up resting her head in her hand. "I heard Cyril say the citizens of Rome wouldn't survive a winter without the grain they import from Auksum. Is that true?"

Marcus drew in a deep breath and exhaled on a long sigh. "I have no reason to doubt it. Auksum also has a large contingent of Christians, much more so than in Rome, which is why I plan to pledge my services to the commander of Lesidi's fleet, this Keleb she talks of."

"But you're a soldier, not a seaman."

He shifted his gaze to the open hatch overhead, his brows converging in thought. "I would think the commander would have use of a soldier on the Demeter. From what I've seen, the great sea is not as safe as it once was if one of a ship in a respected merchant's fleet can be attacked in the harbor of the Emperor's Palace."

Kindra stiffened at the memory of flaming planks of the ship's hull hissing as they crashed into the water around her. Her hands still bore the burns she suffered clinging to one of them. "Let's not talk of such things."

His chest rumbled a muffled growl of agreement, then he rolled on top of her, dropped his lips to her breast and took her nipple into his mouth in a way that made her catch her breath. Careful not to crush her, he straddled her hips, trailed kisses up her neck and then to her lips.

"As you wish," he murmured.

Feeling the tip of his erection at the cleft between her legs, she arched her back, then opened to him once more, and guided him home. She had lost all her tools, the gold jewelry she had made for the Empress, even the serpent bracelet passed down to her from her mother's clan, but she had already received the greatest treasure a woman could possess. She bore the child of a strong man who loved her and would give his life to protect them both, whether in Auksum or any other place on earth.

They rode the tide of their passion to its peak and then rested once again in their makeshift bunk. Kindra lay languidly atop his mountain of a frame, twirling a finger in the hair of his chest when they heard Dracis's voice through the opening of the hold.

"Marcus!" His raspy whisper ripped through their blissful repose. "Marcus. I am sorry to disturb you, but I must speak with you. Now. It is of the utmost urgency. Marcus?"

"Tell him to go away," Marcus complained, nuzzling against her neck.

"Forgive me, my love, but it is not Dracis' habit to badger me unless there is something of dire importance."

"*Arggh.* You are right." He rolled off her reluctantly, stealing a hasty kiss as he dragged the fur around his girth and headed for the ladder. "What is it, boy?"

Kindra could see the boy's crouching silhouette behind a coil of hemp rope, back lit by pale moonlight. Whatever his purpose, he hadn't wanted to be seen. She pulled the blankets around her and sat up, then whispered, "Tell him to come down here."

Marcus motioned Dracis to come down the ladder, which he did quickly, glancing over his shoulder before he ducked his head below deck.

Marcus turned over a heavy woven basket and bid Dracis to sit. "This better be good," he said on a growl.

Dracis took in the intimate scene a moment before he leaned back against the hull of the ship, keeping his face out of the pale light shaft that shown down to where they sat. "That Amari and Fausta. They are up to no good."

Marcus raised a brow and leaned forward clasping his hands between his knees. "You are aware, are you not that I — we all," he said, indicating Kindra, Dracis, and everyone else above decks "— just risked our lives to rescue Fausta from murder at the hands of Constantine's soldiers?"

Dracis frowned and nodded his head several times. "I know that, sir. Yes."

"So why would she do anything to harm the very people who saved her life?"

Now it was Dracis who sat forward, keeping his head low. "Oh, surely that would make sense, Marcus. But it is not us she wants to hurt."

Marcus shook his head. "You better be sure, boy before you accuse Lady Fausta. I have known her as long as I have been in the service of the Emperor. She has many loyal subjects at the palace, not the least of which was her own small army of soldiers. She has never done anything that I know of to harm any person on purpose. Why, my sister has been in her service as well and has assured me she was always treated kindly by her."

Kindra pulled the furs tighter around her shoulders, Dracis' words triggering a chink of doubt.

She shifted her gaze from Dracis to Marcus. "The key here, Marcus, is 'that you know of.'"

He wrung his hands a moment, narrowed his eyes on hers. "Go on."

"Begging your pardon, of course. You may have served the Emperor and Fausta in a public capacity, but I assume you have never spent any time alone with her in her private chambers, as I have."

He straightened, his eyes flying full open. "Certainly not!"

Kindra felt a small charge of satisfaction confirming that fact. "I, however, traveled with her to Moselle, as you know. Like your sister, Anastasia, she treated me well. I occupied a room off her chamber, dressed her and groomed her hair, took meals with her. During those times, she shared some very intimate facts with me that I am sure she wouldn't have wanted shared with anyone else. Let me just say that I developed a certain amount of sympathy for her. Despite her riches and the pampering one would expect, she was not much more than a prisoner in that palace. Those soldiers were just as likely keeping her in her place as there to protect her. And, I might add, the Emperor was just as demanding of her as he was of you."

She kept her eyes trained on Marcus, whom she could see by the change in his expression was starting to understand where she was headed.

She went on. "And you know how this whole thing started. Constantine had his own son, Crispis, killed, then went after her. Do you think she, a woman who had given him four children, who had basked in the riches of his palace, and had no other means of support would just roll over and accept that he wanted her dead? Especially if the accusations about she and Crispis plotting together were true."

Dracis's eyes darted between the two of them, his head bobbing at every point.

Marcus flinched, silenced them with a finger at his lips. They heard slow footsteps on the deck above, like someone was pacing the stern of the ship. They waited until the pacing faded and stopped.

"What do you think?" Marcus asked her, his voice low.

"She told me she was at the bath to meet her lover. She had obviously given her soldiers the time off. Wanted only me to watch the entrances to the caldarium." She trembled a bit at the memory. "Imagine my shock when you barged into the bath."

"You thought—" He started in louder, then caught himself and said in a harsh whisper, "You thought her lover was me?"

"What else was I supposed to think?" Her cheeks flamed. "But then the soldier with you revealed the truth. That Crispis was dead. That's when she lost her senses and started to scream."

Dracis stood now, unable to hold on to his information a moment longer. "She wants revenge. On Constantine, on Rome itself, for killing Crispus and trying to kill her."

Marcus put his hand on Dracis' shoulder, lowered him to sit again. "Where are they now. Amari and Fausta?"

"I had crept away from the mast when I heard them arguing. Making a plan. When I realized what they were up to, I did not want them to know I had heard, so I slipped back up to the mast, then coughed loud enough to get their attention. After that, they went back into Lesidi's quarters. Together.

Marcus frowned and slumped on the makeshift bed like the entire world had come down hard on his shoulders. "Tell me about this plan."

242

Chapter 26 - So Not What She Expected

Newport Beach California - 2019 CE

Lexi bent down to take a look inside the sleek, black limousine. She half expected hot pink seats down one side and a party bar down the other, with neon lights all around, like the one and only time she'd ever been in a limo, a bachelorette party for a college friend.

But this one, a conservative, Mercedes S Class, was like something out of a billionaire fantasy novel. Only one creamy leather seat stretched across the back. There was a modest, mirror-backed bar sporting bottles of sparkling water and fruit juices along with smaller bottles of Tito's vodka and Centenario tequila. They were in California, after all. The lighting was soft blue; subtle, but not neon. The window separating the driver from the passenger compartment was closed.

She flinched at a set of fast chills when Zaire's voice came softly behind her. "I'm not going to jump you, Alexis. I just want to talk to you. Will you please get in?"

He called her by her given name.

So formal.

So proper.

And here she was, a tacky mess, sand in her hair, chatting with an obvious rich dude in the parking lot of a restaurant through his car window like a scene out of Pretty Woman. She glanced toward the restaurant entrance. Already they'd gotten the attention of two Red Hat Society ladies sitting on the waiting bench. As raggedy as she looked right now, they probably already had the wrong idea.

Oh hell. With a glance over her shoulder that caught his half smile, she dropped her rear into the cushy leather seat, swung her legs inside, and slid in.

She caught sight of herself in the mirror behind the bottles. Yes, it was all that. Great. An old heart throb appears in her life after fifteen years and there was saltwater dried in her unruly curls, a smudge of oil on her forehead, and oh yes, that uni-brow? Still there.

He slid in beside her, swept the door closed, and pressed a button on the console at his right arm. The limo purred to life and swooped out of the driveway, leaving her car and every other thing she thought she knew behind.

She was still reacting to the shock -- dry mouth, sweaty hands, heart racing a hundred miles an hour — when they left the Dana Point Marina and headed south.

"Where are you taking me?" As if it mattered. It was the last thing she really wanted to know.

"How much time do you have?"

She rolled her eyes to the roof a moment before she made herself look him square in the eyes for the first time. Bam. She was caught up in amber shot with gold and the blackest of pupils widening on hers. She had to grit her teeth to stop from shivering like a teenager facing her first prom.

She was terrified.

She was excited.

She was a wreck.

Right now, in this moment, every cell in her body wanted to melt into those eyes and disappear; wanted to give him all the time in the world. But the moment passed. The man had been stalking her. That wasn't right. Not right at all. "Wait. Stop. Stop!"

She sat up and braced her hand against the bar.

"You don't just get to waltz in, follow me around in your limo, whisk me out of a parking lot, and take me off to god knows where on a promise not to jump me."

He raised a questioning brow. "Excuse me, but I believe you're the one who marched up and rapped your knuckles on my window."

"Because you've been following me."

He frowned.

She cleared her throat. The reality of the situation was she had gotten in his car voluntarily. She just wasn't sure it was a reality she was ready for. Too much time had passed. Hard, painful time during which she'd felt discarded and alone. She had no reason to believe he would do her harm, but she couldn't help feeling cornered by a stranger.

She remembered a carefree Zaire who would rather spend his time diving off a dingy than cruising around on his father's yacht. She didn't know this Zaire, a grown man wearing a Piaget watch probably worth more than the limo, and a fancy suit so far out of her league she wouldn't even venture a guess at the brand. The ring on his pinkie finger sported a diamond as big as a cherry pit for god's sake; a far cry from the young man who couldn't wait to get away from his parent's pretentious lifestyle.

Nope. This was going to end right now.

"Please. Just … stop the car. I need to know what this is about. What are you doing here?"

He dropped his head a moment, slid his gaze out the window. They were just approaching Doheny State Beach. He pressed another button on his console, spoke to the driver: "Turn in here. Pay the fee if you have to."

They pulled into the state park visitor's area and the driver got out of the car, adding to their privacy.

She let go of the bar and pressed her back into the seat. He lowered the armrest between them. "Better?"

Not really. But this would do for now. She nodded.

"Would you like something to drink? Vodka? Tequila?"

Her mouth was so dry she had to peel her tongue off her pallet to answer. "Water will be fine."

He lifted the lid on an ice bucket, tonged a couple of cubes into a high ball glass, poured sparking water over, then handed it to her.

She swirled the ice cubes with her finger, recovering some of her senses. "What I would like is an answer to my question."

He just smiled, watching her as she gripped the glass with two hands. God, that smile was like time traveling back to the lifetime she had worked so hard to forget. She could almost feel his wet body pressed against hers…Oh no. Do. Not. Go. There.

"I'm sorry," he said "I realize now, I should have called first. Honestly, I couldn't think of an easy way. I was pretty sure you wouldn't have agreed to meet me at my hotel room, so…"

She eyed him over her glass. "So, you thought kidnapping was better?"

He leaned back in his seat, his smile segueing to a frown. "A mistake. Obviously. Again. Please accept my apologies."

It was so strange to hear his voice after all these years, a slightly British accent over rich, deep tones. The King's English, her father had noted, chiding her when she slipped into American slang.

She pulled at her hair, wishing she had taken time to shower at the harbor before she met her new friends for a drink.

He reached up and gently nudged her hand away from her hair, catching her gaze with his. "Don't fret. You look beautiful."

His voice was soft, a hint of longing somewhere in it. The proverbial slippery slope. The giddy teenager lurking somewhere in her psyche would have leapt right over the edge. But the thirty something woman who counseled young women every day had better judgment.

She reached for the door handle. "I have no problem walking back to the Harbor from here, which is exactly what I intend to do if you don't explain yourself right now. What on earth would possess you to track me down after all this time?"

A sudden warmth spread under the necklace where it nestled between her breasts. It spread across her shoulders like warm sunshine in a lifetime lived before this one.

Had she conjured him out of her dreams? She bit her tongue on the thought.

He exhaled on a sigh. "Actually…it was Jamal's idea. I knew nothing about what he was up to until—"

She sat up now, her senses on high alert. "Wait. Jamal? The kid who showed up at my office out of the blue and started grilling me about my family?"

"I'm sorry if he offended you. He's been looking for his birth mother. When he learned I was coming to the states, he begged to come with me. Apparently, he' tracked down his adoption agency and contacted them." He sipped his drink, pulled in a cautions breath. "He seems to think you're the one."

"The one?" The words came out on a disbelieving breath. Lexi stared at him, her arms suddenly heavy.

She took another swallow of bubbly water that went down like a stone. "There's obviously some kind of mistake." Fine hairs rose on the back of her neck, and she hunched her shoulders. "I put a child up for adoption fifteen years ago, but it was a girl."

It was absurd, of course. Yet somewhere deep inside her soul those black crows of doubt peck, peck, pecked at her. She'd seen the resemblance the moment Jamal had walked into her office. Enough to question her denial. Then she let out a little bump of a laugh. The answer was pretty easy. She relaxed her shoulders a little.

He just stared at her with a little quirk at the corner of his mouth, his lips pressed together while she worked it out.

"Well," she said on a stilted laugh, gesturing with her palm. "It's obvious he's your son. He looks exactly like you did when we…" She shifted in her seat. "When you were nearer his age. But, considering I had a girl as a result of our mistake, I have to assume you got some other girl pregnant about the same time as me and she's the one Jamal should be tracking."

Zaire's eyes went dark. His mouth lost all hint of levity. "There was never any other girl," he said softly as if it hurt to admit.

She stared at him, speechless for several seconds taking this in. Of course, that's what he would say. What young guy in his right mind would admit to doing two girls at once? Still, she and Zaire had spent the entire summer together either on his parent's yacht, or on the little dive boat. They had rarely been apart long enough to sleep, or take a meal, let alone be with anyone else. Again, thirty-year-old therapist Lexi knew better. There was likely no greater force in the universe than a testosterone-driven teenage boy. Her heart drummed hard in her chest like she'd narrowly missed a car wreck.

Zaire's jaw clenched once, his eyes zeroed in on hers. "Are you sure our baby was a girl?"

Our baby? "What? Are you insane? Of course, I'm sure. I unwrapped her pink blanket and looked her over the way every new mom does before they snatched her away." She rubbed her temples with shaking fingertips. "In fact," she said with some relief, remembering the moment clearly. "I saw a copy of her official birth certificate three months ago. A girl, born by cesarean section at eight months."

He raised a questioning brow. "Have you talked to your mother about this?"

The question exploded inside her skull. Her lunch threatened to gush out of her stomach. "My mother! Why on earth would I need to talk to her? It was a long time ago, but a young woman, even if she's only fifteen, tends to remember the one and only time she saw her own baby. She was definitely a girl."

Ruby.

He stared at her for several beats before he leaned forward, poured himself a shot of tequila, and tossed it down. "Which brings us back to the question. I understand your perception of what happened. However, Jamal feels pretty strongly about this. I don't want to upend his life without making sure."

Lexi felt gut punched. "Upending *his* life?" She could scarcely catch her breath. "What about mine? You barge into mine with hip boots telling me, what? I have a son I don't know about? How am I supposed to process that?"

He just stared back at her, waiting for it all to sink in.

"You know what?" She pointed at his empty shot glass. "I changed my mind. I'll have one of those."

He poured her the shot, handed her the glass. She downed it in one gulp, followed by a quick sip of water.

"Maybe there were some circumstances of your delivery your mother didn't share with you."

Her defenses went up with knee-jerk precision. But she had to admit, it wouldn't be out of character for her mother. She stared at him now, those amber eyes, that full mouth, that deep dark skin that took her breath away all those years ago. He wasn't stupid. Obviously, he'd done his homework or he wouldn't have pursued Jamal's lead. Denial wasn't going to get this resolved.

And there was Jamal. She couldn't deny she'd liked him the moment she'd seen him. She closed her eyes and took in several deep purging breaths to clear her head.

"Okay. I'm sorry. This is all just such a shock. Obviously, you've had some time to work with this and I'm hearing it for the first time. Jamal seems like a great kid. I don't want to see him get hurt either."

She finished the rest of her water, looking to bring this encounter to an end. "Truth now, Zai. That was you parked behind my house on the island the other night? Not Jamal?"

He hung his head, nodded.

"Why didn't you stop then. Come up to the door? Why all the secrecy?"

Chapter 27 – If Worse Comes to Worse

Zaire studied the face of the girl who'd haunted his dreams since he was a teenager. Those days had been carefree and magical, before the reality of his world came crashing down on his head.

He couldn't complain. Negatu Group, Ltd. was one of the most profitable hotel conglomerates in the world. With a market cap of sixteen billion, it was easy to resist being devoured by the Marriots and Hiltons. NGL shareholders were happy and according to his board of directors, which was all that mattered. Until a month from now, when he at last inherited the majority share of the stock, he would be subject to their direction and opinion. It was bad enough his parents had so much control of his life; they were still at it, even from their graves. The only reason he hadn't bailed on the whole shit show was he didn't want to ruin it for Jamal.

He should come right out and tell Alexis what he wanted and be done with it. It was all for Jamal after all, right? His own future was already a lock; Jamal's life was still ahead of him.

But the moment he'd looked into her amber eyes, he realized this whole thing should have been handled through his legal department. Now it was too late.

The truth pressed so hard against his breastbone he could scarcely take a full breath.

Jamal Isiah Negatu had found his mother. She sat no more than an arm's length away from him, her hand gripping the door handle with white knuckles.

Zaire didn't blame her for having doubts. What woman wouldn't? He'd agreed to meet her at Jamal's urging, if for no other reason than to get her to take a DNA test. In fact, if worse came to worse and she refused, he already had what he needed sitting on the bar; the glasses she'd sipped from.

But now that he'd seen her, he realized that wasn't what he wanted.

"Give me five more minutes," he said, hoping she could read the sincerity in his eyes. "Then if you still want to go, I'll take you back to your car."

She blinked at him a moment, then slowly removed her hand from the door handle and folded her arms across her chest. "Tic, toc."

Now, he sat forward and threaded his fingers together between his knees. "Look. This isn't easy for me either, Alexis. My life is what it is, and I don't have much say in how it goes down. Especially right now."

"I was nineteen when my parents shuttled me off on an extended dive trip. I was over the moon to be working on a world-class project in the Med. You could say it put me on the path to where I am today."

She settled into the seat, pinning him with a skeptical gaze.

"I got back months later to find they had adopted a baby. They never told me Jamal was my son until I was twenty-three. My dad had a heart attack. I guess the lie was on his conscience."

He set his gaze on her; her brow furrowed as she leaned against the door.

He swallowed hard. "That's when I sent you the necklace."

Her chin puckered, and it was clear she was trying to hold back tears. She fished the chain out of the neck of her sweater and dangled it in the space between them. "You mean this one?"

Zaire sat up, shot out his hand and looped a finger through the chain a moment before he lowered his eyes and nodded. "For the longest time, I thought maybe you'd try to find me."

"She never gave it to me," she said, and swiped at a tear that finally spilled.

"What?" Zaire felt gut punched.

"My mother. She never gave it to me." The stricken look on her face nearly broke his heart.

"Once they shipped me off to California, I never heard from her at all until she divorced my dad and shipped all my stuff to me here. I put everything in storage without even looking at it. I mean, why would I? I wanted nothing to do with my old life. I didn't find the necklace until about three months ago when I moved into my house on the island."

Zai felt his jaw loosen, like it would melt right off his face. "Well. That explains a lot," he murmured.

All this time he'd assumed she'd wanted nothing to do with him. He rubbed his eyes a moment, working the truth into his brain. She hadn't known about the necklace, but she was wearing it now. That thought gave him a little twinge of hope.

The limo was suddenly too small to contain the silence between them, which is why she nearly jumped out of her skin when her cell beeped a text notification.

Relief flooded his chest. They could both use a little break. "Go ahead, please," he said softly. At least she wasn't jumping out of the car.

* * *

The text was from Tess, a picture attached. Lexi turned away from Zaire to hide her screen from his view, forcing herself to breathe. She cut her gaze to Zaire to see he was scrolling through his own messages. She enlarged the picture and, holy crap, there were Jamal with Zaire and a beautiful woman on his arm. No, not just beautiful. She was sleek and darkly exotic, draped in a shimmering gold gown. Next to her, Lexi felt like a bleached-out barnacle on the bottom of an old rusty hull. Magnifying the picture further, she read the photo had been taken at an event in the Negatu family's flagship hotel in Bole. With a quick glance toward Zai to see he was still occupied on his own phone, she sent the text to archive. She would read the attached article later.

Tess's text read:

> Hold on to your hat. Your ex-lover-cum-baby-daddy is giving a lecture at the Scripps Institute tomorrow evening. The article mentioned a fiancée. Hope this is helpful.

Lexi texted back:

You have no idea. Talk later.

When she looked up, Zai was staring at her, a vague smile playing at his lips. No doubt he had just heard from miss gorgeous super model and couldn't wait to get back to that hotel room.

Welp. No sense prolonging this any further. Their paths had crossed, but only momentarily. The sooner they resolved the issue of Jamal's mother the better. She had a life to live, and it didn't need any more heartache. She would deal with that later, too.

"Okay," she said, gathering her pride around her. "So, we both got played. There's not a whole flippin' lot we can do about any of that now." Or ever. She needed to get out of this car before her tears betrayed her real feelings.

"As I said, my baby was a girl." She hoped her tone conveyed the finality of her conviction. "I have an investigator tenant in my building who might be able to help Jamal locate his actual mother. In the meantime, I'm assuming you're here on business and you won't be stalking me further?"

He cleared his throat dramatically, clearly taken back by her change in demeanor, then he gave her a respectful nod. "You have my guarantee. As to the business, I'm giving a lecture tomorrow evening at the Birch Aquarium. It's a private event, but, since you still dive, you might be interested."

He handed her a brochure from a stack on the mini bar, fixing his eyes on hers. "It's an indoor event, but dress warmly. Rain is forecasted, but the sunset before the lecture promises to be spectacular."

Those eyes held hers with a power she couldn't resist. It was like being under the thrall of some deep, dark secret that had a physical grip on her soul. She scarcely heard a word he said as she fought not to let her gaze slip to that mouth she remembered so well.

Engaged, she remembered.

Get away.

Get far, far away.

She tightened her grip on the folded brochure and shoved it deep into her bag without giving it so much as a glance.

"Thanks," she chirped. "I'll check my schedule."

No way was she going to subject herself to being in the same space with Zaire Negatu and his beautiful fiancée.

He raised a brow; she looked out the window avoiding any further exchange.

"Right." He pressed the button on the console and told the driver to take them back to the harbor.

Chapter 28 - No Shit Sherlock

Lexi dumped her equipment bag in her own garage and trotted next door, taking the cold brew coffee she'd hastily purchased on the way home with her.

"Tessa?" she called, knocking on the studio workshop door. If she wasn't there, she'd--

"Yeah, come on in," came the reply.

Lexi pushed open the door to find Tessa at her workbench looking through a magnifying glass at a bracelet clamped in a holder. She didn't look up. "Did you get my text?"

"Um, yup." Lexi scooted a rolling stool over next to Tess and sat quietly watching as she squeezed a pair of fine pliers to place a tiny red stone in the empty eye socket on the serpent bracelet.

"Wow, you got those Swarovski's pretty quick."

Tessa exhaled, laid the pliers on the bench, and straightened up, stretching her low back. "Overnighted them. They're going to be perfect." She tipped her head toward the magnifying glass. "Finished. Wanna see?"

Lexi scooted back on impulse, nearly juggling the coffee out of her hands. "No. I just came by to say thank you for pulling me back from the abyss."

Tessa pumped a blob of lotion into her hand and stood, rubbing it in. "The abyss?"

"You will not believe where I was when you sent me that text."

"Oh, that abyss." She turned off the lighted magnifying light. "How about we go out front. I need a rest. I'd forgotten how back breaking it can be to do close work."

Lexi sipped her iced coffee. She held open the shop door while Tessa grabbed an iced tea from her fridge and went out ahead of her.

The tide was at its ebb, their little sailboat resting its bow on the wet sand, the stern afloat. Dangling their legs off the tiny dock in front of their houses, Lexi told Tessa about her confrontation with Zaire and everything she had learned.

"I'm still a little in shock. I mean, I haven't decided about giving my information to the adoption agency and then this…this…Jamal shows up out of the blue…" She waved her cup in the air, unable to finish the sentence because she honestly didn't know how.

Tessa pulled her legs up lotus style, rested her elbow on her knee and propped her head up to look into Lexi's eyes. "So…how was it?"

Lexi scrunched her forehead. "What do you mean, how was it? It was crazy. And confusing, and…I mean, who sneaks up and drops a bomb on a person like that? 'My kid thinks you're his mom'," she mimicked, pulling a face.

"That's not what I meant, and you know it."

Lexi pulled in a long, slow breath. "You mean seeing Zai? After all these years?"

Tess gave her a slow, indulgent nod.

Lexi replayed the image of him sitting next to her in the limo in her mind. "It was like…time travel. No, like revisiting a favorite dream. I can't say that I was thinking straight the whole time. I was torn between shooting out of that limo and running down the street and slithering across that arm rest right into his lap." She sipped the cold brew on a suddenly dry mouth. "Then your text—that photo—brought me back to reality."

Tessa nodded agreement. "Did you read the article?"

Lexi shook her head. "No. Not yet. I literally zombied back here after he dropped me off at the restaurant." She held up the cold brew. "I don't even remember buying this." She threw her head back. "My god, those eyes."

A seagull landed a few feet away from them on the dock railing and padded near, looking for a handout.

Tessa shooed him away. "That's what I thought."

"He's still a hottie."

"Yup. An *engaged* hottie."

"Explains why he followed me around in his car. Probably didn't want her to know he went to see me in person."

Tessa unfolded her legs and let them dangle over the dock again. "Well, according to the article, the fiancée is at home on Bole during his visit. Apparently, in addition to this fundraising tour for his diving expeditions, his company is seeking to expand its holdings in the US time share segment. They have a large group in Carlsbad, near Legoland."

Lexi squeezed her eyes shut. "I'm not sure I want to hear all this." She pulled her knees up to her chin and wrapped her arms around them. "I'm still trying to get my head around the fact he managed to make a boy baby with someone the same time he was seeing me. I mean, we never left each other's sight."

Tessa shrugged. "If it were true, that he never spent any time away, you would have had to have twins. A girl and a boy. That's the only way Jamal could be yours."

Lexi threw back her head and roared. "Twins. Right." The laugh tears streamed down her cheeks. And her mother would have had to lie through her teeth, fake a birth certificate, keep the truth from her for all these years…

Lexi's hands went limp, the plastic cup slid from her fingers and fell to the sand below. She felt suddenly ill. Her eyes shot to Tessa's. "Oh my god. You don't think…"

Tessa's eyes flew wide. She covered her mouth with her hand. "I was…kidding. I didn't mean…"

But Lexi was headfirst, halfway down that rabbit hole. "I know, but I was under anesthetic during the C section, a month early, I don't remember anything except holding Ruby in my arms for just a few minutes. There could have been two babies—twins— and they just didn't bring him in."

"The birth certificate said, 'single birth'." Tessa's words took on a calm tone. She took Lexi's hands in hers. "I remember reading that."

Lexi felt hollowed out inside, like someone had come in with a shovel and scooped everything out of her. Her heart, her soul, her life. The lunch that had threatened to come up when she'd been in the car with Zaire, gurgled up out of her now for real. She leaned over the dock and let it go.

"Oh, god. Here." Tessa put her arms around her shoulders and lifted the iced tea bottle to her lips.

The tea calmed her. She dragged in long, slow breaths, until finally she managed to sit up straight. "It would be just like my mother to do something that devious. But adopt one of the babies to the Zai's family and not the other? Why? They've got more money than god, they could have easily supported both. That can't be true. It just can't."

They stared at each other for a couple of beats, then Tessa slipped her arms over the railing and rested her chin on them. "I know. It's too much to take in. But, let's assume, for just a moment it is true. Your mother may have contacted them. They had been friends, right? Back then?"

Lexi nodded, hanging on to her denial.

"So, she contacts them, giving them a last chance to take some responsibility. Some cultures favor boys over girls. Could have been that simple."

Guilt stabbed Lexi's heart. Twins. How had she not known?

And as if to chime in, the necklace burned between her breasts so hot she needed to slip it out and hold it away from her skin. The images slid in like hot butter sizzling in a pan. Lesidi at the bow of her boat, her twin brother, Amari at her side. It would have been a pleasant scene, except that from Lesidi's point of view—the way she saw everything in her trippy time travel mode—there was seething anger and fear. They were arguing.

"Lex?" Tessa's concerned voice pulled her back. "You're shaking. What's wrong?"

She dropped the necklace outside her sweater and the connection broke. She blinked at Tessa, forgetting for a moment where she was. And then, oh yes. "Twins." A girl and a boy. Like Lesidi and Amari.

Tessa stood, offered her hand to lift Lexi up. "So, what do you want to do? I could ask Phil to—"

"No. He's done enough already." Lexi sniffed and blew out her breath, her stomach recovering, guilt slowly turning to resolve. "We're going to go to that lecture."

*   *   *

In the workshop, with the afternoon sun slanting low, the ancient serpent slithered out of its cubby and off of its shelf, drawn by its twin, gold-filled replica on the workbench. Its ancient ruby eyes glittered as it wound its way up the clamp stand and slowly twined around its sister, scale-by-scale, until it completed the circle.

Chapter 29 - The Birch Aquarium

Located on a bluff high above the Pacific Ocean, the deck at the Birch Aquarium of Scripps Institute of Oceanography offered sweeping views of the majestic La Jolla coast.

"Wow. I've been here before," Tessa said. She craned her neck to see inside the massive glass walls of the Gallerie. The doors were open, the room set up for a theater-style event, with white-tableclothed stand-up reception tables near the entrance where a thick velvet rope still closed the hall. Just outside the door was a life-sized poster of Zaire and another man of about his age, aboard the institute's research vessel, the top half of their dive suits folded down to reveal shining wet six-pack abs. He'd filled out a little since they were kids, but it was definitely in all the right places.

Lexi dragged her eyes away from the poster to scan the diaz. A single podium was set off to the side of the stage, a large theater display screen at the back. The whole thing was bathed in an ocean of soft blue light. A prickling sense of excitement lay low in her belly at the thought Zaire would be standing there in the flesh in just a few minutes.

"I went to a lecture here in my sophomore year," Tessa was saying when Lexi came back to herself. "Ancient Etruscan jewelry found at a shipwreck site." She threaded her arm through Lexi's and led her away from the Gallerie toward the outside railing of the deck. "Probably the seed of my love of the art."

"Probably," Lexi said absently, and squeezed her hand as they wove their way through the gathering crowd. "Thanks for coming with me."

Tess laughed. "Oh, I wouldn't have missed this. Besides, it gave Phillip an excuse to spend some time with his dad without seeming to hover."

"Phillip is a good guy," Lexi said and meant it.

Tessa sent her a little *don't-I-know-it* smile then leaned in close to Lexi's ear and pointed to a tall, handsome guy in the crowd. "Isn't he that sports agent you see around Newport?"

Lexi let her gaze slide to where Tessa pointed. She didn't know much about sports, but she did recognize the man who lived in a lavish house on Lido Island. Now he led a young teen who must be his daughter toward the bluff to see the view.

"There are probably a lot of donors here tonight. Supporters of the Aquarium and the projects promoted by Scripps. Zai said it was a fundraiser, so..."

She recognized one of her former clients and her husband—a prestigious yacht designer—chatting it up with a man who looked like the other guy in the poster by the Galleria entrance. The woman boasted a diamond necklace that could be used as an anchor.

"Definitely out of my league," Lexi murmured as they strolled. She and Tessa were likely the only ones here not invited because of their large investment portfolios.

The real reason gripped her heart in a gentle fist. Her body had known it the moment she set eyes on Jamal even if her brain refused to listen. And last night, as she lay in her bed alone, going over and over all that had happened since that moment, all that must have happened on the day she gave birth, her heart knew it, too. She and Zaire had a son. And Jamal had somehow found her. He wanted to establish a relationship. His father wanted him to have the opportunity. How could she turn her back on that? She couldn't.

It was as simple as that. How it would all fit was going to be a puzzle she and Zaire would have to figure out together. And that started by her being cooperative, providing her contact information, and making time to talk it through.

Antsy, she checked her watch. They had about five minutes before the doors opened. She steered them toward the overlook for a better view.

Zai had been right about the sunset. A low-hung ceiling of sheer clouds curved over the horizon, the whole thing tinted blood orange. "Red sky at night," she murmured to herself.

"Sailor's delight," came a smooth male voice at her ear. She turned to find Zaire close enough to breathe in the fragrance of his aftershave, or maybe it was the ocean spray wafting up the cliffs. His smile spread wide across his face, showing off a row of perfectly straightened teeth. His bearing was gracious and inviting.

"So glad you could make it," he said, offering his hand. When she took it, he pressed hers between his a moment before he let go. She felt the heat of it all the way to her toes.

It took her a moment to find words. "I… yes. Me, too." *I think.* Right then it felt more like she was standing on the precipice of a high sheer cliff with an umbrella in her hand.

Their eyes met and held until Tessa politely cleared her throat. The interruption allowed Lexi to take a breath and step back. "Zaire, this is my neighbor, Tessa Koenig. You were parked behind her garage the other night when you stopped by my house?"

His lips twitched a fraction of a second, but he held his gracious smile.

"Ah, yes." He nodded. "Zaire Negatu," he said, taking her hand.

He looked like he was about to say something else, but the alarm went off on his phone. He pulled it out of his jacket and silenced it. "Sorry. The producer gets upset with me if I don't make it to the podium on time. Will you stay for a drink at the reception afterward?"

Lexi hissed in a deep breath. "Actually, it's a long drive back to Newport so we won't be drinking. But I would like to talk to you privately about … Jamal. How long will you be here?"

"Tonight is the last fundraiser event," he said, his eyes slowly roaming over her face, her hair, her lips. "And I have business in Carlsbad tomorrow morning.

After that, Jamal and I have some research to do. Not sure how long that will take."

Lexi raised her brow. Was he purposefully being evasive? "Isn't your fiancée expecting you back soon? According to the article I read in the Tribune, you are to marry in about a month."

There was a slight tick in his jaw, and his smile faltered a moment before his expression softened, warmed. "I'm … sorry you had to read that in the paper. I should have told you myself the other night."

Yes, he should have, but his sincere response now broke down one of the barriers in her heart. "It's all right. It was none of my business, really."

Zai stared at her a long moment before he pushed forward. "My biggest concern right now is for my son. He's interested in staying in the country. We're looking into private schools."

She nodded. "That's very commendable, Zai. You're putting your son first."

"Anyway…" He held up his phone. "Air drop your contact?"

She retrieved her phone and the ping made him smile. "I'll text you the moment I'm free so we can set up a meeting before I go back."

"Ah, modern technology." She accepted the contact just as a fireplug of a man in a buff fedora hat appeared at his side.

"Excuse me, ladies, but we need Mr. Negatu up front."

He gave them a quick shrug. "Duty calls. Nice to meet you Tessa," he said. "See you both after for a few moments, I hope."

He glanced at Lexi for a second before he turned. Was there a hint of apology there? Did it matter? Another piece of the wall disintegrated as she watched him make his way through the crowd.

The fact that he had been engaged had been a damn big item to leave out of their conversation in the limo the day before, but as he'd said, his first concern was his son. She had to give him credit for that.

A gentle announcement over the crowd that the Gallarie was open for seating, pulled her out of her thoughts.

She led Tess to seats near the back rows. "So we can get out of here before we get trapped in the crowd."

She had come here to set up an appointment with Zai and she'd been successful. There was no point in hanging around afterward.

Lexi fixed her gaze on the empty screen, butterflies having a field day in her stomach. There was no going back now. She had already taken the leap. The only thing left was to see how hard she would fall.

They sat, folded their jackets in their laps, and adjusted their handbags near their feet while the lights came up on the diaz. From the back of the theater seating, it would be difficult to tell Zai from any other handsome black man in the audience. But then, of course, the LED screen lit and there was that handsome face plastered nearly six feet tall all the way across the stage. A moment later his live image was replaced by an eerie underwater scene, a trail of ancient amphora embedded in the sea floor leading to the ghostly outline of a ship's hull.

In bright gold font that filled the entire top half of the screen, the words she read took her breath away:

The Wreck of the Demeter.

Lexi could hardly breathe. The Demeter? Wasn't that…

"In 327 CE, Emperor Constantine ordered his eldest son, Crispis and his second wife, Fausta killed for conspiring to take over the empire. His order to kill the pair was carried out immediately, but according to many accounts, Fausta's body was never found."

Tessa grabbed for Lexi's hand. "That's our story," she hissed in disbelief.

Lexi swallowed hard and leaned forward in her seat. "No way."

But it was true. Zai was telling the crowd about events Tessa had witnessed first-hand and shared with Lexi.

"It was rumored she escaped the Roman army vowing to extract revenge on the Emperor in the worst conspiracy imaginable: the sinking of the Demeter, the last large supply of grain that would make it across the Mediterranean Sea before stormy winter seas made the crossing impossible. Losing the last shipment of wheat would almost guarantee widespread starvation in Rome."

The image changed to a map of the Mediterranean near today's Sicily.

"It is said that the ship indeed went down somewhere off the Skerky Bank, a crossing with a reputation similar to the modern-day Bermuda Triangle because of many converging cross currents. Still, it was the most direct, fastest route to Ostia, the primary port of the city of Rome. This rough, deep-water crossing is the location of a great many shipwrecks reported over the centuries and even unto this day."

In a voice that rolled over her body like warm caramel, Zaire recounted a brief history of ancient trade routes, the goods transported, and the development of deep submergence technology that allowed oceanographers and historians to collaborate in recovering and studying ancient civilizations in a way never before possible.

The image on the screen changed again to show a perfectly round slab of what looked like stone.

"This stone quern was found at 400 feet, a depth that until recently we could only reach remotely."

The young teen they had seen earlier with her father sat in the VIP section in the front row. She boldly shot her hand up like they were in a classroom.

Zaire gave her his wide smile and gestured for her to stand up. "Yes, please. You have a question?"

"I have two questions, actually."

Of course she did. Who wouldn't want the attention of the charismatic man standing not six feet away from her?

"First," she went on, "What exactly is a quern. I haven't heard that term before."

Zaire stepped back to his laptop, zoomed in on the area of the picture with the stone disc.

"So, often in shipwrecks, the wooden elements of the vessel are destroyed by boring worms, and currents and such over time, we just have an outline." He used a stylus to outline what once was a ship. "What we end up with are the iron anchors, rudder connections, and so forth. In this case, we have a stone you would find in a large ship's galley, or in the case of the smaller vessels such as ancient corbitas, it would be out in the open on the fore deck, where the crew would light a brazier without fear of burning through the deck."

Lexi worked the coin necklace out from under her blouse and felt it warm between her fingers. She closed her eyes a moment and could almost see Lesidi, Cyril, and Kindra gathered around the brazier on the deck of Isis. The sounds in the room faded away. She was only half listening.

Up until that moment she'd allowed herself to follow along her dreamlike musings of the past like reading a favorite author's latest series. But Zaire's words pricked her heart with dread. The Demeter? By God, that was Keleb's ship. Fausta was going to try to sink the Demeter? Well, of course, she must have been successful, because, there it was on the bottom of the ocean on … what did he call it? The Skerky Bank?

Oh crap. Was she lapsing into that past life dream or was Zaire's story really about the Demeter? He was talking about Fausta, about identifying pieces of jewelry and coins, about sunken treasure. She needed to pay more attention.

"But I've digressed. What was your other question?"

"How do I get to be on your dive team?" she asked without hesitation. A soft murmur of laughter went up around the room.

Zaire joined in a moment before he answered. "Let's talk a little about that at the reception," he said, giving her dad a friendly nod.

The image on the screen changed again. They were looking at a barge where three men sat in a cramped space, awaiting the moment when they would enter a diving bell in modern scuba gear that would allow them access to deep water finds never before accessible to divers.

Now he was giving figures, costs, timelines; information investors would need to know in order to expand their philanthropic legacies. He was good, had their rapt attention.

"If we can prove this wreck is the Demeter, and that Empress Fausta went down with it, we can solve one of the most long-standing ancient mysteries of the Constantine era."

But Alexis Hill wasn't thinking about solving some ancient mystery, or helping a corporate mogul offload his millions to ease his tax burden. In fact, she wasn't even thinking about Zai or Jamal.

No. Alexis Hill was thinking about Lesidi and Kindra and Dracis, people who lived almost two thousand years ago, and yet somehow lived inside of her. Did she have their actual genes? Their DNA? Or was the necklace the link that joined them together?

The last time she had been present with them, they had been heading toward the Strait of Messina, to meet up with Keleb and the Demeter to deliver the year's last supply of wheat to the city of Rome. If the wreck Zaire wanted to investigate was in fact the Demeter, it would mean they altered course. If Zai was right, and she had no reason to doubt him, unless they did, they were all doomed.

She checked her watch as the lights slowly came up at the entrance to the room where servers were laying out *hors d'oeuvres*, champagne flutes filled with bubbly, and coffee. Tess rested her hand on Lexi's arm. "I need to use the ladies room."

Lexi glanced over her shoulder. "Meet you at that tall top in the corner."

Grateful now they'd sat near the back, Lexi piled her purse on the tall table, expecting to see Tess when she turned at the tap on her shoulder.

Instead, it was Zaire his eyes gleaming with excitement. "Well, what did you think?"

What would he say if she told him everything? That she knew the ancients who went down with that ship? That she'd seen Fausta, and sacks of coins like the one that hung around her neck. Like the one he'd given her all those years ago. She felt the heat drain out of her lips. "I…"

His expression changed at her hesitation. "That bad, huh?"

"No. No. Not bad at all. I just…" She lifted her gaze toward the restrooms. No Tessa in sight, the butterflies going for the Olympics now. She had been bracing for a discussion about Jamal, about Zai's engagement; instead, she had been waylaid by a notion so bizarre, she could scarcely form words in her head, let alone actually say them. But truly, if there was anything at all to the events she'd been experiencing, he was exactly the person she needed to tell.

Chapter 30 - Zaire's Leap

Zaire savored a steaming cup of dark-Ethiopian pressed brew on the balcony of his timeshare suite. It was the only thing regularly brought from home on his travels throughout the world—coffee from home and a French-press to brew it in. The rich blend of dark-roasted coffee reminded him of the people who'd picked and carefully dried and processed the beans with a tinge of guilt. Because of his parents' diplomatic connections, they were able to build a huge hospitality empire. He and Jamal had lived a life of privilege, while most of his countrymen struggled every day.

One of his dreams since becoming more involved in Jamal's life was to expand his non-profit to develop exploration dives for young people from the coffee plantations, something he and Jamal could build together. The idea set a warm glow in his heart as he looked out over eucalyptus trees along a running path below the hotel. The idea wasn't fully formed yet, but it was there, like the vista before him. A cotton-ball fog blanketed the coast, but he knew underneath, was a highway humming with lives and stories, and possibilities.

He drummed his fingers on the arm of his chair, anxious, unsettled, adrenaline pumping through his veins like the first time he dropped through a hole in the deck of an unexplored wreck.

Something inside him had shifted. Where a few weeks ago his future lay before him flat and colorless like the fog, today, he saw something new on the horizon. Something bright and colorful that had nothing to do with getting married, taking control of the family business, or diving for sunken treasure. The prospect of change excited him in a way it never had before.

Ordinarily after a fundraising event, he'd be running scenarios in his head; sizing up investor's wallets, ticking off operations costs, and calculating the potential start dates for the current project. Lately it seemed no matter how hard he worked, or how much he campaigned, without financial support from The Negatu Group, his project—directing, producing, and filming his own deep-water documentary—the start date remained a moving target.

He stood up and gripped the balcony railing, lifting his chin. This morning, and for first time in years, having the corporation's support no longer mattered. There was no point in any of it unless his personal life was in order. *It's not your parents holding you back from making that happen. It's you.*

The thought brought him settling relief, like finally working a festered sliver from a finger. The coastline might be shrouded in a low, foggy blanket, but above it, he could see all the way to the horizon. He stood on the precipice of a seminal, life-changing moment. All he had to do was jump.

He refreshed his coffee from the French press and sat, giving in to the images that had invaded his dreams, woke him in the middle of the night, and refused to be ignored. Images of Alexis Hill.

Fifteen years old and more exciting than any woman he'd met since. Those eyes, so sharp and discerning; the way she actually listened to what he had to say, the way his chest expanded when he heard her voice, the way his blood leapt in his veins when she touched him. Together they had found a magical place where no one else existed and made it their own. He thought it would last forever. What a love-struck fool he'd been, victim of a common, biological urge.

Over the years, he'd come to know the urge was common, but the magic that made you want to soar over the rooftops was rare. The lucky ones grabbed onto it and held on tight, let nothing get in the way. He and Lexi had not been so lucky. He'd screwed that up royally when he'd taken her innocence.

His fault entirely.

His first mistake; one his parents had tried to erase by taking total control.

His second mistake was letting them continue to manipulate him for most of his adult life.

Give up your wild dreams and settle into the family business or give up your full inheritance.

It was mean-spirited and not very forward thinking on their part. Traveling the world filming undersea expeditions may have been his dream, but that dream also identified exotic locations and resources that had expanded Negatu Group's holdings to the global level. He'd proven many times over he could follow his dream and grow the company at the same time. They never acknowledged the fact. Never forgiven him for the one, impulsive, selfish moment in his youth when he'd embarrassed them. Instead, they'd written their punishment into their trust. He was to marry the woman of their choice by age 35 if he wanted to keep his shares in the company.

He fisted his hands, digging his nails into his palm; angry at them for refusing to acknowledge his value on its own merit, angry at himself for letting them.

He hadn't been much older than Jamal when he'd made that fatal mistake. If he could go back in time and speak to his younger self, he would have warned him, and not just to carry condoms wherever he went. No. He would warn him not to trust what others said and did, but to seek out the truth for himself.

His truth was he'd gotten Jamal as a result of that first mistake, and it was a gift he'd only recently begun to fully appreciate. Now he'd learned from Lexi he had a daughter somewhere in the world. That knowledge, and the fact that his parents had kept it from him, left a bloody, gaping wound in his heart.

It was up to him to stop the bleeding. For all of them.

Which is why he would not be going back Abbis Ababa to marry Eyrkah.

It was time someone in this family made decisions for right reasons.

If that meant giving up financing for his diving project, then so be it. His parent's had been right about one thing. It was time he stopped searching for sunken treasure and sought out the things that truly made a man happy.

He had a son to raise, a daughter to find, and, if he was lucky, the possibility of reclaiming the only woman he had ever really loved. What greater treasure could there be?

He scrolled through his messages and clicked on the one from the commercial real estate office he'd been working with in San Diego.

Consider this the official go ahead to make the offer, he texted. **Send paperwork.**

He had friends on the board of directors who knew his value to the company and wanted to preserve the value of their shares. No doubt, they could work something out. If not, so be it. His life, and the life of his family were more important to him now.

Feeling as though a great weight had been lifted off his chest, he hauled in a deep breath and hit the speed dial for his fiancée. It would be late evening in her part of the world, but she was an energetic young woman. She would be awake.

"Zaire? Are you back?" Her last word ended on a sharp squeak. She covered the phone; he could hear muffled words as she spoke to someone with her.

She was likely spending her last free nights with the young man she really loved. The one she would long for in a loveless marriage to him.

"Erykah, sorry to bother you so late. You with Llamar?"

She was sobbing, apologizing. "Zaire, I can explain—"

"Shhhhh, shhh. It's all right. Just listen to me now. Everything's going to be all right."

He ran nervous hands through his hair as he told her his intentions. By the time he'd ended the call, he'd settled into a clear, quiet place; like warm sun had broken through a fog. He could hear the relief in her voice as well. There would be a bit of a fuss at first, but in the long run, he and Erykah would be spared a nightmare marriage. She was a well-educated, beautiful young woman who would have no trouble attracting another young man. And, after finding out Zaire had turned his back on his inheritance, her parents would be all too happy to find a more suitable replacement.

He blew out a heavy purging breath and braced himself for the next step: Lexi. Would she give him another chance? There was only one way to find out. He texted her number.

Can you meet me in two hours for a late lunch?

*   *   *

Bells on the door of The Butterfish Grille jangled cheerily as he went inside. He didn't recognize her at first. She sat with her back to the front window in the first booth, a bright yellow Kente scarf wrapped around her head, a string of large red beads circled her neck. Rich vanilla creme skin glowed under an aquamarine sweater that exposed part of a smooth shoulder.

His breath caught in his throat. With dark eye liner, tomato-red lipstick, and a sultry pout on her lips, she looked like she'd walked out of an ad for one of his elite resort hotels. But when she smiled at him, she was the all-American girl who had captured his heart on a dive boat in the Mediterranean and never let it go. Jamal's mother. Lexi.

Her eyes locked on his as he strode to the table.

"You didn't need to get dressed up for me," he said, letting his eyes feast on that smile. She was as lovely as he remembered the first time he'd seen her when her parents joined his family on their yacht in the Mediterranean. His heart stuttered a bit just the way it had back then.

She twisted a bead on her necklace self-consciously. "I've never worn it before. Not sure the look works for me."

"That's your mother talking, Lexi." He slid into the seat opposite her.

Her eyebrows raised. "I suppose you're right. It's hard not to see myself through her lens."

He studied the face that had lived in his memory for so long. His first impression had been all wrong. She was even more beautiful today than all those years ago. "You know what I see?"

She cocked her head to the side the way he remembered and cricked up the side of her mouth. "What do you see?"

"I see your father's Scottish skin, for sure. But I also see your mother's high cheekbones, a sculptured nose, and a regal chin." His eyes focused on hers. "I see the iconic countenance of an ancient queen."

She dipped her head, her cheeks flushing. He reached across the table and tipped up her chin with a crooked finger until her eyes met his. "Like Queen Zenobia."

She let go a soft laugh.

"I'm not kidding," he said, watching her eyes light up. "Queen Z challenged the Roman Empire back in the day. Got her head on a golden coin."

Her smile faded and she shifted gently away from his reach, touched the edges of the scarf. "It does remind me of that summer," she said, changing the subject.

"Reminds me of that, too. You have the kind of face that can pull it off. Don't let anyone tell you different."

She let go a soft laugh and gave him the sweet smile of her youth. "Anyway. Thanks for meeting me in person," she murmured. "I know it puts you in an awkward position."

"How so?" He was enjoying the high color on her cheeks. The server arrived at the table. "Go ahead and order for us," he prompted. "You know what's good, right?"

She looked nervous, unsettled, happy to have something to do besides squirm in her seat. "Two chowders in sourdough bowls, please, and some of your coleslaw."

"And two glasses of white wine," Zaire put in. "Do you have a preference?"

She caught her bottom lip between her teeth a moment. "I think here, you take what they give you."

He glanced around the space obviously built in the fifties, floor tiles worn from decades of sandy shoe traffic.

"Right." He nodded to the server.

"I don't want to disrespect your fiancée," Lexi went on after the server left. "I'm only here to talk about Jamal, nothing else."

Zaire studied her a moment longer. He folded his hands together in front of him on the table and leaned forward. "Listen. About that…"

The server brought the wine and two glasses of ice water. "Anything else?" Her eyes went to Lexi and they exchanged a look that made Zaire think they were probably friends. She'd brought him into her world. A good sign. "We're good for now, thanks," she said, returning the server's wide smile.

He continued to study her features, settling into his plan. A warm pressure expanded in his chest. This was going to work. It had to.

"You were saying?" she prompted.

Zaire's mind blanked a moment, caught up in the gold flecks in her eyes. How long had he sat there speechless? Seconds, minutes? "There, uh… There is no longer a fiancée."

"What?" Her eyes went wide, she sat forward. "What happened to her?"

"A mutual agreement."

"But the article said—"

"I spoke to Erykah just before I texted you this morning. She's relieved, Lexi. She's in love with someone else. Always has been. Marrying me would have been devastating for both of us. Her parents will be upset for a while, but they'll get over it."

Lexi sat back against her seat. "I don't understand. You would disrespect your parents' wishes?"

"To hell with their wishes. This isn't the dark ages. Besides, my parents don't deserve respect after what they did." He reached across the table and touched her fingertips with his. "They lied to us, Lexi. True, we were just kids and in no position to be parents ourselves, but what they did--my parents and yours-- was unforgivable. I would never do that to our son."

Her eyes went shiny when he said *our son*, and she swallowed hard. She glanced away, wiping a tear with the back of her hand. "Does he hate me?"

"Hate you? No." He slid his hand closer, this time hooking her fingers into his. "He's a private kid. Holds everything in. But he's smart beyond his years. He gets what the situation was back then. It was his idea to try to track you down. Said there was something missing in his life and he needed to find it. Although, I have to admit, looks like he's already moved on to surfing as the missing thing. That's where he is right now with a bunch of kids at some place called Swami's."

She puffed out a laugh, then pulled her hand away gently. "Can't blame him for that."

The server wordlessly slid their lunch onto the table.

She pushed her bowl a little to the side. "My parents weren't any better. I'm still trying to get my head around the fact I had twins and my mother somehow managed to keep it from me."

His mouth went dry.

"Me, too," he said, though he knew it was much different for her. Harder. More visceral. The thought of what she'd been through, both physically and emotionally made his stomach clench. He'd been sent off on a dream trip with a world-famous diving crew, having no idea what was happening in her world. She'd been stuck with the harsh reality of their mistake. Guilt welled low in his belly.

He drank half his water and put it down, then told her the rest of what he'd done that morning; the purchase contract, making the call to Erykah. "I'll be looking into office space in Newport for my non-profit."

She sat silently listening, her eyes growing gradually wider like she didn't believe what she was hearing.

That was okay. He'd make her believe.

"Jamal likes it here," he went on. "I'll be looking into private schools. Honestly, neither of us has spent much time in the compound since my father died."

Lexi was shaking her head, her eyes fixed on her hands.

"What?"

"This is all so … unexpected. I mean, I realize now, I was only thinking about myself." She cut her gaze to the windows a moment before she looked up into his eyes. "When I thought about giving my contact information to the agency, I never stopped to consider how it might impact you. I only thought I might one day get to meet my daughter."

He lowered his head and took that in. When Jamal first told him he'd found his mother, seeing Lexi again had been his first thought. He hadn't considered she might not want to see him. But today had already been a day for truth telling. He'd broken things off with Erykah, something he should have done a long time ago. And he felt better for it. Better to get all his cards on the table.

"Forgive me. I know this is all new to you. I've been stewing on it for some time now. If I don't say what's on my mind, I'm going to explode."

Shoulders lifting a little, she nudged her bowl closer and stirred hot sauce into the creamy center. "That…would be messy. Maybe we should step outside."

That smile again, twisting him up inside.

He leaned in. "Not a chance. Now that I've got your attention, I need to get this said. After that, you can leave if you want to; you and Jamal can make whatever arrangements you want, and I'll stay out of it."

She frowned again. "It sounds like you've already taken some pretty drastic steps."

He took another slug of water. "I wanted you to know I'm serious about this. I don't take it lightly."

She rolled in those luscious lips and nodded, her spoon paused above her bowl, then hit him again with that smile. "Okay."

Zaire blinked at her, caught off guard by her sudden acceptance. "Okay?"

She cocked her head, plopped her spoon into her bowl. "Okay, I want to hear what you have to say."

Her eyes glinted back at him, full of curiosity, patience.

His mind went blank. The silence sat between them like a big, white whale, ready to drag him down without a breath. He sat back and scrubbed his fingers over his mouth like he could dredge up just the right thing to say, but no words magically came to him.

His face heated like a bashful school kid. "Sorry. It's just that…I didn't expect…"

"Didn't expect what, Zai? That I'd accept the truth that Jamal is my son? How could I not?"

He drew in a deep breath and let it go. "Oh, I had no doubts about that. You wouldn't be the girl I once knew if you refused."

If she was uncomfortable, she was doing a good job of hiding it. He, on the other hand was starting to sweat under his shirt collar. *Keep going, idiot, before you lose your nerve.* "I didn't expect to feel the magic after all this time. I told myself I was doing this for Jamal. But when I saw you…"

Her hand went back to the beads at her neckline like they were the only thing anchoring her in her seat. "It was a long time ago, Zaire. You're under no obligation to—"

"Wait. Oh. Forgive me. You're with someone?" *Shit. Shit. Shit.* He'd read this thing all wrong. "I didn't notice anyone--"

"You mean when you followed me around for a week?"

His ears burned on that one. "Well. I had to—"

"No."

"No?"

She laughed out loud and the sound of it released a knot of tension in his gut.

"I'm not seeing anyone. Haven't for a long time, much to Tessa's disappointment." Now she tucked into the chowder with true interest.

"Good. I mean—" He drummed his fingers on the table. Where was that server when he needed a distraction?

"Zai. It's okay. Relax."

"I can't. At least, not until I tell you what I came here to say."

She put down her spoon again. "Okay. So say it. I'm all ears."

"I'm … sorry. I guess that's the most important thing." Just getting those two words out release he tension in his throat. "What happened between us should never have happened. I was old enough to know better. I'd promised my father to uphold our family's legacy. He saw what I'd done as a failure. And you were so young. I should have been the one to put on the brakes, but I didn't, and my actions ruined everything." He gulped down a mouthful of water, ice cubes rattling in the glass.

She looked up at him now from under slightly damp lashes, a liquid sheen in her eyes. "I can't say it was all your fault, Zai. I seem to remember being the one who crawled into your lap and begged to get closer."

His gut clenched now, remembering that moment. It had been like being caught up in whitewater, swept along, catching breath, then plunging down again.

"I've never forgotten the way we were," she went on. "I felt like I was alive for the first time; I would have done anything for you." She glanced away a moment, as if gathering her thoughts. "I was naive, I know. Young. I just followed my heart, too young to understand the consequences."

"And I let you face them alone."

"That wasn't your fault, either." Now it was Lexi reaching for his hand. "You need to let all that go. I'm not that naive kid anymore and I'm old enough to make my own decisions."

It was true. Their age difference didn't matter anymore. She was a grown woman with a solid career, a home, a life. He couldn't just go barging in like he had a pass because of Jamal. He was going to have to earn his way back. Needed to.

Now the blush on her cheeks filled in across what he could see of her clavicles. "I can't say I was only thinking of Jamal when I agreed to meet you today."

Had he heard that right?

"But calling off your marriage?" she continued. "I would never expect you to do that. What about your inheritance? Your legacy?"

"My legacy?" Zaire straightened in his seat, working his jaw to control the rage that word triggered in his gut. He could feel his pulse pumping at his temple. "My legacy is down on the beach with his friends right now," he said, sweeping his arm toward the windows. Resentment stalked him, cranked up the volume in his voice. "… which is exactly where a kid his age should be, not holed up in some compound being drilled on the requirement to fulfill his parent's legacy."

Her eyes went wide, then her expression softened and she nodded slowly. "Like your parents did to you?"

He blinked at her now, the bitterness backing off. She got him. Even at fifteen, she had gotten him. "Yes. I'm sorry. I didn't mean to blast you with that."

She smiled at him, toying with her wine glass. "We always could talk to each other, say anything that was on our minds. Until—"

"Until they ripped us apart." His mouth hardened now, his bitterness dampened with regret. It was doing them no good hashing all that over. He'd done it a thousand times.

They needed a new start.

He got up and came to her side of the table, scooted in close enough to feel the heat of her body next to his. He laced a finger through hers and she finished the move like muscle memory. His heartbeat leapt up a notch.

"Let's forget all that. We need to focus on what's happening now. It's more important to me right now to bring us together. You, me, Jamal. We have a lot of catching up to do. I realized this morning I couldn't do that from the other side of the planet or promised to someone else. Especially, someone who didn't deserve to have her wishes ignored any more than I did. So I called off the engagement."

Chapter 31 - Wait for It

Lexi's heart hammered against her ribs. Or was that Zai's heart thumping into hers? It was impossible to tell. All she knew was the moment that window had slid down on his limo and she saw his face smiling back at her, the world had tilted on its axis, letting in a little more sun, a little more hope. A little more magic.

There was no denying it. The fifteen-year-old inside her wanted to crawl into his lap like she'd done all those years ago. The woman in her was a little more cautious, though no less a captive to his magnetic pull.

The restaurant, just a parking lot away from the surf and almost always cold, suddenly felt like a sauna. Her face flushed. She reached up and slid the scarf off her head, ran her nails through her curls to let in some air.

She had fantasized about meeting Zaire since the night at the lecture. It could have gone down a lot of different ways. They'd exchange contact information, schedules, and meeting places, and she and Jamal would begin the slow process of getting to know each other one weekend a month. Or, she'd fly to the continent and visit the compound in Bole, taking a back seat to Zaire's wife, who would dictate when and how much she would be allowed to visit her son.

But this scenario, the one where Zaire Negatu put his life on hold, came to the States, and gave her full access to his son and himself? That was a dream she hadn't dared entertain. Yet here he was, fingers laced in hers like a favorite pair of sneakers, binding the two sides together, tight and comfortable.

Like they had never been apart.

He didn't just want her in Jamal's life. He wanted her in his.

No one had ever done anything like that for her. Wanted her like that. Ever. It was too much to take in all at once.

Behind the glint of youthful interest playing in his eyes was an earnest, adventurous, deliciously mature man sitting too close beside her in the booth, the same man who had once showed her what it was to want someone so badly you forgot all reason and sanity. Is that what was happening now?

The ever-present counselor in her head spewed out her opinion. *If it sounds too good to be true, it probably is.*

Tessa was right about one thing. The reason there was no magic man in her life was she'd never let one close enough to see it. To feel it. To want it. Seeing Zaire again made her feel it all and she recognized it for what it was. She was needy and vulnerable right now. Decisions needed to be made that affected not only her, but Jamal and his father, even the ex-fiancée. She didn't want her neediness to influence those decisions.

But here was Zai, willing to give them a chance. For Jamal. For all three of them.

All she had to do was crack the door open a little.

She rested her hand on his chest a moment, then gently pushed away from his body, giving them both room to breathe.

She drew in a long slow breath and held it a moment, a sense of calm descended over her. She wasn't that fifteen-year-old kid anymore. She could be hopeful and reasonable at the same time. Had to be. For Jamal, and for herself.

"I hear you've put a lot of thought and effort into this and I can't say I'm opposed to any of it. But, for the sake of … everyone … involved, we need to take it slow. We screwed up all those years ago. We can't let that happen again; to Jamal or to us."

His brows furrowed a moment, then softened into a tentative nod. "What does slow mean in your world? Because in mine, I'm thinking we go straight from here to my place down in Carlsbad, without breaking the speed limits—"

She shoved his side playfully. "It means we focus on Jamal for now. Set up a day to spend together; figure out what comes next. A dive, maybe? This Saturday? He does dive?"

Zai nodded, giving her a knowing smile. "Oh, he dives all right."

"It sounds like you don't approve."

"You want to get to know him? Let him tell you about that himself." Pride in his son's accomplishments shone in his eyes.

"I can't wait."

His grin lit up his whole face. He pulled his bread bowl across the table and tucked into it a few bites as if he hadn't eaten all day.

She watched him a moment before he put down his spoon, eyes glinting again. She found herself loving how he was having fun with this. She hadn't had much of that lately.

He finished the last of his water, wiped his lips, and before she could slip out of the way, he swooped in for a kiss, short, sweet, and full of promise.

And the heat flushed all the way to her toes.

*　*　*

Sitting behind the wheel of her car, she had mixed feelings as she watched the limo pull away from the curb. Her heart felt so buoyant, she thought she might float away; so ambivalent, she was almost afraid to move. Never in all these years had she expected anything like this to happen to her. The people she counseled, maybe, or some oddball family on a daytime talk show. But not her. The prospect of opening her life up to Jamal and Zai had her heart racing in a different direction. She'd agreed to join Zai and Jamal on a private dive trip to Wreck Alley off the San Diego Coast. Something Zai had wanted to do since they'd arrived. It was also just far enough away it made sense to book a hotel stay.

Was she ready for that?

Yes.

And, no. Well, maybe…She would take the ferry home instead of the highway, a route home she reserved for times she needed to think.

Seeing Zai felt like sliding into her favorite pair of jeans, irreplaceable, the perfect fit. True, he'd followed her around for a couple of days, but once he'd owned up to that, he'd been honest about his intentions, and he'd politely backed off when she put on the brakes. She'd set the ground rules and he'd followed them to a T.

The ambivalence was of her own making. She was feeling a little guilty. She was the one who hadn't laid all her cards on the table. What if he learned about her little excursions into the past?

She turned in at the ferry landing and nudged her way into line, only three cars ahead of hers; with three cars per trip, she had time to think.

She shut down her engine and settled back in her seat, blood still pumping fast in her veins. She could not get her mind off the way her thighs heated when he'd gone in for that innocent kiss. It took her all the way back to that summer in the Med when they'd spent every moment together. They were bound up in the ecstasy of youth and teenage lust. A perfect world in which all the stars had aligned just for them. She had never had that feeling again for another man. Never gave one a chance, really. All this time, she'd thought Zai had abandoned her. Why set yourself up for that?

She rubbed her palm against the necklace at her chest. But he hadn't abandoned her. At least, that hadn't been his intent. And that knowledge opened a little crack in her heart. It felt good. It felt really, really good. She wanted all of what he'd told her to be true. Every last word of it.

His presentation had been the final blow to her grip on reality. The fact that they both had a connection to the Demeter had her wondering if she was losing her mind. Zai's dream was to locate and film the wreck of the Demeter. Lexi had seen it real time from several different angles through her link to Lesidi. That simply could not be a coincidence, which meant they were somehow destined to come back together.

Someone behind her tooted their horn. She pulled forward and slipped her transmission into park. Her mind, idling like her engine, took her to a place that sent icy fingers through her veins.

The last time she'd let herself slip through time, Lesidi was on her way to join the fleet and Keleb. The Demeter would soon be headed toward Ostia. From what she'd seen in Zai's presentation, it was likely they'd go down with the ship unless she did something to warn them. What would Zaire say if she told him what she knew? Would he listen? Or would he close the door on what could only seem like a madwoman? Could she even make a difference? Had Tessa?

Gulls fluttered away from the landing as the ferry nudged in and she drove over the gangway. She shut down the engine and got out of the car for the passage, the scent of saltwater mingled with aroma of deep-fried corn dogs and fresh saltwater taffy wafting from the Fun Zone.

But floating across the channel on the ferry didn't bring her any closer to an answer.

She drove off the ferry and the few blocks home with a bubble of anxiety still welling in her chest.

The minute she parked her car in the garage, she got Tessa's text.

Tessa: **How'd it go?**

Lexi: **You in the shop?**

Tessa: **Yeah. Come on over.**

Tessa watched a plate of spring rolls anxiously through the glass front of the little microwave on her workbench. "Want one?"

Lexi shook her head. She'd filled up on chowder at the restaurant; right then the last thing she wanted was another bite of food.

She sat heavily on the day bed, zipped the yellow scarf from around her neck and nervously tied it in a knot. "He broke off his engagement."

"Shut the front door," Tessa crooned. The timer went off and she busied herself with getting the rolls out of the oven.

"I'm not kidding." Lexi kicked off her shoes, folded her legs into lotus on the bed, and told Tessa everything.

"So he's not going back? Ever?" Tessa asked, munching.

"I don't know about ever, but he's definitely not going back to get married. He and Jamal are staying at his time share in Carlsbad for now while they find Jamal a school, preferably in Orange County."

"Wow." Tessa loaded a paper plate with spring rolls, squirted wavy lines of ketchup over them, and sat beside her on the bed. "My first thought was they need to apply for Jamal's citizenship, but then…"

Lexi laughed. "Right. He's a full-fledged American citizen. Born in Washington DC. I'm still trying to get my head around it."

She eyed the spring rolls and changed her mind. "We made a date to go diving on the weekend. The three of us."

Tessa furrowed her brow. "So, why am I getting a sense of hesitation from you? What have you got to lose? Sounds like he's taking all the risk."

"You're right about that."

"What do you mean? You're not worthy? You need to get that thought out of your head right now. You could be some kind of loser addict or mean girl slut. You're not either of those things. You're a brilliant human being with a heart full of love."

"Yeah. And crazy delusional."

"What are you talking about?"

Lexi propped her elbows on her knees, fished the necklace out of her shirt, and dangled it in the air.

Tessa pursed her lips. "Okay. There's that."

"And more."

"More?"

Tessa was going to kill her when she heard what she'd been keeping from her, but she didn't have any choice. She had to tell her or else nothing else she was going to say would make any sense.

"Remember that day you found me in here," she said, gesturing around the workshop. "The snake slid up my arm and I said I didn't remember what happened?"

Tessa looked at her sideways. She went to the mini fridge for some hot mustard. "I knew you were holding back. But I didn't want to force you. So?"

Lexi rubbed her eyes with the heels of her hands a moment then refocused on Tess. "That shipwreck Zaire's pitching his investors? The Demeter?"

Tessa slowly lowered herself to sit. "No way. You were on the Demeter?"

"Not exactly." Lexi squeezed her hands together tight. "Honestly, Tess, you are the only person who would understand. I've seen that wreck, you know … from a different point of view."

Tessa sat, mouth agape while Lexi told her everything she could remember. That Dracis had overheard Fausta's plan, that Lesidi was taking her vessel to meet up with the fleet. "Tess, they're going to sink the Demeter. I've seen it—then and now. And the proof was in Zaire's presentation."

Tessa slowly shook her head. "Oh, man."

"It's no coincidence, right? It can't be." Lexi gripped her necklace now as if to confirm it. "I need to tell Zai. I can confirm his find. But if I do, what if he thinks I'm a nut case?"

Tessa just stared at her.

"Tess! Say something."

"Right," Tessa said, getting up to pace the narrow space again. "First of all, he sought *you* out, not the other way around, so he's not going to think you are somehow after his money."

Lex let out a sigh.

"Second, you can't just spring it on him. It's too…too…"

"Crazy. It's batshit crazy."

Tess stopped pacing, cocked her hands at her hips. "I wasn't going to say that. But it will be a little hard to believe unless you can come up with some kind of proof. Something only someone who'd been there would know, like maybe a piece of jewelry, or…I don't know. But you've got to take it slow, like you already talked about. Get to know him a little better; find out what his mindset is, his tolerance level."

"Tolerance for BS you mean."

"He's a filmmaker, not a scientist. He's into fantasy. There's some wiggle room there, don't you think?"

Lexi shrugged. "I suppose. You're right, as always."

"You need to come to some sort of understanding about Jamal before you wade all the way in. That's the real-world scenario. Like it or not, you have to face it."

Lexi nodded.

Tess sat next to her again and rested her head on her shoulder. "I'm sorry I got you into this, girlfriend."

"What do you mean? It's not your fault I screwed up my life when I was fifteen."

"No, but I talked you into opening that door."

Lexi circled her arm around her friend's waist, noticing it was a little thicker than is used to be. Pregnancy suited her. "Don't beat yourself up about it. I'm glad you did."

"Anyway," Tessa went on. "My take is to keep what you know about Lesidi and the Demeter to yourself until you've spent some time with Zaire and

Jamal. You got yourself a real-time, very present scenario in the here and now. Whatever happened to the Demeter happened a long time ago and there's nothing you can do about it."

"Are you sure?"

"Sure about what?"

"That there's nothing I can do about it. I mean, at least from what I've seen of the past, the actual wreck hasn't happened yet."

"Wait. You're not thinking of going back. You said to keep that bracelet away from you. That you never wanted anything to do with it ever again."

"I know." Lexi wiped her face in the crook of her arm. "I know that's what I said, but, how can I sit here and let Lesidi and her friends go down with that ship? Not to mention the innocent Romans who could starve if they don't have wheat for the winter?" Two hot tears rolled down her cheeks and fell into her lap.

Tessa straightened, her eyes going wide in surprise. Speechless, she just pointed to the wooden shelves above the workbench.

The hairs raised on the back of Lexi's neck when she realized what Tessa wanted her to see. Two serpent bracelets lay circled together on the shelf, their golden scales sliding into a perfect union. Four ruby red eyes glinted back at them before they slithered apart like liquid gold, re-coiled, and rested side by side, completely solidified.

Tessa recovered first, swallowed hard. "Um, Lex?"

"I saw it," she answered, her voice cracking. She picked up her scarf and sidled away from the bench. "Which one is—"

Tessa tiptoed over to the bench. She picked up her needle-nose pliers and gave one of the bracelets a little tap. "I...I don't know."

Lexi's hands were suddenly sweaty. She wiped them on her thighs. "Wha—what if they're both--"

"Lex, I never took that bracelet out of the clamp. And you saw them. They both moved, right?"

Lexi swallowed hard and nodded, a wild-ass idea banging in her head. "So, does this mean two people could travel together? I mean, if the original bracelet infused its power into the new one?"

Tessa gasped, the color draining from her face. "I...don't know what it means."

Chapter 32 - Wreck Alley

Lexi was in shock. When she suggested they go for a dive and Zai volunteered to put something together, she was expecting, well, not this. She was delighted, and not a little impressed. Upon arriving at the harbor near Mission Bay, her gaze immediately went to the sleekest, most luxurious yacht she'd ever seen moored at the end of a dock full of luxury yachts. She had to admire its sleek lines. Probably belonged to some visiting one percenter or rock star. Turned out, it was their ride.

She and Jamal waited on the dive deck for Zai who insisted on supervising the small private crew. It was the first time she and Jamal had been alone for any length of time out of the water.

"So, do you get to go with your dad on some of his dives? It must be pretty exciting."

Jamal sprawled his long legs out the entire length of a bench on the dive deck, arms winged behind his head like he dove off a luxury live-aboard yacht every day of his life. "Waste of funding if you ask me."

Jamal sat up, rested his elbows on his knees and fixed her with an earnest gaze. His resemblance to his father never failed to give her a jolt.

"I'm more interested in saving what's left of the oceans we humans fu—, I mean, messed up. We've learned all we need to know about the past. We need to invest our time and assets in this planet's future."

Spoken like a true modern teen.

"And what would you invest in, Jamal? Right now. Today. If you could?"

A swell lifted the boat as one of the crew cleared the transom and secured the diving platform at the stern. Jamal watched them with hooded eyes; she could almost see the wheels turning in his brain.

"There's not a lot more I can do about climate change. It's pretty much a done deal. Other than conserving, we're pretty much stuck with what is."

They were alone again, the boat's small crew getting ready to move to another location. Lexi had a gorgeous view of the late afternoon sun slanting against the distant shoreline. Jamal's gaze was fixed in the opposite direction, to the Pacific horizon.

The winds had kicked up a couple of naughts since they'd finished their dive for the day; Lexi pulled dry towels from the rack against the cockpit wall and wrapped it around her shoulders and offered him the other.

He shrugged and shook his head. "I'm good." He sat forward, a lively spark built in his eyes as he talked. "There's people in the Florida Keys who have successfully cultivated star corals that do okay at higher water temperatures. They've already spawned on their own. If the new corals survive—"

"So, you want to work on saving the coral?"

"It's better for me, at least, to find something specific to focus on, otherwise I just feel overwhelmed."

Fifteen going on thirty. "I agree."

He perked up. "You do?"

"I tell my patients that all the time. Better to focus on what you can do, rather than something over which you have no control."

He dropped his gaze to the deck, falling silent a moment before he caught her eyes again. "It was fun. Today. Diving with you." He sat up and rubbed his hands on his thighs a couple of times. "It was kind of a dream I had. You know, you and dad and me. Together." A dreamy smile settled around his mouth, his eyes downcast again as he pulled a long draught of air through his nose.

Lexi was stunned, but she shouldn't have been. She didn't know a kid of a single parent who didn't at some point dream about getting his parents back together. "A dream?"

The smile folded in again, his voice lowered. "I only wish…"

They both turned their heads when Zai stepped up on deck, dressed in casual pants and a Henley shirt that showed off his muscular shoulders. "Gear checked and stowed."

Lexi pulled the towel closer around her at a fresh blast of chilly wind. "Isn't the crew supposed to do that for you?"

Zai shrugged. "Survival instinct, I guess. I always check and stow my own gear, and this trip, that includes yours and Jamal's."

He sat a moment near the transom, a broad smile brightening his expression. "So, has Jamal been indoctrinating you in his beliefs?"

"Beliefs?" Jamal let go an eyeroll that would put a fifteen-year-old girl to shame. "Facts, dad. NOAA. Look it up."

Lexi couldn't hold back a giggle. The National Oceanic and Atmospheric Administration was favorited on her computer, along with a link to local conditions. Zai stood, squeezed his son's shoulder, and the look on his face said he was extremely proud.

"Anyway," he went on. "It's getting windy out here. The crew's setting up a meal in the lounge, but if you hurry, you two have time to get a warm shower and change."

In a private suite bigger than her bedroom at home, she sluiced salt water off her skin in an *en suite* bath with golden dolphin faucets and a gilded mirror over a vanity against the bulkhead. A bit gaudy for her taste, but who could complain? Tessa's little sailboat didn't even have a real head, let alone a five-star bath complete with bidet.

She unfurled a pair of white jeans from her roller bag and topped them with a nautical turtleneck sweater, the coin necklace tucked snugly underneath, next to her heart. She twisted her fingers through loose curls and let them fall where they may as she slipped into the pair of white deck shoes she'd bought just for the trip. Remembering how she'd looked like a salty drowned rat the day she'd challenged Zai in his limo, she checked the full-length mirror on the back of the *en suite* door and gave the look a nod of approval. Neither salty nor pretentious, she felt like…well, she felt like herself.

They were waiting for her in the main deck lounge; not the Titanic, but by far, the fanciest vessel she had ever been on.

Zai's eyes said it all when she paused at the doorway. The butterflies were back. Apparently they had multiplied. Jamal, like every teenager, was busy scanning his cell phone, and merely grunted when she said hello.

Annoyance at the boy's response played across Zaire's features, but he let it go; the sign of a parent who picks his battles. Today, Zaire was here for peace and it showed in his smile.

With an ease she hadn't felt in a while, Lexi stepped inside. There was a buffet table set with an array of cheeses and crackers, grilled shrimp and pan-seared scallops, a couple of different healthy salads; and if she weren't mistaken, there was an iced bowl of shiny black caviar in the center of a plate of deep-fried mini red potatoes. Someone in the kitchen had taken the time to pipe a perfect button of sour cream on each one.

She moved on to pick up a plate and selected a few items. "I have to say you were right about staying on the boat. This is much nicer than any hotel in Mission Bay."

Zai nodded. "It was the best I could do on short notice."

"Really? What would it be if you had more time? A hot tub on the sun deck? Cocktails at sunset? Wait. Gambling Casino?"

Zai laughed now, cruising the table while he loaded a plate. "Hardly. I'd love to show you our exploration dive boat. Fortunately for us, she's on assignment right now, earning her keep. Dock fees alone are enough to bankrupt the non-profit if I don't keep her working."

"She?"

"Salacia. The goddess of salt water."

Jamal surfaced from a deep dive into his text messages. "She's from a Greek myth. Salacia hooked up with Neptune and their kid was named Triton," he droned, his voice mocking.

He scraped a half dozen shrimp, a pile of potatoes, and a huge spoonful of caviar onto his plate and dumped cocktail sauce over the whole thing.

Zai sent Jamal a grin. "Triton was supposedly part boy and part fish, like somebody else I know."

Jamal's mouth turned up at the corners no matter how hard he tried to maintain his aloof demeanor. "Yeah, and Salacia rode on a chariot made of shells pulled by dolphins."

Lexi tasted a butter-drenched scallop. Perfection. "Sounds romantic to me."

Jamal snorted. "I think the Greeks ate hallucinogenic mushrooms." He popped a bite into his mouth and slipped a vodka shooter out of the holder. Zai had it out of his fingers before he could blink.

Jamal harrumphed. "Just kidding."

Zai sat in a club chair near sliding glass doors that offered a full view of the mainland in the distance. He patted the cushion in the chair next to him, inviting her to sit.

"My Salacia smells like dead fish and diesel fuel. She has all the technical equipment you would expect, but not many luxuries. We do have an excellent chef on board, but we all eat in the galley on well-worn benches. I don't take it on private dives. She needs a large crew and enough fuel to run five of these yachts."

He popped a caviar-loaded potato into his mouth and chased it with a shot of vodka. "Although," he said with a glint in his eye, "A hot tub might be a nice addition. I'll have to run that by my investors."

Jamal, eyes back on his cell phone, managed to respond, "I'm up for that."

"Hot tub or no," Lexi said, her eyes on Zai. "I really had fun today. Thank you for putting this trip together for us." She glanced at Jamal who was devouring his food in one hand and playing some kind of app game in the other. She set down her plate, her appetite satisfied for now. "I really enjoyed being with both of you."

Zai's eyes were on Jamal, too. "We'll be heading over to Catalina for the night, then anchor off the Farnsworth Bank for tomorrow's dive."

Jamal jolted to attention, his expression lit up like he'd seen his first Christmas tree. "Dog, you didn't tell me."

"*Dog*," Zai mimicked, and ruffled Jamal's hair as he got up for seconds on everything. "The older you get, the harder it is to surprise you."

"I've dived off Catalina a few times, but not on Farnsworth Bank," Lexi said, returning her gaze to

Jamal. "I'm guessing there's some kind of coral there to get you all up and excited."

Watching the two of them, Lexi was overcome with all she had missed. The son she was meeting for the first time at fifteen was definitely an enigma. Part boy, part man. And after trailing him around underwater today, probably part fish.

All pretense of aloofness gone, Jamal was fully animated, excited about tomorrow's dive. She couldn't help wondering if Ruby looked like him. Would they ever know? Her heart squeezed a little ache at the thought and the ache stayed with her for the rest of the meal.

Before long they were rolling through swells motoring toward Catalina. In the harbor, Jamal launched a kayak off the stern, leaving Zai and Lexi alone on the sun deck, mai tai's in hand, their legs stretched out on a comfortable double lounge.

"I want you back before sunset," Zai called out to Jamal as he paddled toward the shore. "And don't go out of the harbor." Jamal waved without turning around.

"You're not worried about him going off alone in the kayak?"

"Sure. But he's capable. And safety minded."

"And fifteen."

Zai sipped his fruit-laden drink, set it on a cocktail table and turned to face her, one eyebrow raised. "So already the protective mom?"

Her face heated, realizing her remark had been almost a knee-jerk response. "I've counseled lots of fifteen-year-olds," she said, tasting her drink for the first time. The liquor slid down her throat, icy smooth rum laced with lime and good orgeat syrup. The butterflies that had been holding a party in her stomach since she'd walked out on this deck had landed, letting her relax for the first time in days.

She rolled her face to his, the low sun highlighting the angles of his cheekbones. "He's amazing, Zai. You've done a really good job with him."

He reached over and took her free hand in his, knitting their fingers together in a loose grip. "I gotta give my folks credit for most of it. The last few years have been…enlightening to say the least. Home schooled. Constant travel. This trip, here in California, it's really the first time he's been around kids his own age for any length of time. I loosened the reins a little and he's been basking in it."

She rubbed her thumb against his, a warmth spreading in her chest. "Teens are tough. I can attest, having been one myself." She gazed in the direction Jamal had headed, thinking she saw him pulling his kayak up on the beach. She pointed, Zai nodded; and they watched him make his way up to the main road, heading for what Lexi remembered was an ice cream shop. She breathed out a long sigh. "I've missed a lot."

He lifted their hands across his chest and up to his lips, planted a soft kiss on the back of hers. Then, he turned toward her, stretched out and rolled up on his elbow, propping his head up with his hand. His wide grin warmed the deepest hollow inside her heart.

"What?"

He shrugged. "Nothing. I just can't believe we're really here. Together. It's one of those things that just doesn't happen."

She pinched her arm, returned his grin. "Well, apparently, I'm really here," she said, though she didn't quite believe it either.

She sipped her drink and put it down, then mirrored his position. He brought their hands up to nestle against his chest, the pupils of his eyes widening.

"Oh. I see where this is going," Lexi crooned.

"You do?" His gaze slipped down to her mouth for a slow moment before it returned to her eyes.

"You sent Jamal ashore so you could get me alone." The prospect excited her in a way she hadn't been in a very long time.

Zai made an exaggerated check of his watch. "I'd say we've got about forty-five minutes before sundown. Give or take."

His words made her insides contract, sending a sizzling charge through her whole body. There was no way she would let this moment pass. She'd been waiting for it—dreaming about it—for fifteen years. She scooted a little closer, reached out and cupped his cheek in her hand, then raised her lips to place a tentative kiss on his mouth. "I think that would be enough time, don't you?"

He slid his arm around her, flattened his hand at the base of her spine, and pulled her against his outstretched body. His kiss was tender, then hungry, then absolutely consuming. He rolled her up onto his chest and ran his hands down her sides, then caught her rear cheeks and pressed her achingly close against his thighs. There was no mistaking his readiness for whatever she'd allow.

"I don't think there will ever be enough time to make up for what we've lost," he said on a low moan.

Well said, still, she pushed away a moment, the palms of her hands gentle against his pectorals, glancing around the sundeck, suddenly aware of their surroundings. They had moored at one of the outer buoys; no other boats were nearby. There was a cruise ship at the other side of the harbor far enough away anyone interested would need binoculars to see any detail about the yacht, and even then, she could see the deck was designed for privacy; probably for moments exactly like this one.

She relaxed a little. "You really did put this together, didn't' you?"

He bent down, nipped a light kiss on the tip of her nose. "Um hum."

Her next breath came in slowly as she circled her arms around his neck and drew him in. Their bodies laced together the way their hands had earlier, muscle memory, heart and soul. A coupling that could have been awkward was instead the fulfillment of a deep-seated longing. Easy and desperate in turns, but completely, impossibly, satisfying.

For the first time in—years—all was right in her world. Well, almost. But it was enough to see light on the horizon and she would take that. When they'd been young, she could tell him anything, and here they were together again. They couldn't be together unless she was truthful with him about her present state of mind. It was time to put all her cards on the table.

"There he is," Zai said, drawing her back to the moment. He had the binoculars lifted to his eyes aimed toward shore. "He's on his way back." He put them down, and she could see his shoulders relax.

"Good." She settled back into the cushions and sought out his hand once more.

He lifted his glass. "Want a refill?"

She shook her head. "Later, maybe. There's something I'd like—I need—to tell you. Before Jamal gets back."

His brows went up. "Oh?"

He put down his glass and sat in front of her giving her all his attention.

She sat up yoga style and took both his hands in hers. "It's kind of…personal."

"Wait. This isn't like some Nicholas Sparks novel where the lovers finally get together only to find one is dying." His tone was only half joking. There was real concern in those eyes as he tightened his grip on her fingers.

She laughed. "No. Nothing like that." *Worse, maybe.* Sharing her secret could mean she'd lose both of her men. "Just listen, okay? I really want to know what you think. And if you never want to see me again or let me near Jamal after—"

"What? Did you rob a bank? Kill somebody?"

She huffed out a sigh. She could see Jamal was about halfway to the boat and she needed to start this conversation at least while he wasn't in earshot. "Just. Listen. Please."

"Okay," he agreed, glancing over his shoulder.

Damn, she should have thought this through more. Where to start? She thought about his presentation, his fascination with the wreck of the Demeter. She should frame it to make sense for him. Tease his imagination. *Yes. That's it.*

"What if I told you there was a way you could find out all that happened to the Demeter without having to deep dive to it? What if I told you I was there? Saw it happen?"

He stared at her, stunned. She studied his eyes which were wide with, what? Disbelief? Concern? Doubt?

He started to shake his head. "So you...dreamed..."

"No. Yes. I mean. This is going to be hard to understand, but both Tessa and I have been caught up in something hard to explain. A past life regression thing is easiest to think about, but...this—the fact that you and I have come together at this moment—this is the part that makes it important."

He held her hands, but there was a deep cleft developing between his brows.

She let go a moment and rubbed her forehead. "Okay. Before you showed up; I experienced what I'll call a vision, for lack of a better word at the moment."

He pinned her with a penetrating gaze. "Go on."

She had his full attention now. There was nowhere to go but forward and take whatever consequences came of it.

"Before I even knew of the possibility that you might come back into my life, I had visions of a fleet of Auksumite ships on the Mediterranean. Their mission was to deliver the last shipment of wheat to Rome. The primary ship, the one loaded with the grain, was the Demeter, bound for Ostia."

His eyes grew wide.

"The captain of one of the transport fleet was a woman. Lesidi."

She lifted the coin necklace out of her sweater and dangled between them. "The fleet commander, the captain of the Demeter, gave Lesidi a coin necklace just like this one."

Just then, Jamal strolled on to the sun deck, rubbing his hair with a towel. "Hey, guys. What's that?"

Chapter 33- Truth Be Told

Zaire's heart thudded in his chest as Jamal padded toward them, pulling a faded T-shirt down over his chest. He recognized the sheepish grin on his son's face.

"Hey," he said, taking in their close proximity with a cagey grin. "What *are* you guys up to?"

Lexi's cheeks, still flushed from their intimacy moments before, reddened even more. She opened her mouth to speak, but Jamal cut her off, his eyes on the necklace dangling between them.

"That's just like this one." He looped his finger around the chain at his neck and brought out his coin necklace.

It was true. It was identical to the one Zaire had made for his son after his first dive, just like the one his dad had given him—the one Lexi wore now.

Just like the one Lexi had seen in a vision of an ancient female mariner. It was a fanciful concept difficult for a man of science to believe. The three coins may not have all come from the same wreck, but they were definitely minted at the same time in the ancient history of his own country. What if they were the key to unlock a door into the ancient world?

Zai's father had always accused him of being a dreamer. Most explorers were. Which was why the notion intrigued him more than he wanted to admit.

It hadn't been that long ago that Jamal had awakened in the night, the t-shirt he'd slept in soaked in sweat, claiming he'd drowned in a storm at sea. He'd described a ship that sounded like so many wrecks in the Med, now worm-eaten and forlorn. They had called it a nightmare, but was it? After the story Lexi had just told him, Zaire wasn't so sure.

Lexi reached out her hand to Jamal's coin. "May I see it?"

Jamal glanced at his father. Zaire's fingertips tingled with a sudden adrenaline prickle. What was the worst thing that could happen? More nightmares? Jamal had so far been able to shake those off. "Sure," he said finally. He hoped including Jamal in the story wasn't going to come back to haunt him.

With a light of excitement in his eyes Zaire had seldom seen, Jamal scooted next to Lexi on the lounge and held the necklace out to her on the end of its chain.

She thumbed it carefully. "Zai, where did you and your father find the coins?"

Zai thought a moment, closing his eyes. It had been the first dive he'd done where they'd actually found something. "On the Bosphorus. In fairly shallow waters off Istanbul. You could see old Emperor's Palace from there. They were minted in what was then Auksum, if I have my facts right."

"You do indeed," she said. "King Ezana, the face on the coin, was the leader of what was then the center of trade in the middle east and Asia." Then to Jamal she asked, "Do you wear it all the time?"

Jamal lifted a shoulder coyly. "I guess so."

Zai watched the two of them, their heads nearly touching as Lexi examined the coin. He started to slip his cell phone out of his pocket, then let it slide back in, realizing he didn't need a photo to preserve the magic of this moment. The intimacy he and Lexi had shared only a few moments before, and Jamal's easy way with her had been his secret dream and now it was playing out before his eyes.

The scientist in him wanted to challenge everything she'd said, especially now, with his son in the mix.

The dreamer in him had to wonder. Lexi had described the feeling of drowning, being sucked down into the depths, the shadow of an ancient ship below. It was almost verbatim what Jamal had told him the night he woke up in a cold sweat. Their stories nearly identical; told from different points of view.

"Jamal. Tell your mom about your dream."

Lexi sent Zai a tender smile before her eyes shifted to Jamal. "What? Did you have a nightmare?"

He shrugged, suddenly self-conscious. "It was stupid, is all. Had it a couple of times. Dad thinks it's why I don't like to dive wrecks."

She raised an eyebrow at Zai a moment before she returned the coin to Jamal. She rubbed her own coin between her fingers as she talked. "Were you wearing the necklace when you had the dream?"

Zaire sat forward, rested his elbows on his knees. He dropped his head and rubbed the back of his neck, then shot his gaze to Lexi. "You think the coins are the key to the place? The time?"

"I'm not sure what to think right now, Zai. Jamal and I had similar experiences. I was wearing the coin at the time."

"Yes!" Jamal blurted. "I was wearing it." He stole to the side of the boat, gripped the gunwale, and looked over the side a moment before he turned and faced them. "I was wearing it every time."

Zai recognized a sudden reticence in his son's tone. He didn't hold back from him often, but when he did, it was written all over his face and the set of his shoulders. He'd been open about the nightmare the first time. And he'd admitted to having another. But every time? That implied it had happened again and Jamal hadn't told him about that. So, how many times it had it happened? When had it started and, why hadn't he told him about it?

Jamal glanced at Lexi now, a new energy burning in his words. "It was just like you said. When I held the coin close, pressed it between my fingers, I could sense…see… a different world."

Zai's stomach plummeted to his toes. It was bad enough that the two of them had some mysterious connection through the necklace, but the fact that Jamal had surreptitiously listened to their conversation was disturbing. He thought he'd taught his son better. Thought he knew him better. Apparently he'd been mistaken and that sent a cold spike through his heart. "Jamal. You eavesdropped on us?"

His son slid his gaze to the deck. "I'm sorry, dad. I was coming up the ladder and heard her telling you...I couldn't believe it. So when I got to the door, I just... I had to hear the rest. I feel like I know some of it. Like, I've seen the same things."

His son's confession sent a chill up his neck. "How many times have you had the dream?"

Jamal let his necklace dangle. He sent Lexi a sheepish look.

She shrugged. "You might as well tell us, son. It's already out there. We just have to figure out what it means."

Jamal sent Zai a wary look. "A bunch. I tried to make it take me somewhere else, but it goes to that shipwreck every time."

Lexi dropped her head in her hands. "I'm sorry, Zai. I didn't know."

Zai shook his head and let himself drop back to the lounge, blew out a rough sigh. "How could you? This whole thing is like some bizarre Spielberg film."

"Cool," Jamal said.

He frowned at his son, but he couldn't deny the adrenaline rush still pumping in his veins. "I've never been one to believe things happen for a reason. Science dictates a more rational point of view." It was one thing to indulge a woman he didn't actually know all that well in a little fantasy. We all have them at one time or another. But it was quite another to have his son pick up the story line and carry it a few more yards. "But, here we are, relating incidents there is no other way to explain." He lifted his gaze to Lexi and pressed his lips together in a tight line a moment before he said, "You and Jamal are linked through the coins."

"And blood," she said. "We're linked through DNA."

The air on the deck seemed to thin and disappear altogether, rendering Zaire speechless.

Jamal speared his gaze back and forth between the two of them, his mouth also working with nothing coming out. And then, like any child wishing to preserve peace in the family, he cleared his throat dramatically, and pointed at the mini fridge behind the lounge. "Can I get something to drink?"

Zaire blinked at him a moment, then exhaled. "Sure. Why don't you get us all something?"

Jamal brought back three cans of Diet Coke and passed them around. He pished open his own can and dropped onto a cushioned bench along the privacy panel. Taking a long drink, he leaned forward and dangled the Coke between his knees. "I learned I could make it happen under certain conditions."

The revelation hit Zai hard in the gut. "*Make* it happen? Like, what conditions?"

Jamal cricked his mouth up to one side. "When I was … thinkin' about … her." He tipped his head toward Lexi.

Zai locked eyes with Lexi, his heart fisted up in his chest. No way he could stop himself wading in. The question had to be asked.

"Lexi, when exactly did you find the necklace? I know it was when you opened the things your mother sent you, but when exactly was that?"

He could see her hands were shaking when she dropped her necklace inside her sweater and grasped her hands in her lap.

"It was about three months ago. I could check my receipts from the storage facility, but right now, I'd say three months. Tessa helped me clear out the storage unit and I found the necklace that night."

"And when did you first get the sense it was connected to your visions?"

She leaned back against the cushions and sipped her Coke. "I think it was that same night. I was at Tessa's and I lost track of time for a little while, I don't remember seeing anything, but I definitely lost track of time standing out on Phillip's deck. When I realized I'd sort of dropped out, I was pressing the coin between my fingers."

He turned to Jamal now, who was staring at his Coke can; his teeth clamped so hard on his bottom lip Zai was afraid he would draw blood.

He went to Jamal and gently caressed his shoulder. "Son?"

Jamal looked up, surprised. Then he squeezed his eyes shut a moment before he refocused on Lexi. Zai's heart pounded against his chest. He had so wanted this trip to be meaningful for them. A new beginning. Bizarre was not part of his expectation.

Jamal straightened, set his Coke on the bench next to him. He rubbed his fingers over his lips a couple of times before he spoke.

"Okay. So…" He paused, huffed out a low sigh. "Everybody thinks I got your information from the adoption agency. But I didn't. I'd thought about trying to find you someday, but I had no idea where to start. Anyway, this woman showed up at our compound. Tall, classy African lady." He sent Lexi an apologetic look, before he shifted his gaze to Zaire. "She asked for you, dad, and, well, you weren't there, of course."

The barb hit hard. Zai deserved it, but he held back a stab of self-recrimination to let his son speak.

"I wouldn't have known she was at the gate except I was just returning from a trip we'd taken to Chobe River." His eyes lit up a moment and he turned once again to Lexi. "There's this cool resort there—"

"Jammer," Zai said, his tone indulgent.

"Um. Sorry." He waved his excitement away. "Anyway, when she saw me at the gate? I thought her eyes would pop out of her face."

Lexi perked up. "Wait, the compound? You mean in Bole?"

"You know about it?"

"Well, of course I do. I visited there a couple of times. With your father. My family and I vacationed with your grandparents." She told him about being expats together in DC. Going on dive trips up to the Mediterranean.

Zai fisted his hands, recalling the last time Lexi had been there with her family. She was probably already pregnant with the twins and neither of them knew it.

"So, this woman said she knew my birth mother. Not only who she was but where to find her if I wanted. She said it was only right."

"My mother," Lexi said, her voice a whisper.

She pressed trembling lips together, lifting her eyes to his. "Jamal. I'm so sorry. I knew she was back on the Continent, but I had no idea she would try to contact you. I didn't even know about you."

Zai moved in next to her, took her into his arms, his heart aching to see she could barely push out the words.

"That night?" Jamal went on. "It was the first time I had a vision with the coin." He shifted his gaze to Zai. "Sorry dad. I never told you. It was just too…crazy. I didn't want you to be worried."

"It's all right, son. Let's just get this all out in the open so we know what we're dealing with."

Jamal nodded and went on. "So that night when I went to bed, all I could think about was I had a mother out there somewhere who wanted to know me," he said. He pulled the coin to the end of its chain. "I was rubbing the coin between my fingers and thinking about her and all of a sudden it was like my room fell away and I felt like I was floating in warm water kind of peaceful, like rocking on a calm swell. And I could hear, like, a heartbeat. Slow. Steady. All around me. It wasn't a nightmare. It was…amazing."

Lexi's hand tightened around Zai's. "Oh my god."

Jamal's eyes glazed over and his voice grew quiet as he relayed his story. "And the craziest thing was, I wasn't alone. I had the distinct feeling someone else was there with me, up against my back, our hearts beating in sync."

He looked up at both of them now, his eyes wide. "Now I know it was my sister."

He bunched his lips, shook his head. "That's when I decided to try to find you," he said to Lexi. "Are you mad at me?"

A laugh burst out of her. "Mad? That doesn't begin to describe how I feel at this moment." She threaded her fingers through her hair, gripped tight for a moment. "Oh, I'm mad all right. But not at you. How could any of this possibly be your fault?"

He lifted a shoulder. "I should have called first or written. Instead, I barged in on you at your work. It was rude, I know. I just …" He dragged in a ragged breath and his eyes brimmed wet, ready to spill.

Lexi got up and went to her son. She sat beside him and put her arm around his shoulder. "Jamal. You did exactly the right thing. You are a curious, exciting, and completely lovable young man. My mother should never have approached you that way. She had absolutely no right to disrupt your life."

She glanced over at Zai. He smiled at her, his heart blowing up like a big balloon.

"Listen, Jamal," Lexi went on. "My whole life I've hoped I'd done the right thing by putting my baby up for adoption. I'm not a religious person, but I prayed my daughter lived in a loving home with parents who could give her the moon. I secretly celebrated her birthdays, even though I'd never seen her since that day. Three months ago I got a form to notify the agency to give out my information if my daughter inquired. I was afraid to send it. What if she rejected me? Instead, I hear from you. A son! One who sought me out. Wanted *me*. That can't be a bad thing. I mean, look at us," she said, leaning over to catch Zai's eyes. "We're here together and it feels right, doesn't it?"

Zai got up and sat on Jamal's other side, slipped his arm around his shoulders. So many jagged, missmatched pieces of his life were starting to fit together and he couldn't think of a better time to get it all in the light. But the primary question remained and he could not ignore it.

"It feels fantastic." He laced his fingers though his son's. "But none of this explains the nightmare. Where does that fit in all this?"

Jamal shuddered a moment. "Those came later."

"And…"

"I was in bed, holding the coin again. I wanted to see if I could go to that warm place, figure out what it was, you know?"

Lexi nodded.

"But instead, when I rubbed the coin, everything around me went suddenly dark and cold. Instead of floating, I was tumbling and my lungs felt like they would explode. I opened my eyes and I saw…" he clenched his eyes tight. "I saw a woman. She was tumbling, too, her clothes swirling all around and I couldn't hold my breath anymore and I opened my mouth and…"

"What did she look like?" Lexi interrupted excitedly.

"What? Ah. I don't—"

"Just think a minute. Was she young, old? Dark, blonde?"

Jamal's brows slammed together; Zai could feel Jamal's heart pounding against his ribs as he held him tight. "She was dark; her eyes glowed like gold lamps; her hair was a hundred braids with gold beads woven in. They flowed out from her head like tiny ropes. And…" He stopped a moment, his eyes wide. "She had a necklace."

He turned to Zai, shaking his head excitedly. "A necklace, like this," he exclaimed, holding his out.

"It was Lesidi," Lexi said with conviction, fixing her gaze on Zai's. "It was the same vision I saw. Only mine was from her point of view. The man with her was Keleb. The commander of the fleet; the captain of the Demeter."

And then the image hit her square between the eyes. "And there was a boy. A young man. Dracis." She fixed her eyes on her son.

Zai sat back a moment, his mind wheeling with possibility. Nobel prize winning physicists agree science is barren without imagination. Who was he to argue with Einstein and Wilczek?

What if… he thought, watching the excitement build in his son's eyes. What if there *was* a way to the visit the past as Lexi had described? What if they were wearing the key around their necks?

Chapter 34 – Lexi Seizes the Sword

Tessa pulled a baking pan of enchiladas out of the warming oven and set them on top of the stove while Lexi prepared a bowl of fresh salsa.

"So how did he take it?" Tessa asked.

Lexi peeked into the front room where Phillip, Zai, and Jamal were whooping it up in Tessa's living room over a highly competitive game of Grand Theft Auto while she and Tessa worked on their feast.

"Let's just say that tonight is the first time I've seen Zaire relax since Catalina."

She'd put in a busy week at the office, not only in her own practice, but now that she owned the building, she had a ton of other issues to deal with. And, after learning of Zai's intention to open an office for his non-profit in California, she and Robbi had begun clearing out a suite abandoned by its previous user in somewhat of a mess.

One thing was certain: Zai was serious about supporting her relationship with his son. And with his newly minted friendship with Phillip who was using his extensive knowledge of the law to work on his immigration status, Zai had settled into the idea of making himself available as well.

The dive trip had been a fabulous opener. In fact, she'd been surprised how well the final day went after all they'd shared the night before. Watching Zai and her son together was beginning to fill a hollow place in her heart. And every now and then, when Jamal stole a look at her, the corner of his mouth curled, punching a dimple in his cheek. They were good for each other and that was worth nurturing. She felt hopeful for her future as well as theirs.

She stirred a pot of black beans she'd brought over from home, replaced the lid, and lowered the heat. Like she'd said in the beginning, they should take it slow. But she couldn't help remembering how amazing it felt to have Zaire's body next to hers after all this time. He even smelled the same; the thought of it sent a delicious heat wave through her body.

She put down the spoon let out a sigh. "I just hope I haven't ruined everything by telling him the truth."

Tessa pulled oven mitts off her hands and put an arm around Lexi's shoulders. "Judging by the way he looks at you, I'd say you were in no danger of that."

"You think?"

"Tell you what. After dinner, we'll take him down to the workshop and show him the photos of the jewelry and Phillip can tell him his version of it. Coming from another guy, he might take it a little better."

"Honestly, I don't think he's as worried about what happened to you as much as he is about Jamal's involvement."

Tessa mushed up some avocado in a *molcajete*, dropped in some of Lexi's salsa, and squeezed lime over the mix. "Grab those chips," she ordered, and headed for the other room which had grown suddenly quiet.

"So, with that snake bracelet on her arm and the cloisonne brooch nearby, she actually went back in time?" Jamal's eyes flashed with curiosity.

Lexi stopped in the doorway and held her hand up for Tessa to do the same.

Zai had the game controller, headphones clamped over his ears, deep into his game session. Phillip and Jamal had their heads together.

"Not exactly," Phillip went on, unaware of their presence. "Her body was here, but her mind was definitely somewhere else."

"Wow."

"It's not to be taken lightly, son. There's more to it. People have gotten hurt. It's important you don't try anything on your own. We're not exactly sure…"

Lexi had heard enough. "Damn right we're not sure." She plunked the bowl of chips on the coffee table and Tessa put down the guac.

Jamal jumped to his feet, stabbing his gaze back and forth between the women. "Can the bracelet really move on its own?"

Tessa huffed out a sigh. Phillip looked up and shrugged, face turning crimson. "He asked me what I knew and I wasn't going to lie to him."

Tessa gave him eyeroll. "What if Lexi doesn't want him involved?"

"He's already involved, Tess." He shifted his eyes to Lexi, gave her a hang dog look. "Better he knows what that means than blundering through into something he can't get out of."

Zai hollered a victory score, oblivious to the conversation behind him.

"That should be Zai's decision, not yours," Lexi added.

Phillip rubbed his hands on his thighs and looked to his wife for support.

Jamal shoved his hands into his pockets. "Dad already knows. We talked about it earlier."

"Funny," Lexi said, "I don't remember that conversation."

"That's because it was just us guys," Jamal said, chin up.

Lexi huffed out a long sigh. "And what did you learn?"

"That the bracelet helped Tess find that brooch. That the lady in the past made it."

Tessa's eyes cut to Phillip. "And that's *all* you told him?"

Phillip lifted a shoulder. "Pretty much."

"I just want to see it. I won't touch it, I promise." He helped himself to a handful of chips and tucked into the guacamole.

Lexi's hands turned suddenly old at the memory of a woman's body lying in the courtyard below because of that damned serpent bracelet.

She took his shoulders in both her hands. "Lexi's workshop is off limits to you. It's like Phillip said," she went on, "We don't exactly know what the bracelet is capable of."

After all Jamal had done since coming to California with his father, she knew he was quite capable of taking matters into his own hands.

"I want that promise," she said solemnly, having no idea whether he would honor it.

Jamal fell silent and, after a moment, nodded, but turned away. She gently touched his chin with a finger, turning his face to hers. "I need you to say it. Right now, in front of all of us."

"Ok-ay. I promise," he said, petulantly.

She glanced at Phillip, then Tessa, then back to her son. "Okay. Poke *Franklin* over there and tell him dinner is ready."

"Franklin?" Tessa asked on the way back to the kitchen.

"A character in the game. There's a trio of thieving criminals roaring around in crash cars. It's actually kind of fun."

Tess raised a brow. "Can't blame Jamal for being interested in the bracelet. Kids are so into role play scenarios these days."

"Yeah. Well, we both know that damn snake is more than just a little role play."

Tessa loaded the first plate with tamales, rice, and some of Lexi's beans. "Let's hope we don't have to find out how much more."

The evening progressed to Lexi's balcony for dessert—a little flan, a little banana coconut cake. It was the first time since taking over the property she'd entertained anyone at home. The essence of Audrey nearly shimmered in the room. Lexi beamed at the thought. *This is what you wanted to happen, sweet lady. Thank you.*

Tessa offered Lexi another piece of the cake.

"Oh gosh, no I'm stuffed." She nodded toward Jamal who had crashed in the lounge chair in a quiet corner of her deck. "I need to make the up the bed in my spare room. Zai says after all the drinks this evening, he doesn't want to drive back to Carlsbad tonight and I agree."

Tessa's eyes went wide. "*Oooooh.* That could be fun."

Lexi grinned back at her. "One can only hope."

A half hour later they'd said their goodbyes to Tess and Phillip, and Zai guided a half-asleep Jamal up the stairs and into bed.

He stood on her deck now, gazing across the Grand Canal.

"Jamal sure likes his Mexican food," Lexi crooned. "I thought we'd have enchiladas left over for lunch tomorrow. But they're gone."

Zai let go a laugh. "Welcome to my world."

She came up behind him and in a move emboldened by what was left of a tequila buzz, circled her arms around his waist, and pressed her cheek into his warm back. "I'm beginning to like your world."

Zai set his glass on the railing and turned in her arms. He pulled her close, rubbing his fingers gently up and down her spine until her knees went nearly liquid.

He slid a hand up between them and tilted her face to his. "I like your friends, Lex."

"Family," she corrected. "Phillip and Tessa are my family. I don't know how I would have gotten through the last few years without them."

"Phil says the same about you."

"He does?"

He leaned his cheek on top of her head, turning so they could both see the lights wiggling their reflections across the Grand Canal. "He told me everything, Lex."

She tipped her face up to look into his eyes. "Everything?"

"How they found the jewelry in the walls of the house. How the bracelet affected Tessa. How she found the cloisonné brooch, the *accident*."

Lexi swallowed hard, realizing the depth of the conversation Zai and Phillip had had. "That's what he said it was? An accident?"

Zai frowned at her. "Wasn't it?"

Lexi's stomach did a little tumble. "A woman died in a fall off Tessa's top floor balcony. But it was no accident. That bracelet made it happen."

Zai leveled his gaze at her. "You believe the bracelet has some kind of dark power."

His tone was skeptical, but not accusatory.

"I don't know whether it's altogether dark, but it's something for sure. Still, I don't want you thinking I'm some kind of nut case you don't want around our kid."

He leaned in, pressed a tender kiss on her lips. "Not going to happen," he whispered. He guided her through the sliding doors and closed them behind her, then sank down on the L-shaped sofa, his legs stretched out, hers lifted over his. She hadn't felt so comforted, so cared for, since, well, maybe never. She snuggled into him. The feeling was so worth waiting for.

He ran his fingers down her arm, threaded them through hers a moment as they settled into a familiar body meld. "So, Tess was wearing the bracelet when all this happened?"

Lexi nodded. "That's why Valerie trashed her entire bedroom. She'd been up there looking for it. Slashed her mattress, the wallpaper. Who knows how far she would have gone had Tessa not shown up when she did?"

He fingered her hair lazily with his fingertips. She nestled into his touch.

"You have to understand, though, Zai," she said, keeping her voice low. That woman? The one who fell? She was a real person in this timeframe. But when Tess was under the influence of the bracelet, who she *saw* was a woman from the past. Valeria."

He blinked, taking it all in.

"We think she needed the bracelet to get back to her own time; instead, the bracelet protected Tessa and sent her over the railing."

"It shifted its loyalty."

"Or maybe it was never Valeria's to begin with. All I know is when Tessa did a past life regression with the snake on her arm, she went straight back to exactly the time she wanted to be." She tucked her legs under her Yoga style and took his hands in her. "What if we could get it to take us to the Demeter?"

His eyes focused on hers and he bit his bottom lip a minute before he spoke. "You're serious."

Breathing deep, she pictured Lesidi at the prow of her ship, and Keleb on his, unaware of the disaster that awaited them. "I think we could use it to break through to Lesidi and Keleb, warn them somehow. We may not be able to keep the Demeter from sinking, but maybe we could keep them from going down with it."

He blinked back at her, his pupils crowded the center of those amazing amber eyes. "And you need to do this because…"

"Because, if Lesidi is my ancestor, and she dies on that ship before her time? Me, Jamal, my parents, theirs; they might never exist."

"But you *are* here, which means if that's true, they didn't go down with the ship."

"Because they were warned!" Her voice came out louder than she planned. Her eyes shot to the hallway, hoping she hadn't awakened Jamal with her outburst.

He threaded his fingers behind his neck, winging his elbows; his brows converged in a deep cleft down the middle, stretching his back. "Not sure I—"

"I want you to do it with me. Tessa's made a duplicate bracelet, and we've already seen it do some…stuff." That stuff made her nervous, but so did the original golden serpent. "After everything that happened to Tessa, she's here, safe. Pregnant for that matter. We've got nothing to lose, really."

"It sounds like you're convinced."

She couldn't help thinking about her daughter, about never having the chance to see her, to know her. To love her. "I don't have a choice in the matter." She hugged her stomach with both arms, grounding herself in her conviction. "I have to try or everything I know and love—you, Jamal, even our daughter -- could disappear, poof!" She snapped her fingers. "Like that."

He swung his long legs off the couch and pulled her up with him, into in his arms. He smoothed his fingers over her cheek, then brought her face close to his and kissed her gently, then thoroughly, spreading his big hands over her back, then sliding down. She wrapped her arms around his neck and returned his kiss, savoring the taste of him, the memory of him, the very present reality of him as he backwalked her down the hall to the master suite and closed the door. He lay her on her bed, and slipped alongside her, and stared into her eyes, his expression unreadable.

Her heart seized up in her chest. "You think I'm crazy."

He framed her face in his hands and locked those amber eyes on hers.

"I do not think you are crazy, Alexis Hill. I think you are still the most amazing person I have ever met." He kissed her gently and gazed at her again. "I love you."

She pulled in a breath and swallowed hard. "You do?"

"I do. And, I agree with you. I think we should try. Together."

CHAPTER 35 - YOU JUMP, I JUMP

Zai lay next to Lexi on the thick area rug in her front room, their heads propped on pillows, more pillows propped under their knees. The solid gold bracelet coiled against the skin on his biceps, neither particularly warm nor tight. Just there, like the copy Lexi wore on her arm. He doubted he could be hypnotized, he had too strong an ego to let someone manipulate him in that way. But there was no harm in trying, right? Even if he could be hypnotized, they had no idea whether the bracelets would work together; there was only one way to find out. He gripped Lexi's left hand with his right and caught her gaze with his, giving her a reassuring smile. "I'm good. You?"

She looked a little stiff, her breathing a bit shallow, but she bravely gave his fingers a squeeze. "You jump, I jump," she said, "Like Jack and Rose." It seemed a fitting response given their goal.

"You guys ready?" Tessa asked. If she was nervous about doing her first official regression, she was doing a good job of masking it.

"Yeah," Phillip said, sipping a coffee, his expression neutral, as Zai would expect.

Tessa gave him a playful smack on the arm. "Not you, Sherlock," she teased. "Our time travelers."

Time travelers. Zai couldn't hold back a short laugh. What they were about to do was probably nothing more than a parlor game for entertainment on a Saturday afternoon. A self-guided role play with an Ouija board.

A lark.

His father would be vindicated about now. His worthless, wanderer of a son had completely lost it. It's what came of hanging out with scientists and dreamers instead of sticking to the business of making money.

But another part of him—a part that seemed to grow more dominant by the second—felt like he was about to leap off the transom of a dive boat into unexplored waters. *That* part bubbled with anticipation. He and Lexi had agreed they would grip the necklace in their fingers and they'd both concentrate on the Demeter. Whether or not it would work remained to be seen.

He relaxed into the steady, even cadence of Tessa's voice, embracing the heated connection between them where Lexi's fingers entwined in his. The ancient coin was pressed between their palms, a serpent's coil snug on each of their biceps. He turned his head to find her looking back at him and squeezed her hand tight. "We're ready," he said.

Lexi sighed, turned her head back on the pillow and closed her eyes. "Okay. To the Demeter."

"To the Demeter," Zai mimicked, and straightened his head.

"Now," Tessa started in, speaking slowly. "I want you to breathe in and out on the count of four."

Shelving his natural skepticism, Zai relaxed into the floor, deeper with each count.

"Now imagine you're holding the book of your life in your lap. As you turn the pages you can go back in time to memories stored there. As you continue to deep breathe, turn the pages back to a time in your recent past that made you feel warm. Loved. As you think about that time, an image will begin to appear on the page."

Zai felt the book on his lap. It was heavy. Thick. He remembered the day he, Jamal, and Lexi dove together for the first time. He had never felt so free, so hopeful.

"The longer you look at the image, the clearer it becomes. See every detail, feel all the feels of that day."

Zai drew in another deep breath and let it out slowly. Had he really been alive before that day? He didn't think so. Everything had changed--the way the light shown through the water, the way his heartbeat when he saw them together, the way he breathed. A new sense of calm, of permanence, enveloped him and he sank deeper into the warmth of it.

"Good. You guys are doing really well," came Tessa's voice. "Stay relaxed. Breathe slowly, in...and...out."

As he let himself be guided by her voice, he felt increasingly heavy, sank deeper into the carpet.

"Now, turn another page and remember a time in your distant past where you were free and easy and totally happy, relaxed and at peace. Each breath on a four count will bring that time into focus until you can see it clearly."

Zai let himself go, deeper, deeper, until an image began to take shape on the page. He was with Lexi, on a dive boat. The air was warm, the sea around them was quiet and his desire for her filled every cell of his being.

"Now stay with that feeling, wherever you are, and relive the experience of what it was like to be in that moment. Tell me when you are there."

Zai squeezed Lexi's hand and wondered a moment if she were seeing the same thing he was. He was definitely there, feeling the warmth of the Mediterranean sun on his body and in his soul. "I'm…there," he said. His voice, barely a whisper, carried a sluggishness that surprised him.

He vaguely heard Lexi's murmured reply, "Yesss."

He couldn't have turned his head if his life depended on it, he had sunk so deep into the floor.

"Good. Stay there as long as you want, then tell me when you're ready to move on."

He didn't want to move on. Peace filled him like it had never done before, like everything he'd done up until that moment had been leading up to this one.

"Go," Lexi moaned. "I'm ready."

"Good," Tessa answered softly. "Zai?"

Reluctance dragged him down, but a moment later, he felt the heat build at his biceps, saw the serpent's red eyes sharpen in his mind.

"Yes," he whispered. All hesitation dissolved.

"Now take a moment to breathe again and get ready to turn another page."

Heat spread up his arm and across his chest. There was a faint moan like the wind somewhere in the distance.

"Now, I want you to turn the page to a lifetime lived *before* this one. It will be no more difficult than recalling your memories in this life. When you come to the page you want, stop and let the image appear."

The heat intensified, spread to his torso, his thighs. There was a sound of wind racing in his ears. Then suddenly it snapped like the unfurling of a jib on the windswept ocean, grabbing the sheet, taking hold, driving him forward, driving him ...

Chapter 36 – Fausta's Revenge

Lesidi tossed through the night in her makeshift bed under the watchful eye of the swan at the Isis's stern. She lay awake now giving in to the siege of visions that came in wave after ghostly wave, brought on by Dracis's report about Amari and Fausta's plotting. She had spent enough time with Kindra to know that while the young man was impulsive and sometimes incorrigible, he was not a liar. Both Marcus and Kindra vouched for his veracity. If *he* believed Amari and Fausta were planning some kind of outrage, then she would take him at his word.

There was no doubt in her mind that Amari could be led to perform all manner of reckless acts if there was a pile of gold as his reward. She had seen him in action in her dreams. Knew what he was capable of. Raging against him in her head to the point she could not go to sleep wasn't going to resolve the issue. She vowed to confront him at first light about what she had learned, then pulled the heavy furs over her head and gave into to the exhaustion that had overtaken her.

After what seemed like hours of listening to the wind rattle in the sails, at last she floated, buoyant, weightless, her mind drifting into the peacefulness of a dark-blue universe.

Denizens of the deep nosed at her with curiosity, weaving through eerie landscapes bereft of trees or plants or sunlight. The only sound that reached her ears was the sound of her own breath in deep, regular intervals.

The current that had teased her into sleep grew more insistent, more powerful. Where once there was a pleasant pull, now the force of it dragged her onward against her will. Peaceful landscape gave way to tumbled rocks that spilled over a sharp cliff. The current pulled her down, down, down, until what had looked like a tumble of random rocks took the shape of amphorae. Like Ariadne's thread, the amphorae spread out in a trail, one leading to the next and the next, until a larger shape dominated the scene below.

Her heart lurched when her brain caught up with the scene. She was looking at a great ship, resting on the muddy bottom, broken in two, cargo spilling haphazard out of its broken hull—amphorae, ropes, crockery and a great pile of what she now recognized as bales of winnowed wheat. The scene was dynamic, mud still settling around as if the ship had only landed there just a few minutes before.

Her heart caught in her throat. Lifeless bodies were trapped under planks of the broken ship, their hands still gripping the oars holding them in place. Other bodies were caught up in rigging, or drifted, their eyes forever frozen in shock.

The main sail near what was left of the ship's prow unfurled on the current, then billowed wide to reveal the identifying insignia. Her father's trademark, one of the great obelisks of Auksum. *My god, it was the Demeter.*

It took every ounce of her strength to hold her breath and not gasp at the sight, an act which would rob her of life like the corpses that floated below her.

She flinched at a touch on her shoulder and turned to find a body floating right next to her, its arms outstretched. Her heart broke anew when she recognized those shoulders, the hauberk and short knife at his belt. Shaking her head, she gingerly pushed a shoulder, turning the body around enough to bring its face into view.

Keleb, eyes wide, unseeing, mouth frozen in death.

Lesidi could hold her breath no longer. Lungs on fire, she gazed up to the surface. It was impossibly far away. *Why even try, when Keleb was lost to you?* She gasped, expecting a rush of saltwater to invade her soul, but instead, she found herself safe on the Isis, wrapped in furs on the deck where she'd fallen asleep. The Dream again.

"Keleb!" she cried out loud, grief sharp and hollow in her chest.

She sat up and rubbed at the ache. Maybe it was just worry, all the doubt and suspicion she had endured since the Leto went down. She was fine, wasn't she? Alive here on the Isis? And Keleb was fine, too. The Demeter was a strong vessel with a skilled crew; fast and seaworthy. It would take more than a winter storm to sink her. She pulled her furs around her and fought to get her breathing under control.

The voice came at first as a distant echo. *It's real, Lesidi.*

She strained to hear. Then it came again, closer, louder this time. It was Lexi, the goddess who spoke inside her mind.

The dream is my past, but it's your future—yours and Keleb's—unless you do something now to prevent it. Fausta has convinced Amari to help her take revenge on Constantine by sinking the Demeter.

Lesidi shook her head. "But how do you know?"

I have seen it, Lesidi. It is as your dreams show you. Unless you act soon, the Demeter will go to the bottom of the sea with you, and Keleb, and the empire's last shipment of wheat onboard.

* * *

Lesidi drove herself toward the prow of her vessel, the echoes Lexi's words roaring in her brain. *Unless you act soon... Unless you act soon... Unless you act soon...*

"Cyril!" She whipped her head around, where was that man? "Cyril!" She shouted again as loud as she could.

"Here, captain; I didn't expect you to be up so early," he said, quickly fastening his robe around his shoulders. "I'll get the brazier going for some warming tea."

She stalked toward him, her heartbeat thudding hard in her ears. "Forget the tea. Bring my brother to me. *Now.*"

Lesidi paced the deck, her mind racing with images of the lost Demeter. A crisp, cold wind whipped the front mast, but it was Amari's apparent willingness to betray everything her family stood for that chilled her to the bone. She was almost grateful her father had not lived to see it. Her only hope was to make Amari see for himself how he had strayed from his duty.

To the Leto. To the fleet. To himself.

Perhaps there was still a part of him with a conscience. A part of him that could be made to see Fausta was using him to her own ends and could care less how it impacted him. By the gods, she wouldn't let his insolence deter her from her mission. She would have him lashed below decks if she had to.

"Lesidi!" Cyril called, his voice anguished, strained. He stalked to stand facing her with a brow furrowed more deeply than she'd ever seen.

"What is it?" But she needn't have asked. She saw by the expression on his face, and her heart sank. "They're gone."

Cyril bowed his head, scuffled his feet, averting his eyes. "Sometime during the night. Took supplies from the galley and the launch."

Lesidi's stomach clenched tight. She should have known. A sudden memory of the Demeter broken on the bottom of the sea seared her heart.

Unless you act soon…

"Wake the crew, Cyril, and make ready to sail." She gripped the coin necklace Keleb had left on her pillow tightly in her hand. "If they get one of the Emperor's galleys, they could overtake us before we reach the fleet, even in a storm."

Chapter 37 - Anywhere But Here

Amari slid the launch past the lesser dock, under the pilons as close to the shore as he could get.

"Duck down, woman," he hissed. "I'm going to get the nose up on the shore so you can step onto dry land." It was the least he could do for the empress, who had insisted he not treat her with any deference, lest someone become suspicious.

Dressed in clothing he *borrowed* from one of the Isis's crew, she had poled the long boat with him under cover of darkness from the shallow cove where the Isis was anchored, returning along the same route they had followed after the Leto went down.

Breeching the palace to get into Fausta's quarters would be more difficult. They had already noted increased guard activity along the main quay.

Without her actual body to put on display, Amari doubted that woman, Valeria would accept the fact that Fausta was dead, which was a condition of getting the rest of the money she had promised him. Now he had the woman, alive. How much more would Valeria pay to dispatch her with her own hands?

He considered that possibility now in light of Fausta's offer. If he could get her into her chambers where she could access her secret treasury, she could pay him handsomely and bribe enough guards and crew to defeat Valeria and take control of her private galley. With that, they could go anywhere.

She studied him now as if she could read his mind. "Second thoughts, Amari?" She sent him a querulous look and stepped off the launch.

"There is the possibility the guards are loyal to the emperor no matter how much gold you offer," he answered in his defense. "You might just as easily be dead before night fall."

He lay their poles inside the boat and stepped over the bow onto the shore next to her.

She lifted her chin and gave him a mirthless grin that chilled his blood. She might be dressed in a poor sailor's clothing, but there was no disguising the determination of a woman accustomed not only to adoration, but to obedience. Now she leveled a piercing gaze on him.

"We are a lot alike, you and I, Amari. You have been robbed of your place in life, stripped of your station, am I wrong?"

She rested her hand on his forearm, her gaze intensified. He thought of Keleb now commanding his father's fleet, the fleet that should have been his; and his vessel at the bottom of the bay. Two bags of gold coins tied at his waist did not come close to replacing what he had lost.

He pressed his lips into a hard line and shifted his gaze toward the palace walls where torches marked supply entrances from the docks. Was Valeria out there waiting for him?

Fausta squeezed his arm. "Your chances of regaining what is rightfully yours will not be improved by turning me over to Valeria."

His eyes snapped back to hers. She tipped her head slightly, her eyes catching the glimmer of the torches, reminding him suddenly of his sister—questioning his motives, doubting his worth. A spike of dread stabbed through his soul. He had traded one witch for another, and right now, he wasn't sure which was worse. Regardless, he would have to be on his guard.

"You say there is a way to get into the palace without using those gates?" He nodded toward the torchlit colonnade as he bent down and picked up the supply bags from the launch.

She took one of them and looped it over her shoulder, assuming a slumped posture as further disguise. "You have coins on you, right?"

By the gods this woman would be the death of him. "I do."

She gave him that crafty smile again. "Then yes. There is a way."

*   *   *

The distant horizon was tinged in purple light when Amari emerged with a party of five guards from the castle sanitation exit, ten coins lighter and smelling like excrement. Two more guards headed for the quay under cover of darkness. Amari marveled at the power Fausta wielded over the guards. In all cases but one, the moment a guard recognized his empress, he took a knee and spoke with an air of relief. The one guard who did not immediately pay homage was dispatched by those already pledged to help get her to safety.

Now they stood in the shadows assessing the activity on the quay. They were not the only ones hurrying to beat the dawn. Two helmeted soldiers were piling supplies into a handsome galley whose bow and stern gleamed gold in the torchlight. The galley was not nearly as large or magnificent as the one the Emperor used to travel to Rome, but what the Empress's galley lacked in grandeur, it would gain in speed because of its smaller, sleeker size. There were already enough oarsmen sitting in their positions to get the galley swiftly away from the palace.

Fausta scowled at the scene. "I never liked that hateful woman, Valeria," she hissed.

Amari knelt beside one of her men. "I count three soldiers including Valeria. Can they best us?" He was a sailor not a warrior and had no qualms about admitting it.

One of the two men they sent ahead rejoined their tiny cadre, breathing hard, a rough sack over his shoulder. "Not without these," he announced with a toothy grin, spilling a pile of short swords and spears on the ground. He was a man Amari recalled as being in possession of three of his gold coins. He had just earned them.

"All right then," Amari growled. "Let us go."

* * *

Two of Valeria's soldiers were cut down before she saw what was happening. She looked up from her position at the stern of Fausta's galley in time to see the third's head lopped off. She watched in horror as it rolled down the embankment and into the water, ten oarsmen in their positions behind her screamed in terror.

Standing proud as pale dawn threatened to crest, a woman pulled back the hood of her cloak and stalked forward, her head high, her teeth bare, a sword brandished before her in both hands.

The Empress.

She raised the sword to shoulder level and stalked closer, one foot in front of the other until she stood not more than ten feet away. "You are finished, vermin. Get off of my ship. Now."

Three soldiers and that ignorant fool she had paid to get rid of Fausta and Marcus stood behind the Empress adding strength to her words.

Valeria swayed on her feet, still weak from the injury to her head. So this was the way her life ended. She had failed the Emperor. Failed herself. She drew her arms around her chest, her right hand covering the golden bracelet she had stolen from Kindra. She took a step backward, nearly losing her balance.

Fausta stepped onto the gangplank, the men moving in behind her. She had no knowledge of whether Fausta knew how to skewer an opponent with a sword, but right now it didn't matter. Unarmed and weak, Valeria doubted she could best her in a common cat fight.

She retreated another step, the bracelet burning hot under her grip. "No," she cried, weakly.

Fausta stepped onboard the galley. "I will teach you to betray the Empress of Rome," she said, her voice smooth and regal and menacing all at the same time.

The bracelet was blistering under Valeria's fingers, more than a distraction. A curse. But she found she could not let it go. She moaned into the dawn, accepting her fate. "By the gods, take me away from this death!"

Fausta stepped within striking distance. "Stand where you are, traitor and I will make your death swift and painless."

A woman's voice, canny and sly, crooned in Valeria's ear. *Where do you wish to go?*

Gasping for breath, she was caught in Fausta's raging glare. The woman had every intention of doing exactly what she claimed. Resigned to her fate, Valeria sucked in three burning breaths, then threw her head back and roared, "Anywhere but here!"

*   *   *

If Amari hadn't seen it with his own eyes, he would not have believed what happened.

Fausta charged at her foe, closed her eyes and lunged, striking Valeria straight through the chest. There was shriek, a flash of some sort of serpent's tail coiling between the two women, and a second after that, Valeria was gone. Vanished.

Fausta held her sword high, looked over her shoulder into the water, the back to Amari. Her men rushed the gangplank now, shouting in alarm.

She turned to Amari whose face must be ashen because it had turned icy cold. "What in Hades just happened?" she asked breathlessly.

He shifted positions with her, careful to stay away from the sword that hung from her limp arm.

"I don't know, my lady." He inched away from her, unsure as to whether it was safe to stand so close. "You struck at Valeria with your sword and there was a swirling flash of blue light, like Astrape at the left hand of Zeus! I expected to see a gusher of blood. Instead, she was gone!"

"Gone?"

"Disappeared!"

"Disappeared?"

"We can marvel at it later," he said, still shaking from the sight of blue lightening swirling around the two women. "Give that cursed sword to your guard and come with me." He gestured to the guard who took the sword gingerly by the hilt and passed it arm's length to the man behind him, who did the same with the man behind him.

"Right now, we have to leave before the light betrays us." And like the sailor he was, he set a man to call the oarsmen to haul, another to hoist the mainsail, and they slipped away from the palace harbor without drawing further attention. With any luck they could stay just out of sight of the Isis until they caught up with the fleet.

Chapter 38 - Lesidi's Coin

Loose rope lashed across Keleb's face as the wind took hold of the mainsail in a sudden, capricious blast. He caught it in his fist and slid his hand up its length to get it under control, then tied it off at the base of the sheet where it had come loose.

"By the gods," he complained to no one, "I should never have waited so long." Already the winter storms threatened and his hold was still heavy with a full shipment of grain and olive oil. They should have been on their way back to Auksum by now. He could come up with a dozen excuses, but if he were honest with himself, only one would be true. He had given Lesidi twenty-four hours to catch up with the fleet before they left without the Isis. But she didn't arrive, and he could not bring himself to leave. He couldn't afford to lose another transport vessel, but more than that, if something happened to Lesidi, he could never forgive himself. He'd promised her father to keep her safe.

Now, he stalked across the deck past the empty oarsmen's stations and on to the Captain's block.

"To your reckoning, Captain, when do you expect this storm will hit?"

His captain returned his glare for a moment, then pulled his heavy cape tighter around his hauberk and looked up into the back sail rigging. "Seems to me, Commander, it has hit already. We should have left for the strait yesterday."

The wind ripped through the rope rigging overhead, setting up a fearful wail, confirming the truth of the captain's words.

"We've been dragging anchor for a while now," he went on. "The men are fed and ready to take up their oars." He strode to the commander's side and placed a heavy hand on his shoulder. "We cannot delay any longer," he said, pinning his gaze under furrowed brows. "If you wish to make your delivery without endangering the entire fleet, you will have to let Lesidi fend for herself. From what I've seen of her skills and courage, she's perfectly capable of doing just that."

Keleb planted his feet wide apart, his neck muscles tightened, strained to their limit as he took this in. He hoped to the gods his captain was right.

"All right then," he said, the words burning in his throat. "Order the men up on deck and signal the transports to set sail."

"Right away, sir."

He watched his captain make his way below decks, shouting orders as he went. Dread hunched on Keleb's shoulder like an albatross, heavy and cold and wet. He planted his hands on his hips. As commander of the entire fleet, which this trip, comprised the 150-ton merchant ship on which he stood and six, 70-ton transports, he had the sole authority over their enterprise. He had already lost one of the vessels, the Leto. And if Lesidi failed to show with the Isis, he'd be down to four. Their success, truly, the future of

Negasi's fleet, depended on his leadership, his knowledge of the sea, and his courage in the face of the inherent dangers of navigating these waters in good weather. A winter storm could blow them off course enough to miss the Strait of Messina altogether, forcing them into deeper, more treacherous waters.

He felt he had already failed the mission. He should have taken control of the Isis when he had the chance. Instead, he let Lesidi talk him out of what he knew was right. Now they would all pay the price.

He paced to the prow of the ship as the oarsmen took their positions, ready to bend their backs against the wind. The four transports had already begun to set their sails and draw their anchors.

"Commander!" The shout came from behind him and he turned to see the first mate making his way down the keel line between the oarsmen. "We've sighted her. At least, it looks like one of our fleet, off the stern."

Keleb pushed past the mate, striding over coiled ropes and water buckets, and around the open cavern of the main hold to make his way to the stern. Bracing his hands on either side of his eyes to cut the glare, he scanned the distance, saw nothing.

"There, commander!" The mate shoved past him, pointed off the starboard side, and shouted into the wind. "You can see the square sail, just there."

Doubt had Keleb holding his breath. "How can you be sure?"

The mate stood tall, tucked in his chin. "We've got four transports off the port, sir; one lost," he said, cutting his eyes away a moment, "so that leaves only one of our fleet unaccounted for. The Isis."

"I know that much," Keleb growled, but as he searched the distant horizon, he finally saw what the mate described. A white sheet bulging with a strong wind materialized as if out of nowhere and appeared to be growing larger. He reached out to the gunwale and let his weight sink into it.

Dare he believe it was true? "It could be a transport from another fleet."

"If you don't mind my saying commander, you are the only one foolish enough to wait for a lagging transport at this time of year."

Keleb turned and fixed the mate with stern glare, surprised to see the man was little more than a youth. While youth didn't excuse his audacity, it did explain it. He would question his captain about the lad later. But right now, the cold ice stone that had settled in his chest when he realized the Isis had not made her appointed rendezvous started to melt and break apart.

"You're right, lad. Not likely to be any other but the Isis in these waters." And, as the vessel moved even closer, he thought he could just make out the obelisk on the sail that would identify it as one of Negasi's transports.

"Go tell the captain to hold steady the oarsmen and prepare the gangplank for boarding."

The young man sprinted across the deck toward the captain's cabin. Keleb turned back to the gunwale, threw his head back and blew out on long-held breath of relief. Six ships would insure a successful delivery allowing for some mishap along the way. That had already happened. Four ships were definitely going to make his delivery difficult and take much longer, but five ships, including the Isis, would be sufficient to get the job done.

Again, if he were honest, it wasn't regaining the Isis that had his pulse quickening. From the moment he'd rejoined the fleet after leaving the Isis behind, Lesidi's eyes glowed back at him. He longed for the feel of her supple body next to his, to hear her steady breathing, her heartbeat. He had made a mistake. One that could cost them a cargo, and even the fleet. But losing Lesidi now that he'd made her a part of his soul would be the greatest disaster of his life. By the gods, he would be damned if he would ever let that happen again.

Chapter 39 - Keleb's Call

Lesidi could see him standing at the stern of the Demeter, wind lashing his robe around his shoulders. The gangplank was lowered halfway, waiting for Cyril to maneuver the vessel close enough to the Demeter for a safe boarding. Though, the way the chop tossed and the wind blew, she feared it would be impossible to join the ships for a safe boarding. She would have to swing across on a rope instead. The idea would strike terror in her soul accept that she had already seen her death, and it wasn't from swinging on a rope. The real question was, would Keleb welcome her aboard? Or would his anger at her disobedience be insurmountable?

Her answer came in a flurry of activity at the stern of the Demeter. Keleb's captain and mates lowered the gangplank the rest of the way, and before she could make her way to the front of her vessel, Keleb had bounded across the yet unsteady transom and scooped her into his arms in front of the crews of both vessels.

"Lesidi," he growled into her ear, his arms gripping around her torso so tight, she could scarcely breathe. "I was afraid I had lost you."

She pushed away just enough to see into those sharp, gray eyes, saw something there she had only dreamed existed. "And I you."

She wrapped her arms around his neck and held on with all her strength as the wind whipped around them.

Men on both vessels whooped and howled, until Keleb turned and glared at them. "What are you gawking at? Get back to your preparations. We leave at once!"

Satisfied the crews were responding to his commands, he turned to accompany her to her quarters and ran straight into Marcus.

A giant of a man, armed with a heavy sword, his arms folded over his chest. Marcus wore the heavy gold circlet around his neck, a clear sign of a Praetorian Guard of the Emperor.

Keleb scowled at him, suspicion hardening his jaw. "A Roman soldier aboard one of our vessels?" he questioned, turning a raised brow to Lesidi. "What manner of treachery is this?"

Lesidi was speechless, struck by the vehemence in his voice. She had been so concerned how he would receive her after holding up the fleet, she had not considered he hadn't officially met Marcus.

"Keleb, this is Marcus. The man I told you about who was with Amari after the Leto—"

Keleb held up his hand to stop her explanation, and considered the man another moment, scanning him head to toe.

Marcus cocked his hands at his hips, then returned the appraisal. "At your service, Commander," he said with a guarded deference. He was a soldier of the highest rank, despite the fact that he had left his post.

Keleb strode forward, leveling his gaze on the man. "I cannot decide whether you are the luckiest man I've met, or the best strategist."

"Commander?" Marcus stood at ease once more.

"First you survive your betrayal of the Emperor, then you survive the sinking of the Leto."

Marcus studied his face. "My goal was to protect the mother of my child. I expect you would do the same." He lowered his arms and took a less threatening stance. "I am in your debt, Commander." He brought a fist to his chest and slightly bowed his head.

"How so?" Keleb asked, glancing at Lesidi.

"For allowing my women safe passage to Auksum. I understand you are not in the business of transporting passengers."

Keleb nodded, accepting the thanks. "And what of Amari? Lesidi tells me you were with him when the Leto went down."

Marcus's brow furrowed and he glanced at Lesidi. "Forgive me, Lesidi," he said, then to Keleb, he said, "Her brother…his allegiance is…changeable. It seems Fausta was willing to pay more to save her own skin than Valeria was to burn it."

"He's right, Keleb," Lesidi answered. "I fear Amari made a deal with Valeria to destroy the Leto."

Keleb stepped forward, offered Marcus his hand. "Amari's recklessness is not news to me, I fear. I will of course honor Lesidi's wishes. You and your family will transfer to the Demeter at once. There will be more room—"

"No!" Lesidi shouted over the wind that seemed insistent to drown out their words.

"No?" Keleb raised a brow. "You question my authority again?"

Lesidi drew in her breath. She hadn't thought about how she would handle this moment but handle it she must, his authority be damned. "Commander," she said in a deferential tone, "We need to talk."

*   *   *

The moment they gained their privacy in her quarters Lesidi closed his hand around the necklace and squeezed her hands around his.

His grey eyes narrowed. "What is this?" He started to pull away. "You are returning my gift." She held firm.

"You know what they say about me. That I have the sight?"

Brows furrowed, he gave her a slow nod. He did not believe her now, but he would.

"Forget everything you think you know and do exactly as I say."

He raised a brow, silently questioning her.

"Close your eyes, Keleb."

*   *   *

Keleb stared at her for another long moment, marveling at the conviction with which she ordered him around. Even in the direst of times, she tested him, and yet he could not disobey. He closed his eyes, gripping the coin tightly in his fingers, her hands warm around his. A moment later, he sat under a shaded colonnade, the most beautiful woman in the world at his side, three young children playing at the water's edge, one of Auksum's great obelisks visible in the distance. His heart had been open and full at the same time. But in the next moment that vision was swept away by another vision—the Demeter with a broken back. He had heard Lesidi had a gift from her own father. But this power—the power to make him see life and death in the blink of an eye?—This had to be magic of the darkest kind. What manner of mayhem had she set upon him?

Not magic or mayhem, my friend. What you've seen will definitely come to pass if you stay on your current path. You can ignore the vision, or you can listen to what Lesidi has to say. Choose wisely.

It was a man's voice, coming first from afar, then so close he could almost feel the heavy breath of it against his ear. He whirled around, but there was only he and Lesidi inside her chamber.

Lesidi gripped his shoulders, leveling her gaze on his. "Keleb. What did you see?"

"I am…not sure what I saw," he admitted, his shoulders hunched around his ears, fending off disbelief. He squeezed the back of his neck to release the stiffness there, searching her eyes for some kind of explanation. "Maybe just my own fears?"

Lesidi shook her head, and he recognized anew what anchored her image in his heart—not only that glowing skin, compelling green eyes, and the regal lift of her chin, but the soul-deep power she had over him. The thought of losing her threatened to tear him apart from the inside out. Like Marcus, he was willing to do anything to protect her.

She gripped his forearms in her hands and squeezed hard, bringing his eyes to hers. "What you saw will come to pass unless we can contrive a way to change it. We can save the Demeter if—"

Her words unleased his anger. He stalked away from her, ready to leave.

"Save the Demeter?" He fisted his hands at his sides to keep from striking the bulkhead. All his adult life he'd put the protection of someone else's property ahead of his own welfare. His own desire. Loyalty, honesty, integrity, and strength. Protecting Negasi's fleet had been his sacred duty and he had done everything in his power to save it. After seeing his future—their future, he realized his passion had never been to protect Negasi's fleet, it was, and had always been to protect Negasi's daughter, Lesidi. Without her, there was no passion, no purpose, no life.

"To Hades with the Demeter!" he roared. "I lived in agony fearing I would never see you again, that I wouldn't have you in my life. If your fool of a brother wants the Demeter, so be it! Let him ride it to Neptune's depths!"

"But—"

He closed the distance between them in two great strides and took her by the shoulders, his chest heaving with conviction. "He can have the whole goddamned fleet if it pleases him, but I will never let us be separated again."

"Keleb!" she cried, her shoulders pressed tight against her ears in his grip. "The grain. What about the people of Rome? Think. Think what you are saying."

He caught his breath, realized he was clenching her too hard, then loosened his grip. He threw back his head and blew hot breath. His eyes went back to her face to see tears streaking down her cheeks.

"What of your oath," she drove on. "Loyalty, honest, integrity and strength. What good is our life together if we throw those away?"

He stared at her another long moment, his mouth working but nothing coming out. Once again, he knew why he could not live without her. He pulled her against him, held her tight. Her arms wrapped around his body and they stood that way, their heartbeats melding as one. Conflicting emotions settled like and ebb tide around them while a new cascade of images flooded his mind.

There was a way to save the grain if they weren't already too late. He had seen all he needed to see. He pushed the necklace into her hands. "Where is your brother now?"

Lesidi blinked at him in surprise. "It doesn't work that way. I cannot always—"

"Make it work, Lesidi. Your part in this is to *make* it work."

She shook her head at him. "Your head is like a block of stone." She ground her teeth at him. "The necklace is my connection to you; I do not need it to feel my brother."

He threw up his hands in exasperation. "Then do whatever it is you do!"

She covered her face in her hands and sat on her bunk. "Just, give me a moment."

He settled himself, stepped back, and waited.

After a moment, he did see a change in her. It was almost as if she were in a sleepwalker's trance.

"What do you see?" he demanded impatiently.

She held up her hand to silence him. He rolled his eyes to the planks of her ceiling. Great gods she would be the death of him.

Several more interminable moments passed before she at last lifted her eyes to his.

"They have breached the palace and seized the Empress's ship. Depending on the number of oarsmen Fausta could enlist, they could already be on the way to intercept us." Then, like a foresail with broken lines, she dropped into her bunk, exhausted, her eyes barely open. Never had the sight taken so much out of her.

He stood another moment taking inventory of his resources, considering the storm, her reckoning, her condition, a plan forming in his mind. It would be painful and difficult, but it could work. If saving the grain and Lesidi meant giving up the Demeter, then that's what they would do. He could get another ship. But he could never replace Lesidi.

He knelt beside her and took her hands in his. "This Marcus. He's a good man?"

Lesidi furrowed her brow. "Kindra puts all her trust in him."

Keleb nodded. "All right then. I am going to need his help. Indeed, I will need the entire fleet to make this work."

"But, what are you going to do?" She sat up, some of her usual vitality returning.

He pressed his lips together in thought, determination fisting his hands. "Can you make it up on deck?"

She swung her legs to the floor and rose with his help. Looking into her eyes, he saw fatigue, but also her characteristic determination and grit.

He led her up on deck, supporting her with an arm wrapped around her waist. Marcus and Kindra stood side-by-side, his mother, Flavia, and Dracis nearby. "There seems to be a lull in the storm," Marcus said.

Keleb scanned the distant dark clouds. "Yes. But it is likely temporary. I have a plan and I will need your cooperation."

Marcus nodded. "At your service, Commander."

Keleb acknowledged Marcus with a heavy hand on his shoulder, then shouted for Cyril.

The mate came running across the deck. "Commander."

"You will take charge of the Isis." Lesidi stiffened in his grip; he squeezed her hand tightly. "We will offload the grain and oil from the Demeter to the other four transports. They will continue through the Strait of Messina and on to Ostia. The Isis and Demeter will draw Fausta and Amari to the Skerky Bank."

Cyril raked his watch cap off his head. "But that is madness, Commander. The currents at the Bank are deadly."

"Which is why it is the fastest route to Ostia."

"But, Lesidi——" Cyril protested.

He held up his hand to stop the argument and turned his gaze on Lesidi to intercept what he saw as a protest forming on her lips.

"The Demeter's Captain, Felix, will command the transport fleet to Ostia. He's my highest-ranking officer and can be trusted to ensure the grain is delivered and the fee is paid."

He pulled her against his side. "Lesidi will take Felix's place as Captain of the Demeter." He felt her relax, sending a wave of relief through him.

Marcus lifted his eyes to Keleb. "What are the odds of the mission's success?"

Keleb squared his shoulders and answered truthfully. "The grain will make it to Ostia. The Messina Strait is easily navigable, close to shore, and protected from the strongest currents. I cannot say about the Skerky Bank. The Demeter could be lost. Many ships have gone down on the bank trying to make the faster run."

"So, Kindra and her mother would be safe with the fleet?"

"As safe as is possible traveling these waters."

Marcus sent a sorrowful look to Kindra and stepped forward, his shoulders erect. "Then I will stay with you. Help ensure you prevail against your foes."

Spoken like a true soldier. Keleb appreciated the offer, but he couldn't accept. "You have sacrificed too much already, Marcus. Go with your women and protect them. Once the cargo is delivered to Rome, Felix will see that you and your loved ones get to safe harbor in Auksum."

Dracis leapt between them. "Take me, Commander. I have nothing to lose."

Marcus smiled at the boy. Keleb nodded. "All right then, you will continue to crew on the Isis under Cyril's command."

He shifted his gaze to Lesidi, images of loss still playing in his head. It was true. If he put Lesidi on another vessel, his mind would be preoccupied with her safety. His mind was made up.

"All right. We have our plan. Once the cargo is transferred, we will head around Sicily, keeping the regular routes. The Isis will trail us at a distance. Watch for any vessels approaching from the east. Once we identify the traitors, we'll set the Demeter to free sail and abandon the ship for the Isis."

May the gods be with you, came the voice in his head.

Chapter 40 - The Skerky Bank

Keleb breathed the briny air of the Mediterranean, wind in his face, Lesidi by his side. He pulled her under his arm, one hand gripping her shoulder, the other on the gunwale of the powerful merchant ship. Excitement prickled through his arms, his legs, his soul. Under her command, all sails were furled and the full complement of oarsmen worked in perfect unison. Without her heavy cargo, the Demeter was capable of carving through the water at substantial speed. The grain shipment was safe on its way to Ostia and Lesidi was safe in his arms. If they made it past the Skerky Bank alive, he would count himself a god. Or at least the luckiest man alive.

They had left the loaded fleet at the entrance to the Messina Strait, then sailed past Syracuse bound to round Sicily. As ordered, Cyril followed in the Isis, keeping closer to the land, his cargo bay empty, extra launches lashed to the deck should the Demeter fail to traverse the Banks in one piece. Keleb could not see the Isis, but he trusted she was there.

Already he could feel the pull of the current that would propel them toward the deep-water channel, whether they chose to go or not, if Cyril's warning held true. He had no reason to doubt his experience. Once there, how the ship would behave would be anyone's guess. For now, he ordered his men to ship their oars. If they went any further ahead, it was likely no ship could overtake them. If indeed Amari had procured a worthy vessel the night Lesidi left the harbor, say a galley with sail and oarsmen, they wouldn't be far behind.

By the time they rounded the southern tip of Sicily, it was nigh on full dark. He ordered all lanterns lit. It made them a target to any seaman looking for a fight, but that's exactly what he wanted. As long as they went after the Demeter, the grain shipment would be safe. Seeing dark circles under Lesidi's eyes, he ordered her to the captain's quarters to rest before the danger surely to come.

The first assault, a lighted bolt, hit the deck and burst into flame. Laden with oil, its fire spread quickly, increasing with the next and the next until the oarsmen had to abandon their posts and take up water buckets to quell the flames. They had little experience fighting soldiers, but they had fought fire many times and knew the drill.

Keleb rushed to the captain's quarters and roused Lesidi. Together they clamored to the stern to see an elegant galley coming alongside fast, it's swan's neck prow covered in gold sheet.

"My god, they've taken the Empress's ship!" Lesidi cried.

Keleb rushed her along the rail away from what looked like a probable collision. Indeed, it was the Empress's galley. He had seen it during a previous trip to the Bosphorus, a thing of beauty. Knowing what lie ahead of them, it would likely join the Demeter on the bottom of the sea tonight.

Looking over his shoulder as they pushed along, he recognized Amari. He and a handful of soldiers were lobbing lit torches at the Demeter, one after the other. Fausta, egged them on while her oarsmen fought to hold the boat steady. About one third the size of the Demeter, its decks lay well below theirs, but it didn't stop them from their attack.

"Burn! Burn!" Fausta shouted to the heavens, her head thrown back like a madwoman. "The people of Rome will starve for betraying me, Constantine." She climbed precariously high on the swan's neck, straddling the point where the gunwales came together, her peasant's robes lashing her legs. "Burn!" she wailed, again and again.

Flames engulfed the middle of the Demeter, driving the oarsmen to split into two groups. He could not see the men at the front of the ship, but those nearest them, led by Dracis and Cyril worked frantically to douse flames converging on the long boats they had lashed to the deck, their only means of escape.

A torch landed two feet away from him. He picked it up and lobbed it back toward the galley, without taking time to see if it hit its mark.

The wind that had quieted long enough to get their cargo transferred over the gangplanks to the transport ships had since wound up to gale force, tearing at their sails and driving huge swells at them from three different directions, just as Cyril had predicted. Keleb's stomach lurched as the two ships slid together on the face of a giant swell, then collided, sending three of his men overboard. He grabbed a hold of the boathouse rail. "Lesidi! Where are you?"

"Here!" she cried, holding on to the tiller as it threatened to swing free. The swell broke over the deck and washed her off her feet. "Keleb!"

*　　*　　*

Lesidi slid across the deck, her screams drowned by the wailing wind, until she hit the gunwale at the stern. The Empress's vessel rose on another swell and for a fleeting moment, Fausta's eyes burned into hers, mouth open in terror. In the next moment, the two ships collided again. To Lesidi's horror, Fausta lost her grip, and flailing against the hull of her galley, her foot tangled in a lashing rope for an agonizing moment before the wave washed over the prow and took her and the rope with it. Lesidi watched helplessly as her body disappeared into the churning black water. Despite shock and horror, her heart broke for the woman. She had once been the Empress of Rome. But for vengeance taking over, she might have been safe on her way to Ostia at this moment. Instead, she was sinking to the bottom of the sea forever.

Heat seared Lesidi's skin, smoke stung her lungs. Men screamed, their clothing aflame as they jumped overboard, choosing to drown instead of burn to death. She backed away from the railing. Had her vision been a lie? Was this the end of all things?

Smoke engulfed her, she threw herself to the deck, seeking clearer air. Where were Keleb and Dracis? She lifted her head one more time, trying to get her bearings and caught a brief glimpse of lights in the distance. Was it the Isis? Or some light from the shore far away? It was impossible to tell.

The two ships continued to swirl in a slow, sickening spin like they were being stirred in a frothing, salty stew.

"Keleb!" Lesidi cried out as the sea lifted the ships up again, sliding the Demeter sideways. "Keleb," she moaned, her voice was so weak and choked with smoke she doubted anyone could hear. And then, almost a relief, the sea washed over her, tumbling her like a rag doll, over and over and over…

"Keleb," Lesidi sobbed, then coughed seawater.

Someone wrapped a blanket around her shoulders. She opened her eyes to see her friend, Dracis's smile. "He is alright, my lady. He and your brother. We got them before…before…"

She sat up now, looked around her. They were sawing along the coast, pushed by a gentle breeze in the early morning sun. "The Demeter?"

"It is as you predicted, my love." Keleb's baritone voice rolled over her, sad and also sweet. He stood in the bulkhead, a bandage circling his head, covering one eye.

"Oh my god. You are hurt!"

"I will survive. And so will your brother."

"My brother?" Her heart gave a little pinch of shame. In all the swirling, flaming, raging turmoil they had just been through, she hadn't given a thought to her brother. She rubbed at a bump on her own head. "Is he—"

"I managed to pull him out of the drink before the flaming mast he was holding on to carried him down. He suffered a few bruises, the greatest of which I believe, to his ego."

Lesidi reached for her necklace, finding solace in its touch had become a habit. But it wasn't there. "By the gods, I have lost it."

Keleb pulled her into his arms. "I will buy you a hundred necklaces. A thousand."

"But the Demeter. She is gone."

"Insured for more than she was worth, I assure you," he said on a bitter laugh.

She just looked at him, mouth agape.

"We will build another, Lesidi. It is you that cannot be replaced."

"Four, three, two, one, and you are feeling alert and…"

Lexi blinked and sat up. Tessa, Phillip and Zai stared back at her. She swallowed hard, her mouth dry as roadkill. Tessa handed her a bottle of water.

"Well, I guess we're still here." She pinched herself on the arm just to be sure. Her hands were still shaking a little.

Zai scooped her onto his lap. "That we are."

Zai glanced at Tessa and Phillip before he turned back to her. "How long were we gone?"

Tessa checked the clock on Lexi's mantel. "About ten minutes, give or take."

Zai slowly shook his head. "Ten minutes? It felt like days."

Phillip scooted his chair closer to Lexi. "So, tell us. What did you see?" He shot excited glances back and forth between Lexi and Zai.

Lexi blinked at him. "I'm…actually, I'm feeling a little overwhelmed. I feel more like taking a nap than talking."

Tessa circled her arms around Phillip's neck from behind and hung her chin over his shoulder. "She's right, Sherlock." She glanced over her shoulder and nodded at Zai who looked like he was about the fade. "Let's leave these two alone to sort this out." She rested her hand over her belly. "Me and junior here are jonesing for some pizza."

Chapter 41 - What Doesn't Kill You

The first thing Lexi noticed when she burst through the doors to her building was the giant bouquet of flowers—ivory lilies, peach roses, and creamy sweet mini carnations tied with a huge satin bow.

"Wow!" Robbi with an 'i' was making progress in her new world. "Aren't you the special one!"

Robbi grinned at her under a fresh haircut, that gorgeous smile beaming. "Yes, I am special, but no. They're not for me. They're yours."

She stood and pointed out the card.

Lexi opened it and read:

Thank you for sharing with me. Minh and I have had a lovely weekend. Thought you would like these instead of my usual emergency Monday visit. —Cam Tran.

Lexi drew in a breath, whispered, "Oh, my," on an exhale. Guilt pinched a raw spot in her heart.

Robbi sighed. "When I grow up, I wanna be just like you."

Lexi looked up, surprised how far away that pinch had taken her. "What?"

Robbi blinked at her a moment, then shook her head. "Never mind. You have a visitor upstairs. Hope it's okay I let him in. It's Monday, I know but…"

"Jamal?"

She nodded.

"It's okay. He told me he was going to come in."

She wrapped her arm around the flower vase and headed for the elevator.

For the first time since the regression two weeks earlier, she actually felt a little settled. It had been an eventful two weeks. First off, she and Zai had agreed to write down everything they could remember about their adventure without talking about it first.

They were both a little undone to learn their accounts meshed almost perfectly, except for their points of view. Lexi taking Lesidi and Amari's part and Zaire taking Keleb's.

If you believed in the magic of it, they had successfully done what they set out to do. Bring Lesidi and Keleb together and deliver the wheat to Rome. If you didn't believe, no harm, right?

Jamal had been upset at first that they'd done it without him. But his upset was quickly reversed when they let him read both their accounts.

"The *dopest* thing is," he'd explained after reading, "You guys know something nobody else knows."

They'd been sitting on the seawall eating frozen bananas and swinging their feet, watching the tide creep up the bank when Jamal started an excited steam-of-consciousness chatter.

"Yeah, what's that?" Zai asked.

"The Empress's galley is down there, too. Under the Demeter."

Lexi tangled her leg with his a moment, stopping his nervous swing. "Thought you weren't interested in wreck diving." She winked at Zai over his head.

He shrugged. "I don't know. Maybe I could be persuaded, someday."

Zai's meeting with the board of directors had gone better than expected. In light of his contribution to the company's growth—nearly quadrupling their value in the past two years—the members took advantage of their option under the revokable trust and voted to extend the deadline for marriage an additional year without any stipulation as to who that partner would be.

Zai had other plans. He'd already waited a lifetime to be with Lesidi and he hadn't wanted to wait another day. That evening he had surprised her with an engagement ring, a cabochon ruby surrounded by a star of diamond baguettes that looked suspiciously like one of Tessa's ancient designs, and plane tickets to Las Vegas for a quickie marriage.

In the end, he and Lexi had come up with a compromise. They agreed to wait until his Carlsbad acquisition officially closed escrow, allowing Lexi and Tessa time to plan a sweet wedding and a honeymoon trip to the Med.

Zaire had sent for Jamal's teacher to continue his home school classes until the end of the school year, after which he wanted to enroll in a local public school with his friends.

It was true, it had been a whirlwind of events, but Lexi was good with all of it. She had waited a long time, too.

From the top of the mezzanine, she could see her office door stood open. She stepped inside to find Jamal feeding her fish.

"Good morning again. How'd you know I was here?" She put down her flowers on the windowsill behind her desk.

He rolled his eyes at her and sauntered over to one of the chairs in front of her desk. "Just a guess," he said, humoring her.

She stared at him. Would she ever get used to the way he was the spitting image of his dad at his age?

Since the night of the regression, Zai and Jamal had spent most of their time at her house, making themselves at home. Jamal had taken over the spare bedroom while Zaire set up temporary office at her kitchen table. It was cluttered, it was messy, and it felt absolutely perfect.

Zai's office in her building was nearly ready, so the kitchen office would soon go away, but in the meantime, she was happy to have Zai's company and share her space. This was the first time Jamal had come to her office since that first day when she had no idea who he was.

"Sit, sit," she told him. "Give me a minute." She pulled open a drawer, and dropped her purse in, then shoved it closed with her foot and gave him her full attention.

He plopped into the chair like he owned the space.

"So, you wanted to talk to me?" Lexi opened her laptop and logged in. Her schedule popped up on her screen. She scanned it absently. "Okay," she said, lifted her gaze to his. "What's up, Jammer?"

He hesitated a moment….."What do you know about twins? I mean, besides the obvious."

Her heart stumbled. "Twins." She slid her eyes to the fish tank a moment her heart stuttering a little, hollowing out. Where was this going?

She opted for the most direct, factual route. "Well…there's identical and paternal. With identical, one cell splits; with paternal, two eggs are fertilized, and…"

"I feel her," Jamal butted in, teenage boy voice breaking high. "She's like, in my head, my heart. Every day, Lexi. Like a missing piece of me."

Tears welled in his eyes.

She stared at him a moment, the hollow in her chest expanding. She got up and came around her desk, sat in the chair next to him and took his hands. "Jamal. Honey."

"It's not fair," he went on, ignoring the tear streaking down his cheek. "I got everything I wished for. Everything I ever wanted. You, Dad. A chance to live a normal life like other kids. And she's out there. Somewhere. Alone."

"I know, baby. But she's got her family. People who love and care for her. She's—"

Jamal shot out of his chair, paced across the room, and turned on her. "How do you know that?"

She shook her head, speechless. She's asked herself the same questions over and over, but she hadn't seen it coming from him. It knocked her sideways.

"What if they don't care? What if she needs us?"

"She——"

"…could be in trouble. I feel it. She could need us. You don't know. But you could. All you have to do is file those papers."

"Papers."

"Dad told me about the papers. For the agency."

His words hit her like a stake in the heart. "I——"

"What are you afraid of?"

She stared at him. Her son. So young. So vulnerable. So wise. What was she afraid of? Rejection? Hate? Recognition she was a failure at being a mom?

Phillip had forwarded the paperwork to her email. She'd red flagged it. Filled in all the blanks. All she had to do was frickin' hit SEND and she hadn't been able to bring herself to do it. Now Jamal, of all people was standing in front of her, rubbing her nose in it.

He came back, sat down beside her, and took her hands again. "Was it so bad to find out about me?"

Oh god. How had she been so blind. Of course he might think that. Blame himself. That's what kids did.

She slowly shook her head. No. Discovering she had a son had been shocking, monumental, and life affirming. The discovery of Jamal and Zai in her life had been the most amazing miracle. Better than any fiction out there.

"No. It's been…incredible." She threw her arms around his neck and pulled him in close. "You are the most amazing person I've ever known."

He hugged her tight then pushed back enough to look into her eyes. "I've got a twin out there. Somewhere. Mom. I think we should give her a chance to see who we are."

It was the first time he had called her 'mom' and the sound of it made her heart bloom like those time-lapse videos of a flower opening.

"You really think I should do it?" She tugged in a breath and blew out her doubt.

"What have we got to lose?"

We.

A tiny two letter word that suddenly felt as big as the universe. Tears spilled and she wiped them with the backs of her hands. She sucked in halting breaths as she got up and went around her desk, punched keys on her keyboard.

Jamal bit his bottom lip, watching her.

She found the paperwork file on her computer, opened it, looked it over. Everything was in order. All she had to do was attach it to the email and hit send.

She glanced at Jamal. He sat forward and gave her a nod.

She pulled in a long slow breath and hit the button.

*   *   *

Morning light filtered through the window, tracing a path along the ceiling, then lower to the tops of the bookshelves. At precisely ten a.m., an unfiltered light beam warmed the scales where she rested in her nest of tissue.

The violin-string tone inside her head played a sweet, resonant note that grew louder, sweeter with each degree of temperature rise in her skin, until the siren call became an unbearable, glowing ache from the base of her skull, down her sleek body, and all the way to the tip of her tail. Once again, the Mistress called. Eyes alight, she uncoiled her body and wound her way among the half-finished gold rings, pins, and broches, down to the workbench, then to the windowsill, where she coiled up once more, lifting her eyes to see the world outside. The voice grew more insistent, compelling, enticing. Not the angry voice of greed or power, or the melancholy blue of lost love, but soft whimper of a child.

Oh, that pesky snake! **Time to grab Book 3, The Serpent's Coil,** because, you know darn well, Jamal's not going to refuse the call. You'll find links to The Serpent's Coil and all my books on my web page at www.katdrennanbooks.com, or grab a pic of the QR Code:

Thank you so much for reading Lesidi's Coin. Writing this series has been a great adventure for me. Indy authors thrive on reviews, so dear reader, it would make me so happy if you would take a few moments to leave an honest review.

About the Author

Kat Drennan writes sensual stories from the heart of the Golden State.

From the curling surf at the edge of the continent, to the granite sculptures of the Sierra Nevada; from San Francisco to Death Valley and all the way to the Mexican border and beyond, California's unique landscape and colorful, dramatic history step forward as characters in each of her novels.

She is an alumna of the Squaw Valley Community of Writers, as well as a past Secretary of the Contemporary Romance Writers Chapter of RWA.

Based in Ojai, California, Kat loves the beach, a challenging bike ride, cooking with a friend, and watching her two granddaughters grow.

She loves to hear from her readers. You can follow her at www.katdrennanbooks.com, sign up for her newsletter to find out about new releases, or follow her <u>Facebook page</u> to hear about, freebies, and other promotions, or just have a chat!